RESURRECTION

Sue Yockney

For my father from whom I inherited my love of writing and storytelling

Chapter 1

13/06/3042   12:05 hours
SARAH

The first thing I notice about the Council Chamber is the dark, and the quiet. I wasn't expecting that. And then there's the smell, not stale as I first thought, but different from the Colony. It has an unused quality about it, feels cold against my face. It's not completely dark either, there's a persistent orange flash of light coming from somewhere in front of me, enough for me to make out that I'm in some kind of food preparation area. Not that there's any food here, only piles of empty trays stacked up on the work surfaces. As my eyes adjust to the gloom, I wonder why I didn't bring a flashlight with me. I make my way towards the door and look about for some kind of opening mechanism. But there's nothing. It must be an automatic door but there's nothing *automatic* about it now.

'Hello...is anybody there?' I say, banging on it, in frustration.

I'm met with only silence. The quiet unnerves me. All I can hear is my own staggered breathing and something else, hovering beneath the stillness, a buzz regular and insistent, coming from the other side of the room. I move towards the sound then realise that it's linked to the amber light. Now I'm closer, I see that the flashes of light are coming from the direction of a large metal hatch. I grab the handle at the bottom and push it upwards. At first, it won't budge but then it gives way and I'm able to coax it up about half a metre. A rush of cold air is released, ruffling my hair. Easing myself through, I slip down onto the floor. I *feel*, the scale of the space, before I see it. Through the amber flashes I make out rows of tables and chairs, in a high-ceilinged room.

'Is anybody there?' I call out.

My voice, feeble and tremulous, breaks up in the void in front of me. I realise for the first time since I jumped out of the food chute, that I'm scared. I step forward, my hand clasping the screwdriver out in front of me. This looks like a refectory but one that hasn't been used for a long time. I weave my way across the room, through the tables. A light on the ceiling flashes on and off, a buzz punctuating each one. None of the other lights are working. I glance behind me at the serving hatch. Would it be better to go back to the food chute? I've got nothing with me apart from the screwdriver. No food, no water, nothing.

Approaching the door in front of me, I notice that it's partially open and stick my head out of the gap. My heart pounds in my chest as I peer into the corridor. In one direction, there is only blackness, thick and featureless. In the other, about fifty metres from me, another flashing light. Hoping that it continues to cling onto its tenuous existence, I edge my way along the wall of the building. Every cell in my body screams at me to go back, but I continue. I call out again, but my voice seems too loud in the emptiness of the corridor. Now that I've left the relative security of the refectory, I feel reluctant to draw attention to my presence, to my vulnerability.

I creep forward, pressing my right arm tight against the wall of the building for comfort. Moving in small bursts, a few metres at a time, I use my hand to feel my way. The light is ahead of me now, on the opposite side of the corridor. I count the flashes in my head, the rhythm gives me something to focus on other than my fear and how very alone I feel. My fingers curl round a corner. Ahead of me is what looks like a connecting corridor and the familiarity of this structure is reassuring. Is the Council Chamber built to the same design as the City? Of course, it's the top half of the Colony's vast cylindrical structure. If I keep following the buildings, I'll return to my starting point. I can't get lost.

This comforting thought is snatched from me, as the flashing of the light falters. It gives out three or four bursts before it fails and I'm plunged into darkness. Then it buzzes and flashes on again. But I know it's only a matter of time before it stops altogether. I have to get across the connecting corridor to the next building before that happens. Launching out into space, I walk forward in, what I hope, is a straight line. Another flash and, as I predicted, it's the last. I'm stranded in the no man's land between buildings, with no light to guide me. I step forward, my arms out in front of me but it's an act of faith and I know I can't do it. Turning one hundred and eighty degrees, I walk back to the refectory building. My hand touches cool metal again and I gulp in a breath, relief flooding my body. I work my way along to the corner and slip around it. Then, with my left arm brushing against the face of the building, I make my way back. I hear a whimper and look behind then realise that it's coming from me. The sound of defeat. I thought it would be so easy. Go up in the food chute to the Council Chamber and they would take control of the situation. I would be lauded as a hero, looked after. But instead, I'm stranded here in this dark, cold place, alone.

Pushing my self-pity away, I stretch out my hand in front of me and creep along the building searching for the doorway, hoping that it will still be open. It comes up quicker than I was expecting and I slip inside and rest against the refectory wall. I feel safer here, I don't know why? Perhaps it's the light that continues to cling onto life. I weave my way back to the serving hatch and climb through. A search of the shelves and cupboards for anything edible, confirms my fear, that there's nothing here. In the corner, I notice something I'd missed before. It looks like a water dispenser. Rushing over to it, I press the button but it's not working, like everything else. *Useless.*

Now, despite the danger, trying to get back down to the City is looking like my best option. But I can't do it on my own, or *can I*? I stare at the control panel next to the food chute. It looks identical to the one in the Food Production Unit below. I press the start button and, to my surprise, a green light illuminates and the doors of the chute slide open. I climb inside and wait for them to close again. For a few seconds, nothing happens. Then there's the faintest of clicks and the doors creep towards each other. I watch as the light from the refectory reduces and a familiar feeling of panic takes me in its grip. No, I *can't* do it. I push my way through the diminishing gap between the doors and fall out onto the floor, my whole body shaking. Another click and the chute galvanises into action. I jump to my feet and pound on the doors, in frustration. It's going back down to the City. *You idiot.* I stab, in anger, at the buttons on the console but it will not be stopped. All it needed was a little bit of courage, that's all. Sliding down to the floor, I stare at the serving hatch, mesmerised by the on-off, on-off pulses of the light.

After a while, I curl up on the cold hard surface, my ear picking up the soft vibrations of the City beneath me, and weep.

Chapter 2

14/06/3042   19:35 hours
JONATHAN

I look across the room, full of Colony Re-habs preparing for their new life in the city. Resurrection, it's called, the process and the city. The dining hall is packed with people finishing off their evening meal. Marilyn and Kyle are deep in conversation, over the other side of the room, as far away from me as they can get. Marilyn glances in my direction but looks away when she sees that I'm watching. I don't have to hear what they're saying, I know they're talking about me, trying to assess if I meant what I said outside the Renaissance Gate. I should go over and tell them right this minute, that they're wasting their time. *I do mean it.* I've never meant anything more in my life.

I stare down at the cup cradled in my hand, the bitter smell of its contents assaulting my nostrils, and fight off the nausea. My tongue circles one of the ulcers on the roof of my mouth, caused by the scalding liquids I've been given since I arrived. I'll never get used to hot food and drink. I feel a hand on my shoulder and look up. The girl called Oli, short for Olivia, a fact that she insisted on telling me earlier, sits down on the empty chair next to me. I do only enough to acknowledge her presence then return my attention to my untouched drink.

'Hello, my name's Oli, short for Olivia,' she says.

'I *know*,' I say, without looking at her.

She sighs.

'What is your problem, Jonathan? You're safe. You've got more food and drink than you've ever seen in your entire life. You've got your whole future ahead of you. And yet, here you are, looking like you died anyway.'

'I don't want to talk about it.'

'Yes, so you say. But I think you should. You could be suffering from depression. Post-traumatic stress, they call it. They'll give you something to help you, in the short term.'

'I don't need any help,' I snap.

I shoot a glance over to Marilyn and Kyle, pleading with them to rescue me. To my surprise, it works. Marilyn gets up and walks across the room, followed by a plodding Kyle. They sit opposite me, ignoring Oli's presence. I can't bear the pity in their eyes.

'Jonathan, we've been wondering if...' Marilyn says.

'Yes, I do mean it.'

'It won't achieve anything,' Kyle says. 'You'll end up dead. What possible use is that? Sarah wouldn't want that, would she?'

I jump up, pushing back the chair and lean into them across the table.

'Don't you *dare*, tell me, what Sarah wants. You don't know her like I do.'

'Who's Sarah?' Oli asks.

'This is a private conversation,' Marilyn says.

'I'm not asking *you*. I'm asking Jonathan.'

'She's…she's…' I say, wanting, needing to talk about her.

But I can't find the words to describe what she is to me.

'She's his girlfriend,' Kyle says.

'Oh,' Oli whispers, picking away at the edge of her nails, head down.

'When…?' Marilyn asks.

'As soon as possible,' I reply.

'They won't let you do it,' Kyle says, glancing at one of the Re-hab assistants.

'They won't know about it, will they?'

He's stopped looking at me.

'*Will they*, Kyle?'

'Look Jonathan, if you insist on going ahead with this crazy idea then we'll have no option but to tell the authorities what you're planning.'

'*We'll* have no option,' I look at Marilyn. 'I thought you were my friend. I thought you were Sarah's friend.'

'I am, you know I am. But Kyle thinks and I agree, that…'

'I don't care what Kyle thinks,' I say, 'because, if it wasn't for *him*, we wouldn't be in this situation. *Sarah* wouldn't be in this situation. He's to blame for it all. He gave the information to Zack.'

'That's unfair, Jonathan,' Marilyn says.

'And you…you played your part too,' I say.

My stabbing words are designed to wound. I want them to experience the pain, the crippling pain, I'm feeling.

'If either of you had any sort of moral integrity,

you'd go with me. Help me rescue her.'

'Go with you,' Marilyn says, 'is that what you're thinking?'

'Yes,' I say, 'I thought…I *hoped* you'd come with me.'

Chapter 3

I open my eyes. I have no idea where I am. A sharp pain stabs me between my shoulder blades, as I roll my stiff, cold body over onto my back. I sit up, alarmed and feel behind for the screwdriver. My breaths come in rapid, nerve-driven bursts. My eyes strain to see through the semi-dark, punctuated by a pulse of orange light. And it all comes back to me. *Everything*. The hopelessness of my situation. I draw my legs up to my chest and hug them close to me, feeling the chill of my knees against my chin through the thin fabric. I'm thirsty, hungry and cold but, worse than this...quite alone. How long have I been asleep, minutes...hours? I have no way of knowing.

A faint noise cuts through the low level thrum of the City below. It's not a rumble or vibration, this is something more tangible. And it's moving. A Council member? Maybe. But something about it doesn't feel right. The sound is creeping, uncertain. I grab hold of the screwdriver, its handle cool against my palm then get to my feet and approach the serving hatch. The sound is louder here but not loud enough to be coming from the refectory. Loneliness winning out against fear, I weave my way through tables and chairs towards the door. With every step, the noise gets louder. When I reach the door, I peer out. I don't want to go out there again, it's dark, intimidating. The light, that guided me before, has failed. I strain my ears against the silence. The noise has stopped. Perhaps I imagined it, made myself believe that someone else is here.

Then I hear it, a soft rustle and, it's close. At the same time, a beam of light splits the blackness of the corridor, bobbing up and down as it approaches. I step back into the refectory and wait. After a couple of minutes or so, nothing has happened. No one has passed the doorway. I peer out again. The light has disappeared and I can't hear a thing. Puzzled, I shuffle along the wall towards the corridor, feeling my way with my right hand, my left grasping the screwdriver thrust out in front of me. My fingers edge forward down the side of the refectory building. If I maintain contact with it, I'll be able to find my way back. Sliding my hand about half a metre forward along the wall, my middle finger comes up against something. I allow my hand to travel over it. It's warm...it's *alive*. I scream. The screwdriver falls from my other hand and clunks onto the floor. I listen, dismayed, as it rolls away from me. Then I hear a gasp in front of me and the sound of items, falling to the floor. I don't wait, to find out, what.

'Who's there?'

I increase my pace. I've lost the screwdriver. I'm defenceless.

'Stop!'

Then I'm caught in a beam of light from behind, my shadow stretching out in front of me, long and sleek. I freeze.

'Turn around,' a voice commands, 'show

yourself.'

I shuffle round on my hands and knees, blinking against the light.

'Who's there?' I say, putting my hand over my eyes to block out the glare.

'Sarah? Sarah, it's me, Stuart.'

'Stuart!'

I reach out my hand and feel it grasped. Lunging forward, I misjudge it and our heads collide. Then I cling onto him, my head aching and cry with relief.

'It's alright, Sarah, I'm here now.'

'I can't help it. I'm so happy to see you. How did you get here? Was it the Council? Did they get you up here?'

'Slow down, Sarah, one question at a time. When there was no response from you, I got worried. I came up via the Maintenance elevator, bypassed the console to reach this floor. I wasn't sure it would work but here I am.'

'So where's the Council?'

'I haven't come across anyone, except you Sarah.'

'But they must be here somewhere.'

'What's that way?'

He points behind me.

'It's a refectory but there's nothing there. Have you got any water, Stuart, I'm so thirsty?'

'I *did*,' he says, 'but I've dropped it. We should go back and find everything I brought with me then continue the search.'

'Why is there no power up here?'

'There was a major power failure in the City

yesterday. I think Zack must have tried to hack into the computer system again.'

He directs the beam of light out in front of us then, with me clinging onto his arm, we make our way towards the corridor. The first thing we spot is a glint of metal on the ground in front of us.

'That's the screwdriver,' I say.

The bag of food and the water is close by. Stuart produces a water bottle and I fumble with the top, my hands too eager.

'Here let me,' he says, unscrewing it for me.

I gulp down water, letting its coolness seep into every pore of my body.

'That feels good,' I say.

'Right, lets continue searching,' Stuart says, striding ahead.

It's all so much easier with the flashlight. I gaze about me, taking it all in, as I go.

'It's just like the City,' I say, 'a cylinder.'

'Yes, it is up to a point. There's a Jojo running around the edge of the Council Chamber and buildings with connecting corridors linking the perimeter with the centre. But there's something very different up here.'

'What?'

He points the beam of the flashlight across the corridor.

'See.'

'See what? All I can see is a blank wall of metal.'

'Exactly. There's no Solarium in the centre.'

'But that's impossible, how can they live without a source of sunlight?'

'I don't know. It's a mystery. Behind that metal wall must be the top of the Solarium dome but they don't appear to have any access to it.'

When we reach the end of the refectory building, Stuart shines the flashlight into the connecting corridor.

'That's odd,' he says.

'What?'

'There's no building there, only empty space.'

'Perhaps it's a wider corridor.'

Stuart edges forward and I follow, clinging onto the back of his tunic top. But the end of the beam hits, nothing, but a solid wall of blackness.

'I don't like this Stuart, shouldn't we go back? We've been walking for ages and there's nothing here.'

'I don't understand this.'

'I'm scared,' I say.

'Alright, we'll try again when the lights come back on.'

We turn and make our way back but, without corridors, it's hard to work out whether we're keeping to a straight line. After about ten minutes of tentative progress, the beam of the flashlight catches a wall in front of us.

'Right now,' Stuart says, 'we need to go back to the building I came up in. I'm hoping there will be a sub generator there.'

On more familiar ground, Stuart marches forward. Passing the refectory, we cross to another building then slip inside, training the light around the entrance. At the end of the corridor, we reach a door with a spark symbol on it.

'That's the generator room,' Stuart says.

The door is open a little but not enough for us to get in.

'We need to make the gap bigger.'

Stuart grabs the edge of one of the doors then indicates that I should do the same with the other. I push my fingers in below his then, using every bit of my strength, I pull. But it won't budge. Not one centimetre. I look up at Stuart's red face. He's struggling too. *This isn't going to work.* I'm about to give up, when I feel a slight movement.

'Keep going, Sarah, keep going.'

Then, as if it's given up the fight, the door shifts, making a gap big enough to squeeze through. Stuart pushes through first, without hesitation. I'm not so keen, thinking it could close up again and trap me. Taking a deep breath to make myself smaller, I slip in.

Stuart is already across the room, standing in front of a large metal box set into the wall.

'The first thing to try is the trip switch.'

He pulls down a red lever and the room floods with light.

'I didn't expect that to work,' he says, surprised.

'I did,' I say, patting him on the back.

'I've searched this building already,' he says, trying to hide a smile, 'but there's only offices and this maintenance area. I think we should have a look at the next one.'

I follow him back out into the corridor. Getting the power back on hasn't been a total success out here, only a few of the lights are working. They stand out white against the flashing amber of the faulty majority. Despite this, there is more than enough illumination to get around. The first thing I notice is the space.

'There's so much room,' I say.

'Yes, well it's only catering for a fraction of the people in the Colony.'

The space, intimidates me, as we approach the entrance of the next building.

'That's better,' Stuart says, as the door slides open.

It's not obvious straight away what this building is, from the sparse furnishings. It could be anything.

'Looks like more offices,' I say, disappointed.

'I think we should have a proper look,' Stuart replies.

We exit the foyer area then enter a corridor lined with small offices. Stuart marches off and I plod behind him, unimpressed. At the end of the corridor, there's a much larger room that looks more interesting. In the centre of it, in a sealed rectangular half-glazed compartment, is the biggest array of computer equipment I have ever seen. But, it's what's around the walls of the room that grabs my attention. Lined up, row upon row, are dozens of screens, some flickering, others blank. Most, display images.

'What are they?' I say, spinning around, taking it all in.

'Look more closely.'

I go over to one of the screens and squint at the

dim amber-lit image displayed.

'It's the corridors outside this building,' I say.

'No, Sarah, it isn't. This is the Council's surveillance facility. What you're looking at…is a corridor, in the City below.'

Chapter 4

14/06/3042   19:51 hours
JONATHAN

I watch, fascinated, as a single tear appears in the corner of Marilyn's right eye, slides down her cheek and onto her chin. It hangs there, gaining momentum, then splashes down onto the table top. She holds my stare, with her tortured eyes, then her hands are over her face and she's sobbing.

'Now look what you've done,' Kyle says, putting his arm around Marilyn's shoulders.

'Don't you think…don't you think, I know…' she stutters, 'that I owe it to Sarah to try and rescue her? But I can't do it, Jonathan, *I can't*. I'm too scared.'

'Just supposing,' Kyle says, struggling to control his anger, 'that there was a way of getting back into the Colony. That all the generations of ex-colonists who have ever tried to get in, have all failed because of some reason other than…that it's impossible.'

'You want to go *back* into the Colony?' Oli says.

'Shut up,' Kyle snaps at her, then continues. '*If* there was a way, then you'd only rescue Sarah, would you? You'd leave the rest of the colonists down there at the mercy of Zack and the Fulcrum?'

'I haven't thought that far,' I say.

'No, you haven't thought at all. That's the problem. Have you even got a plan?'

I stare down at the table.

'I thought not,' Kyle says, as if that's the end of

it.

'*Have* you got a plan?' Oli asks.

'How can he have a plan? He's got no idea what to expect,' Kyle says. 'Who knows what measures the Colony has taken to protect itself?'

He's right. I stay silent.

'You're still going to do it, aren't you?' Marilyn says, wiping her nose with the back of her hand.

'Yes.'

'You're an idiot,' Kyle says, turning away from me.

'Maybe. But I'd rather be an idiot, than a coward.'

'Getting yourself killed, that's the *coward's* way. You think that you can't live without Sarah and you haven't got the courage to even try.'

'Don't go back, Jonathan,' Marilyn says.

I stare at her.

'Let me ask you something. If it was Sarah here safe and I was trapped down in the Colony, with no way of escape, don't you think she would do the same, Marilyn? Think about it. Don't you think she would try and rescue me?'

'Yes…she would.'

'You can't say that with any certainty,' Kyle says, 'she might not…'

'She would,' Marilyn insists, 'I *know*.'

'Come with me, Marilyn,' I say, 'help me rescue Sarah.'

'I can't. I'm so sorry, Jonathan. I just can't.'

'Of course she's not going and neither am I. You're on your own, Jonathan.'

'I'll go with you,' Oli says.

'What?' I say, surprised because I thought she'd gone.

'I'll go back into the Colony with you, rescue this Sarah and anyone else who wants rescuing.'

'Why would you do that?' I say, turning to face her.

'I have my reasons.'

'You do realise how dangerous it's going to be and that we'll probably end up…'

'Do you want me to go with you or not?'

'How do I know I can trust you?'

'You don't.'

'Then I'd rather go on my own.'

'Alright, but the offer's still there, if you change your mind.'

She gets up to leave.

'Wait,' I say.

'Let her go,' Kyle says, 'it's, all talk with her. She has no intention of going with you, why would she?'

She stops, turns and walks up to Kyle, thrusting her face into his.

'Don't you *dare*, tell him, what *my* intentions are. You don't know what they are.'

'But why would you risk your life by going back into the Colony,' I say.

'Revenge,' she whispers.

'Revenge, against *who*?'

'Sean,' she replies.

'*Sean*?'

'He's one of Zack's sidekicks.'

'I know who he is, but what's he have to do with

you?'

'That's my business,' she says.

'If you're coming with me, it makes it *my* business too.'

'Don't listen to her,' Kyle says, 'she's making it up.'

'No, she's not,' Marilyn says.

'You know nothing about it, Marilyn,' Oli says, '*nothing.*'

'It would have happened before your Deathday. Either the night before or on the morning leading up to the ceremony,' Marilyn says.

'How do you know that?' Oli says.

'Can someone tell me what you're talking about?' I say.

'He attacked you, didn't he?' Marilyn continues.

'Yes, but....'

'You're not the only one, Oli. It will happen to them all...all the girls.'

'*What* will happen?' I say, panicking.

Marilyn's look tells me that this is something she's kept from me. Something I need to know. She turns away, avoiding my eyes.

'He forced you to take it, didn't he...the tablet? Leonard must have made it up for them, while I was stalling. That means that...Sar...'

Oli stares at her puzzled.

'No, I hadn't taken anything.'

'They didn't give you the rape drug?'

'The *what?*'

'How did he do it, then?'

'With brute force, Marilyn, that's how. He

dragged me screaming through the corridors to his pod, I fought him every step of the way. But he was too strong…too strong for me. I watched him, that nervous tick flickering in his eye the whole time, as he pushed me onto the floor, tearing at my clothes. Then he…'

She gulps down a shuddering breath, at the memory.

'I went to my Deathday, covered in bruises, my scalp raw where he'd torn at my hair, a swollen cut on my lip where his teeth had bitten down on it. I stood, on the podium at my ceremony, shaking, not with cold…but with humiliation. I felt degraded…beaten. Not *one* person…not *one* of my colleagues said a word. They just stared at me.'

Marilyn places a hand on her shoulder.

'I don't want your pity,' she says, shrugging it off, 'all I want is revenge.'

She gets up and walks away from us towards the door.

'Now do you get it?' I scream at Kyle and Marilyn. 'Why I have to go back!'

My flailing hand knocks over the cup in front of me and I watch, as a pool of brown liquid pours off the table onto the floor.

Chapter 5

14/06/3042   04:23 hours
SARAH

'I thought the Eyes in the City were turned off at night,' I say, peering at the muted orange image in front of me.

'Yes, so did I, so did *everyone*,' Stuart says.

'So they've been watching us at night.'

'Yes, it looks like they have, Sarah. I think we need to search the whole Council Chamber.'

'Yes, okay, let me just…' I say, distracted.

'*Now.*'

I turn and stare at him, surprised by his tone.

'I don't want to leave you up here until we're sure what the situation is.'

'You're going to leave me here?' I say, alarmed.

'I've got to keep working, behave normally, if I don't, they'll get suspicious and…'

'Yes, of course, you're right. I hadn't thought it through.'

'We'll do it together, find out what's beyond the buildings, see what...'

I don't hear what he says. *He's going to leave me.*

Collecting together the screwdriver, flashlight and some of the water, we walk out of the surveillance room and into the corridor. At the exit, I notice that the doors open and close without any intervention from us.

'That's good they're working,' Stuart says.

'I was hoping that they'd stay open,' I say, 'so that we can get back in.'

'They'll open again,' he says, with a confidence I don't share.

The lighting in the corridor is a mixture now of, the bright, fully functioning units and the amber pulse of the faulty ones.

'We need to cover as much ground as we can, in case the lights fail again,' I say, quickening my pace.

'Yes, but we don't want to get separated, Sarah, slow down.'

I wait for him to catch me up.

We pass the building that Stuart came up into then reach the refectory and walk along its length, knowing what's at the end. I stare out at the empty space in front of us. There are no other buildings in sight. Common sense tells me to turn back, to keep away from this void, but Stuart doesn't hesitate, he charges into it like he knows where he's going. The addition of light does nothing to make it less menacing, as we launch out into the emptiness, following the path of the Jojo. I run my hand along the top of the guardrails, their familiarity filling me with a new confidence and stride forward, humming to steady my nerves. After ten minutes of brisk walking, I spot something in front of us.

'What's that?' I say.

Stuart peers out at it, his eyes squinting through the gloom.

'I have no idea but it looks interesting.'

As we continue towards it, I make out a number of small buildings.

'Pods?' I say.

'Well, if they are, they're a lot bigger than anything down in the City.'

Now that we're almost upon them, I can see that they are one storey buildings arranged in three rows, with paths between them. I've never seen anything like it before. Curiosity takes over from fear, as I walk up to the first of them.

'This must be the residential area,' Stuart says, his head moving from side to side.

I glance down one of the pathways, at the uniform buildings stretching out in front of us on either side.

'Should we call out?'

'No, don't do that, Sarah?'

The caution in his voice worries me. We move forward at a steady pace, scanning the buildings as we go. The hairs on my arms are standing on end, as I hone my senses, expecting to catch a movement or hear a noise from one of the buildings. I'm gripped by the eerie silence of the place, as if eyes watch our every move. But, if anything's there, it's not human. This place is devoid of life.

'Where is everybody?'

'I have no idea,' Stuart says, 'but if this is the Council's living quarters, these pods are huge compared to the cramped boxes, we live in.'

We reach the end of the row and stop.

'I counted twenty buildings in this row and there are three identical ones,' Stuart says. 'Sixty individual buildings, sixty Councillors, one for each, it makes sense.'

'But where are they all, Stuart, the place is

deserted? I don't like it.'

'Let's take a look,' he says, walking over to one of the buildings.

I follow, not wanting to be left exposed in the middle of the path. To my amazement, the door of the unit slides open when Stuart reaches it.

'That's interesting,' he says.

We step inside into a small foyer. Beyond this, we can see a spacious living area with padded seats. I walk over to one of them.

'This is comfortable,' I say, bouncing up and down on it.

The swish of the main door closing, surprises me, but before I have time to comment, there's a click as the main lights dim. A number of smaller lights scattered about the room on tables, come on, creating in an instant a more intimate atmosphere. Another click and the strains of music surround us, rising and falling.

'This is incredible,' I say.

But it hasn't finished yet. The white wall in front of me flickers into life, displaying a life-sized scene of dappled woodland. It's as if I'm looking through a huge picture window. Stuart's busy, picking up and examining the unfamiliar objects that cover all the available surfaces in the room. I leave him to it and walk into one of the three areas coming off the main living space. One, is a food preparation area the other, a luxurious hygiene unit and separate sleeping area. I stare at the bunk and two things hit me. First, it's huge and second, it's spread with a cover of the most exquisite material, so different from the coarse fabric of my bunk. I climb onto it and sink into its soft embrace, letting the silkiness of the material brush my cheek. If I'm going to get any sleep at all in this Council Chamber, then this is where it's going to happen. I call out to Stuart in the next room.

'Come and look at this.'

He appears at the entrance to the sleeping area.

'I'm going to finish looking around,' I say to him, as he walks over and slumps down next to me.

'Alright, I'll be out in a minute.'

Walking back into the living area, I notice a glass partition door at the far end that leads into a space beyond it. It's too dark to make out what it is. All I can see is my own reflection in the glass, as I walk up to the doors. They glide apart and I step through them. A bank of lights flash on above my head, blinding me. My eyes, adjusting to the glare, see in front of me, a rectangular area about twelve metres long by six metres wide. *A miniature solarium?*

'Stuart,' I shout, 'you'll never guess what I've found.'

My attention is drawn to a fountain in front of me but there's no water coming from its parched nozzles. There are statues dotted about the area, a bench on a paved courtyard with a path weaving through the space, following a design that no longer applies. This is a garden, but a garden with no plants. All that remains are shaped beds of dry earth. I sit down on the bench, close my eyes with my face tilted upwards and soak up the revitalising sunrays.

After a while I decide to go back inside. I hear the swish of the doors as they seal up behind me.

'Stuart,' I call out, but there's no reply, no sign of him.

Walking towards the sleeping area, I hear a noise coming from inside.

'Stuart…is that you?'

I creep forward and peer in. Straight away, I know that the noise is coming from the bed, or to be more precise, from Stuart, on the bed. A regular tremulous wheeze as he breathes in, followed by a whistle as he exhales. I've heard this racket before.

'Stuart, wake up, we need to get back.'

But there's no waking him. And there's no way I'm going back out there on my own. Rolling him over onto his side, I pull at the cover beneath him. There's a slight stutter and I think he might wake, after all, but the rhythmic snoring resumes, undeterred. With the cover released, I climb in beside him and pull it over us. Despite the size of the bunk, I move across and nestle in next to him, resting my head against the rise and fall of his back. The last thing I see, before I drift off, is the slow fade of the lights.

Chapter 6

14/06/3042   20:18 hours
JONATHAN

'Are you angry with me?'

'*Why*, Kyle, would I be angry?' I say.

'Well, for a start, you launched *that* across the table.'

A Re-hab assistant pushes me out of the way, as she uses a cloth to try to hold back the flow. She gasps then drops the brown sodden wad, as the hot liquid scalds her hand.

'I wish you'd calm down, Jonathan,' she says, shaking her burnt hand, 'if you hadn't been arguing, waving your arms all over the place, this wouldn't have happened.'

'*He* started it,' I point, like an angry child, at Kyle.

'It doesn't matter who started it, grow up,' she says, marching off.

'You made an error of judgement,' Kyle says, 'it happens to us all.'

'What do you mean by *that*?'

'Nothing.'

'No, come on, if you've got something to say, *say* it.'

'Jonathan leave it,' Marilyn chips in, 'don't you think you've done enough already?'

'Oh, so you *can* still speak.'

She looks away and stares over my left shoulder,

her new found verbal skills silenced again. I turn my attention back to Kyle.

'*Well*?'

'Well what!'

'What did you mean by an *error of judgement*?'

'Jonathan…' Marilyn tries to intervene.

I put my hand up to silence her.

'I'm talking to *him*,' I say.

'Alright, if you must know, you've made Marilyn and I feel bad about not agreeing to take part in your crazy scheme.'

'By *crazy scheme*, I assume you're referring to my plan to rescue Sarah, your friend,' I stare at Kyle then, Marilyn, 'and *yours*.'

'Yes,' he says.

'Well, for your information, I've got no problem at all with that. I'd be lying if I said I wasn't disappointed, but it's your decision and I respect it. I don't understand it, but I do respect it.'

'But you're quite happy to take a complete stranger with you, someone who doesn't strike me as either reliable or trustworthy. You're happy to do *that*.'

'She was the only one who offered,' I say, bitterness tainting my words.

'But she's not doing it for Sarah.'

'No, and neither are you two.'

Kyle is about to reply, when we're interrupted by a commotion by the door. I turn to see what's going on. A man, I don't recognise, helps a young boy wrapped in a grey coat, through the door. The coat flaps open and I see, as everyone sees, that he's naked underneath it. His legs are bruised with the cold and he looks barely alive. Forgetting her scalded hand, the Re-hab assistant rushes over to him, followed by another, who appears from across the room.

'Found him wandering about,' the man says, 'stark naked he was, about five hundred metres from the Renaissance Gate. Can't get much sense out of him but he's come up from the Colony, that's for sure.'

One of the assistants thanks the man then guides the boy to a chair. The other places a cup in front of him. The boy reaches out, his eyes dull and wraps his shaking hands around it. He looks surprised but also, comforted, by the warmth. After some encouragement, he takes a sip. A spray of brown liquid shoots from his mouth and lands on the male assistant's shirt. He jumps back in alarm.

'What is it with you CB's?' he shouts, furious.

A hush descends over the room. The female assistant shoots a warning look at him, as he rubs at the splatters patterning the white cloth.

'Well, it gets on my nerves,' he says, quieter now.

Confused I glance round at Oli.

'What's a CB?'

'Colony Born, that's what they call us,' she says.

'We do *not* use street talk like that here,' the female assistant says.

'Tell *him* that, not me,' Oli says, glaring at the male assistant.

'Water,' the boy whispers, through parched lips.

I grab the jug in front of me, pour some water into

a cup and take it over to him.

'Here,' I say putting it into his hands.

He drinks it down in one, then holds the cup out for more. I pour him another, then another. After three cups, he stops. He looks a little revived but he's still shaking. I watch as his eyes dart about the room. Someone replaces the coat with a large blanket and gives it back to the man, thanking him as they do.

'Anyone, would've done the same,' he mutters, as he walks out of the door.

'He needs a counsellor,' the female assistant says, as she rushes off.

'You're safe now. Everything's alright,' I say, sitting down next to the boy.

'I don't understand…' he says.

'They'll explain it all to you. What's your name?'

'Carlo,' he says.

'What were you doing wandering around like that?'

But he's not looking at me. His gaze is transfixed on something behind me. I turn and see that what's caught his attention is a container of fruit.

'You want some?' I say, pointing.

He nods. I pick an apple and put it into his hand.

'Go on, it's good, try it.'

He bites into it, plays with it in his mouth a while, then swallows. He takes another bite. I wait for him to swallow that then, try again.

'Why were you wandering…?'

'Late…my Deathday ceremony…was late,' Carlo says.

'Late? How late?'

'Four hours, maybe more.'

'Come away from him, Jonathan,' the female assistant says behind me, 'the counsellor will deal with all that. He needs to rest now.'

'*Why* was it late?' I say, shaking off her hand.

'There was a power failure. The Ascendor…would not work…I…I was ready…but…I could not get in.'

He takes in a sharp breath, his chest shuddering with the memory.

The counsellor arrives and Carlo is helped to his feet. As he's led through the door, he looks back at me, fear in his eyes.

'You're safe now, Carlo, I promise,' I call out to him.

But I don't think he hears me.

'You know what that means, don't you?' I say, turning to Kyle and Marilyn.

'You should have let the counsellor deal with it, Jonathan,' Marilyn says, 'you upset him with all your questions.'

I ignore her.

'Zack has tried to break into the computer. I can't delay going in, not now. It has to be tomorrow.'

'Please don't do it, Jonathan, *please*,' Marilyn says.

She takes hold of my hand, pleading with her grasp. But I've made up my mind.

'Wish me luck,' I say.

Kyle gets up, silent and walks away from me. Marilyn pauses then throws her arms around my shoulders. I can feel her tears wetting my cheek. Then, without a word, she releases my hand and follows. She catches him up, as he marches out of the room. So, he isn't even going to say, goodbye.

Chapter 7

I wake and blink at the unfamiliar surroundings. It's alright. You know where you are. It's fine. I breathe deep into my chest and let the cool air calm my thumping heart. I go through it in my mind. I'm in the Council Chamber, in the residential area. Yes, but something's wrong. The sound? *What* sound? There is no sound. The sound has gone. I sit up and stare at the empty space next to me. *Stuart's gone.* A hand, my hand slaps into my mouth and I gasp. He's gone, left me on my own. How could he do that to me? How could he? No, think about it. Stuart has to go to work, has to act normally. Zack will be searching for me. He knows I haven't left the Colony. They'll be watching everyone, watching for unusual behaviour. He had to go. But why didn't he wake me? Because he knew I'd plead with him to stay. Stuart did the right thing, the logical thing and I hate him for it.

I pull back the cover and get off the bunk. Something senses my movement and a light comes on. Then, making my way over to the hygiene unit, I dash over to the waste unit and relieve myself. When I get up, I hear the sensor activate, as it sucks down my offering. In no time, I discover that it all works, the waste unit, the ultrasound cleaner, *everything.* I take my time over my hygiene routine, I'm in no hurry to go out into the empty corridors again. When I've finished, I walk into the living area and a soft light comes on followed by the wall screen. Spotting Stuart's bag on the floor, I sit down opposite the screen, take out the water bottle and take a gulp. Alarmed, I see that it is only half full. It's alright, Stuart will be back tonight. I'll need to ration it, but it'll be fine. I rummage around and find the remains of the food and sit, staring at the screen, chewing. Was that a movement? My whole body tenses as I peer at the image in front of me. Something scurries through the fallen leaves, a creature with a curved bushy tail. And that's not all. The tree branches sway, buffeted by a silent wind and dappled sunlight filters through their leaves, illuminating the blue flowers at their feet. What I thought, last night, was a static image is full of life, full of movement. I stare at it, entranced.

After a while, I come round. I've been here too long. I have to get back to the surveillance room, do something useful. I pack up the bag and walk over to the door. Disappointed, I watch it open onto the pathway. I don't want to leave here. Outside, I look back at the drab exterior of the building I've just exited, and marvel at the comfort and luxury I know is within. I make my way along the walkway looking at the identical buildings in the row. Are they all the same, like the pods in the City or...? I can't resist taking a look. I approach the door to the third one along the row and it opens. As I'd hoped, this one is quite different from *mine*. Different furniture, garden area, artefacts, even the layout is different. But most surprising, it has a different scene displayed on the wall screen. I go from building to building, excited. In one there's a seaside view, in another, a snow-topped mountain range. I look at ten in all and everyone shows a different view, each one personalised to the desires and needs of its occupant. A little bit of the Earth transported into their lives. The urge to stay here is strong and I have to force myself to leave. But, as I march down the corridors towards the business end of the Council Chamber, I'm filled with a new confidence. It's as if I've visited the homes of ten individuals, ten human beings with hopes and dreams, kindred spirits.

The first building I arrive at, is vast. I glance through tinted windows and see that it's full of laboratories and that it's some kind of science block. The next is the computer block, containing the surveillance room. So that makes five work buildings in all and a residential area. I approach the entrance to the computer block, as if I've done it many times before, instead of, only once and make my way to the surveillance room. Once inside, I settle down in front of the screens and play around with the switches, flipping through images. I dart about the Colony, from corridors to pods, to the inside of buildings. There's a fascination about watching people going about their business. The City is busy with colonists on their way to the Solarium. I look at their expressionless faces. I recognise many of them. My eyes dart from screen to screen, searching. The face I'm looking for, the one I want so much to see, isn't there. I look away. *Jonathan's dead*. I will never see him again and the pain of that terrible truth, sears into my heart.

Then something, *someone*, forces my eyes back to the screens, Stuart, walking towards the Security Response Unit building. He strides along the corridor, his head held high, the timidity he had when I first knew him, gone. I will him to walk past the entrance but instead he punches his ID code into the door console and is admitted without a problem. I switch cameras and watch as he walks across the foyer and talks to an SRU officer at the desk. He waits while she punches something into her console. He glances around and looks up at the Eye. For a fleeting moment, I think that our eyes meet but then he looks back at the officer and I convince myself that I was mistaken. A novice arrives and escorts him out of the foyer and down the corridor leading to the offices.

They exit the sightline of the camera and I fumble with the switches, trying to pick them up again. Images of SRU officers flash across the screen but there's no sign of Stuart. Then I spot something and go back to the previous screen. I recognise that office it's, Zack's. I make a mental note of the switch position and watch fascinated as Stuart enters and walks over to the desk. Zack sits behind it, facing the Eye. Stuart has his back to me. I zoom in on Zack's face but I can't read his lips, however hard I try. He looks calm, in control. Stuart sits quite still, apart from an occasional nod of his head. They could be two colleagues talking about the day's work programme.

I don't know how long they talk together like this, twenty minutes, maybe more. Then Zack gets up, followed by Stuart, and walks around the desk. Stuart turns to go and I catch his expression, hoping to glean something from it but it's blank. Zack places a hand on his shoulder with the light touch of friendship and leads Stuart over to the door. As he walks out of the office, I switch cameras and follow his progress out of the SRU building and into the City corridors. I try and rationalise what I've witnessed. A terrifying thought germinates in my brain and keeps on growing. *Can I trust Stuart?*

Chapter 8

14/06/3042   20:45 hours
JONATHAN

'We're better off without them,' Oli says.

'I'm going in tomorrow.'

'*Tomorrow*,' she says.

I see it at once, a flash of fear in her eyes.

'You're still coming, aren't you? You haven't changed…?'

'Of course I'm coming. I wasn't expecting it to be so soon, that's all.'

'Good, good,' I say. 'We'll need things like tools, a flashlight and a bag to put it all in? Do you know where we can get hold of all that?'

She smiles.

'I certainly do,' she says, 'follow me.'

Then she makes off in the direction of the corridor.

'And food and water. We'll need that too,' I call after her.

'Alright, alright, one thing at a time.'

In front of an office door, she stops and beckons for me, to join her.

'Stand guard.'

Then she's inside, hauling something out from behind the desk, a bag. Unfastening the pockets, she turns the whole thing upside down. The contents cascade out onto the floor, in a heap. She rummages through it, throwing things behind her, as she goes.

'Nothing there of any use to us,' she says, 'but it's a good bag.'

Out of the corner of my eye, I see a movement.

'Someone's coming,' I whisper.

Oli dives behind the desk. I recognise the person now, as the physical re-hab instructor. She glares at me, puzzled.

'Good evening,' I say, blocking the view into the office, where the floor is littered with an assortment of rejected items.

'What are you doing hanging around here at this time of night? You should be in the dormitory.'

'On my way,' I reply, as she passes without stopping.

I turn and look back into the office.

'Right,' Oli says, emerging from behind the desk, 'let's get this filled.'

She marches off in front of me, as if the incident hadn't happened, with the bag slung over her shoulder. I follow behind. I have to admire her nerve. Reaching the end of the corridor, she pushes open the fire exit and races down a flight of stairs.

'Where are we going?' I call after her.

'The basement.'

When we get to a set of heavy double doors, she peers through the small, wired window. I look over her shoulder into a large room lined with workbenches. Standing by one of them is a young man, wearing a set of blue overalls.

'Wait here,' Oli says, thrusting the bag at me. 'I won't be long.'

As she approaches him, the first thing that strikes

me, is that he doesn't look surprised to see her. Their lips move. Oli smiles at him. Then she pulls him to her and kisses him on the lips. Her hand travels down his back, caressing his buttocks through the material of his overalls. I watch mesmerised, as her fingers slip into his back pocket. Then she stops, says something in his ear. He looks about him, nervously, then walks off in the direction of the door opposite and walks through it. As soon as he's gone, Oli runs over to me and pushes a set of keys into my hand.

'See that cupboard,' she points, 'you should find everything you need in there.'

'What are you going to do?'

'I'm going to be the distraction, so you'll need to be quick,' she grins, 'shouldn't take more than ten minutes, tops.'

I stare after her, open mouthed, as she runs across the room after the man.

I walk in, expecting a light to come on automatically. I wave my hand about in front of me, but nothing happens. Then, I remember seeing people here switch lights on, using a console on the wall. I feel around by the door and find a small square box with a switch on it. I push it down and the cupboard fills with light. Straight away, I see a screwdriver lying on the bench in front of me, grab it then look about for anything else that might be useful. But I can't see the most important thing, a flashlight. I start pulling out drawers, aware that time is running out. I'm on the verge of giving up when I find, at the back of one of the larger ones, several flashlights of various sizes. I pick the biggest then test that it's working, by playing the beam around the cupboard. It's much more powerful than Stuart's but it's also heavy. I decide to go for a smaller one, which is lighter. I stuff it into the bag with the other items.

'Got what you need?'

I look up, startled. Oli stands in the cupboard doorway, her face flushed, her short blond hair sticking out from her head.

'Yes, I did. What about you?'

'Well, *Larry* did,' she says.

Something about her expression warns me against asking for any further information. I switch off the light and step outside, leaving the keys hanging from the lock. Then she's off again, out into the stairwell and back up the stairs. I follow behind, accepting that she's in charge here and that I have no idea what's going on.

'What now?' I say,

'Well, I'm going to get us some provisions, food and water,' she says.

'How are you going to do that?'

'I have a contact in the kitchen.'

'Do you need any help?' I ask.

'I *shouldn't* think so, Jonathan, would you?'

I shrug my shoulders.

'Probably not,' I say, my cheeks reddening.

'So what's the plan then?'

I look at her, puzzled.

'The plan…for getting back into the Colony?'

She still thinks I've got a plan. She's going to be

47

an asset, that's clear. I have to sound convincing.

'I'll explain it all to you later,' I say.

But I'm not getting away with that.

'You haven't got a plan, have you?'

'No.'

'Fine, I just thought I'd check. So I know what I'm dealing with.'

'You knew didn't you?'

'Yes, of course I did. I'm trained to watch people. I notice things, weigh things up, remember.'

'*Trained*?' I say.

'Yes. I was an SRU officer in the Colony.'

I stop dead and stare after her, astounded.

'Does it make any difference?' she asks.

'I don't...'

'If it's any consolation, being in the Fulcrum didn't stop Sean raping me before my Deathday ceremony.'

'*You were in the Fulcrum*?'

'Yes, Jonathan, I was,' she says, striding off in the direction of the kitchen.

Chapter 9

However hard I try, I can't stop thinking about Stuart. I keep going back to it, turning it over and over in my mind. Zack's hand on his shoulder, the ease of it. The way they slotted together, like two parts of a puzzle that begin to make sense, to fit. I know that if I go on like this, I will drive myself mad. I have to concentrate on something else, relegate my worries to a less accessible place in my mind. I need to find a distraction. Looking across the room, I spot a screen that I haven't noticed before. It's separate from the others with its own operating console. Intrigued, I walk over and sit in front of it and press the 'on' button. I jump, my pulse racing, as the screen flashes on revealing a seated man. His shoulders slump forward and he leans to one side, as if the effort of sitting upright is too much for him. His face is ashen, drained of all natural colour except for the red flare of his cheeks. A bead of perspiration on his forehead catches the light, as he moves. His hair falls in lank strands over his protruding ears and he struggles to breathe. He coughs with a violent retch into his hand, looks up then speaks.

I do not know who I am addressing but I have very little time to convey this message to you, perhaps only hours. My name is...is Professor

49

Martin Cusack, head of a team of computer scientists...but this is not important. I am the last...and so it has fallen to me to ensure that...despite what has happened here, the breeding programme will carry on...without us.

I do not blame the outsiders...those left behind...those left to face the apocalyptic events, angry...in despair. Is it any wonder that they smashed the only visible evidence of the Colony's existence...of its salvation, the UV sensors on the surface? But, in doing so, they put the whole future of the Colony and its mission, in jeopardy. One of our engineers...I will tell you his name, Daniel Carter...such a brave man, risked his life to go up to the surface and repair the sensors, so vital to our survival. He was successful. He returned in triumph to the Council Chamber. But we were not to know that his survival was to seal our fate.

He coughs into his right palm, his chest heaving against the force of it. Then, composing himself, he continues, his voice choked with phlegm.

Two weeks after his return, some of us started to display flu-like symptoms. At first, we were not unduly concerned. Every one of us had been inoculated against all viruses and disease, before entering the Colony. We had medical experts who had been given the task of eliminating all possible threats to our health. But this mutated virus that we identified as H15N13...such an innocuous name...proved stronger than any of us. One by one, it picked us off. Against its ravages, we were defenceless. It became an unspoken pact that victims, faced with certain death, should go up to the surface and offer their diseased bodies to the relentless heat...to the flames. It is vital...absolutely vital that we leave no trace of it behind.

The Council was made up of the finest brains in every scientific field. It was our task to oversee...to protect the breeding programme...but we failed in this endeavour. There was only one way that we could save the Colony and we worked night and day, despite our illness, to achieve this. A group of the best computer scientists in the world, led by myself, programmed the computer to carry on the breeding programme. It has been set up on a loop of eighteen years duration...that it will repeat for as long as it can. It will continue to report that the surface is uninhabitable, so that the Colony can continue...until...until what? I do not know. Now, the computer functions independently. How long it will continue is unknown. I hope...it is long enough.

Sometimes, in my darkest moments, I think that we have been punished for 'playing God'. I can only hope that you...you are the saviour...that we have succeeded in clutching the Human Race from the arms of extinction. That is our hope...my hope.

Now, I must prepare myself, to leave...to go up to the surface. The responsibility, that has burdened me for so long, is no more. I wish you farewell, whoever you are.

The screen goes blank and switches off. I can't

move, I can't breathe. Seconds before it went black I noticed, in the top right hand corner of the screen, a date, 18/09/2535. A surge rises in my stomach. Jutting my head forward, I vomit onto the floor. Then I slump down onto the workbench, my forehead resting on my hands.

After a while, I get up and fetch the water bottle. I gulp it down, trying to get rid of the burning sensation at the back of my throat. The sour-smelling puddle at my feet creeps under the workbench and I know that I should clear it up before it disappears out of reach. But, transfixed by the blank screen in front, I'm unable to switch it back on…to check…to check that what I saw is real. I haven't got the courage to do that yet because, I *know*, it's real. 2535. That means the Colony has been in existence for… I struggle to do the calculation in my head, translate the solid weight of dread that's pressing down on me, into concrete figures. It's too big for me, paralysing, terrifying. I have to leave it be.

I walk over to the sealed computer area and stare in at my captor, at the *Colony's* captor. The lights dance about the consoles in rhythmic patterns like the beat of a gigantic heart. For centuries, it has calculated the path of our enslavement, connecting and transmitting impulses to achieve ultimate control. It has outperformed itself, adjusted, and learnt. It is both our salvation and our nemesis. There is no Council, only the Computer…*only the Computer*. I slump down onto my knees before it and feel the vibration of its life force through the floor. Please don't fail us, *please*.

After a while I get up and go back to the screens. I stare at them, hypnotised by the flickering images, watching the business of the City unfold. But the weight of the information I've discovered is too much for me to handle, on my own. I need someone to talk to – *anyone*. Without actual physical contact, all I can do is interact with the people on these screens. People going about their work, with no other thought than whether they will manage to complete their daily quota of work. I want to be part of that community again. I want to rid myself of the destructive knowledge that is gnawing at my guts, leaving only a void where my vital organs should be. I'm being eaten alive, by words. Soon there will be nothing left of me, the Sarah, who once walked these City corridors. I need someone to comfort me. But there's no one. I've never felt so alone in my life and it hurts. It hurts so much.

The swish of doors opening, nearby, cuts into my thoughts. I jump off the stool and run over to the door. Hearing footsteps approaching, my body tenses. The screwdriver is over the other side of the room. I make a dash across to the workbench, grab it and sprint back, holding it in my hand like a weapon. I keep very quiet, very still and listen, as the footsteps get louder. Somebody is outside now. I raise my makeshift weapon ready to use it if I have to. The door slides open and I leap across it.

'Stuart!' I gasp. 'It's you.'

'Who else were you expecting?' he says, eyeing the screwdriver poised above his left eye socket.

'I…it's so early, how…?'

'Can you stop pointing that at me, it's making me nervous?' he says and pushes past me into the room.

'I came straight up here from work,' he continues, without looking at me.

'I collected some food and water and waited for all the Maintenance personnel to go up to the City, then made my way here.'

'I see.'

'You don't look very happy to see me. I thought you'd be pleased.'

'I am…pleased…you surprised me, that's all.'

'So, what have you been up to since I left,' he says, placing the food and water onto the workbench.

I think about what's happened in a few short hours, the enormity of it all.

'Not much,' I lie. 'What about you? Have there been any developments?'

'Developments?'

'Have you seen any evidence that the SRU are making progress with their plan to take over the Colony?'

He hesitates. 'Have *you*?'

'What?'

'Have you seen anything going on down there?'

He looks across at the surveillance screens.

'Not really,' I say.

'Are you alright Sarah, only you seem a bit on edge?'

'It's been frightening being here on my own.'

'Well, there's no real alternative. You're safe up here.'

'Am I?'

'Of course, nobody knows you're here.'

'No,' I say, eyes lowered, 'I suppose you're right.'

'Don't you want some food? I thought you'd jump at it.'

'No,' I say, 'I was sick earlier.'

The words are out before I can stop them. He turns around from rummaging in the bag and stares at me.

'Sick? You mean vomiting?'

'Yes, a little.'

'Why would you be sick? What caused that?'

'I don't know, nerves, or something. I'm fine now. I'll have some water.'

'It's still a worry,' he says.

'It's *not*, Stuart. It just happened,' I snap.

'Alright, fine.'

He sits on the stool, the stool from which I heard the terrible truth and starts eating from one of the food packets.

'So, you haven't seen any SRU officers then?'

He looks up at me, stops chewing, then swallows, hard.

'I didn't say *that*,' he says.

'So, you have then?'

'No...yes...obviously I've seen SRU officers but I didn't notice anything unusual.'

I look away from him. I've given him the chance to tell me the truth, to tell me about his meeting with Zack and he's lied to me. The only person I thought I could trust, has betrayed me.

Chapter 10

Where is she? The welcoming party will be here any moment. She knows that we have to be in position before then. She's had second thoughts. I'm not surprised. Telling her I had no plan didn't help. So many people have tried to do what I'm planning, and failed. Why do I think that I'll do any better? Kyle and Marilyn are right. It is suicidal. A menacing buzz resonates through my left ear and I dive sideways, banging my head against the branches above me. It won't leave me alone. Five minutes I've been here and it's attacked me three times already. I know what these things are capable of. I've been on the receiving end of one of their stings. In the Colony, there are no live insects. I always thought that was a shame, until now.

'Ow!'

I jump, as the flying menace collides with my right cheek.

'Jonathan?' I hear someone call out.

'Is that you?' I say, rubbing the spot where it made physical contact with me.

Peering out of the foliage in the direction of the voice, I spot Oli approaching. She stoops forward under the weight of the bag on her back. How much stuff has she got in there?

'Over here,' I call out, shuffling over to make

space for her.

'Here take this.'

She crouches down on her knees, thrusts the bag at me then crawls in. But there's no room for her *and* the bag.

'Hold on, while I put the bag up above me on the branch,' I say.

Next thing I know, she launches herself on top of me, her fingernails biting into my arm.

'What was *that*?' she screams, her hands beating at her hair, in panic.

'I don't know, but it's very persistent.'

She burrows down next to me still flicking at her hair. I can feel her warmth through my jacket, her smell, strange and intoxicating.

'Plenty of room,' she says.

Her head is so close to me that her hair brushes against my right ear.

'Did you see the welcoming party, on your way up?' I ask.

'No, but according to my contact in the kitchen, there's been a big discussion about what happened yesterday with Carlo.'

'What do you mean?'

'Well, now that things are getting so erratic in the Colony, they're considering having someone posted here all the time.'

'When are they going to start *that*?'

'There'll be a roster, but I think someone will stay on, today.'

'So we need to get in…'

Her hand slaps across my mouth.

'Someone's coming,' she whispers.

We watch as a group of three people, one man and two women, settle on the mound facing the Renaissance Gate.

'Supposing nobody comes up like yesterday,' Oli whispers in my ear.

'Then we stay here until they do.'

'You're mad, do you know that?'

'I wonder what the time is,' I say, ignoring her.

Without a word, Oli pulls up her sleeve and pushes her timepiece up against my eyes. I push it away so that I can read it. 14:05.

'When am I going to get one of those?' I ask.

'Well, you won't get one *now*, will you?'

After a few minutes, the welcoming party approaches the Renaissance Gate. The smaller of the two women is in front, with a blanket and visor. The other, behind her, carries a water bottle. The man stands back a little.

'When the Gate opens, we stay put, okay?' I say. 'We move when it starts to close and *only* on my signal.'

She doesn't answer.

'Understand?'

'Yes, of course, I'm not an idiot. Gate opens, don't move. Gate closes, move.'

'*On my signal*,' I stress.

'On…your…signal,' she spells out.

'Good.'

I reach up and dislodge the bag from the branch above my head. It's so heavy, it falls down with a sharp crack, as a dead twig snaps off under the weight. I freeze. The man looks behind him straight at us and I wonder how hidden we are. But he seems unconcerned and turns back to the Gate. I grab Oli's wrist and look at the timepiece, it says 14:15.

'Get ready,' I say.

Oli manoeuvres onto her haunches ready to move. I can't get the bag onto my back, there's not enough room, so I crouch down holding it in my arms. Oli nudges me and I look up and see the Renaissance Gate's massive metal doors slide apart dwarfing a pale, naked girl standing behind them. Her arms are crossed over her chest, her hands clutching onto her upper arms. She has her eyes closed. Then, unable to hold her up a second longer, her legs buckle under her and she collapses in the doorway straddled across two worlds. The women approach, coaxing her onto her feet. The visor and blanket are put on. The doors won't close until there's no obstruction. I watch as the women, one either side, help the girl out but she seems reluctant to move. I feel Oli next to me tense, ready.

'Now?' she says.

'No, wait until they're free of the doorway.'

But she doesn't. She launches herself out of the bush and runs towards the Renaissance Gate. I have no choice but to follow. *It's too soon.*

She darts around the group and in through the Gate. The doors are moving together now. The man leaps forward and grabs her arm. She lashes out at him, as the gap gets smaller. I have to go *now*. I push past the two women and the girl, whose eyes are now, wide open with fear. Using the bag, I come up behind the man and barge into him with all my strength. He stumbles sideways, away from the door, away from Oli. The gap is only forty-five centimetres wide now and I throw myself towards it. But it's too late, I'm not going to make it. Oli grabs the bag and throws it behind her. Unburdened, I turn sideways and push with all my strength through the gap, lose my balance and end up on top of it. I lie on the ground panting, my heart, racing. Then Oli helps me up. We stare up at the engraving above our heads, listening to the pounding on the closed doors. *It is your destiny*, it says.

'What have we done?' Oli whispers.

Chapter 11

I woke up late this morning and found that Stuart had left for work. This time, I was glad of his absence. Since yesterday, I've felt uncomfortable in his presence. I've scrutinised his every move, analysed his every word, searching for clues, signs. *Anything.* I want to trust him, but I can't. I'd glance up, see that questioning look in his eyes, as if he needed to ask me something but didn't know how. I ran all the way to the surveillance room. I felt I had to watch him, spy on him. It's the only way I can find out the truth. The first thing I did when I arrived here was to check, make sure he's where he's supposed to be, down in the Maintenance Department. And, of course, he was. Safe, reliable Stuart. Even so, I kept going back. But, every time I did, he was there, going about his duties as usual. It became an obsession. I couldn't go for more than ten minutes, without going back there to check on him. It had to stop. So now, I've decided to concentrate my efforts on the insides of the other City buildings.

I switch all the screens, from views of the corridors, to images of interiors. I scan them looking for one particular interior and there it is, second screen in from the left on the bottom row, the foyer of the SRU building. That's where I'll start. The images move around the building as I play with the switches. One by one the offices come into view. I flick through them so fast, they become a blur then I see something interesting and go back. Clarissa sits hunched over a computer console, with Zack standing behind her. Her facial muscles are tight with concentration. Every now and then, she glances over her shoulder, her face seeking his approval but he stares down at the screen, emotionless. About twenty minutes elapse, maybe more and I think about moving on to another area. Then the lights in the office flicker. It's barely noticeable. But it's enough to make Clarissa look back at Zack and this time, he smiles. And that's when everything goes black. I grip onto the edge of the workbench, every nerve in my body alert. I count the seconds, one, two, three, four... Then, I'm released from the dark fear, as light floods the room again. I fight to slow my breathing, calm my thumping heart but I'm too shaken and it takes me several minutes to regain my composure.

I look back up at the screen, where the image of the office has been restored. But now it's empty. With trembling fingers, I track through the screens but they've disappeared. Then an image appears that I recognise, the outside of the cellblock. Two figures make their way down behind it, Zack and Clarissa but they're going out of the camera's range. I try other switches and various views of the cellblock area flash onto the screen. I stop at one that points at a dark, featureless area. I play with the zoom function to get more detail. Now, I can see that it's an open doorway into a dark storage area. *The arsenal*?

I watch, as several SRU officers come into the camera's view and run up to it. But, as if there is some kind of invisible barrier, they stand quite still in a row in front of it, facing into the black void. Zack and Clarissa appear behind them. One jolts forward, then another, as Zack thumps them in the back. But they will not be moved. They seem paralysed by something much stronger, darker than Zack's fury. He pushes through the line and marches up to the entrance, hesitates for a moment then enters. He reappears seconds later, his mouth gaping with authority. He points into the vault then at the officers, still standing motionless, outside. Two galvanise into action, as if a switch has been thrown and run inside. Lined up against the walls, I can make out the shadowy shapes of what I assume to be weapons, glints of light from the corridor catching on the hard shine of metal. This is what they're after. Clarissa has succeeded in generating an intruder alert. But why aren't they getting the weapons out? They must know that the computer will detect that it's a false alarm and seal the arsenal again. They'll only have minutes. It doesn't make sense. Then two figures appear in the doorway, bent over double, one is Zack. They drag something out backwards, their whole bodies straining against the weight. I zoom in. Not something, someone. Finn. *Finn's dead body.*

Chapter 12

15/06/3042   14:20 hours
JONATHAN

I pick up the bag, swing it onto my back and start walking away from the Renaissance Gate.

'*Come on*, Oli,' I say.

Getting no response, I go back to her. She stands, rigid, the fingertips of both hands pressed against her mouth as if to suppress a scream, her eyes transfixed on the engraving above the door.

'Come on.'

She turns and stares at me. But I can't bear the look in her eyes, it's too close to what I'm feeling inside. I turn my back on it and carry on down the tunnel. Oli catches up with me, clings onto my arm. Ahead, I can see the next doorway, about two hundred metres in front of us.

'How many Gates are there?' she says.

I try and recall the journey I made only three days ago, but terror fogs my memory.

'Apart   from   the   Renaissance   Gate...I think...there's four.'

Oli stops dead.

'Did you see that?'

'What?'

'The lights...they flickered, didn't they?'

'I didn't notice,' I say, as we're plunged into blackness.

'Get   the   flashlight,   get   the   flashlight,'   Oli

screams.

I slip the bag off my back, unzip it and grope around inside, but it's crammed with so much stuff that I can't find it. The lights flash on and then off again.

'Where is it?' I shout.

She's not listening.

'*Where's* the flashlight?'

'In the front pocket,' she says, at last.

I find it, flick the switch and a shaft of light pushes out in front of me. Oli's face, caught in the beam, is contorted with fear, her features picked out with shadow. I take hold of her hand, it's clammy, cold and we walk on in silence.

We approach the door in the first Gate and I help Oli onto the ground. Then we sit with our backs against the cold metal, the beam of light illuminating the way we've come.

'Why are the lights going on and off?' she says.

'I don't know, it could be something to do with an intruder alert being triggered.'

'An *intruder alert*…as in, the Colony defence system?'

'Yes,' I say, 'you know about it, do you?'

'No, not really. Do you?'

'No…I don't,' I lie.

Isn't she terrified enough?

'You know, Jonathan, don't you?'

'I know *something*, not all the details.'

'Well, tell me anyway. What does this defence system do exactly?'

'I don't know.'

She pulls my face around to hers, trapping my eyes with hers.

'That's the truth, Oli, I *really* don't know.'

'Nobody's managed to get past it though,' she says, releasing me.

'No.'

'So, it must be effective.'

'Nothing's happened yet, has it?'

'Not *yet*,' she says.

We fall into an uneasy silence.

'Oli, I think we're going to have to turn off the flashlight. We'll need it later.'

'*No*, Jonathan, please don't turn it off.'

I ignore her and turn it off anyway. We've got no choice. We huddle together, held by the enveloping darkness. After a while Oli speaks.

'What if nobody else comes up…from their Deathday? We'll be trapped here…we'll die here.'

'Someone will come up.'

'You can't know that,' she says.

'They will, they *must*.'

I put my head back, close my eyes, defending myself from the fear.

'*Sarah.*'

'What?'

Oli's voice cuts into my dream. Her head rests on my shoulder, her arm draped across my chest. I keep my eyes shut tight, disappointed.

'Jonathan, are you awake?'

I stay silent, but she must be able to feel my heart pounding through my jacket. She changes position and I sense that she's in front of me. Her kneecaps press against my thigh, her hands cradle my face. I keep my eyes closed. But she moves in closer and I feel her breath on my cheek. She places her lips against mine and my body reacts.

'So, you're not asleep,' she says, her hand travelling down my leg.

'Get off,' I shout, pushing her away from me.

'Alright, alright.'

Oli picks herself up from the floor. I notice the lights in the tunnel are back on, as she thumps the metal door with her fist.

'I'm sorry, Oli,' I say, 'I don't feel that way about you.'

'Well, it didn't seem like it to me.'

She looks down.

'I thought you were Sarah,' I lie.

'Yes, well...*lucky* Sarah.'

She moves several metres away from me and sits down again, her arms folded across her chest. Neither of us speaks. I don't know what to say.

'Oli...' I say, breaking the silence.

'Don't bother, Jonathan. I get it. Sarah is the love of your life etc...etc.'

'You're upset.'

'I was having a bit of fun, that's all, taking our minds off imminent death, that sort of thing.'

'I see,' I say.

But I'm not sure I do.

'I'm hungry.'

She pulls the bag towards her.

'Oli, I've been thinking about the food situation.

If we have to wait for somebody to come up from their Deathday, to get through each Gate, it will take us four days to get to the Ascendor.'

'*Four* days!'

'I thought the intruder alert would force matters, speed things up. I didn't expect *this*.'

I stare at the closed door. She looks in the bag, takes out the screwdriver and marches across to it. Then she's pushing the blade into the gap between the edge of the door and the armoured wall, trying to prise it open. But it's hopeless. The screwdriver slips out of the groove, screeching across the surface of the metal.

'You won't get it open like that,' I say, irritated.

She throws it down and it clatters along the stone floor, almost hitting my leg.

'*Calm down*, Oli, what's the matter with you?'

'I'll tell you what the matter is, *Jonathan*. I realise that I've made a big mistake, a huge mistake, in fact.'

'Well, don't take it out on me. It's not my fault, is it?'

She goes to say something, but stops.

'*Is it?*' I insist.

'I thought...I thought we had an understanding,' she says.

'What do you mean...an understanding?'

'That us...doing this...*thing*...together...meant something.'

'What?'

'You haven't got a clue, have you?'

'No I haven't, so help me.'

'You're going to make me spell it out?'

I don't know how to answer. There's a vein pulsing away on her left temple. Everything I say is making it worse. I don't need this, not now.

'Do you like me, Jonathan?'

'Yes…but you seem a bit edgy, all the time. That makes it difficult to…'

'I'm not talking about whether we're going to end up the best of friends. Do you find me *attractive*?'

'Attractive?'

She sighs.

'Let me put it another way. Do you feel the same way about me as you do about this…*Sarah*?'

'No…*no*, of course not. Why would you think that?'

'Forget it', she says and starts making her way back down the tunnel.

'Oli, wait.'

She doesn't reply. She keeps on walking.

'Where are you going?'

'As far away from you as I can get.'

'We need to stay together. What if the lights go out again?'

'Then I'll keep going until I hit something.'

'Why are you acting like this?'

She doesn't reply, just keeps marching away from me. I follow behind her.

'Oli, let's talk.'

'Leave me alone.'

I try another tack.

'I'll need your help.'

She slows down and I think that maybe I've got

through to her.

'I can't do it on my own, you know that.'

'*Do* I?' she says.

She stops walking and turns to face me. I can tell even from this distance, that she's been crying.

'I'm sorry I upset you.'

'You haven't.'

'Good, then you'll come with me, help me rescue Sarah.'

'*Sarah?*'

'Yes, Sarah, that's what it's about, isn't it? It's never been about anything else.'

'No, I suppose not,' she says, 'it's always going to be Sarah…always Sarah.'

'I've made up my mind, Jonathan. I'm not going with you. I'm going to stay by the Renaissance Gate and as soon as the next person triggers it to open, I'm out of here. Back to civilisation, back to safety and *you*…you can do what you want, because I don't care anymore.'

'Is there anything I can say, or do, to make you change your mind?'

'Yes, there is, but you won't *say* or *do* either of them.'

'So, you want me to leave you here, on your own?'

'Yes.'

'Do you want me to leave you some food and water?'

'No, you'll need it.'

'Oli…'

'Just *go*, Jonathan.'

I turn and walk back the way I came. Every now and then, I glance back at her to see if she's following. But she sits, huddled up against the Renaissance Gate, staring out in front of her. I'm on my own.

Chapter 13

I shudder at the sight, at the *thought* of the tormented death he must have endured, trapped inside that place, alone and terrified. They pull him out into the corridor. The other SRU officers gather round the body. Zack crouches down beside it. Clarissa appears, with a bottle of water and a cloth. She kneels down next to Finn. I zoom in and watch as she wets the cloth, places it over his lips and squeezes. A trickle of water runs over his mouth, down his chin and onto his neck. Zack grabs her arm, but she shrugs it off. She wets the cloth again, but this time she prises his lips apart a little and squeezes water into and around his mouth. It runs out onto the floor. Zack gets up and turns his back on the group. The rest exchange glances then, one by one, get to their feet and follow Zack into the vault. I recognise one of the first to move, as Sean. Only Clarissa remains kneeling beside Finn's grey, twisted body. She turns to Sean and I see her lips move. She points to Finn's feet. Sean grabs one in each hand and drags him, down the corridor, out of sight.

It's over thirty minutes since they hacked into the computer and triggered an intruder alert, but still the doors to the arsenal remain open. The SRU officers who, earlier, were frozen with fear are now carrying weapons out, piling them up against the walls of the corridor in a metallic heap. Zack has made no attempt to shift the position of the Eye, to hide their actions. Does he know that the Council doesn't exist? If he does, then only one person could have told him that. I push this thought to the back of my mind and study the pile of weapons. There are about twenty of the elaborate metal objects, outside the vault. I'm struck, by the angry mass of levers and handles, jutting from them.

Now the group turn their attention onto something else. Jevon emerges from the dark with a box in his arms. Although it's not that big, I can tell by the way he's holding it, knees bent, that it's heavier than it looks. Zack emerges with another one. They place them on the ground and study the labels. I zoom in as far as I can but I can't make out what's written on them. Jevon shrugs and walks across to the pile of weapons and crouches down beside them. He examines one, then consults the label on the box again, squinting at the words, his brow furrowed with the effort of thought. Another officer appears from the vault struggling with another two boxes and half drops, half places them down beside the weapons. They stare down at the collection. Something's not right. They look puzzled, their previous enthusiasm gone.

I flip switches trying to find them again. An image comes up on screen of the inside of one of the cells. I see Naomi and the other SRU rebels, inside. They sit hunched over, on the floor around the walls, heads down. I watch them for a while, remembering how it felt to be crammed together in such a small space then move on. The male SRU prisoners occupy the adjacent cell. So, they're all holding out against Zack, despite the temptation to join forces with him. The next six are empty but something makes me move to the last one, the one at the far end of the block. It's occupied. A boy lies on the bunk, arms rigid at his sides. He's alone and wears an SRU uniform. I zoom in on his face then jump, realising that it's Finn. A morbid fascination makes me linger there. I've never seen a dead body before. He has a grey peacefulness about him. Guilty at my curiosity, I go to switch cameras. Then his eyes open, wide with alarm and a fountain of liquid shoots from his mouth, as he coughs up water. Unable to control his jerking limbs, he rolls over and crashes to the floor, his whole body shaking. *He's alive.*

Chapter 14

15/06/3042   18:41 hours
JONATHAN

I'm trapped in a rock-hewn prison, thirsty, miserable, with a bladder that's full to capacity and ready to burst at any moment. This can't wait a moment longer. I jump up and look around me through the subdued lighting, desperate to find somewhere to relieve myself. *But where?* Walking over to the wall furthest from the door, necessity driving me, I stand as close to it as I can. I relax the muscles that have been clenched for hours and watch, as a stream of golden liquid splashes down onto a metal channel in the rock floor running along the edge of the wall. On and on it goes, in an endless torrent that I think will never stop. Glancing sideways towards the Renaissance Gate, I worry that it will reach Oli and hope for her sake, it doesn't.

Back at the door, I give up the battle against my thirst and gulp down a couple of mouthfuls of water. I feel better. I can make out Oli's figure lying next to the Renaissance Gate. Perhaps, now she's had time to think things through, she might change her mind. *Perhaps.*

'Oli,' I shout.

The last consonant ricochets off the walls on its way down. There's no response, so I try again.

'Oli, what time is it?'

Still no response. Is she alright? There's no

movement that I can see from this distance. It would be madness for me to leave the door, but I need her timepiece. At least that's what I tell myself as I pull out some food, a bottle of water and the flashlight from the bag and make my way towards her. As I approach, I see that she's lying on her side facing me, her eyes open, trained on me. Has she been watching me the whole time? A sharp, acrid smell hits me and I look guiltily across at the far wall.

'Yes, I know, it's disgusting,' she says, 'but I was desperate.'

I stare at her in surprise.

'Anyway,' I say, 'I came down here because I need to know the time, in fact, I need your timepiece.'

'Okay,' she says, removing it from her wrist.

'Unless…you need it…unless you've changed your mind.'

'I haven't,' she says, passing it over to me.

I strap it on and admire it from different angles, glancing down at the face. *19:05*. I stare at it bewildered.

'Still a very long time to go,' I say.

Getting no response I carry on.

'I must have dozed off for a few hours,' I say, trying to assess her mood.

'What about you…have you managed to get any sleep?'

She gets up, rubbing her back.

'Jonathan, what do you want?'

'I don't understand,' I say.

'Why are you here?'

'I came to get the…'

'You've got it. So now you can go back to your door and your suicide mission.'

'Oli…'

'Don't waste your breath, or your time. I'm a couple of steps away from a normal life, a future, and I intend to take it. Good luck Jonathan. You're certainly going to need it.'

I look at her, then the Gate. The temptation to take that step too is almost overpowering but I ignore it and walk away from her, away from safety and back down the tunnel to the door. I didn't give her the food or water. But she won't need it.

Not *now*.

Chapter 15

I search the screens for any SRU officers near the cells. Finn's alive and alone. He'll be terrified too. But even if I find somebody, what can I do about it? They think they've left a dead body there. No one's going to go back, not unless they have to. Sean, crouches down by the pile of weapons, in front of the open door of the arsenal. An SRU officer, I don't recognise, brings out another of the boxes and places it next to him then squats beside him. Sean seems annoyed by the intrusion and pushes him aside. Then he takes the lid off one of the boxes and takes out a black object about fifteen centimetres long. Next he picks up one of the weapons and inspects it, turning it around in his hands. He tries to force the black object into one of the protruding handles but can't make it fit. He hurls it back into the box then glances up, with guarded eyes. Someone moves towards him into the sightline of the Eye. The unhurried walk of authority, tells me that it's Zack. Sean says something, as if answering a question then gets up, grabs the box and takes it back into the arsenal. Minutes later he emerges with another. Zack pushes him to his knees onto the floor. Sean fumbles with another of the black objects trying to ram it into the weapon. But it doesn't fit, either. He shoots a nervous look up at Zack.

Zack waves his right arm and two other officers make their way towards the arsenal. One steps through the opening, with the other following. The first stops dead, as the lights in the arsenal flash off. He flies out of the darkness back into the corridor, the other close behind, as the door begins to close. Zack rushes forward and tries to hold back its progress but it will not be halted. He pulls his hand away in time to avoid it being crushed then thumps his fist against the sealed door. I recognise that look, it's one of fury, of frustration but I don't understand why. Then he's waving his arms at the officers again. They pick up a weapon each and carry them off.

I switch screens back to the cell. At first, I think I've made a mistake because there's no sign of Finn. I zoom in then see a movement under the bunk. A hand appears then another, clawing their way across the cell floor. The head of this slithering creature clears the legs of the bunk and Finn appears into view. I think that maybe he's trying to get back onto the bunk. But that isn't it. He crawls away from it. I can't see his face, as his head is too low, almost touching the floor. When he reaches the corner, he slides himself around it with his back to the wall and curls up in a foetal position, pushing himself as far back into it as he can. I zoom in on his face. Two wild, staring eyes fill the screen. I can't imagine what horrors are fuelling that look. There's something else in those unblinking eyes. Survival. It's as if by closing them, he will accept the fate he's already escaped once, and die. I can't bear to watch his suffering. There's nothing I can do for him.

Then I notice his expression change. His stare loses the blankness it had before. There's recognition there…and fear. He cowers back against the wall but there's nowhere for him to go. Two SRU officers come into view, carrying weapons. Spotting Finn, they drop them, soundless, onto the floor then turn, wide-eyed and bolt out of the cell. Finn is up on his haunches, his arms splayed out either side of him, pinned to the wall by terror. A group of people, led by Zack enter the cell. He moves over to Finn whose arms flail around in front of him, preventing any further approach. Two officers join Zack and approach Finn, one either side, in a pincer movement. They edge forward through a barrage of punches and grab his wrists then hook their hands under his armpits and drag him across to the bunk. Zack watches, as they push him up and onto it. Somehow, Finn manages to loosen the hold on one of his wrists and his fist shoots up, making contact with Zack's face. Clutching his battered nose, Zack jumps back.

Then two people wearing the tunics of Health workers enter the cell, pushing a stretcher trolley in front of them. In a deft movement, one takes hold of Finn's loose arm and holds it down, while the other administers an injection. They wait, holding him down, until there's no more resistance then release their grip. He lies motionless, his eyes closed. He looks almost peaceful. A feed line is fitted into his other arm, coming from a fluid bag, attached to the trolley. The two Health workers manoeuvre the trolley around so that they can push it out of the cell, but are stopped by Zack. There's a discussion. The Health workers return the trolley to its previous position. One slumps down on the bunk. They watch Zack and the SRU officers leave, their bodies sagging with resignation. *Has Zack locked them in?*

I watch them for a while to see what they'll do but they sit motionless, defeat in their eyes. I switch cameras to Zack's office. He stands by his desk, one of the weapons in front of him. He picks up a black object, resting beside it and tries to push it up into one of the handles, as Sean had done earlier. It doesn't fit. He tries another, then another, banging his hand flat on the desk with each failed attempt. Ten minutes pass like this. Then he takes hold of one that looks the same as all the others but, this time, it slots easily into the handle. Zack stares down at it, smiling. At last he seems satisfied. He lifts the weapon up from the desk, his finger curled around a lever under the main body and points it out in front of him.

His eyes dart up. Jevon charges into the office then, seeing the weapon directed at his head, thrusts out his arm, pushing it away from him. Zack loses his balance and the weapon takes on a life of its own. It veers up and to Zack's left, spewing out flames, jerking his body up and down, as he fights to keep control of it. Jevon dives under the desk. A shower of particles rain down from the ceiling through the smoke that now fills the room. Then, as fast as it started, the flashes stop and the weapon is still again. Zack hurls it away from him. It crashes into the wall.

He sits up, puts his hands over his face, then through his hair. Jevon crawls out from under the desk, watching the discarded weapon all the way, his face drained of all colour. He slumps down onto the seat next to him, stunned.

I remove my hand from my mouth. The implications of what I've witnessed are too terrible to contemplate. If that, is what *one* of the weapons is capable of, then they've got enough to take over the Colony. It's irrelevant if they get the others to work because, *one will be enough.*

Chapter 16

My eyes open and meet a solid wall of metal. I sit up disorientated, my mind racing, as I try to make sense of it through the foggy remnants of sleep. What time is it? I look for the COMSET. No, that was...the dream. Back in the Colony, Sarah by my side...*only a dream*. I push away the leaden weight of disappointment. I want to go back there, but I'm wide awake. This is reality – *face it*.

Then I remember. I look down at the timepiece on my wrist, trying to focus my eyes on its illuminated face. That can't be right. *It can't be*. My pulse quickens as I stare down at it, unable to believe what my eyes are telling me. *14:12*. I look at it again but it hasn't changed. My heart hammers in my chest, as I watch the seconds tick over with a relentless accuracy. Then I'm on my feet, grabbing the bag, panic gripping me. I press my ear up against the metal door but all I can hear is the pounding of my own heartbeat. Then I hear something else, the faintest of sounds...a whimper. The door clicks and I watch, mesmerised, as it creeps open. The gap widens and I step in front of it, confronted by the ashen, screaming figure of a wide-eyed boy. He falls forward, rigid. I manage to catch him before he crashes to the floor. The door is fully open now and I put my arm against its edge, as I lower the pale, limp

83

body across the doorway opening, onto the stone floor. Feeling no resistance to my hand, I take it away, ready to shoot it back if it starts to close again. I turn my attention back to the boy lying at my feet.

'It's alright, I promise, it's alright,' I say, patting him on the cheek. 'Wake up, quick, wake up!'

His face looks sickly grey in tone. I take the bag off my shoulder and search for the water bottle. I pour a little into the lid and trickle it onto his lips. His eyes open and he raises his head. At the sight of me his arms go up, hands beating at the air as if he's trying to erase me from his view. He hits my hand and I almost lose my grip on the water bottle.

'Stop that!' I shout, giving him a sharp slap on the face.

He stares goggle-eyed at me.

'Listen to me, you're safe, do you hear me? You're *not* going to die, do you understand what I'm saying to you? *You're not going to die.*'

I'm not sure he understands but, at least, he's stopped fighting me.

'All you've got to do…'

I'm interrupted by a shout behind me.

'What's going on up there?' Oli screams down the tunnel.

I daren't lose the boy's attention now. I ignore her and carry on.

'…is walk down to the next Gate.'

I raise his head and direct it towards the Renaissance Gate.

'Do you see it? There's a girl there.'

He nods.

'Good. You must stand in front of it and it will open.'

He whimpers.

'It's alright, you're not going to die. There will be people...on the other side of it...people to help you. I promise.'

'But...' he whispers and I know what's coming.

'The ozone layer...it's *fine*. It's repaired. You'll be safe. The girl by the door and me, we came from the *outside*. We're safe, look at us, we're perfectly alright.'

A flame of hope burns in his eyes. He wants to believe me. His breathing has steadied now.

'Jonathan, what's happening,' Oli shouts, a note of panic in her voice.

The boy clutches my arm, picking up her anxiety.

'You need to get up and walk to the last Gate,' I say.

I help him to his feet. He's shaking, I prise his hand off my arm and encourage him forward. But he won't move and grabs my arm again.

'I have to stay here but I'll watch you every step of the way and the girl, her name is Oli, she'll help you.'

He loosens his grip and stumbles forward.

'That's right, take it slowly, step by step.'

I stay in the open doorway, watching as he staggers away from me. Every so often he glances over his shoulder and I give him an encouraging smile. He's making some progress now and I begin to relax a little. Then he stumbles on the uneven ground and falls onto his knees.

'Oli,' I shout, 'help him. I can't leave the door.'

She rushes forward, puts her hands under the boy's armpits and lifts him to his feet. Then, with him leaning into her, they move towards the Renaissance Gate. His head is inclined towards her, as if he's listening. Whatever she's saying to him is helping. His pace has quickened and there's more purpose about him. They arrive in front of the Gate. Oli pushes him forward then takes up position several metres behind him. They wait. The boy looks back at her. Then the doors of the Renaissance Gate start to open. A shaft of light cuts into the gloom, as the doors move apart. Oli shouts something to the boy and he steps forward, then freezes. There are a number of silhouetted figures moving around in the white light but I can't make out what's happening. I screw up my eyes against the glare and see the boy being helped outside by two black shapes. Then the doors start to close. But there's a figure standing in the doorway. It's Oli. Sensing a presence in their path, the doors stop. She turns around and looks at me.

'Jonathan, quick, come on, get out, *get out*!' she screams.

Then I see a figure dive through the gap from the outside, knocking Oli to the ground, away from the opening. Unobstructed, the doors creep towards each other. Seconds before they close, another figure squeezes through. The subdued lighting of the tunnel is restored. My eyes, blinded by the previous brightness, have difficulty focusing but I can make out shapes in front of me.

'Jonathan!'

Running towards me is Marilyn and behind her, Kyle. She jumps at me, almost knocking me out of the doorway, her arms around my neck.

'Why…?' I say.

'Don't ask,' Kyle says, 'she can be very persuasive.'

'Quick,' I say, pushing Marilyn through the door then Kyle.

For the first time since the Renaissance Gate closed, I look up and see Oli standing several metres away from us, staring.

'Oli, are you coming with us,' I shout.

She doesn't answer, just runs towards us. Then, without a word, she pushes past me through the doorway, I follow. I turn and watch as it seals up, behind me.

'Thanks for that,' she says, glaring at Marilyn and Kyle, her arms folded tight across her chest.

'Sorry, but we weren't expecting anyone to be…'

She stops speaking. The lights in the tunnel flash on and off following a precise rhythm. Then an ear-piercing noise assaults our ears as a siren starts up.

'What's happening?' Oli screams.

I don't get a chance to answer because that's when we hear, *the rumble*.

Chapter 17

Stuart hasn't turned up and I don't know what to do. I sit in front of the surveillance screens and search the corridors, the buildings, the pods, but it's useless, I can't find him, I can't. When he failed to turn up last night, I tried not to panic…tried not to think the worst of him. All day, I've worried about what I'd say when he arrives…about confronting him with his treachery. But *now*, now all I want, is to see him…his familiar face. I don't care what he's done. He's my only human contact. I miss him.

Without looking, I reach across to the water bottle but the light feel of it, makes me take notice. I change my mind about taking a drink. This is serious. After everything I've found out, everything I've witnessed it's agony to sit here doing nothing. I've become a spectator. I collapse onto the workbench, my head resting on my arms. I will die up here, alone. No, not alone. There's the computer, my only companion, with its constant bleeps and flashing lights reminding me that it and only it, keeps us…*me*, alive. I walk over to its half-glazed prison and peer in through the glass. I am nothing more, than an intruder in its kingdom. I don't belong here. I'm as much a prisoner as this inanimate machine. What use are my legs, if I have nowhere to go?

I have to think about my options. I must have some. The elevator? No, only Stuart can make that travel from the City to the Council Chamber and he's not here. *He's not here*. Stop that. The food chute? Of course, the food chute. It's the only way. I go back to the workbench, with renewed hope, grab the bottle and gulp down the last of the water. I'll need the screwdriver and the flashlight from the bag. They're extra weight, perhaps too much. I look at the two objects in front of me. Which of them can I afford to leave behind? It's no use, I need them both. I take one in each hand, march out of the building and into the corridor.

With every step, I imagine that I can hear the voices of the lost Council, see them going about their work, discussing, analysing and planning. Their presence fills my mind and I don't know if it comforts, or frightens me. I quicken my pace, past the administration building and the health centre. I'm on familiar ground, as I enter the refectory building and stride across the dining room. One or two of the lights have come on in here, but the faulty one continues with its dying amber pulses. The door to the food preparation area is still closed. I try again to open it, but nothing I do, works. It isn't going to budge, so I go round to the front and climb in through the serving hatch. I stare at the wall in front of me. It's not how I left it. The doors of the food chute are closed. *The food chute isn't there*. Of course, it isn't. It will have gone back down to the Food Production Unit. I press the button on the control panel and wait but I can't hear anything.

Putting my hand onto the door, I detect through my fingers, the slightest of vibrations. It's coming. I hear a clunk on the other side of the door and a faint click from the control panel. After a couple of seconds, the door opens and I stare, open-mouthed at its contents. It's full of food packages. Water? I unload it all onto the floor, but there's no water. *Of course there isn't.* The City has its own supply. Now, I have no choice. I have to go down.

The dark, cramped space in front of me brings it all back, the fear...the panic. My heartbeat speeds up. *I have no choice.* I climb inside and shuffle round so that I can reach the control panel outside, with my right hand. I place the screwdriver down onto the floor of the chute then transfer the flashlight into my left hand and stretch out my right arm, as far as I can behind me. I feel around for the start button, gulp down a lungful of air and press. The doors begin to close and I snatch my arm back into the chute, as they click and lock. As darkness engulfs me, I grope around beneath my legs for the flashlight. My hands are shaking, as I locate the switch. Then my tin box is flooded with light. At the same time, there's a jolt and then a vibration, as it starts to move downwards. I'm not sure whether the light is a welcome addition, or not. It has the strange effect of making the space look bigger, and smaller, at the same time. My shadow, picked out on the metal wall, gives the impression that I'm not alone, that I have a dark companion with me. Now, I can see, as well as feel my body bent and twisted against the inadequate sized container. The chute creaks and groans its way down, struggling with the load.

At last, I feel it slow down. I grab the screwdriver and turn off the flashlight. Before it stops, I swap hands so that the screwdriver is in my right, ready to use to defend myself. The chute jolts to a halt and I wait for the doors to open but nothing happens. I press my ear up against the cold metal and listen. A thump vibrates through my head and I pull away from it, stunned, stifling a scream with my hand. *Someone's there.*

Chapter 18

'What is it?' Kyle says, his face animated with fear.

'I don't know, but it's getting louder,' I reply.

'It's not just the noise,' Marilyn says, crouching down, with her right hand flat on the stone floor, 'there's a vibration too. Can you feel it?'

I stand quite still and allow the buzz to run up my legs from the soles of my feet.

'It could be doors opening or closing in front of us,' I say, with little conviction.

I turn round to see if Oli's behind us. She's only metres away. She walks, with her arms still folded across her chest, her lips pressed together in a sullen pout. She doesn't look happy. Not one bit.

'Come on, Oli, keep *up*,' I shout.

'You and your *friends* go ahead, don't worry about me. My plans for a quiet life have already been ruined.'

I sigh. Let her sulk. There are more pressing things to sort out right now, like what's going on in front of us. Above the vibration from the floor, I can feel Marilyn trembling, as she clings on tight to my left arm.

'Is Oli alright?' she asks.

'Who knows? She's a complete mystery to me.'

'Sorry to interrupt,' I hear Oli say, behind us.

I spin round, not realising she was that close.

'Does anyone else think, that *maybe* we ought to be a little more concerned about what's making that noise…shaking the floor?'

In front of us, Kyle stops about ten metres from the next Gate and stares at the metal wall in front of him. The vibration is so strong now, that it feels as if the floor will crack beneath our feet. The rumbling sound has become deafening. Kyle spots it first. He swings round to us, eyes dark with fear. I stare in disbelief and watch as the entire armoured wall, begins to rise into the rock ceiling. Centimetre by centimetre, it creeps upward, across the entire width of the tunnel, taking the door with it. *The whole wall is disappearing, before our eyes.* When the gap at the bottom is about one and a half metres, I run forward, pulling Marilyn with me.

'Quick, get under it!' I shout.

But Kyle isn't moving. Kyle is frozen to the spot.

'Look,' he shouts, pointing a shaking finger in front of him.

The armoured wall is now above our heads, revealing, what we were too close to see before, another wall of glistening silver metal, spanning the width of the tunnel. Our mirrored reflections stare back at us, distorted by its uneven concave surface, as it trundles, relentlessly, towards us. A monster machine pushing everything in its way. *And we're in its way.* Kyle turns and stumbles away from it in the direction of the Renaissance Gate. Marilyn screams something in my ear. I don't hear it. I'm searching for a way round. But the gaps down the side, between the rock wall and the edge of the machine, are too narrow. *Far too narrow.*

'Jump,' I shout, as the metal beast rears up in front of us.

I launch myself at it, getting a foothold on the slight curve at the bottom edge and hook my fingertips over the top edge. Then, swinging my body from side to side, I try to get my foot over the rim but, the mechanical vibration, is making it hard for me to maintain my grip. Mustering all my strength, I try again. This time I manage to get my right foot, then my knee, over the top. I push myself up onto the scoop and shuffle around, so that the top of my body is leaning over. Below me, I see Marilyn running away from the machine, with Kyle about five metres ahead of her, screaming encouragement. She falls forward onto the floor.

'Get up, Marilyn,' I shout, '*get up!*'

She scrambles to her feet, sobbing. Then she turns to face her pursuer, arms flailing about from side to side, as if she's trying to push it back.

'Grab my hands!' I shout.

She looks up, stumbling backwards and sees me perched on the top edge of the scoop.

'Jump and grab my hands!'

The machine is almost on top of her. She jumps off the ground, a second before it touches her feet and clings onto to me with her left hand. My arm muscles strain to hold her swinging weight. I'm not sure I can keep my grip on her, not with one hand.

'Grab my other hand!' I scream.

She reaches up to it but misses.

'Try again!'

She lurches to the right, pushed by the momentum and then back again. This time, she manages to get a hold on my hand and I pull with all my strength. Her hands are clammy and I can feel them slipping through my fingers. I look down at her. She has her teeth clenched in determination. She makes one last effort, a fraction of a second before I feel her about to drop. She hooks her leg over the rim and I pull her over.

'Kyle,' she whimpers.

He's stands a few metres in front of us. It looks like he's decided to face down his mechanical enemy.

'Jump!' I shout.

I can see Gate 4 behind him and it's coming up fast.

'*Jump!*'

His eyes dart from side to side trying to find an alternative then, realising that he has no choice, he jumps. But he's a lot shorter than me and doesn't manage to reach the top rim.

'Try again!' I scream.

He jumps again. The machine is almost on top of him but, this time, he succeeds in hooking his right hand over the top. His body swings in jerky movements below me and I can see the agony on his face. I clutch at his left wrist on the next swing across and, with Marilyn's help, he claws his way up, panting with exhaustion.

Then I look up and spot Oli at Gate 4. She has her back to the wall, her arms stretched out either side of her. She looks as if she's trying to push herself through its armoured plating.

'Oli, when we get near to you, jump!'

'I won't make it,' she shouts, her eyes wide like a trapped animal, 'I'm too short!'

I peer through the flashing light. We're only metres away from Gate 4 and there's no sign of any movement. *It isn't going to open.* I sense the machine slowing down. Then a scream splits the air around us. Marilyn gasps.

'It's moving!' she says.

But there's no movement in the wall. Oli looks down at her feet and I see what she's staring at. She's standing on *metal*, not stone, a metal plate. It creeps *under* Gate 4, revealing a pit running the full width of the tunnel. There's nowhere for her to go. The last thing I see as the machine moves up to the wall and comes to a stop, is Oli's expression, picked out by the flashing light. It's the same expression I saw on Finn's face, as the arsenal doors closed on him. The sirens stop their wailing, the lights stop flashing.

'Where's Oli?' Marilyn whispers.

'Let's get off this thing,' Kyle says, ignoring her.

'No, wait,' I say, as I feel the vibration start up again through the metal, 'it's not finished.'

There's a sharp jolt. Kyle, who has relaxed his grip, almost falls off. He scrabbles to regain his hold on the rim.

'What's happening?' Marilyn says.

'It's going back,' I say.

The machine edges away from the wall, its job

done and I peer down into the gaping space below us. I can't make out how deep it is. It doesn't matter. There's no sign of Oli. As the machine clears the pit, I take one more look over the edge. I can't believe what I'm seeing, Oli, clinging onto the near edge of the pit. She looks up at me. Her eyes have gone past fear, now they stare out with the terror of the inevitable, as the floor creeps forward from the wall, closing the gap. I watch, helpless, as her lips form the words. *Help me.*

I wait a few seconds, then ease myself over the rim of the scoop and hang down. I close my eyes and release my hold and jolting my left knee as it twists away from me, I fall hard onto the uneven floor. There's no time to worry about the stabbing pain. I turn and run towards the edge of the pit.

'Hold on, Oli, hold on!' I shout.

The floor creeps forward. In seconds, it will reach her. Falling onto my knees in front of her, I force my brain to focus. I try to hold her gaze but I can't. There's a faint spark of hope growing there now. It paralyses me. I lean over her suspended body and grab her upper arms.

'I can't hold...I can't,' she cries.

'It's alright, Oli, I've got you...I promise, I've got you.'

'*No...*'

'Oli, you *must* let go, so that I can pull you up.'

Her eyes lock into mine. She has to trust me. I feel the weight on my arms increase, as she loosens her grip on the edge.

'Don't let go of me!' she screams.

'I've got you, Oli…I've got you,' I say, as I pull with all my strength.

But my arms have been weakened, by hanging from the scoop and I'm not sure I can hold her. The unevenness of the floor helps as I gain a purchase on it with my feet and, centimetre by centimetre, haul myself backwards, dragging my load with me. The unbearable strain eases as she hooks her arms over the edge and scrambles out. She pulls her left foot out as the floor closes up. Then she's sobbing, deep and uncontrollable, her whole body racked by it. I haven't got time to comfort her because I can see the machine is approaching Gate 3.

'Quick Oli, we've got to run *now*!'

'No…leave me alone.'

'*Get up*!' I shout.

Grabbing her arm, I drag her to her feet. We stumble after the machine, Oli protesting all the way. Marilyn and Kyle move away from us, their elbows hooked over the top rim. I can see that Marilyn is concentrating all her effort on keeping her grip. Only Kyle can help us now.

'Kyle, help us up!'

He stretches over as far as he can, his hands dangling a metre above my head. I jump up and grasp hold of them. I hear him panting above me, as he hauls me little by little upwards. When I think it's safe, I let go with my right hand and slam it onto the rim. Kyle guides my other hand next to it. Over my shoulder, I see Oli below me staring up.

'Don't leave me,' she screams.

'Grab my legs, Oli. *Now*!'

For once, she doesn't argue. I feel a wrench downwards as her entire weight tries to prise me from the rim of the scoop.

'I don't think I can hold on any longer,' Marilyn says, beside me.

Her voice has a tremor to it. She's struggling. But I can't help her. My arms can't take much more. Oli and my combined weight is, too much. I'm finished. Perhaps Oli senses I'm at breaking point because she starts to climb up my body. Then, when I know I can't bear the strain a moment longer, her right arm shoots up and she hooks her fingers onto the rim.

'Look,' Kyle says, 'all the doors are open, *all of them*. It's going right to the end.'

I glance behind. The doors are sealing up behind us, too.

'Where's the bag, Oli?'

'Where do you *think* it is? I'm sorry, but when the floor opened underneath me, I didn't think to pick it up.'

I look over to Kyle. He shrugs. 'I dropped ours when I jumped onto this thing, had no choice.'

'So, we've got nothing, no food, no water…nothing,' I say. 'We've got a real problem then.'

'I think,' Oli says, pointing, 'that we've got a real problem *now*.'

The end of the tunnel is in view, but it's not a solid rock face as I'd thought. It's a gaping dark hole, the entire width of the machine and it's coming up fast. As we approach, I can make out the back of it. This is where the machine came from. This is where it's stored, when it's not sweeping people to their deaths. This is where we're going to end up, if we don't get off this thing right away.

'Jump!' I scream, as the roof of the storage hangar looms up above our heads.

Oli goes first. Kyle and Marilyn scramble over the rim so that they're facing the same way as me, into the hangar. Kyle lowers himself down and hangs by his hands then jumps backwards. I help Marilyn to do the same and, with Kyle's help she drops down to the floor. I watch as she loses her balance on landing and falls back onto him.

There's a jolt. The machine stops and I hear it engage with the back wall of the hangar. There's a grinding noise above my head. It's getting darker. The wall of the hangar is lowering, closing up, behind me. I jerk backward but something is preventing me from moving. My right arm is held fast. In the increasing darkness, I spot that the fabric of my right sleeve has caught on a raised edge of metal on the rim and won't budge.

'Get out!'

They're shouting at me. But I'm not going anywhere. Panic has taken me in its grip. I can't think. My brain refuses to cooperate. It's easier to give into it.

'*Jonathan*!'

Sarah? No, not Sarah. My mind's playing tricks. But it's enough, enough to galvanise me. I tug at the material but it's stuck fast. There's only one thing I can do. I ease my right arm out of the caught sleeve, hanging onto the rim with the other. Then I pull my top over my head, allow my left arm to slip through the sleeve and let my body drop to the floor.

I turn in the narrow space between the machine and the hangar door. The gap between the bottom of the wall and the floor is now only half a metre. I drop down and press myself flat against the ground. I can see three silhouetted heads against the narrowing strip of light from the tunnel.

'Jonathan!' the heads scream.

But it's too late. I'm not going to make it. Then I feel hands grab hold of my left arm and leg and I'm pulled through the gap. I feel the bottom of the door brush my back, as one last effort shoots me through to the other side.

I place a quaking hand onto the floor and push myself up. I'm a mess but I'm alive. Then Marilyn lets out a loud snort. I look up at her surprised. Then Oli's face crumples and she bends forward her whole body shaking.

'Don't!' Kyle splutters.

'What's so funny?' I say, confused.

'*You*,' Oli says, tears dripping off her nose.

'What?' I say.

'Look at you,' Marilyn says, as she collapses onto her knees, holding her stomach.

I look down. I've lost my tunic top and one of my shoes and I have a few cuts and grazes on my arms. I don't look *that* funny. But it's no use. It's contagious. It starts as a chuckle then I lose control and my chest burns with the effort. I can't stop, my whole body, fuelled by relief, spasms with laughter.

'What…now,' Kyle gasps in air, as he speaks.

'We settle down…here…for the night and…' I manage to say, choking between laughs, 'and…wait for the Deathday candidate.'

'*What*!' Oli says, losing her sense of humour.

'That won't be until 14:00 tomorrow.'

'How else did you think we'd get down to the City?' I say, intimidated by their cold stares.

There's no reply. I shrug. No one's laughing *now*.

Chapter 19

16/06/3042 23:42
SARAH

'It won't open,' I hear a voice say, from the other side.

'Don't be an idiot, of course it'll open.'

The door is thumped again. I press myself as far back against the wall of the chute, as possible, my grip tightening on the handle of the screwdriver. Adrenalin pumps around my body. I feel sure that they must be able to hear it coursing through my veins.

'What's the matter with it?'

Another assault on the door makes me gasp.

'Did you hear that?'

'What?'

'A noise, coming from the inside.'

'No, I didn't and neither did you. Just go and find something to prise this thing open.'

But he will not be deterred.

'Who's in there?' he shouts, louder this time.

Alarmed, I jump, my head smashing against the roof of the chute. At the same time, I feel a jerk upwards and the whole thing starts to move. It's going back up. No, it's not. It's continuing *down* to the Maintenance Department. I switch the flashlight back on and get into position as best I can in the confined space. As soon as that door opens, I need to be ready to pounce. The chute slows and I feel every muscle in my body, tense. When it stops, I wait, with thumping heart. For a few agonising moments, nothing happens then there's a click, the lock releases and the hatch rises. *Someone's there.* I can see the bottom half of their body. When the gap is twenty centimetres, I can't bear the tension any more. I drop the flashlight, place my left hand underneath and pull upwards. Then I thrust the screwdriver out of the opening. There's a shout and a figure flies backwards away from me then crashes onto the floor. I half jump, half fall, out of the chute. A searing pain shoots up my left calf. Aware of nothing but the pain, I hobble about, groaning.

'Sarah!'

I turn around, still clutching at my lower leg. Stuart looks up at me from the floor, grinning. I lunge towards him.

'Put that thing down, will you,' he says, panic in his voice.

I stare at him confused. He points at the screwdriver, I'm still wielding.

'Sorry…sorry,' I stutter.

I drop it with a clunk onto the floor and hold out my hand to him then stop, doubt taking hold of me.

'What's the matter?' he says, puzzled.

'Nothing,' I say.

'So, why have you left the Council Chamber?'

'I…I ran out of water.'

'But I was about to bring you some supplies. Why didn't you wait for me to arrive?'

'You were late, I panicked. I thought you weren't coming.'

'I would never do that, leave you, you know that.'

'Do I?'

'What do you mean by that?'

'I saw you…in Zack's office.'

It's out and I'm glad.

'Oh.'

'Is that all you can say…*oh*?'

'You have to trust me, Sarah.'

'But that's the point, Stuart…I don't.'

With that, I walk away from him down the corridor towards the workshop.

'Where are you going, Sarah? Wait!'

I hear his footsteps behind me, but I'm not stopping.

'Sarah, please,' he says, as he places a hand on my shoulder.

I try and shrug it off but he keeps his hold on me. I turn and face him.

'Sarah, I've convinced Zack that I'm helping him.'

'*What*?'

'It was the only way to keep you safe. They're watching my every move. They suspect me of helping you but they've got no proof. They have no idea where you are.'

'You must have been convincing, Zack's no fool.'

'I told him that you trust me. That you'd seek me out, ask for my protection, now that Jonathan's gone.'

'Poor trusting Sarah. I don't need your protection, Stuart!'

'Listen, you don't understand.'

'I *do* understand, Stuart, I can't trust you anymore. I'm in more danger than ever.'

'No, you're not, Sarah, listen. Zack believes that I'm on his side, that I'll bring you to him.'

'And I'm supposed to be comforted by that, am I?'

'He's completely blind when it comes to you. He wants to believe me, despite what he knows.'

'So, you're going to hand me over to him?'

'Yes…well no, not exactly. I've got a plan. I promise I'll keep you safe. The same promise I made Jonathan.'

'He trusted you, didn't he?' I say, my voice softer now.

'Yes, and so should you.'

'I want to,' I whisper.

'Then *do*.'

I look at him. He's still the same Stuart, more confident, wiser, but the same. I can see it in his eyes. I step forward and throw my arms around his neck.

'Steady on,' he says, laughing.

'Stuart, I've got so much to tell you…terrible things.'

'Come on, I'm taking you to my pod. You can explain it all to me there.'

'They all died, Stuart…the Council. They died of a virus…a very long time ago.'

'Yes…it had to be something like that.'

He takes my hand in his and leads me back to the elevator.

Chapter 20

17/06/3042   13:13 hours
JONATHAN

My right foot spasms with cramp and I let out a groan. It's difficult to assess how awful I feel. There is no way that you can get to sleep on a solid rock floor, in a freezing tunnel, with no cover and only half your clothing. But I've been trying to do, just that, for hours. Marilyn and Kyle are cuddled up together about a metre away from me. There's no movement, except for the gentle rise and fall of their chests. At first, I was full of admiration that they could manage to sleep at all, under the circumstances. But, as the hours dragged by, that admiration turned to annoyance. I had to stop myself from shuffling across and prodding Kyle in the back to wake him up.

Last night, Oli decided that she was going to sleep with me, *not in that way*, as she put it, only for warmth. I pretended that I didn't know what she meant and went along with it, too tired to argue. But all night, I've had to listen to her complaints – I'm cold...hungry...thirsty. My head hurts...my back hurts...my whole body hurts. Ignoring her made it worse, because then she started with the recriminations. You don't care about me...I could freeze to death and you wouldn't be bothered...I don't know what Sarah sees in you. *That did it*. I sat up and glared down at her. She cowered beneath me, most likely from cold, than fear. I rescued you, Oli, *remember that*, I said to her in a teeth-clenched whisper, my lips brushing her ear. She shut up after that, except for the occasional whimper. I felt bad that I couldn't provide her with the comfort she needed after the shock she'd experienced. But I didn't have the will, or the energy.

What's the point of getting up? We've got no food, no water. All we've got is time, hours, until the Deathday candidate comes up from the Colony. I roll over on my side, trying to find a comfortable position, expecting to feel Oli's body against mine but she's not there.

'Come on Jonathan, wake up,' I hear Kyle say, above me.

I force my eyes open and look up at him, struggling to focus on his face, or rather, his chin and nostrils. They move in and out of my vision. Then I understand why. He's jumping up and down and, behind him, Marilyn is doing the same.

'Go away,' I moan.

'You've been asleep for hours, goodness knows *how*,' Kyle says, panting. 'Marilyn and I were awake all night, weren't we?'

He turns to her and she nods.

'Too cold and uncomfortable to sleep,' Kyle continues, 'but not you.'

'I didn't get...'

What's the point, they're in no mood to listen.

'What time is it?' I say, instead.

'13:43.'

'*What*!'

I sit up a little too fast and the tunnel walls spin around me. 'I feel awful,' I groan.

'Try some exercises, Jonathan, they really help,' Marilyn suggests.

I stare, as they bob up and down, waving their arms up and over their heads in sweeping movements.

'Why are you so cheerful?' I ask.

'Well,' Marilyn says, between breaths, 'we decided that we needed to keep our minds off food and keep warm. This seems to work.'

'Doesn't it make you thirsty?' I say.

She stops dead. 'I hadn't thought of that. Kyle, we should stop.'

I sigh.

'Where's Oli?'

'Over by the gate, sulking,' Kyle says.

I look down the tunnel and make out her figure about halfway to the next Gate, sitting against the wall, her head resting back on the stone. She looks small and alone.

'She's going out with the Deathday candidate,' Marilyn says.

'Is she?'

Not this, *again.*

'That's what she said,' she replies.

We fall into an awkward silence.

'We could do with her help,' I say, after a while.

'There's no time, leave her,' Kyle says.

'I'm going to speak to her, check she's okay.'

'Why?'

'Because...I don't know...I feel responsible for

her and…'

'You're wasting your time, with that one,' he says.

'Perhaps,' I say, getting to my feet.

I don't want to walk too far away from the Ascendor. After all I've been through to get here, walking back down this tunnel, however short a distance, seems all wrong to me. I compromise and go about thirty metres, then stop.

'Oli!' I shout.

The name bounces off the walls towards her. It sounds too insistent, too aggressive.

'Leave me alone.'

I lower my voice.

'Come over here, I need to talk to you.'

'Why should I? If you want to talk to me, come down here. Otherwise, leave me alone.'

'I can't.'

'Why not?' she says.

'Because…we need to stay by the Ascendor…it's nearly time…'

'Well, that's too bad, because I need to stay *here*.'

Stalemate. Kyle's right, I'm not going to get any sense out of her. Let her go, if that's what she wants. I turn my back on her and walk back to the others.

'Didn't think you'd give up that easily.'

I continue walking.

'Can't have that much to say to me then.'

There's a note of concern in her voice. Maybe she doesn't want to go.

'Oh, alright, if that's how you want it, I'll come to you. But it won't do you any good because…'

'Jonathan, quick, I can hear something!' Marilyn shouts.

I swing round and see her by the Ascendor, her ear pressed up against the door. I charge towards her, forgetting Oli.

'It's coming,' Kyle says, as I run up behind him.

'This is it then,' I say.

'In case anyone's interested,' Oli says, pushing past me, 'I've decided I'm coming, after all. You don't have to thank me.'

Chapter 21

Something punctuates my dreams, a voice, clipped and cold. A familiar voice, but not human. I feel I must take notice of it but I don't know why. I force my eyes open and the light sears into them.

'*...The date is 17/06/3042 and it is Leander Day.*'

'Sarah, are you awake?' I hear Stuart ask from under the bunk.

'It's so bright,' I say, blinking.

'Welcome back to the City.'

I sit up and look puzzled at the cover tangled around my legs.

'I don't remember...'

He smiles.

'You sat on the bunk last night, clutching the flashlight, ready to tell me everything but your eyes kept drooping. I told you to lie down, turned my back on you for a few seconds. Then the light in the room dimmed and, when I looked round, you were fast asleep with the flashlight lying on your chest, shining up at your chin.'

'How much did I tell you?'

'Enough to keep me awake for most of the night,' he says.

'I still can't make myself think about it without

panicking.'

'You don't need to think about it, Sarah. The Colony is as old as it is. Nothing can change that. It's the only thing we know, the only thing we have. Our priority is to keep it functioning.'

'But the way Zack and the Fulcrum have been abusing the computer, it has to be undermining it.'

He says nothing.

'I'm right, aren't I?'

'I don't want to worry you, Sarah, but yes, the computer system has been showing signs of instability.'

'Could it fail completely?'

'I don't know.'

'If it did, that would be the end.'

'Yes, it would.'

We sit, silent, both lost in our own thoughts.

'But we're not at that point, yet,' Stuart says, 'there are things we can do to make that less likely.'

'Like what?'

'Well, we need to stop the Fulcrum gaining control. We have…'

'But didn't I tell you about the weapons?'

'What weapons?' he says.

'Clarissa succeeded in triggering an intruder alert. I saw it all, on the screens. The arsenal opened and stayed open long enough for them to get weapons out.'

Stuart's whole body deflates like a burst balloon, in front of me.

'How many?' he says.

'Fifteen, twenty, I'm not sure. But I saw it, Stuart,

the destruction that only one can cause.'

'They're *already* using them?' he says, alarmed.

'Zack managed to get one working in his office. It was an accident that it went off. It's…horrific…what these things can do…devastating.'

'That's where we have to start then,' he says.

'What do you mean?'

'We have to get the weapons away from them.'

'But how can we do that?'

'I'm not sure, but the first thing we have to do, is get you to Zack. Distract him. You're his only weakness, Sarah, we have to exploit that.'

'I'm not sure…' I say.

'You have to do it, Sarah, for the Colony.'

I nod.

He walks into the hygiene cubicle and returns carrying a pile of clothing.

'Here put this on.'

'That's a Maintenance tunic,' I say, surprised.

'Yes,' he says, tossing the tunic and an ID badge at me.

'How did you get hold of these?'

'Don't ask,' he says.

'Come on, I'm intrigued.'

'I gained access to one of the female Maintenance workers pod,' he says averting his eyes.

'*And*?' I ask, eyebrows raised in anticipation.

'I stole them.'

'Is that it?' I say, disappointed.

'Yes, that's enough isn't it? I felt terrible. What did you mean by…*is that it*?'

'Nothing. Well, turn round then, so I can put them

on.'

'Oh, yes of course. Sorry, wasn't thinking,' he says, redness flooding his cheeks.

I pull my Museum and Archive tunic top up over my head and catch a stale waft coming from it. I step out of my tunic bottoms and lay them on the bunk with my top.

'Sarah…there's…er…some clean underwear…in the pocket of the tunic,' he says.

I look up at him, surprised.

'You thought of everything.'

'I hope…you don't think that…'

'Stuart, I don't *think* anything, except what a genius you are.'

I remove my dirty underpants and hide them under the pile on the bunk, then scramble into the clean clothing.

'It's a perfect fit, Stuart. How did you manage that?'

Stuart turns and looks me up and down.

'I looked round for someone who I thought matched my calculations.'

'Calculations?' I say.

'Yes, calculations about your size, shape, that sort of thing.'

'You never cease to amaze me, Stuart,' I say, grinning.

He blushes then glances up at the COMSET.

'Time to go,' he says. 'Now, remember to keep your head up. You have to look official, confident, if you appear unsure, people will notice.'

I nod. The door clicks and glides open and we

step out onto the walkway. Stuart walks across to the stairs and down into the corridor. I follow, a little behind him. He marches off, then slows, to allow me to catch up with him. We walk side by side down Corridor C, looking like any other work colleagues.

It's busy with the morning rush. Colonists pass us on the other side of the corridor but I look no one in the eye. They march past, staring ahead, uninterested. Stuart's pod is situated at the back of the Eugenics Centre, the building next to the SRU, so we don't have far to go. When we get to the perimeter corridor, we turn right. My heart speeds at the sight of its impressive façade. This seems like madness. Stuart turns to me, as if sensing my apprehension then gives me an encouraging smile. He marches up to the entrance and keys in his ID. There's a pause.

'Good morning, Stuart,' a bored sounding female voice says, 'what can we do for you?'

'I need to see Zack,' Stuart replies.

'I see,' she says, 'I have no record of an appointment.'

'I have an *open* appointment with Zack.'

I notice that his voice has lost some of its previous confidence. I stare at him with a questioning look.

'An *open* appointment?' the voice says.

'I have someone here with me.'

'Who is this person?' she asks, a touch of irritation tinging her words.

'Sa…' Stuart says, staring at my name badge, '…Georgina.'

'So is it Georgina who has the appointment with Zack?'

'Not exactly,' Stuart says, floundering.

I push him out of the way and lean into the console.

'Tell Zack that Stuart has brought the girl he needs to see. He'll understand.'

'Well, I'll try,' she says. 'Please wait.'

Stuart claws at his bottom lip, his brow lined with worry.

'He'll see us,' I say, squeezing his arm.

A minute later, the intercom clicks on.

'Zack will see you both.'

The door unlocks and slides open and we walk into the foyer. The owner of the intercom voice sits at the desk in front of us, her head down. A novice approaches us and directs us to follow him. I glance at the girl at the desk but she won't acknowledge me. The three of us go through a set of doors and down the corridor.

'Isn't that one Zack's office?' I say, pointing to the familiar door.

'Not now,' he says, 'that one's being refurbished. He's moved.'

Stuart and I exchange glances. The novice slows down and stops outside an office close to the end of the corridor. She knocks on the door.

'Enter,' Zack says, from the other side.

I'm overcome by anxiety, as I follow Stuart into the room. My mouth is dry and my heart thumps as it pumps blood out to my trembling limbs. I know that he's staring at me, even before I look up. His

117

presence burns into every pore of my body. He holds me with his eyes as I walk towards the desk. Stuart is ignored.

'Hello Sarah,' he says.

Chapter 22

17/06/3042 13:50 hours
JONATHAN

The four of us face the Ascendor door, Marilyn and Oli in front, Kyle and I behind. We've had plenty of time, to devise a plan, in fact several plans. We've been over and over it many times. We've amended, revised, argued and amended again but the one thing we all agreed on, from the start, is that we must not alarm the Deathday candidate more than we have to. That's why I suggested that Marilyn go in front. The fact that Oli insisted on joining her was unfortunate. But who was going to tell her that she's more likely to traumatise the poor girl. *Not me.*

'We still don't know if the Ascendor will take us all,' Kyle says, again.

'We've been over this,' I say, exasperated. 'We have to take the chance, do it in one go.'

'But, it's not only the size issue, Jonathan,' he persists, 'it's the weight.'

'Yes, we've been over that too,' I say, '*numerous* times.'

'But...'

'If the Fulcrum has taken over the Colony already,' Oli says, 'the first thing they'd do, is stop the Deathday ceremonies.'

Kyle and I exchange looks. She's right.

'Which means,' she continues, 'that we'll be trapped up here.'

'To die,' Marilyn whispers.

'It's just a thought,' Oli says, glancing sideways at Marilyn's anxious face, 'it's not *likely*.'

'Then why mention it,' I say, annoyed.

'To stop you two idiots from arguing.'

'It's nearly 14:00 hours,' Marilyn says, looking at her timepiece.

I push between Oli and Marilyn and press my ear up against the cold metal of the Ascendor door.

'Can you hear anything?' Kyle asks.

'No…but I can feel a faint vibration…nothing…'

A mechanical sigh makes me stop. I press my ear harder against the door. I can hear a muffled noise from the other side. There's a click. We all hear it. I jump back behind Marilyn and push her forward. The door swishes open. I peer over Marilyn's shoulder, the Ascendor looks empty but then she steps forward and crouches down, revealing a frail, dark haired girl curled up on the floor. Marilyn reaches down and touches her pallid arm. The girl looks up, surprised and screams. Her terrified cries bounce around the tunnel walls in diminishing circles.

'It's alright,' Marilyn says.

But the girl is trapped in the grip of fear. She's on her feet now pressed against the back wall of the Ascendor, her gaping mouth pouring out the screams, over which she has lost control. Oli steps inside.

'Stop it!' she shouts, slapping the girl's face hard with the flat of her hand.

The girl stops screaming and stares, transfixed at

her attacker.

'That's better,' Oli says. 'Now listen to me. You are safe. You're not going to die, do you understand, you're not...going...to die?'

The girl looks over Oli's shoulder at the three of us.

'Look at me, not them,' Oli says, pulling the girl's face back to meet hers. 'Do you understand?'

The girl nods.

'Good, now this is what's going to happen.'

She lays an arm over the girl's shoulders and helps her out of the Ascendor. Straight away, I push Marilyn in and stand holding back the door, so that Kyle can join her. The girl lets out a sob that comes from so deep inside, that her whole body heaves with the strain. Her head goes down.

'You haven't got time to snivel. You have to concentrate,' Oli says, lifting up the girl's face and pointing down the tunnel.

'Do you see that doorway, down there? That's Gate 1. Walk up to it and put in your ID code.' Oli waits for the girl to nod before continuing. 'Good, now there are three more Gates like that. Then you'll get to, the Renaissance Gate, that's different. That one leads to the outside.'

The girl whimpers.

'Stop that,' Oli says. 'Look at me, look into my eyes.' She waits for the girl to do as she's says. 'Do you trust me?'

The girl nods.

'Good. You stand in front of the Renaissance Gate and it will open but you'll be safe, I promise.'

With that, she shoves the girl in the back, propelling her in the direction of the first gate. After a few steps, the girl stops and turns. 'Come with me,' she says.

'Sorry, can't,' Oli says, 'I've got a Colony to save.'

With that, she jumps into the Ascendor. The last thing I see, before I jump in, is the arched back of the girl as she staggers away from me.

'So much for the gentle touch,' I say, my face only centimetres away from Oli's.

She shrugs.

We wait for the doors to close but, after several seconds, they're still open.

'You're obstructing it,' Kyle says to me.

'What am I supposed to do?' I say, trying to push myself away from it.

'It's not going to close,' Marilyn says, panic edging her voice. 'We'll have to…'

But, before she can finish, the doors glide shut. Now, we're wedged solid, inside the stationary box. I can't breathe. *I can't breathe.* I shut my eyes. Please start. Then, as if I willed it to, there's a jolt and it begins its descent to the Colony…and *Sarah.*

'You alright, Jonathan?' Oli says.

'Yes,' I snap, moving my lower body away from her abdomen.

'Only asked,' she says, a grin in her voice.

There's more room in here than I first thought. Despite this, I feel her press up against me again. Marilyn and Kyle have shifted away from me, finding some additional space. Oli, however, remains glued to my back. The Ascendor comes to a halt and I sense the bodies around me tense in anticipation. Marilyn will be the first out. But nothing happens.

'First it won't close, then it won't open. This is ridiculous,' Kyle says.

'Is there a button?' I ask, knowing there won't be.

'It's not going to open,' Oli says.

I stare at her, puzzled.

'Why?'

'Think about it, when it returns to the Colony, it should be empty. Why would it open?'

'A pity you didn't think of this earlier,' Kyle says.

'Well at least I'm thinking,' she snarls.

'I've got an idea,' Marilyn says, 'it might work. If I...'

'Look Marilyn, do it, whatever it is,' Oli says, 'otherwise we're going to suffocate waiting for you to explain.'

Marilyn, hesitates, then taps on the door.

'What...?' Kyle says.

'Shhhh,' Marilyn says, her ear pinned to the door.

She taps again, louder this time.

'Leander?' a voice says from the other side.

'Yes, it's me. Open the door, *please*.'

'How...?' the voice starts.

'Open the door,' Marilyn insists.

All goes quiet. The doors slide open. We spill out into the Ceremonial Chamber, sucking air into our lungs, as we go. But it's stale, stuffy from the Deathday ceremony. Oli's the first to recover her composure. She grabs the arm of the attendant, who stands frozen in front of us.

'Get the other one,' she shouts at me.

I leap across the room, as he reaches the door.

'Oh no you don't,' I say, pulling him back.

'Who are you,' he says. 'Where have you come from?'

'We haven't got time to explain,' I say, 'all you need to know is that we're not going to harm you.'

I push him down onto one of the seats. Oli brings the girl across and pushes her down onto the one next to him.

'Right, what I want you to do is call in a male and female Administration worker from the offices. Make sure the male one is tall and slim,' I add, assessing the size of the one in front of me.

'Why?' she says, eyeing my bare chest.

'Don't ask questions,' I glance down at her ID badge, 'Sherryl…just *do* it.'

She fixes me with a glare then gets up and marches across to the intercom. She glances back to her colleague.

'Who's the tallest?' she asks.

'Tyler?' he replies.

She presses a button and speaks.

'Send Tyler and Fearne to the Ceremonial Chamber.' There's silence. 'Did you hear me?'

'Yes,' the voice replies.

'I need them to help me clear up,' Sherryl adds, detecting the query in the voice.

She returns to her seat. I signal to Kyle to take up position on one side of the door, I take the other. Oli guards the prisoners, holding them with only a menacing stare. Marilyn is at the back of the chamber, searching for something. I don't get the chance to ask her what she's doing because the door opens and two people walk in. I can see straight away that Tyler is shorter than me but he'll have to do. Kyle and I grab them from behind and push them, protesting, towards the other two.

'What's going on?' Tyler says.

'Shut up and take off your tunics,' I command.

Four sets of eyes stare at me, astonished.

'Don't just stand there, *move*!'

Scrabbling out of their tunics, they stand in their underwear, in a quivering row.

'Now, we're going to swap clothes,' I say.

Kyle and Oli are already undressed. Marilyn comes over and takes her clothes off too. They hand them over to the bewildered group. Only Tyler seems reluctant to go along with our plan.

'You have no tunic top,' he says, stating the obvious and looking at my chest, 'and only one shoe.'

'Doesn't matter,' I say, 'get undressed.'

I throw the clothes, I do still have, at Tyler and he puts them on and stands with his arms crossed tight over his bare chest. Scrabbling into the Admin tunic, I stare down at the gap between the bottom of Tyler's tunic bottoms and the shoes. It will have to do. I glance over to the others. We look the part…we've become four Administration workers.

'We'll need something to tie them up with,' Oli says.

'No, we don't,' Marilyn says, going over to a small table at the side of the Chamber. She picks up a container of water and fills up one of the cups laid out next to it then returns.

'Marilyn, what…?'

But before I can finish my question, she opens up her hand and reveals eight small tablets. She gives each prisoner two.

'But…' Sherryl starts.

'Take them,' Marilyn says.

They don't move. But Oli does. She charges across the room, fist clenched.

'*Do* as she says,' she snarls, towering over them, despite her size.

She watches as they take the cup of water from Marilyn then put the tablets in their mouths and swallow hard.

'What was that all about,' she says, walking back to the door.

'Sedatives,' Marilyn says, 'double dose. They'll be out for hours.'

Chapter 23

17/06/3042   09:05 hours
SARAH

I stand in front of him, like a novice being reprimanded for some minor offence, my palms sweaty and my chest battered from the inside. I can't speak, my arid mouth isn't capable of it yet. All I can do is stare in bewilderment, hating him for reducing me to this husk of what I am. I force my eyes away from his and turn to Stuart for help.

'Here she is,' he says.

'Yes, here she is, indeed,' Zack says, his eyes still fixed on mine. 'And where, may I ask, have you been hiding?'

I don't answer. He'll never get that out of me whatever he does, whatever he says. Let him stew in my silence. Seeing perhaps the glimmer of defiance building in me, he turns to Stuart.

'*Where* has she been hiding?'

'The deal was that I should bring her to you, that's all,' Stuart says, the tremor in his voice giving away his nerves.

'Still the protector, even in betrayal,' Zack says, smiling.

'He doesn't know where I've been hiding. He found me down in the Maintenance Department.'

'So she speaks,' Zack says, 'but forgive me if I don't believe that.'

'I don't care what you believe,' I say, folding my

arms across my chest.

'Defiant, as ever. You know I can make you tell me, don't you?'

'Yes,' I say.

Stuart approaches the desk.

'You promised that you wouldn't harm her. You gave me your word.'

'He won't harm me.'

'So, you think that I'm an honourable person, Sarah?'

'It wouldn't be in your interests to harm me.'

His eyes dart away from mine then, back again. It's the smallest of movements, but enough for me to know that I've touched a nerve. For the first time since I entered this office, I feel in control.

'My interests?' he says.

There's something now at the edge of his words but is it fear, or excitement?

'Yes,' I say, 'I couldn't go on hiding forever, could I? I had to make a decision. And what I decided was to give myself up. Stuart may have brought me to you, Zack but I come of my own free will.'

'And why…why would you do that?'

The hope coming from him is tangible. It's as if I could reach out, grab it in my hand and crush it. But, I need to keep something in reserve.

'I had no choice.'

He lets out the breath he's been holding, disappointment flooding his features and I know I've gone too far.

'Loneliness got the better of me,' I add.

'I see,' he says. 'So tell me, does this mean that you will be joining the Fulcrum, Sarah?'

I don't respond. He's taken me by surprise.

'Stuart, what about you? Will you be using your considerable skills to help me gain control of the Colony? Because that's what we're talking about here, as I'm sure you realise.'

'I...' Stuart says, giving up under Zack's scrutiny.

'You won't ever gain control of the Colony,' I say.

'Why do you say that?'

'The Council will...'

He interrupts me before I can complete the lie.

'The Council does *nothing*. They're weak, ineffective. I already have everything I need to take over their precious handiwork. But do they try and stop me? No, they don't. And why is that, do you suppose,' he pauses, not expecting an answer, 'because they know what they'd be faced with. They know the consequences of intervening. They'd rather see the Colony under my control than risk it being destroyed completely.'

'You don't know that,' Stuart says, 'they may be waiting...waiting for the right time.'

'They may be,' Zack says, 'but before you get your hopes up, I want to show you both something.'

He walks out from behind his desk and pushes past Stuart on his way to the door.

'Follow me,' he says.

We leave the office and trail behind him to the end of the corridor, then through a set of doors towards the back of the SRU building. In front of us,

129

I can see the cellblock and, as we approach, I look behind and up at the ceiling. And there it is, the camera from which I viewed this very scene, only yesterday.

'They're not going to help you, Sarah,' Zack says, noticing the direction of my gaze, 'you know that.'

I turn away from it, flustered and follow on behind him. He stops outside the second from last cell and keys his ID into the console. We walk in. The cell is empty apart from a stack of weapons piled up on the floor against the back wall.

'Do you know what they are?' Zack says, pointing.

'No,' I say, a little too fast.

'Stuart, what about you? You're a man who appreciates a well-designed piece of machinery.'

'I haven't come across anything like that before,' he says.

I realise that, unlike me, he's telling the truth.

'Let me show you.'

Zack bends down and picks up one of the weapons.

'This,' he says, holding it across his chest, 'is a gun.'

My eyes fix on the sleek blackness of it. I had not appreciated its dark beauty through the camera lens. Now I can see that it's designed to impress. To strike awe into those who gaze upon its intricate construction of interlocking parts, knowing what it's capable of. Zack smiles. Then he manoeuvres it into position, pointing out from his body, his finger poised over the lever underneath. He sweeps it from left to right in a semi-circular motion. Instinct takes over and I dive to the floor under its path. Zack lowers the gun and looks down at me, surprised.

'So you *do* know what it is, what it does,' he says.

He steps towards me and places the tip of the gun at my temple.

'What's going on here?'

'Zack, *please*,' I whimper, every cell in my body focused on the small circle of cold metal pressed against my head.

'*Tell* me!' he shouts.

I feel the point of contact press harder into my skin and all I can think of is what will happen if he pulls that lever, when he pulls that lever.

'Please Zack, I beg you.'

Then, there's a scream, piercing, terrified. I think at first, that it's come from me. But Zack isn't looking in my direction. The point of the gun drops, as he stares at the wall between this cell and the next, Finn's cell. Zack's body jerks forward and Stuart pushes the gun away from my head.

'Drop it,' Stuart shouts.

Zack doesn't move.

'*Drop it*, I said.'

He does what he's told hearing, like me, a menace I've never heard before from Stuart. The gun thumps down on the floor only centimetres from my feet. I jump up and move behind Zack. Now, I can see that Stuart has another of the guns pushed up against Zack's back. His arms are shaking so much that I know he won't be able to hold it there for much longer.

'Sarah, pick up the gun,' he says.

I crouch down in front of Zack and, without looking up at him, lift it and myself back up again, my thighs muscles straining with the effort. I carry the gun cradled across my outstretched arms and place it on the pile.

'Good,' Stuart says, his voice shaking as much as his arms. 'Now Zack, I want you to go to the other cells and release the prisoners.'

'What prisoners?' Zack says.

'The SRU officers that wouldn't go along with your scheme.'

He laughs. 'You're too late, there aren't any left. They all came to their senses in the end and joined me.'

'You're lying,' I say.

He glances across at me, with a questioning look. 'Am I?'

'I…I don't believe you,' I say, trying to divert his suspicion.

'It's irrelevant what you believe.'

'Move,' Stuart says, pushing the gun into his back.

'Look, Stuart,' Zack says, 'you know and I know, that you're not going to pull the trigger of that gun. So why don't you stop playing games and put it down.'

'*Don't* push me Zack.'

'If you're going to do it, just get on with it,' Zack taunts.

I stare open-mouthed at Stuart. His eyes dart from side to side and I see a sheen of perspiration form on his forehead. He looks close to tears.

'Stuart, put down the gun,' I whisper.

'*No*,' he says.

I watch as his arms brace and his finger quivers above the lever. And I know, at that moment, that he's going to do it. He's going to kill Zack. I launch myself at him, pushing him sideways. He slams into the cell wall and drops the gun to the floor. I fall on top of it, as if it might move of its own volition.

'Run Stuart!' I scream. 'Run!'

He stares down at me with his traumatised eyes and then, as if he knows he has no choice, he scrambles to his feet and flies out the cell door into the corridor. I hear a quiet moaning coming through the wall. Poor Finn, poor terrified Finn. Then I'm sobbing for Finn, for me and I can't stop. I cling onto the gun and cry.

After a while, I don't know how long, I feel a hand on my arm.

'Sarah, it's alright.'

I raise my head and there's Zack, kneeling down beside me. He strokes my hair, brushes the tears from my face with his fingertips.

'It's alright,' he says, 'I was in no danger.'

'What do you mean?' I say.

'The gun…it wasn't loaded.'

'What?' I say, sitting up.

'None of them are loaded, Sarah, not yet. We'll load them when we need to.'

He takes my face in his hands and lifts it, so that I can't escape his eyes.

'You saved my life,' he says.

'No,' I say, 'you weren't in danger.'

'But you didn't know that, Sarah,' he says, 'you didn't know that.'

Chapter 24

'There's a foot sticking out,' I say.

Oli sighs and kicks at the leg protruding from behind the podium.

'He won't fit,' she says, 'there's not enough room to hide them all here.'

'They need to be out of sight, Oli,' I say, 'can't you pile them up a bit.'

'They're dead weights, Jonathan. If you think you can do any better, *you* try,' she says, marching over to a seat.

She flops down on it, making as much noise about it as she can.

'Kyle, guard the door a minute,' I say.

I walk over to the podium, glaring at Oli, as I go. Behind it is a tangled mass of bodies. I look across to Oli.

'If you put them in position one at a time, they'll fit.'

'Go ahead then,' she says, disinterested, drinking from the cup of water Marilyn's given her.

I pull the two girls out of the way first. I know Oli's watching me, so I keep my eyes down. Now the girls are to one side, I can deal with Tyler. I kneel down and half push, half roll him right up against the back of the podium. As I do, I notice a thin line of saliva running from the corner of his mouth, off the side of his face and onto the floor. His feet are out of view now and I glance up at Oli, ready to gloat, but she's not looking. Just as well, because then I see that, at the other end, the top of his head is sticking out.

'I can still see him,' she says.

Irritated, I crouch down, grab the back of his knees and bend his legs a little. Now he's hidden. Then I drag Oscar and Sherryl as close to Tyler as I can but that still leaves Fearne. She's the smallest and there's only one place she can go. I pull her on top of Oscar, draping her over his body. Her left hand touches his face in a light caress. I wonder what they'll make of *that* when they come round. I cross over to the others.

'Nobody should enter the Ceremonial Chamber now,' I say, looking behind me at the podium, 'but if they do, the four of them are out of sight from the door.'

'So, now what?' Kyle says.

'I'm going out.'

'You can't go yet, you'll be spotted straight away.'

'I need to find Sarah.'

'I know, but you need to wait until 17:30, when people are coming out of work. Going now is too dangerous.'

'I can't wait that long.'

'So you're quite happy to put the rest of us in danger,' Oli says.

I don't reply.

'…for your *precious* Sarah,' she adds, under her

breath but loud enough to be heard.

'Leave him alone,' Marilyn says, 'even if he's spotted, they won't know there are others here.'

'But they *might*,' Oli insists, 'it's not worth the risk.'

'Nothing we say is going to stop you, Jonathan, is it?' Kyle says.

'No.'

'Well, you'd better go then. But we need to arrange a time and place to meet up.'

'It'll have to be the Gym,' Marilyn says, 'at 18:00 hours.'

'Small flaw in that plan,' Oli says, 'even if we manage to remain undetected in the Gym, what are we going to do when the Silence begins? We haven't got pods we can go to.'

'We'll need Stuart for that,' I say. 'You'll need to find him, tell him...'

'Who's Stuart?' Oli says.

I stare at her, realising my mistake. They don't know Stuart, of course they don't. Only *I* do. Before I can reply, Marilyn states the obvious...the obvious that I don't want to hear.

'Jonathan, surely it would be more sensible, if Kyle and I search for Sarah and you find Stuart.'

I'm trying to think of *anything*, anything at all that could counter that logic, but I can't.

'Much more sensible,' Oli says, smirking.

'Alright, *I'll* find Stuart,' I say, marching across to the door.

I don't stop. I charge through the building, past a blur of offices and Admin workers, until I reach the foyer. Only one door left now between me and the City corridors.

'Excuse me…' I hear, from the reception desk behind me.

I ignore it and exit the building without slowing my pace. As soon as I'm outside, I know the others were right. The perimeter corridor is deserted. I step into it, feeling swamped by the space around me. Hesitation will be my downfall. I must keep moving. I turn right and make my way along the front of the Administration building. But I haven't got a clue where I'm going. My body, hunches up with indecision. I've forgotten how quiet it is during work hours. All that I can think is, why would an Admin worker be roaming the corridors at this time of day? Official business? Maybe. But *what*? *Think*.

'Is everything alright?'

I stop, my pulse racing and force myself to look over my shoulder. Behind me, I see the black of an SRU uniform. But the wearer is unknown to me, a girl. Her ID badge tells me that her name is Alaise. I start to breathe again.

'Are you alright, Tyler?'

I stare at her, puzzled then see that she's looking at my badge.

'Yes…yes, I am.'

'Only, your walk seems unsteady, as if you are unwell.'

Unwell. That's it.

'Yes…I feel unwell…I'm on my way to the Health Centre.'

'You're going in the wrong direction then,' she

says.

I give her a blank look.

'The Health Centre is *that* way.'

She points, in the opposite direction, to the one I've been going.

You *idiot*.

'Sorry…' I whisper.

'There is no need to be sorry.'

She sounds sympathetic enough but there's note of suspicion in her voice.

'Would you like me to help you there?'

'No,' I say, 'I…can manage…thank you.'

'If you are sure,' she says.

'Yes, yes, I'm sure.'

I turn and walk, as slowly as I can, away from her.

I approach the entrance of the Health & Wellbeing Centre and stop in front of the door console then lean out and glance down the corridor. Alaise is talking to another SRU officer. Even from this distance, I recognise Jevon. She turns and points in my direction and he looks up. I thrust my head forward out of view. Out of the corner of my eye, I catch a flash of black. They're coming this way. I don't know if Jevon recognised me, but I'm not hanging around to find out.

I bolt towards Corridor D, turn into it and charge down to the esplanade without stopping. At the end, I swing right and run along the backs of the SRU and Eugenics buildings. Another right turn takes me into Corridor B and back to the perimeter corridor. I pause, then dash across to the Jojo and throw myself onto the floor behind the barrier, out of view. I shuffle forward, feeling the vibration through my knees and hands, as it trundles its way round the City. I peer out through the gap in the barrier. There's no sign of either of them. But halfway along the Eugenics building opposite, I spot Jevon as he shoots out of Corridor C. He doubles over, clutching at his midriff. I pull my head back. A few seconds later, when I think I've passed him, I peer out again. Alaise is with him now but they're not going anywhere. Jevon's face is screwed up with pain. Perhaps I'm safe, for a while. But they're bound to report the incident. They'll be looking out for me. I've been careless, stupid. I need to calm down, act rationally. I take in a deep breath.

The Jojo is passing the SRU building now and my brain half registers a figure standing by the entrance. *Sarah*? That *was* Sarah, I'm sure. The hair, golden, cascading down her back. It was Sarah. I stick my head out further. Yes, she's there.

'Sarah…' I call out.

She looks up surprised but her attention is taken by something else, someone else behind her. An arm drapes across her shoulders, as she's guided out into the corridor. She turns her head and smiles at the SRU officer beside her. Such a smile. A smile, she once gave to me. And I know, before he comes into view, that it's Zack. A lead weight crashes into the pit of my stomach. I watch, as he removes his arm from her shoulders and returns it to his side. I catch a glimpse as his hand seeks hers and they walk away from me, arms touching.

Chapter 25

17/06/3042   15:00 hours
SARAH

'I've brought you another cover, Sarah,' Zack says, entering the cell through the door that has remained unlocked, since he led me here this morning.

'Am I a prisoner?' I'd asked, as he scurried around never taking his eyes off me for a second.

'No, of course not...no,' he'd said. 'This is the safest place for you. I can protect you here, Sarah. I'll look after you now.'

Now. That word has punctuated every sentence he's uttered since the gun incident. It's as if, for him, there was no before, only *now*. But what does he think *now* is. What does he think has changed? I know the answer, of course. I'd be lying if I said I didn't. The truth is that *everything* has changed. As far as he's concerned, I saved his life. He's come to his own conclusion about what that means. He doesn't seem to need any confirmation from me. And to be honest, however much I try, I haven't been able to come up with anything that explains my actions. We had the fate of the Colony in our hands. One death, to save thousands of deaths, to save the Human Race. Stuart *knew*. It doesn't matter that the gun wasn't loaded. He was prepared to do what had to be done. But I threw that chance away. *Why*?

'Where do you want these?'

I look up and see Sean enter the cell. He glowers at me, with that surly look he's been nursing ever since he barged into Zack's office and caught him stroking my hair. His astonished expression, as he was ordered out, went unnoticed by Zack, but not by me.

'On the table,' Zack says.

'There's no room.'

Sean looks down at the array of food packages in front of him.

'*Make* room,' Zack barks at him.

Sean nudges the opened packets to the edges of the table and puts the four new ones in the space he's made then glances across to Zack.

'Why is she…?' he begins.

Zack swings round to face him.

'Get out!' he shouts.

Sean doesn't move straight away but instead, holds Zack's stare, his eyes narrowed for long enough, to register his protest. His expression is a mixture of anger and disappointment. Then he turns and walks towards the door but, at the last minute, stops and looks back at him.

'We just want to know what's going on, Zack,' he says, 'that's all.'

'*We*?' Zack says.

'The other officers, the Fulcrum.'

Zack moves over to him.

'All *you* and the *others* need to know, is that Sarah's with me now, with us and you'll treat her with the same respect, as you do me. You can tell the *others* that's how it's going to be from now on.

142

Understand?'

Sean doesn't respond. Zack takes a step towards him.

'*Understand*,' he repeats.

'Yes,' Sean says, then marches out, flashing a final glare in my direction.

'Zack, I'm not sure that…' I say.

'They'll get used to it. Come on, eat up, you look so thin.'

He brushes his hand down my arm. Then falls into silence. After a while he speaks.

'Where were you?'

Not this again.

'I've told you, Zack, I won't tell you that. I won't put anyone in danger.'

'They won't be in danger, Sarah, I only want to know.'

'Stuart helped me. You already know that.'

'He couldn't have done it on his own. We watched him. He went to work, he came back from work and he went to work again. How…?'

'I promise you, Zack,' I cut in, 'Stuart was the only one who helped me.'

I hold his look because I'm not lying and he knows it.

'It frightens me that I lost you, Sarah, that I couldn't find you however hard I tried. I don't want that to happen again, not now.'

'I'm not going anywhere,' I say.

I know he's not satisfied but he doesn't push me further.

'Stuart's dangerous,' he says.

I look up, surprised at the apparent change of subject.

'No, the gun wasn't loaded, you knew that.'

'Do you think I would have taunted him like that, if it was? I pushed him to find out what he was capable of and now, I know.'

'He panicked.'

'He didn't panic, Sarah, he knew exactly what he was doing. And, what's more, he'll do it again if he gets the chance.'

'I'm not sure he would,' I lie.

'Look Sarah, you have to make a choice. It's him or me, it can never be both, not now.'

'I…'

'You don't have to answer straight away, but think about it, Sarah.'

'Perhaps I will have something,' I say, getting up and walking over to the table.

I open one of the packets, grab a handful of rice and suck it into my mouth from my palm.

'That's right,' he says, coming over and sitting next to me on the bunk, 'eat up. Is there anything else you'd like, anything at all?'

I swallow.

'I need some sunlight, Zack, I haven't had any for days,' I lie.

'Yes, of course. We need to get you to the Solarium,' he says, smiling.

'I could go on my own.'

His smile disappears for a second, then creeps back.

'No, I'll take you.'

'Don't you trust me?'

'I...'

'No, of course you don't. That's understandable. These things take time.'

'Yes, they do.'

He glances at me.

'Sarah, I...'

'*Don't...*' I say.

I'm not ready for this.

'Let's go then,' I say, getting up.

He doesn't move just stares down, grinding the palms of his hands together, all the tension in his body focused there.

'Come on,' I say.

He gets up and follows me out. When we reach the foyer, Zack goes over to the girl at the reception desk and says something to her. As he leans over her, she glances across at me over his shoulder. I notice the contempt in her gaze. Zack is oblivious to it. He beckons me over to him then follows me through the doors. Outside, he comes up behind me and places an arm over my shoulders, as the doors close behind us. I look up at him, surprised.

'Sorry, I wasn't thinking.'

'That's fine,' I say and smile, 'it's not a problem.'

His eyes have a vulnerable quality about them and I hold them longer than I should. Then, I hear my name. Someone calls out my name. Not someone. *Jonathan.* I look behind, guilt taking me in its grip. But there's no one there. Jonathan is dead.

'Sarah, what's the matter,' Zack says, 'you're trembling?'

I can't speak, the loss I feel is too painful. I feel sick with loneliness.

'Come on,' he says, 'let's get some sunlight onto you. You'll feel much better then.'

I manage a nod, as he guides me away from the entrance. We turn right and make our way towards Corridor D. I raise my right hand in front of me and stare, fascinated, at the way it shakes. It's moved by a force, separate from conscious thought. I feel Zack's hand enclose round it. Then we let our clasped hands fall down between us.

'That's right, Sarah, hold onto me.'

We walk, our movements synchronised, his body so close to mine that it's as if we're one person. And I feel safe.

Chapter 26

17/06/3042   22:38 hours
JONATHAN

'Aren't you going to eat that, Jonathan?' Oli says, eyeing the unopened food packet on my lap.

'I'm not hungry,' I say, pushing it across the floor of the Jojo towards her, 'you have it.'

'You need to eat, Jonathan,' Marilyn says.

She gives Oli a look of disapproval.

'Mustn't waste the Colony's precious resources,' she says with her mouth full.

'Why do they put food in the service elevator every night anyway?' Kyle asks.

'Zack's got an arrangement with somebody in the Food Production Unit,' I say, 'it's his way of getting extra rations to the Fulcrum, keeping them on his side. It seems to work.'

'So, it's only a temporary arrangement then. It might stop at any time.'

'Look Kyle,' I snap, 'it's not worth worrying about. *Anything* could happen at *any* time.'

He folds his arms tight across his chest, his shoulders hunch up against the attack.

'Sorry, I spoke,' he mutters.

I can't be bothered to apologise. All I want is to be left alone.

'So, what do we do next,' Oli says, 'now that this Stuart hasn't materialised?'

I don't answer.

'Jonathan?'

'What?' I say.

'I said, what do we do now?'

'*I* don't know. Why is it always down to me to decide what we're going to do? Isn't it about time one of you contributed something?'

'That's a little unfair,' Marilyn says, 'you know your way about at night in the City. We're doing what we can to help.'

'Marilyn's right,' Oli says, 'it's not our fault that your precious Sarah has betrayed you, is it? So don't take it out on us.'

I stare at her. Then, overcome by a mixture of fury and frustration, I launch myself across the metre or so between us and push her shoulders hard up against the Jojo barrier. Her eyes fix on mine, wide with surprise.

'If you say *anything* about Sarah, anything at all, I'm going to make you wish you hadn't. Do you understand, Oli?'

'Are you threatening me?'

I apply more pressure on her shoulders. 'I *said*, do you understand?'

'Yes, I understand.'

She hasn't taken her eyes off mine, for a second. I release her shoulders and she pushes me away from her.

'You've got to face up to it sometime,' she mumbles behind my back.

I pretend I didn't hear and return to my place beside Kyle.

'There's no point fighting amongst ourselves,' he

says, 'we need to concentrate, work out our next step.'

'And that would be…?' I say, knowing he hasn't got a clue.

'We could follow the SRU officers,' Oli says, looking at Kyle not me.

'What?'

'The SRU officers that have been walking down towards the Solarium.'

I crawl over Kyle's legs and peer around the gap in the barrier. The corridor's empty. I turn back to Oli.

'What officers?'

She glares at me for the first time since our confrontation.

'They've gone *now*.'

'How many did you see?'

'I don't know, seventy, eighty maybe.'

'Why didn't you say something?'

'I just did.'

'There must be a Fulcrum meeting tonight,' I say, glaring at her, 'which is probably over by now.'

'I doubt it,' she says, 'the last group I saw went down about twenty minutes ago.'

I grab the food packet out of Oli's hand.

'Hey, I haven't finished yet.'

'You have now.'

'We'll come back for this lot later,' I say, piling the packets up against the barrier.

I look up and down the amber lit perimeter corridor. There's no one around. Beckoning to the others to follow, I dash across to the entrance of

Corridor C. One by one they come up behind me.

'We need to go now, while the corridor's empty.'

'Where are we going, Jonathan,' Oli says, 'only it's quite important that we know.'

Irritated by her tone, I still have to concede that she's right.

'We're going straight down to the end then up the steps to the top walkway on the SRU building.'

'When...?' Oli starts.

'*Now!*'

I bolt down the corridor as close to the side wall of the SRU building, as I can. I reach the stairs then, without looking to see if they're following, charge up them and wait. Oli's the first to arrive, followed by Marilyn, then Kyle. He flops down next to me, gasping for breath. I lean over the railing and look to my right down the esplanade, nothing, then to my left. In the gloom, I make out a sizeable group between the Administration block and the Solarium. I pull myself back in and go across to the others.

'OK, I can see them, they're two buildings away. We'll need to get closer.'

'How are we going to do that without being seen,' Marilyn asks.

After a quick explanation on how to travel across the walkways, we set off, across the length of the SRU and down the stairs into Corridor D.

'From now on,' I say, 'we need to be as quiet as we can. Follow me.'

We dash across to the Health & Wellbeing Centre and creep up to the top walkway. I get down on all fours and signal to the others to do the same. Then we crawl the length of the walkway and stop at the stairs going down to Corridor E. Now, I catch snippets of what they're saying, below me.

'...we have the weapons...entry to the Council Chamber...via the service elevator...we need a volunteer.'

'What's happening?' Oli whispers behind me.

'I'm not sure. I need to get closer. Wait here.'

I make my way down the steps into Corridor E, creep across it and hide myself under the stairs. An impenetrable wall of heads confronts me. I need to get higher. Holding my breath, I walk up to the top walkway, a step at a time. Each one I take clangs out, breaking the ominous silence that's developed below. At the top, I crawl along the walkway then get on my knees and peep out over the top of the railing. The only person I see, at first, is Sarah. She stands next to Zack between Sean and Jevon. I'm mesmerised by the sight of her. I notice that everyone's eyes are fixed on her, too. Then she speaks.

'How else can I prove my loyalty, my allegiance to the Fulcrum?'

'Well, well,' a voice whispers behind me. I swing round and see Oli, half a metre away from me looking out on the scene below.

'Get down, you'll be seen.'

'I wouldn't miss this for the world,' she says.

'I told you to wait over there.'

'It is agreed, Sarah will go up tomorrow night,' I hear from below.

I shuffle round and slump down with my back to

the railing, and the betrayal. I stare at the pod door in front of me.

'You were right,' Oli whispers, 'she is the enemy now.'

She settles down next to me, knees up, her arm touching mine. I feel her body trembling against mine. Then her head goes down to her knees.

'What's the matter?'

'Nothing,' she says, but the shake in her voice, gives her away.

'Come on, tell me.'

'Seeing Sean…down there…brings it all back.'

I turn round to her, puzzled.

'The last time I saw Sean's face, it was pressed up against mine, covered in sweat, his breath hot on my neck. I…couldn't move…he…he had me…pinned down. There was nothing…nothing I could do.'

'Oli, I'm so sorry,' I say.

She says nothing for a while then raises up her head and takes a deep breath.

'If you promise not to feel sorry for *me*, Jonathan, I won't feel sorry for *you*.'

'And revenge?' I say.

'Oh yes, I still want that.'

Then she gets onto all fours and crawls away from me along the walkway.

Chapter 27

'You may have fooled Zack,' Jevon hisses as he pushes past me on his way to the front of the meeting, 'but we don't trust you, Sarah, not one bit.'

'I'd be careful, Jevon, if I were you,' I say, leaning in as close as I dare, 'I've only got to tell Zack and you'll...'

'Tell Zack *what*.'

I look up. Zack's next to me. He places a hand of ownership on my shoulder.

'Ask *him*,' I say, staring at Jevon, a shadow of fear crossing his face.

'*Well*,' Zack says.

'We're ready for you now,' Jevon says, looking at me rather than Zack.

'Good, we need to get started, there's a lot to get through.'

Jevon slopes off to join Sean. Then Zack's hands are gripping my shoulders from behind, guiding me through the crowd towards the front.

'Can't I stay back here? I don't need to be at the front, do I?'

I feel his fingertips tighten on me through the fabric of my tunic and I know I've made a mistake.

'You're with *me* now, Sarah.'

But it comes out as a question more than a statement.

'Yes, of course, you know that.'

'Do I?'

'What do you mean?'

I guess what's coming.

'This evening...' he begins.

'...I'm not ready for that yet,' I say, remembering his fumbled attempt to kiss me.

He brushes my cheek with his fingers, unaware that people around us are staring.

'The only thing I've ever wanted, Sarah, is for you to come to me...of your own free will.'

'Then you won't push me into anything until I'm ready.'

His disappointed eyes drift to the side, unfocused, over my right shoulder.

'Give me time,' I whisper, 'that's all I ask. A little more time.'

He doesn't say anything, doesn't look at me. As we pass the colonists that now make up the Fulcrum, I catch muttered comments. I can't make out the individual words. I don't need to. Their hostile tone reinforces the fact that I'm not wanted here. I'm still the enemy. Nothing has changed. Zack, either doesn't notice, or doesn't care, he looks straight ahead. When we reach Sean and Jevon, Zack takes up his position between them.

'Make room,' he says.

He beckons to me to join him. But there's not enough room.

'Move!' Zack barks at Sean.

Sean makes just enough space for me to wedge myself in next to Zack. Trying not to make actual physical contact, I look up. The first thing I notice is how much the Fulcrum has grown since last I saw it. There can be only a handful of SRU officers who have not joined its ranks. I fix my eyes above their heads and wait.

'Salute!' Zack commands, startling me.

Without hesitation, the entire gathering breaks into the aggressive arm movements of the Fulcrum salute. I stand, awkward and intimidated and watch. When they finish there's a silence, so complete, that it's as if we are confronted by rows of statues rather than living beings. Zack's voice pierces the hush.

'As you can see, we have a new member...Sarah.'

He turns to me but there's no emotion in his look.

'You will recognise her, as the same Sarah, we have until now, considered an enemy of the Fulcrum.'

A buzz travels round the gathering.

'So, it is even more significant that she has joined me...us...in our mission to take over the Colony and free ourselves from the tyranny of the Council.'

Tyranny of the Council? That's new.

'She will play an important role in this mission and that's why I want her close by my side. Any questions?'

Nobody speaks and I feel Zack's arm relax. Does he feel he's passed a test of some kind?

'I have a question?' Sean says.

Zack's head swings round to him. I can't see his face but I can see Sean's, and it's pinched with worry.

'Well?' Zack says.

'How do we know we can trust her?'

'I *know*.'

But Sean isn't leaving it there. 'But *how* do you know.'

'Because…' Zack says, '…and I want you all to know this…Sarah saved my life.'

Sean stares at me, stunned. I hold his eyes long enough to stamp my authority on Zack's words.

'Does that answer your question?'

'Yes…yes, it does,' Sean manages to get out.

'Good, then if there are no further questions, we'll continue with the business of this meeting.'

'As you will know,' Zack addresses the crowd again, 'we have successfully broken into the arsenal and taken out a number of weapons. However, because of limited time, we were unable to retrieve from the vault the corresponding ammunition.'

He turns to Sean.

'How many of the weapons will be functional?'

'Well…we…that is Jevon and I…have been…' he stammers, under Zack's glare.

'How many?'

'Three.'

'*Three*?'

'Yes, the rest are useless to us,' Sean says.

'Why didn't you tell me this before?'

Sean's face reddens but he stays silent.

'Three will be enough,' Zack says, although he sounds as if he's trying to convince himself, as much as the others.

'So now we have the weapons, we need to gain entry to the Council Chamber and take control.'

'And the only way we know of getting up to the Council Chamber is via the service elevator in Corridor G. And, with the help of our new contact in Maintenance,' he points to a boy in the first row, 'this will be achievable.'

He scans the impassive faces in front of him.

'So we need a volunteer,' he says.

His statement is met with a wary silence.

'*Well*,' Zack says, picking out the smaller officers in the front row whose eyes are now glued to the floor beneath them.

'I'll go,' I say.

Zack swings round to me.

'No,' he says, 'not you.'

'How else,' I say, addressing the crowd, not him, 'can I prove my loyalty, my allegiance to the Fulcrum?'

I hear shouts of agreement from the back. Several officers in the front row are nodding, relief etched on their faces.

'Why?' Zack whispers.

'It's the only way, Zack, the only way I can prove myself to *you*, to *them*.'

He nods then turns back to the Fulcrum.

'It is agreed. Sarah will go up tomorrow night. You are dismissed.'

We watch as the SRU officers slowly filter away from the meeting then fall into an uneasy silence.

'Zack, I'm tired. I need to get some rest.'

'Yes, of course,' he says, pushing a stray strand of hair from my face and behind my ear.

'Where…?' he whispers.

'The cell, Zack, I want to go back to the cell.'

'You could come to my pod.'

'I *could*, Zack but you know I won't, not tonight.'

'Not tonight,' he whispers, as he takes my hand and leads me along the esplanade, in the direction of the SRU building.

Back in the cell, I sit on the bunk waiting for Zack to leave but he seems reluctant to go.

'Is there anything I can get you?'

'No, I need to sleep,' I say.

With nothing to keep him here, he walks across to the door and I think he's about to leave.

'You did very well tonight, Sarah,' he says, turning to face me.

'Thank you.'

'You're sure there's nothing…'

'Zack, I'm fine. I'll see you in the morning.'

'Goodnight,' he says.

I watch him disappear through the door and wait for the familiar click but it doesn't come. So, I'm not a prisoner. Waiting five minutes, I creep over to it and stare, as it slides open, then I step into the corridor and make my way along the front of the cellblock. I press my ear up against the smooth surface of a door. All I can hear is a rhythmic breathing punctuated by an occasional groan. I tap on the door, keeping my ear against it, but get no response. I tap again, louder. This time the breathing falters then returns to its previous rhythm. I give up tapping and knock as loud as I dare.

'Who's there?' a groggy voice says.

'Naomi, is that you?'

There's no reply.

'Naomi,' I whisper.

'Who is it?'

The voice is close and full of suspicion.

'Sarah,' I say.

My name is met by silence. I can feel the presence of a person on the other side.

'Naomi, I know you're there. It's Sarah.'

Still nothing. Could she have forgotten who I am?

'It's Sarah, remember me, we…'

'I *know* who you are,' she says, at last.

Grateful for any response, I continue.

'I'm in the cell second from the end.'

'As a prisoner?' she says.

'Not exactly.'

'What's that supposed to mean?'

'Well, I'm not locked in, I…'

'Come to a special arrangement with Zack, have you?'

'In a way,' I say, 'I've tricked him into thinking that I've joined the Fulcrum.'

'You must have been very convincing,' she says, 'because the last time we heard anything about you, Sarah, the SRU were scouring the City searching for you.'

'I hid from them.'

'Yes, and we were the ones they took it out on, when they couldn't find you.'

'*We*?' I say. 'How many of you are left? I noticed at the Fulcrum meeting that…'

'You were at a Fulcrum meeting?'

'I...have to get Zack's trust, Naomi.'

'What about *my* trust, Sarah, is that important to you, anymore?'

'Of course it is, but things are escalating. There's so much you don't know, things you need to know if we're going to defeat the Fulcrum.'

'*We're* not going to do anything, Sarah.'

'What do you mean?'

There are only eight of us left...*eight*. How do you suppose we can defeat them with that number? I assume you know about the weapons?'

'Yes.'

'And you still think we can defeat them?'

'Look, I'm going to get you and the others out of here. I'll have access to one of the weapons.'

She doesn't respond. 'Naomi, did you hear what I said?'

'Yes, I heard. I'm just wondering why they would give you a weapon.'

'They want me to go up with it to the Council Chamber, in the food chute.'

'The food chute?'

'The service elevator.'

'To overcome the Council?' she says.

'No...yes...well, that's what they *think*. But Naomi, there *is* no Council.'

'No Council?'

'I've been up there. It's empty. That's where I've been hiding.'

'In the Council Chamber?'

'Yes,' I say.

'You must think I'm an idiot, Sarah, a complete

idiot.'

'It's true, I promise, you have to trust me.'

'That's just it, Sarah, I *don't* trust you. Not one bit. Whatever warped little scheme you and Zack have come up with, I…we want no part of it. Do you understand?'

'Naomi, please listen. *Naomi*?'

But she's gone. I press my ear up closer to the door.

'Who was that?' I hear another voice say.

'Nobody,' Naomi says, 'nobody at all.'

Chapter 28

I poke my head over the railing and look down into the esplanade. The meeting is finally breaking up. SRU officers peel off from the crowd and disappear into the amber gloom. Then I spot Zack and Sarah deep in conversation and my heart goes up a gear. I battle to control my breathing but it comes fast and shallow. I see her lips are moving but it's not Zack she's looking at, it's me. I dive down onto the walkway and hold my breath. Did she see me? I can't take the risk. I need to move. I scurry along the walkway floor towards the stairs, keeping as low as I can. A few steps down, I catch sight of people turning into Corridor E. A soft murmur of intimate conversation drifts up to me then Zack and Sarah come into view. I creep backwards up to the walkway, my eyes fixed on the corridor. He has his arm across her shoulders. I fight the urge to jump down and rip it away, to push him hard against the wall of the Administration Block. Instead, I watch them pass with an all-consuming feeling of helplessness.

Before I start down the stairs again, I wait a few minutes but there's someone else there. A boy, and I can see from his tunic that he's not an SRU officer. His face comes into view and even, through the dim lighting of the night corridors, I can make out that it's Zack's new Maintenance contact. I let him pass the stairs then, two at a time, I charge down them and jump into the corridor behind him. He doesn't have time to turn because I'm up behind him bending his arm up his back.

'Don't hurt me,' he screams.

'I'm not going to hurt you as long as you do *exactly* what I say, understand?'

'I'm going to help the Fulcrum, I promise.'

'That's good, because Zack has asked me to give you your first task. Call it a way of proving yourself.'

'What…what do you want me to do,' he says.

'We're going down to the Maintenance Department.'

'*Now*?' he says.

'Yes, now. This can't wait.'

'Why?'

'You're asking too many questions…move.'

I yank his arm up further, to emphasise the point.

'Alright, alright, don't hurt me,' he whimpers, trying to turn his head.

'Keep looking straight ahead.'

His head shoots back. When we get to the perimeter corridor, I push him out into it, maintaining my grip on his arm.

'Anyone there?' I say.

'No…no one.'

'That's good. Now we're going to turn right and make our way to the Maintenance elevator, understand?'

'Yes,' he says, nodding.

At the elevator in Corridor F, I manoeuvre him so that he's facing the console.

'Key in your ID.'

He hesitates.

'Key it in,' I repeat, my lips against his left ear.

I detect a shudder running through his slight body, as he raises a trembling finger up to the keypad and puts in his code. There's a pause, much longer than I remember and I start to think that maybe it isn't going to work. Then the elevator door slides open and I push him inside. I press the button and it jolts into life, moving downwards to the Maintenance Department. At the bottom, I shove him out and then pull him to a standstill.

'Right, into the store cupboard,' I say, pushing him across the corridor to the door opposite.

'Why…?'

'Remember, you don't need to ask questions.'

Inside the cupboard, I wait for the lights to respond to our presence. Our eyes are assaulted by flashing images of its contents, as the lights flicker on and the space is flooded with light.

'Right, flashlights.'

He points to a shelf unit on our left and I push him over to it.'

'Grab one.'

'Can you let go of my arm, it's hurting.'

'Nice try, use the other arm.'

He picks up a flashlight.

'Test that it's working.'

He switches it on and a faint circle of light hits the wall, almost invisible against the brightness of the overhead lighting.

'Over to the screwdrivers.'

'Screwdrivers?' he says.

'That wasn't a question was it?'

'No…no, it wasn't,' he stammers.

I look at the bewildering selection, I'd forgotten how many different sizes there are. He puts the flashlight down on the bench and picks one of the larger ones off the rack.

'No, not that one…smaller.'

He points to another.

'Yes, that'll do. Now hand the flashlight over to me, without looking.'

He picks it off the surface and passes it to me over his shoulder. I slide it into my tunic pocket.

'Grab the screwdriver,' I say.

He does what he's told.

'Now, down to the offices.'

We exit the store cupboard and walk towards the main workshop situated right at the end of the corridor. When we reach the first of the offices, I stop.

'In you go,' I say, 'and switch on the console.'

I guide him over to the desk and, in a few minutes, we're staring at the garish red and green colours of the Maintenance welcome page.

'Find out the maintenance override code for today.'

'What?'

'You heard,' I say, tightening my grip on his arm.

He winces and I loosen my hold on him, feeling a pang of guilt. He keys his ID into the access screen.

Once inside the system, he clicks on the Maintenance Override icon and a four-digit number appears, 8047. I repeat it to myself several times until it's fixed in my memory.

'Are these offices lockable?'

'Lockable?' he says, surprised. 'We never lock them.'

'That's *not* what I asked. I asked *if* they are lockable.'

'Yes,' he says, 'there's a key somewhere.'

'A key? You mean a code.'

'No, a *key*.'

He opens a drawer at the side of the workbench, rummages around at the back of it for a while then pulls out a metal object.

'The key,' he says, holding it out in front of him.

'How…?'

'We have to go across to the door.'

'Well move then,' I say, pushing him forward.

'You put the key in here.'

He inserts the square-pronged end into a hole under the door handle and turns it anti-clockwise. Nothing happens. This must be some kind of trick. But then he grabs the door handle and rattles it up and down.

'See, it won't open,' he says, 'it's locked.'

I stare at it over his shoulder, with no idea, how that could work.

'Unlock it,' I say.

He turns the key clockwise.

'Now, give the key to me.'

He hands it over and I put it in my pocket with the

flashlight.

'*And* the screwdriver.'

'It's next to the console,' he says.

I guide him back over to the desk and pick up the screwdriver with my free hand.

'Right, I'm going to let go of your arm. Then I want you to walk right to the back of the office. Don't think about looking back because I'll be watching you all the way.'

He nods. I release his arm and it flops, a dead weight, down to his side.

'I can't feel my hand.'

'Just move.'

He plods towards the far wall, wriggling the fingers of his right hand as he goes. I walk backwards to the door, turn and open it without a sound. Out in the corridor, I close it behind me and turn the key anti-clockwise to lock it. But it won't budge. *Wait, I've got this wrong.* Then I see the handle of the door move. I drop the screwdriver, grab it with both hands and pull with all my strength against his attempt to open it from the other side.

'Let me out!' he screams, thumping the door.

Keeping my left hand in position, I use my right, to turn the key clockwise. There's a clunk as I feel it lock. I watch as the door handle flaps up and down. Satisfied that it's going to hold, I pick up the screwdriver and make my way back to the elevator and the City.

Using the Jojo for cover, I make it to the SRU building without being seen. In front of the entrance I take a couple of deep breaths and key in the

167

override code, the code that I've repeated over and over to myself since I left Maintenance Department. 8...0...4... What was the last digit...9? I key in 9 but nothing happens. *Visualise it.* The sound of voices approaching focuses my thinking and I see it...a...7. I jab the code in again with a 7 at the end and wait an agonising couple of seconds. There's a click and the doors glide open. I dive through into the SRU foyer and scrabble along the floor out of sight. The doors close as a group of three SRU officers walk past. Through the darkened glass, I see that the one nearest the door glances sideways at it as if he's caught a slight movement. But it isn't enough to make them stop and I roll onto my back and stare up into the dark. I take the flashlight out of my pocket and switch it on. A beam of light cuts through the blackness, picking out pillars, the reception desk and, above it, the giant COMSET, less powerful now in its blank silence.

I get up off the cold marble floor and direct the flashlight beyond the desk. Then I march across the foyer through the doors. I'm on familiar ground now and I make good progress. Another door, another corridor and I'm at the cellblock, looking down the row. I've only ever accessed the cells from the air vent system but I'm certain I know which one I want. I direct the beam of light at the door console and key in the override code, wondering if it'll work here. The door slides open and I take in a deep breath. I'm hit by the stale smell of unwashed bodies and something else that I recognise, as urine. A chorus of heavy breathing, the occasional snore and quiet moans, accompanies the smell. I pick out two bodies on the floor in front of me, and another three pressed up against the cell walls. I step over the first body but my heel clips her shoulder and I hear a groan from beneath me. Two eyes, wide with surprise, stare up at me. Before I can say anything, she opens her mouth and screams. Then the other four are on their feet, each revealed in turn, as I swing the light across the cell.

'Who's there?'

I move the light in the direction of the voice and pick out Naomi's ashen face.

'Naomi, it's me…Jonathan.'

'Jonathan's dead,' she says, shielding her eyes from the glare.

Of course, *she can't see me*. I shine the flashlight in my face.

'See, it's me, Jonathan.'

She screams. There's a bang on the wall that separates this cell, from the next.

'What's happening,' a male voice calls out. 'Naomi, what's going on?'

Something brushes against my foot, as one of the girls scurries past me to the back of the cell. I point the flashlight out in front of me and pick out the five of them pinned by fear, up against the back wall. Naomi stands a little to the front of the group. I take a step towards them.

'Stay back,' she shouts.

'Naomi, I know this is a shock but…'

Another thump. 'Naomi, are you alright?'

I go across to the wall. 'There's nothing to worry

about, they're fine.'

'Who's that?' a different voice, this time.

I turn back to Naomi.

'Nothing is as we thought, the ozone layer…it's repaired. There are people…living outside. It's perfectly safe. There is no Council, Naomi. The Colony is being run by the Computer.'

'That's what *she* said.'

'Who?'

'Sarah, she said…she said there is no Council. I didn't believe her…I don't believe you.'

'You're right not to trust her,' I say, 'she's with Zack, with the Fulcrum. She doesn't know I'm here, that I'm alive. Has she told Zack about the Council?'

'I don't know.'

'He mustn't find out. When did Sarah tell you this?'

'About an hour ago. She's in the second from last cell but not as a prisoner.'

'Can you get us out of here?'

'Yes, but not yet.'

I point at the connecting wall. 'Tell them what I've said. I'll be back for you all. And Naomi,' I say, walking over to the door, 'don't say anything to Sarah about this.'

She nods but I can see she's not convinced.

I walk out into the corridor and the door closes on their fetid world. I look along the cellblock. I should get out of here fast, but I can't. Instead, I allow myself to drift down to the second from last cell. I stand in front of the door, knowing that this is madness and watch it open, as Naomi said it would. I direct the beam of the flashlight down onto the floor so that there's enough light to see and creep in. There's no sound coming from the mound on the bunk, as I approach. The first thing I notice is a cascade of hair falling over the side of it, almost to the floor. I can't see her face because she's lying on her side, so I move round to the other side and crouch down, hardly daring to breath. My face is only centimetres from hers. I could lean in a little and kiss it. I could but I don't. Instead, I lift up a strand of her hair, press it onto my lips and draw the scent of her into my body. Then I get up and walk away from her…away from her betrayal.

Chapter 29

I wake up with a start but keep my eyes shut tight. There's somebody in the cell with me. My heightened senses track their every movement, from the door to the bunk and around it. I struggle to regulate my breathing, quell the pounding of my heart because I know that they're staring down on me. I feel their eyes burning into my skin. A twitch starts up in my right eyelid, it's the slightest of movements, but it feels huge. I resist the urge to press a fingertip to it and so it continues with its involuntary pulsing. Why don't they *do* something? Their hovering is unnerving me. Anything would be better than this. They've moved closer to me now. I feel the faintest of breaths brush against my cheek, their head only centimetres away from mine. I battle against my nerves, knowing that I won't be able to keep up the pretence of sleep, for much longer. Then the tension on my scalp lightens, as a section of my hair is lifted up towards where their face must be. At this moment, I know, that it's Zack.

I hear a gentle murmur coming from him. Part of me, wants to open my eyes, acknowledge his presence but not the logical, thinking part. That part, is telling me to keep still, to wait until he's finished, to leave well alone. A whimper from Finn's cell seems to distract his attention and I feel the follicles on my scalp take up the weight again, as he lets go of my hair. His arm brushes against my face and I sense that he's got up. I strain to listen, as he moves away from the bunk and out of the door. I wait a few minutes to make sure that he's gone then open my eyes. I'm alone again. But the intimacy of the encounter remains. I lie, staring into the gloom and wonder why it felt familiar, comforting.

'*Wake up, Sarah.*'

A voice penetrates my dream. My eyes flutter open and I look up, yawning. He's there beside me, still.

'What time is it?'

'Time to get up,' Zack says, smiling.

'Did you sleep well?' I ask.

'You mean, did I sleep well despite your rejection of me.'

'I didn't rej…'

'I know. You're not ready. I understand that. But, in answer to your question, yes, I did sleep well, very well indeed.'

'Did you?' I say, puzzled.

'Yes, I dreamt about you, all night. If sleep is the only way I can be with you, why wouldn't I?'

A possibility nudges its way into my consciousness. Perhaps I was dreaming too. I sense my cheeks filling with colour.

'Do you dream of me, Sarah?'

'No, no I don't,' I say, banishing his smile.

He places a bundle at the bottom of the bunk, his eyes averted now.

173

'I've brought you this.' he says.

'What is it?'

'An SRU uniform, you'll need it now that you're one of us.'

'Is that necessary?' I say, taken aback.

'*I* think so, what do you think?'

His voice has an edge to it that I recognise, that I'd forgotten.

'Yes, you're right. I'll put it on straight away.'

I wait for him to leave.

'Good,' he says, then notices my reluctance to get undressed in front of him, 'I'll get you some food.'

I watch him leave then pick up the tunic top. The ID badge with my name on it, catches my eye. This isn't some fleeting whim of Zack's, he's serious about this, about me. I pull it over my head and wriggle my arms into the sleeves, hoping that it won't fit. But, of course, it fits. I get off the bunk and step into the tunic bottoms and my body responds to its black authority.

'Look at you,' Zack says, entering the cell carrying two food packages and a bottle of water, 'you look like you were born to it.'

No, I want to scream at him. I was born to the Museum and Archive Department, not this. But my back *is* straighter, my shoulders *are* pulled back, I *feel* taller.

'It's just a tunic,' I say, 'like any other in the Colony.'

'That's not how other people see it, Sarah. All they'll see is an SRU officer,' he pauses, '…with the most beautiful hair.'

'I'll need to tie it back.'

'I don't see why,' he says, disappointed by my response to his compliment.

'I want to look more official, like the other female officers.'

'If that's what you want.'

He sighs.

'I'll bring you a hair tie. Hurry up and eat your food, I have a job I want you to do, your first as an SRU officer.'

'*What* job?'

'I'll explain later.'

'Zack, tell me now.'

But he's already left.

After about fifteen minutes, he returns with a hair tie and a male SRU officer. As I struggle to gather up the unruly mass into a neat ponytail, Zack introduces him to me.

'This is Gerard,' he says, 'do you know him?'

I look up at the familiar face then glare at Zack in disbelief. Is he testing me? Do I know Gerard, the SRU officer who betrayed me, betrayed Jonathan, my friends and the SRU rebels?

'Yes, I do,' I say, staring into Gerard's unflinching eyes.

'Good, you'll be working with him this morning.'

'Doing what?' I say, my mouth dry with a rising dread.

'One of the female SRU rebels is to go to her death today. I want you to escort her with Gerard.'

He turns to go.

'Where are you going?' I say.

'I've got things to prepare for tonight.'

'What about my weapons training?'

I grasp at this small lifeline.

'They'll be plenty of time for that, this afternoon.'

His eyes tell me that, he's not open to discussion.

'I'll see you later,' he says then marches out of the cell.

'Well, well,' Gerard says, as soon as he's out of earshot, 'it seems we have something in common, after all.'

'What do you mean?'

I watch his eyes travel up my body.

'*Betrayal*, Sarah.'

I can't speak. My tongue is swollen with guilt. What am I doing here? *What*?

'Come on, we've got work to do,' he says, smiling.

He walks over to the door then turns and stares at me. I haven't moved.

'Come *on*, Sarah.'

Resigned, I follow him out of the cell and down the corridor. He stops outside the female rebels' cell and keys in his ID code. A thought hits me.

'Have *I* got an ID code?'

He turns and smiles.

'Not yet, Sarah, you'll need to prove yourself a bit more for that, even to Zack.'

I don't give him the satisfaction of a response. The door opens and I'm appalled by the conditions inside. It was bad enough when I was in here but *this*, this is far worse. Gerard walks in, his nose wrinkled in disgust. I stay at the door. The inmates stand in a tight group in the middle of the cell, Naomi in front. Apart from the defiant look in her sleep deprived eyes, I barely recognise her. Her hair hangs in limp strands around her colour-drained face. She seems shorter than I remember. The others look no better, cowed, behind her. And the smell, like nothing I've ever experienced before in the Colony, is fetid, engulfing. I gulp down the saliva build-up in the back of my throat.

'Naomi...' I say, shocked.

'Don't speak to me.'

I take a few steps towards her. Her head goes back and she launches a glistening ball of spit at my face. It falls short and lands at my feet. I look down at it, dismayed.

'That's no way to treat an SRU officer,' Gerard says.

'She's *not* an SRU officer.'

Gerard ignores her. 'We've come for Andrea.'

There's a whimper from behind Naomi.

'Take me instead,' Naomi says.

'You know I can't do that,' Gerard says, stepping towards her, 'now move out of the way.'

'I'm warning you,' she says.

'*You're* warning *me*.' He laughs. 'Sarah, over here, help me.'

'Don't do it, Sarah,' Naomi says, 'you can stop this.'

Gerard grabs at Andrea's hand and pulls her from behind Naomi. I rush forward as Naomi's hand swings up towards his face. He shoves her hand with his right arm and she stumbles back and crashes against the wall. I look across at her. Then, moved by something alien to me, I grab Andrea's other arm and haul her, screaming, out of the cell.

'*Traitor*,' Naomi hisses, as the door closes.

Chapter 30

The bright light, filters to a red glow, through my closed eyelids. The temptation to pull the cover over my head and go back to sleep is strong, but I resist it and open my eyes. The glare sears into my eyeballs and I groan. I'm tired, so tired. But not as tired as I would have been, if I hadn't come back to Stuart's pod, used the override code and fallen, exhausted, onto his bunk. I peer across at the COMSET ignoring its attempts to draw me back into a world, of which, I'm no longer a part. 08:19. Doing a quick calculation, I know that I've only had four hours sleep, at most. Not enough, but more than the others will have had out on the Jojo. I tried to find them. That's a lie. After a quick look around the area of the SRU building, I gave up, too tired to care. But I need to find them, *now*.

I sit up, yawn then stagger over to the hygiene unit. I look down at my Administration tunic, a crumpled imitation of the immaculate garment I took from Tyler. It will have to do, I decide, removing it and trying to smooth out the creases. I stand on the ultrasound cleaner and wait for it to start up. An unwanted image of Stuart naked, doing the same thing, jumps into my mind and refuses to leave. *Stuart*. He didn't come back to his pod last night. *Where is he*? I should have checked the other cells. I

179

can't believe I didn't do that. He's in the Colony somewhere and I have to find him.

After my hygiene routine, I feel better, fresher. I dispense some food and water and gulp them down with alternate mouthfuls. It's 08:34, as I stand at the door waiting for it to open. But it stays shut. I wave my hand over the sensor, annoyed at myself for forgetting the correct procedure. Still nothing. I stare at it, puzzled. Then, I realise my mistake. Only a pod's occupier can open the door this way. *I'm trapped here.* I go back to the bunk and slump down on it, my head in my hands. The COMSET punctuates my misery with a stream of trivia.

'Shut up!' I scream, at its cheerful indifference.

But it continues to communicate to its captive audience, unmoved by my outburst. *Communication.* Of course, that's it. I jump up, cross over to the intercom and press the button.

'Good morning, Stuart, what can I do for you?'

For one second, I think about attempting to copy Stuart's voice then decide against it.

'Something's wrong with my pod door…it won't open.'

There's a pause.

'Did you notice anything unusual when you entered it last night,' she says, suspicion all over her words.

'No, I didn't. It opened without a problem.'

Another pause, longer this time.

'Can you not deal with this yourself, Stuart?'

He's a *Maintenance* worker of course he'd deal with it himself. I spot his toolbox on the floor up against the wall.

'Yes, I *could* but…unfortunately…I left my toolbox in the Maintenance Department…yesterday evening.'

'I see,' she says, 'so you want me to contact the Maintenance Department and get an engineer to you?'

Yes, yes, of course. Are you stupid?

'Yes,' I reply, 'thank you so much.'

There's a click as the intercom switches off. I rush across to the hygiene unit and retrieve the flashlight I left there in the early hours of this morning and shove it into my pocket. The screwdriver will have to stay put, it's too difficult to hide. Ten minutes later and I'm pressed against the wall on the opening side of the door, waiting. Then I hear a sound outside and brace myself. The door glides open and I push past the engineer without a glance, and fly out onto the walkway.

'I'll leave you to it!' I shout over my shoulder and make for the stairs.

At the bottom, I compose myself then filter into the flow of colonists in the corridor. Keeping my head still, my eyes dart from side to side scanning the area for the others. I cut down Corridor C to the perimeter. As I pass the SRU entrance, I glance sideways into it then face forward again, in time to stop myself colliding with the back of the Food Production worker I've been following. Like those in front of her, she's slowed down. Moving a little to my right so that I can see round her, I spot the problem. About twenty metres in front, two SRU officers are escorting, no not escorting, *dragging* someone down the corridor. From the length of the hair, it's a female, a female dressed in the black of the SRU. Her uniform is soiled and her hair matted and I know that it has to be one of the SRU rebels. Not Naomi, one of the others and she's fighting every step of the way. Her two escorts struggle to keep their grip on her, as her arms and legs flail about her. We trail along behind them in a passive line watching the battle being played out ahead. At the Administration Block, they come to a complete stop. So, she's to be sent to her death. I smile, knowing she'll be safe.

They're opposite the entrance now, attempting to hold up the flow of traffic down the corridor so that they can cross to it. For the first time, I concentrate my attention on the SRU officers. One, I recognise straight away, as Gerard. The other is hidden from view but, as Gerard moves forward to enter his ID code, I catch a glimpse of the face. *Sarah's* face. With her hair tied back like that in a loose plait, she looks so different. But it's the tunic that fooled me...the uniform. It puts the seal on her treachery. I can't bear to look at it. My head goes down and my pace slows.

'Keep moving, Admin boy,' I hear Oli's voice behind me.

I go to move my head.

'Don't look at us, get inside that building. We need to get to the Ceremonial Chamber before they do, otherwise our cover's blown.'

'But...'

'*Do* it, Jonathan,' she says, taking up position by my side.

'We're right behind you,' I hear Kyle say.

We cross over to the entrance and Kyle puts in his code. I notice the creases in his tunic sleeve.

'Sorry, I didn't find you...'

'Not now, Jonathan, you can explain later.'

Through the darkened glass of the entrance, I see the prisoner on the floor, her feet kicking out in all directions. Sarah and Gerard still have a hold on her but, in order to avoid her feet making contact with their legs, they're forced to jump from side to side in a strange syncopated dance. The door opens and we charge across the foyer, past a distracted novice at the reception desk, her mouth gaping in astonishment at the scene in front of her. We don't stop. We don't look back. We head for the doors behind the desk and straight for the Ceremonial Chamber. Inside, I breathe in, detecting mustiness in the air then look over at the podium. Tyler is slumped over the back of it, his elbows supporting his head. There's no sign of the other three. Marilyn runs across and crouches down behind the podium.

'Tyler's coming round but the others are still out,' she says.

'We need to gag him,' I say, looking round for something to use. 'There's nothing.'

'There's *this*,' Oli says, pointing to the Deathday sash laid out on a long table next to the podium.

'We *can't* use that,' Marilyn says.

'Why not?' Oli asks.

'Use it,' I say, 'we haven't got time for

sentiment.'

She peels the silken fabric off the surface and ties it several times round Tyler's drooping mouth. His head lolls sideways, as she does. He's too dazed to complain.

'Oli, you'll have to deal with them, Sarah doesn't know you.'

'Sarah?' she says, puzzled.

'Yes…she's one of the SRU officers…with the prisoner,' I say, keeping my eyes away from hers.

'*Is* she?'

I sigh. There's nothing else to say.

'Marilyn, stay behind the podium, keep them quiet and still.'

'I'll try, 'she says, 'but the rest of them will come round, any minute.'

'Kyle stand over there by the table, keep your head down and don't look at them, whatever happens.'

'What are you going to do?' he says.

'I'm getting into the Ascendor.'

I run over to it and punch in the override code.

'Quick,' Oli whispers from the door, 'I can hear them coming.'

Inside the Ascendor, I press my ear up against the door and listen. Oli's is the first voice I hear, although I hardly recognise it. Somehow, she's managed to inject it with a convincing air of authority.

'Ah, you have the prisoner,' she says, 'Zack told us to expect you.'

Nice touch.

'If you could escort her over to a seat, we'll deal with her.'

'She's out of control,' Gerard says, 'you'll need our help to get her into the Ascendor.'

There's a silence.

'Yes, I see,' Oli says, 'however…we are trained in dealing with situations of this kind. We'll sedate her. She'll calm down in no time.'

'Well, if you think you can manage,' I hear Gerard say.

For a while all I can make out is the scrape of chairs being pushed around the Chamber floor and the occasional cry of pain.

'Prepare a sedative,' I hear Oli say…to Kyle?

'Hold back her head.'

A series of muffled noises follow but I can't tell what's happening.

'Swallow,' Oli commands. 'Keep hold of her until it takes effect, it should only be seconds.'

'There,' Oli says, 'you can let go of her now. We'll take it from here.'

'What will happen to her?'

That was Sarah's voice. Before Oli can answer Gerard takes over.

'She'll go the way of all the rebels.'

'Yes,' Oli says, 'a traitor's death is all she deserves.'

Then I hear something, almost inaudible, a moan. *They're coming round.*

'What was that?' Gerard says.

'I didn't hear anything,' Oli says but I can hear an edge of panic in her voice.

'There it is again.'

'So sorry,' I hear Kyle say, 'I have a touch of indigestion.'

Indigestion?

'Oh, I see,' Gerard says and, even through the door, I can detect his embarrassment.

I hear the swish of the Chamber door as it opens and closes again.

'*Indigestion*,' Oli says, 'brilliant!'

She laughs, stops, then a spluttered explosion, confirms she's out of control.

'Can someone let me out?' I shout, banging my fist on the Ascendor door.

But it's no use. No one can hear me.

Chapter 31

18/06/3042   11:13 hours
SARAH

'Is it done?'

Zack looks up from his desk as we enter.

'Yes, but next time, can we sedate them *before* they go to the Ceremonial Chamber?' Gerard says, rolling up the left leg of his tunic bottoms. 'Look what she did to me.'

A row of red marks run up the length of his shinbone, framed by ragged white skin.

'You're quiet, Sarah,' Zack says.

'I'm fine…it was…difficult, that's all.'

'The females are far worse than the males,' Gerard continues, 'vicious little thing she was.'

'Perhaps, being locked up in a crowded cell in appalling conditions, didn't help,' I snap.

Zack shoots a look at me then turns back to Gerard.

'Yes, stop whining Gerard. She was an exception, they're usually a lot quieter than that.'

Gerard smiles. 'That's true, even Sean didn't fancy *that* one.'

Zack's eyes flash Gerard a warning look, but it's too late.

'What's that supposed to mean?' I say, breaking the silence.

'Nothing,' Zack says. 'Get *out* Gerard!'

'No, wait. What did you mean?' I say, grabbing

Gerard's arm as he walks past me to the door.

'You'll find out soon enough, Sarah,' he says, shaking me off him, still grinning.

There's a clatter behind me, then a crash. I turn and see Zack's chair on the floor behind him. He charges across the room towards Gerard who steps back, his eyes, wide with surprise. Zack dives at him and shoves him by the shoulders against the wall.

'If *you*, or any of the others, touch her,' he says, his face only centimetres away from Gerard's, 'you're going to be very, *very* sorry.'

'I didn't mean…' Gerard says.

Without giving him a chance to answer, Zack pulls Gerard's shoulders away from the wall then slams them back again.

'*Do* I make myself clear?'

'Yes, yes.'

Zack lets go. Gerard slumps forward, rubbing the back of his head.

'Get out!' Zack shouts.

Gerard doesn't hesitate. He dashes to the door, stands in front of it jiggling his legs up and down, waiting for it to open wide enough to get out, then he's gone. Zack makes his way back to the desk, bends to pick up the chair, then sits down. He runs a hand through his hair.

'Zack…'

'I don't want to talk about it,' he says.

'Well, *I* do.'

'He was talking nonsense. Forget it.'

'Quite a reaction from you, for *talking nonsense*.'

He doesn't respond.

'I know what happens to the female Deathday candidates.'

'Nothing happens to them.'

'Don't bother to lie, Zack. Marilyn told me.'

'Marilyn's long gone.'

'So, are you telling me that it doesn't happen anymore?'

'I'm not telling you anything, Sarah.'

'Then it *is* still happening.'

He stares down at the surface of the desk, as if fascinated by something he's found there.

'Whose Deathday is it tomorrow?'

'I don't know.'

'*Find* out!' I shout.

'This is ridiculous,' he says, glancing up.

One look at my expression and he's pushing a button on his intercom.

'Whose Deathday is it tomorrow?'

'Beatrice,' a male voice replies.

'Beatrice,' Zack says to me, '*satisfied*?'

'*When* and *where* does it happen?'

'Come on, Sarah, please drop this nonsense.'

'That word again.'

He sighs. 'Look, Sarah, what do you want from me?'

'I'll tell you what I want, Zack. I want you to prove yourself.'

'Prove myself?'

'Yes. I'm wearing the SRU uniform. I'm going up to the Council Chamber for the Fulcrum, tonight. I *saved* your life. What have you done, Zack?'

'Sarah...I...'

'*What* have you done?'

'Nothing,' he whispers.

'Right, well now is your chance. You're the only one who can stop it.'

'Sarah…I can't.'

'You *can*, if you want me *on* your side, *by* your side.'

'It's too late.'

'What do you mean…it's too late?'

'For Beatrice, it's too late. Because of the takeover of the Council Chamber tonight, they've moved it forward.'

'*They*?'

'Sean and Jevon,' he says.

'*Both*?'

I stare at him, horrified.

'Sometimes…and sometimes…it's others. I don't get involved with it now, Sarah.'

'But you are involved, Zack. You *started* it,' I scream at him, 'and now you're going to finish it.'

'Sarah…'

'I mean it Zack. If you don't do this, you've lost me. Yes, you can force me to do anything but that's not what you want.'

'Alright, Sarah,' he says, pushing himself up from the desk with his arms, 'alright, you win. Follow me.'

'Where are we going?'

He doesn't answer, just marches out into the corridor. I stumble behind him, struggling to keep up, as he makes his way to the rear of the building.

'The cellblock?' I say, but he's not listening.

We go through the first set of doors and into the cellblock corridor. He stops outside a cell in the centre of the row and thumps his ID code into the door console, tugging at his eyebrow as we wait for the door to open. When it does, the only person I see, is Beatrice. She lies half-naked on the bunk, her right arm, hanging limp over the side. And all I can think is…we're too late. Sean stands behind the bunk, frozen. Jevon has his back to us, his tunic bottoms in a heap around his ankles. He swings round at the sound of the door opening, his brow furrowed with guilt, or perhaps irritation. Charging in, I push him sideways. With the fabric binding his legs, he loses his balance, crashes to the floor and lands heavily on his elbow.

'Get away from her, Sean,' Zack shouts.

I look down at Beatrice. She stares out from her paralysed body, with wide-eyed terror.

'Beatrice,' I say, stroking her face, 'it's alright.'

I swallow against the tightness in my throat and turn to Zack.

'Look at her,' I scream, 'do you *condone* this?'

'What's going on Zack,' Sean says, regaining his composure.

'Get out,' Zack commands, 'and you Jevon.'

'We haven't *started* yet.'

Jevon gets to his feet.

'Get out,' Zack repeats, quieter this time.

'So *she's* in charge now, is that it?' Sean says.

'They'll be no more of…this,' Zack says, pointing at Beatrice.

Sean approaches Zack.

191

'*What*? We've earned this, Zack.'

'You've earned *nothing*. Don't you think there are plenty of others who would jump at the chance to be my deputies?'

Sean stares at Zack, his expression unreadable.

'Alright,' he says, 'this stops…if that's what you want.'

'We still get the rest of it, though,' Jevon says, tugging up his tunic bottoms, 'the extra food…the drugs.'

Zack says nothing.

'Zack?'

'Get out of my sight, the pair of you.'

They don't push him further. As Sean passes me on his way to the door, I catch the hate in his eyes. Jevon, still adjusting his tunic bottoms, ignores me and hobbles out. I pick up Beatrice's clothes from the floor and try to pull them over her unresponsive limbs but, it's hopeless. They're like dead weights and I can't get her tunic bottoms past her knees. I turn to Zack. He walks over to the bunk and, without a word, lifts up her torso a few centimetres, enough to allow me to slide them under her buttocks and up to her waist. Zack lays her back down on the bunk.

'It's over,' I say, 'you're safe now.'

I see the fear building again in her eyes.

'Don't worry, Beatrice, I'm not going to leave you, I promise.'

I look over my shoulder. Zack stands by the door with his back to me.

'I'm staying here with her, until the drug wears off. The weapons training will have to wait.'

'Yes,' he whispers.

The door glides open and he goes to walk out.

'Thank you, Zack,' I say. 'I won't forget what you've done here today.'

I see his shoulders relax, as if the tension he's been holding there has been released then he walks out into the corridor, without a backward glance.

Chapter 32

'Sorry about that, forgot all about you,' Oli says, as the Ascendor door opens, 'nothing personal.'

I step out and gulp down air.

'Are you alright, Jonathan,' Marilyn asks, 'it must have been a shock seeing her…Sarah, like that.'

'He didn't *see* her, did he?' Oli says.

'*Hear* her, I mean,' Marilyn corrects herself.

'What was there to hear,' Oli says, 'she just stood and watched. I couldn't believe it. Pathetic.'

'I was impressed with your performance, Oli,' Kyle says, 'very convincing.'

'Well, you have to step up at times like that.'

She glances over in my direction. I know what she's trying to do.

'Yes, you did well, Oli,' I say.

Her mouth drops open in surprise and, for once, she's speechless.

'Right,' I say, taking advantage of her silence, 'we need to get moving.'

I walk across to where Andrea sits slumped in a chair, her face softened by oblivion. Her head is hooked over the back of it, to stop her from sliding off.

'When will she wake up?' I ask Marilyn.

'In about an hour, maybe less. I gave her a grade two sedative. A grade one calms you down. A grade three knocks you out for hours and a double dose, well...'

Her eyes dart sideways, 'Jonathan...'

I spin round and see Tyler making for the door.

'Oh no you don't,' I say, leaping across and grabbing his arm.

'Let...go of...me,' he says, his words sliding out of his mouth, semi-formed.

I haul him back and push his loose body down onto a seat.

'Marilyn, Kyle check on the others.'

Marilyn rushes over to the podium while Kyle fetches the water container and cups.

'Oli, guard the door,' I say.

But she's already there.

'You, Tyler,' I say, '*you* stay put.'

'My head,' he groans then jerks sideways and throws up onto the floor.

'Great,' I say, 'that's all we need. Kyle, give me that water.'

He hands me a cup. I grab it from him.

'Drink this,' I say, thrusting it towards Tyler.

He's having difficulty focusing on it and I know he's not going to manage by himself. I put the cup to his lips and pour in water. He coughs, spitting it out at me. I jump backwards and spill a third of the cup's contents on Tyler's lap.

'Let me,' Kyle says, pushing me aside.

Then, supporting the back of Tyler's neck, he trickles water into his mouth and most of it stays put. Tyler swallows it down into his dehydrated body.

'More,' he murmurs.

'Only if you promise not to try any more stunts,' I say.

'I promise.'

'Help me Jonathan,' Marilyn calls out.

I leave Kyle with Tyler and go over to where Marilyn is supporting a dazed Fearne. Grabbing hold of her under the armpits, we drag her, toes brushing the floor, to the seat next to Tyler.

'Get some water into her,' I say.

I turn round in time to catch Oscar as he descends to the floor.

'He insisted on walking himself,' Marilyn says.

'Come on, Oscar,' I say, 'sit down.'

Fearne's head, too heavy for her to hold up anymore, rests on Tyler's shoulders. He seems unaware of it. Oscar moves a chair away from her. It must have been a shock for him to open his eyes and discover that he'd spent an intimate, but unconscious, night with her.

'She's still very groggy,' Marilyn says, as she walks Sherryl over to the seat next to Oscar.

She's upright for almost three seconds before her torso begins its gradual descent onto the three chairs to her right.

'No, Sherryl, you have to wake up now,' I say.

I lift her reluctant body into a vertical position.

'Leave me alone, I'm tired.'

Kyle dabs some water onto her face. She watches him through half-closed eyes.

'Tyler,' I say, noticing that he's looking towards the door again.

'All you're thinking at the moment,' I say, as he

jumps and faces forward, 'is how can I get out of that door and report what's going on. I'm right, aren't I?'

He nods.

'I know that because I'd be thinking the same in your position. But it wouldn't be the right thing to do, at least, not before you've heard me out. Are you willing to listen to what I've got to say before you make any decisions?'

He nods again.

'Good.'

'Fearne?' I say, noticing that her eyes are open now.

She gives me a bleary nod.

'Right,' I say, taking a deep breath, 'where did we come from?'

Tyler looks puzzled.

'From the Ascendor?' Fearne says, raising her head up.

'Yes exactly, *from* the Ascendor. So how did we get there?'

They stare up at me, open-mouthed, the answer hovering on their lips.

'From...the outside?' Tyler says, at last.

'Yes, from the outside.'

'But that's impossible,' Fearne whispers.

'Look at the clothes you're wearing, the clothes you swapped with us. They're not Colony clothes, are they?'

'No,' she says.

'But the Council...' Oscar begins, sliding across to sit next to Fearne.

'There is no Council,' I say.

With Kyle and Marilyn's help, it takes me almost an hour to convince them of this stark fact. Oli huffs her impatience from the door, the whole time. They go through the full range of emotions - disbelief, anger, fear, despair. Everything, we've had weeks to grasp, they have to deal with in less than sixty minutes. There's a lot of crying.

'So, we can get into the Ascendor, go up to the surface and *live*?' Sherryl says.

With these words, I know that we've got through to them, that they understand.

'Yes,' I say, 'you *could*.'

'So, we need to contact the SRU, organise an evacuation,' Tyler says.

I glance across to Oli.

'There's something you need to know about the SRU.'

I take some time to explain about Zack and the Fulcrum, how the fact that they still think that there's a Council, has held them back. I tell them about the weapons.

'We need to deal with Zack first,' I say, 'if we're going to get everyone out.'

'We can't get many into that Ascendor,' Oli says, 'it will take days, to evacuate over six thousand people.'

I stare at her, digesting what she's just said.

'So we can't wait, we have to start the evacuation now. And it will have to be co-ordinated from here.'

'We'll have to get as many people out before

Zack and the Fulcrum realise what's happening,' Marilyn says.

'Couldn't we tell Zack about the outside,' Sherryl says, 'surely he'll jump at the chance to leave the Colony?'

'You don't get it,' Andrea says.

'You're awake,' I say.

'I've been awake for a while, listening, trying to take it all in.'

'What do you mean, we don't get it?' Kyle says.

'It's all about power with Zack,' she says, 'it's all he thinks about, all he craves. Down here, he can be somebody. That's what he wants. He wouldn't give that up to become a, *nobody*, on the outside. He'll do everything he can to stop an evacuation. Believe me, he'll fight for it. And now he's got the weapons, there's nothing to stop him.'

She's right. I turn back to the group.

'Now that you know everything, I'm not going to stop any of you getting into that Ascendor and leaving,' I say.

'I'm staying,' Andrea says.

'You'll need us to organise the evacuation,' Tyler says, looking around at the others.

'Don't speak for them Tyler, they need to make up their own minds,' I say, 'Fearne?'

'Yes, I'll help.'

'Oscar, what about you?'

'I don't know...it's hard,' he says.

'Sherryl?'

'Yes, I'm staying.'

'I'm outnumbered,' Oscar says, 'alright, I'm in

too.'

'Good, we'll need to get the whole Admin Department involved, if it's going to work, but not yet. You need to carry on as usual.'

'The Deathday ceremony?' Oscar says.

'Yes, it must go ahead today.'

'But look at us,' Fearne says, glancing down, 'we need our tunics.'

'And we need your tunics, too,' I say.

'Tell Kyle where your pods are. He'll use the Maintenance override code to get fresh tunics for each of you.'

'Marilyn, you'll need to go with him.'

'Why?' Kyle says.

'To hold open the pod doors, they can only be operated from the inside, by the pod occupier.'

'Are you sure?' Kyle says.

'Oh yes, I'm sure.'

'We'll need our ID badges back, as well,' Sherryl says.

'I hadn't thought of that,' I say, annoyed at myself for missing the obvious.

Oscar gets up and walks over to a small white cabinet in the corner of the room to the left of the podium. He opens one of the drawers and takes something out then returns to the group.

'Look,' he says, 'ID badges.'

'How?' Marilyn asks.

'They're from the Deathday candidates. We hand them over to the SRU at the end of each week. Here you are,' he says, pushing one into my hand.

I look down at it. *Ryan*, it says.

'Just when I was getting used to being, *Tyler*.'

Chapter 33

'Remember, Sarah, only pull the trigger as a last resort.'

'We've been over this, Zack. I know *exactly* what will happen if I do.'

'How?' he says, glancing up from loading the weapon.

'What?'

'How do you *know*, Sarah, what will happen? You didn't explain, yesterday.'

'Yesterday, I panicked…I…*sensed* the danger that's why I dived to the floor. I didn't *know* for sure. This afternoon's weapon training has shown me that I was right to trust my instincts.'

I wait for more but he remains silent. If he's not satisfied with my explanation, he doesn't show it and continues to make a final adjustment to the weapon.

'Are you ready?' he says, after a while.

'Yes, I think so.'

'Tell me what you're going to do when you get up there.'

'Not again, Zack.'

'I want to make sure you're clear about it.'

'Alright…I make sure the gun is ready before the service elevator arrives at the Council Chamber.'

'By…?'

'By taking off the safety catch.'

'Good.'

'Then I jump out, grab the first Councillor I come across and hold them as a hostage.'

'If necessary…' Zack prompts.

'If necessary, I fire the gun up into the air to show that I mean business.'

'Then…'

'Then I round them up in one place and keep guard.'

'After…'

'After what?' I say.

'After you've made them unlock the Council Chamber access to the Ascendor. No, wait,' he says, 'that won't work.'

'Why not?'

'Because you can't keep guard and get someone to unlock the Ascendor on your own.'

'I'll think of something,' I say, knowing that I won't have to.

'No, you need someone with you. I should have realised earlier.'

'Look Zack, I'll manage.'

'I'm worried,' he says.

'I know you are but look…'

I take the gun off his desk and point it out from me, adopting the most intimidating pose I can.

'Would you argue with this?'

He smiles, his complete trust in me, obvious.

'No, I wouldn't, Sarah,' he says. 'I'd do anything you ask.'

He takes a step towards me and I know what's coming but he's stopped, by a knock at the door. His eyes darken with annoyance and the moment is lost. Sean and Jevon enter.

'They're ready,' Jevon says. 'Eight down in the Ceremonial Chamber by the Ascendor.'

He flashes me a look as he speaks, eyeing the gun in my hands. I turn away and place it back on the desk.

'All of the SRU officers have got weapons,' Sean adds, 'but only two are loaded.'

'But what if the Council has its own weapons?' Jevon says.

'They haven't,' Zack says, a little too fast to be convincing, 'weapons are only needed to defend the breeding programme from attack. That's the territory of the SRU, not the Council.'

'Look, I'm the one going up there and I'm willing to take the risk.'

Zack takes hold of my hand.

'Someone else can go, Sarah.'

'The rest of the Fulcrum are lined up in Corridor G, waiting,' Sean says, 'waiting for Sarah.'

'Yes, Sean's right,' I say, relishing his surprised eyes, 'this is my way of proving myself to *you*, to everyone. I won't back out now.'

'Right, let's go,' Zack says, picking up the gun and laying it across his outstretched arms in an attitude of ceremony.

'This is an important day for me…for the Fulcrum.'

We make our way to the foyer then get into position, Zack with the gun in front. I follow, with Sean and Jevon at the rear. We exit the building, turn right and, march along the fronts of the SRU, Health & Wellbeing and Admin buildings. Zack's pace slows as we turn left into Corridor F. Members of the Fulcrum line both sides of the corridor, all eyes on us, on me. I feel them sear into my face but refuse to be intimidated by their reluctant respect. I stare out in front of me, keeping my head high, as we slice a path through their silence and make our way towards the service elevator at the end of the corridor. Before we reach it, Zack stops and turns to face Sean.

'Is Daniel ready to override the elevator from the other side?' he says.

Sean and Jevon exchange looks.

'What?' Zack says, noticing.

'It's nothing, Zack,' Jevon says, 'there was an incident, that's all, down in Maintenance, in the early hours of the morning.'

'What sort of incident?' Zack says.

'Daniel was forced to give over today's override code to someone. They also took a flashlight and a screwdriver.'

'Stuart!' Zack says, looking across to me.

Stuart? Why would he involve Daniel, in something he's able to do, for himself?

'Yes, Stuart,' I say.

'He was shaken up by it, but he's fine now.'

'Does he know what he's doing?' Zack says.

'Says he does,' Jevon replies, watching Sean pull up the food chute door.

Zack lays the gun inside. Then, as instructed, I step forward look down the length of the corridor then I raise my clenched fist and shout.

'I do this for the Fulcrum.'

'For the Fulcrum!' they repeat, giving the full salute.

Zack helps me into the chute. If I thought it was cramped the last time I did this, now is far worse. I push the gun as far as I can against the back wall and arrange myself next to it, checking again, that the safety catch is in place. I feel the hard metal pushing into my right knee, as I stare out into the corridor, dreading the moment when the door closes. Zack leans in.

'Good luck, Sarah.'

His lips brush my cheek in a light kiss. Then he pulls his head and shoulders out and grabs the handle of the hatch. I gulp down a lungful of air, as the darkness descends and I'm left alone with my metal companion. I wait, blackness pressing in on me, for the chute to move. But will the weight of the gun be too much? I wait for something to happen. Then, when I'm about to give up hope, there's the slightest of jolts, as the chute takes up the weight and moves upward in a stilted ascent. I hear the whine of the lifting mechanism and I know it's at breaking point. But still it continues, complaining every centimetre of the way. But then the mechanical high-pitched scream is replaced by, a faltering groan and I know it hasn't got much left to give.

Then it stops. But I don't know where I am. All I can do is wait. I've practiced taking off the safety catch with my eyes closed, all afternoon, but leave it alone now. Instead, I take hold of the gun, easing it out from under my leg and sit with it perched on my bent knees facing away from me. There's a faint click. My heart's racing as the elevator doors slide apart to reveal the familiar pulse of amber light from the food preparation room and the Council Chamber. Relieved, I push the gun out, swing my legs sideways then jump the short distance to the floor. I walk towards the serving hatch in front of me, my arm muscles quivering in protest at the weight of the gun, after the hours of training they've endured.

All I want to do is put it down. But before I can, I'm pushed forward with such force that the gun crashes into the edge of the work surface and slams into my stomach. Every bit of air inside me is expelled in one heaving gasp. I let go of the gun and it falls, with a dull thump, onto the floor. Bending over double, I clutch my battered stomach, struggling to draw breath into my lungs. A wave of nausea takes hold of me and I fight the pressure at the back of my throat. Then I'm grabbed from behind, my arms pulled up my back in an impossible angle as if they'll snap off at the shoulders. I let out a moan, as I'm pulled backwards and turned around so that I'm facing the food chute again. Shoved in the back, I stumble forward, fighting to keep my balance. When I do, I turn to face my attacker.

'Stuart?' I say, transfixed on the barrel of the gun pointed at me.

My eyes travel up to his face. His gaze is steady, unfaltering and there's no look of indecision about him now. Then I hear a click and know that he's removed the safety catch.

Chapter 34

'Get back, Oli, you'll be seen,' Kyle says.

She jerks her head away from the gap in the barrier and takes up her position on the floor of the Jojo, next to Marilyn. She kicks my leg as she sits down then glances up at me, her face lit up with excitement and I realise that she's enjoying this.

'They're all lining up down Corridor G,' she says, 'looks like they plan to make an occasion of it.'

I don't give her the satisfaction of a response.

'So, do you think she'll go ahead with it?'

I pretend I don't know she's talking to me.

'…Jonathan.'

'How should I know,' I snap, giving away too much.

'I'll tell you one thing,' she continues, 'she's got guts, volunteering like that. I was impressed. Well, either that, or she's stupid.'

'Sarah's not stupid,' Marilyn says.

'Even so, she'll be going up there alone. That's going to be scary and…'

'Shut up, Oli,' I say, crawling across to the gap and peering out.

'It's alright for Jonathan to do it, but not me?' Oli complains.

'What's going on?' Kyle says, ignoring her.

I struggle to focus my eyes, through the amber

gloom, on the Fulcrum members at the end of the corridor, the ones nearest the esplanade. Then I notice some activity, heads turning, as a wave of anticipation travels down the corridor, along the two rows of SRU officers, towards us.

'Something's happening,' I say.

There's a shuffling behind me, as the three of them jostle for positions so that they can see. Kyle and Marilyn scurry across the gap, facing me. Marilyn lies flat on her stomach with the top of her head, poking out. Kyle's legs straddle her back and he leans over her so he, too, has a view.

'Let me see,' Oli says, pulling at my arm.

'Find your own position,' I say, shaking her hand off me.

'Fine,' she says, 'I will.'

Then I feel her pushing her way through my legs from the back, forcing them apart as she edges her way forward.

'Oli don't,' I say.

But she's not listening. Instead she nestles into position underneath me then peers round the gap in the barrier, in a mirror image of Marilyn.

'That's better,' she says.

Twisting her head, she flashes me a provocative grin over her shoulder.

'Alright?'

I don't get the chance to tell her what I think of the arrangement because I spot Zack turning into Corridor G from the esplanade, carrying the gun out in front of him across his outstretched arms. His elbows are tucked into his torso, braced against the weight. Any heads that had deviated to the side, are now back in position as he approaches, and remain unmoved as he passes. Behind him is, Sarah. I swallow hard at the sight of her wearing the SRU uniform with such ease. Her arms hang loose at her sides. She stares straight out, no hint of emotion on her face, eyes blank with indifference. Behind her come Sean and Jevon. Sean's face is tight with anger. Jevon looks more resigned. They march side by side, united by something, not yet fully identified. About halfway down the corridor, Zack's eyes go up and appear to stare right at us.

'Did he see us?' Kyle says, pulling his head back behind the barrier.

'No,' Oli says, 'he's not looking at us. He's too caught up in the moment, wallowing in the power. Look at him.'

'He looks worried to me,' Marilyn says.

'Sean doesn't look happy,' Kyle says.

'Good,' Oli says, shifting position under me, 'let him sweat.'

As they reach the end of the corridor, Sean and Jevon take up position either side of the service elevator with Sarah standing in front of them. Zack stares down the length of the corridor his back to us then turns to Sean and Jevon. I watch his lips move. There's an exchange of worried glances between them then Jevon steps forward. He's not looking at Zack when he speaks. He shifts from foot to foot looking down at the floor. The more he says, the more Zack's expression, darkens. Then, dismissing Jevon with a flick of his right hand, Zack steps forward, raises the gun above his head then turns and walks across to Sarah. Sean lifts up the hatch of the elevator, as Zack places it inside, then steps back. He takes hold of Sarah's hand and leads her into the centre of the corridor so that they face down towards the esplanade. I see Zack glance at Sarah and, without a second's hesitation, her right arm shoots up, fist clenched.

'I do this for the Fulcrum!' she shouts.

The SRU officers, ranged out in front of them, take up the cry. I hear Marilyn's sharp intake of breath, as she turns her head away from it.

'I wasn't expecting *that*,' Oli says.

'None of us were,' Kyle says, stroking the back of Marilyn's hair.

'That was quite something,' Oli continues, 'if you're going to do betrayal, do it in style, that's what I say.'

'Do you ever get sick of the sound of your voice, Oli,' I say.

'It's not my fault your girlfriend is betraying you in such a spectacular way.'

'She's only saying what we're all thinking,' Marilyn says, raising her head from her hands.

The disappointment in her voice is far worse than any barbed comment from Oli. She didn't know Sarah and neither, it appears, did I. I stare back out and watch as she's helped into the elevator, Zack's hands all over her. It's been Zack all along. As soon as she thought I was out of the way, she ran to his arms. He leans in and I fight back the image of the intimate moment that I imagine passes between them, in that confined space. Oli is saying something but I can't hear her words. I don't want to. I don't want to return to that world. The world where I have to accept Sarah's betrayal because everyone, even Marilyn, has accepted it. I want to stay where I am, clinging onto one last hope that Sarah will prove me wrong. That she'll jump out of the elevator with the gun in her hands and force Zack to surrender. But he pulls down the hatch and she's gone.

'She's gone,' Oli says, pushing her body out from between my legs.

'What now?' Kyle says.

I stare at him with empty eyes, empty heart. What now.

'Nothing's changed,' Oli says, staring at me, 'we're still here to save the Colony, aren't we?'

'Oli's right,' Marilyn says, 'that's what we need to focus on…now that Sarah…'

'We need to forget Sarah,' I say.

'*You* need to forget Sarah,' Oli says, 'I've forgotten her already.'

I've been clinging onto something that's not there anymore, because I couldn't accept the truth, wouldn't accept the facts before my eyes. I haven't been concentrating on what's important. Sarah's been a distraction.

'We need to get as many people out before things turn ugly,' Kyle says, 'because they will.'

'I want you all to go back to the Ceremonial Chamber when things have quietened down,' I say, 'try and get some rest.'

'What are you going to do?' Marilyn asks.

I don't answer. I'm already on all fours, making my way along the Jojo.

'Jonathan, where are you going?' I hear Kyle call out behind me, '*Jonathan.*'

I don't stop. I know what I have to do.

Chapter 35

SARAH

'Stuart, what are you doing? I say, stepping forward, my hand raised in defence.

'*Don't* move,' he commands, 'until I say so.'

'I don't understand…'

'I've been watching you, Sarah.'

'Stuart, let me explain. It's not what…'

'What I saw doesn't need explanation.'

He raises the gun up a few centimetres. It's pointing straight at my heart. It will only take one twitch of his finger, that's all.

'It's loaded,' I say.

'I know,' he says, his eyes fixed on mine.

I notice a new hardness about them.

'But it wasn't loaded before…with Zack.'

I gabble out the words through trembling lips.

'I want you in the surveillance room,' he says, confused by my comment and moving round behind me, 'where I can keep watch on you.'

'Stuart…'

'Just walk.'

He prods me in the back and my spine turns to water. I know what he's capable of.

'I'll *do* anything, *go* anywhere you want, but please stop pointing that at me.'

But he's not listening. I push the air from my lungs and cry with noiseless, hot tears. He pushes me forward with the gun, unmoved. So, they'll be no mercy. Nothing that I say will convince him that I'm still on his side. I walk forward, the gun's dark presence, behind me. Allowing the wet to roll off my chin, unchecked, I remain silent and stumble down the half-lit corridor towards the computer block. We pass beneath one of the faulty lights, its pulsating rhythm presses down onto the top of my head, disorientating me. I slow down.

'Keep moving,' he says.

I quicken my pace but feel sick. I swallow hard, fighting back the nausea. An overpowering tiredness takes hold of me. It's all I can do to stop myself from dropping to the floor and curling up in a tight ball. With no flashlight, our progress through the corridors is slow and I start to think that my legs won't hold me up long enough to get me there. Only the gun in my back, propels me forward. After a while, I see the corner of the computer block in front of me. We walk past the rows of brightly lit windows. The backup generator seems to be doing its job here, at least.

'Get in,' Stuart says.

The doors slide open and I step inside but can't remember the way.

'Left,' Stuart says.

We reach the door of the surveillance room and I feel the point of the gun jab into my back, as I'm pushed inside. I swing round.

'When did you become a bully, Stuart?' I say.

'When, you betrayed me, Sarah. You did this to me…no one else.'

'But Zack…'

'Zack, I can deal with. But *you*, you're something else.'

His damning words leave me stunned, open-mouthed. Nothing could have prepared me for *that*. In Stuart's eyes, I'm worse than Zack. He moves in front of me, the bank of screens, behind him. I can't look at him, not now, so I stare over his shoulders at the amber corridors of the City, searching for any sign of activity. There's none. I wait for him to speak. For a while, he says nothing. I keep my averted eyes from his but I know he's staring at me.

'So, what happens now?' he says.

'You've got the gun, Stuart, only you can determine that.'

'Yes, but what would you have done, if I hadn't been here?'

His question takes me by surprise. Then I realise that I had no plan, have no plan.

'I don't know,' I say, 'I hoped you'd be here to help me, like you always do.'

For a second, no more than that, I see the old Stuart standing in front of me. The Stuart, I used to trust with my life, *still* trust with my life.

Something pulls my attention away from him, a movement on one of the screens, at the far right of my vision. A figure has come into view. I can see only the top of their head. They glance up and, even through the night gloom of the corridor, I see the eyes, the *eyes*.

'*Jonathan*,' I whisper, pointing a shaking finger at the screen.

The effect on Stuart is immediate. His grip on the gun, that had begun to relax, tightens and the look he directs at me, is searing.

'That's a cheap trick, Sarah, even for you.'

'No, Stuart, please believe me. It's Jonathan, it is.'

I glance back up at the screen but he's not there. Of course, he's not there.

'Using Jonathan…who fought to protect you, right to the end…to gain an advantage…that's low, Sarah. You *disgust* me,' he says, turning away.

I fall down on my knees, the pain as I hit the floor is nothing to the pain that I feel in my gut, in my heart.

'I can't bear it,' I say, 'I can't.'

My head crashes down onto my knees, my arms fold tight over the top of it.

'Sarah, get up.'

I hear Stuart's muffled voice above me but I can't move, even if I wanted to. Despair has taken a hold of me, I'm engulfed by it. Then a hand takes hold of my arm and I'm pulled to my feet. Stuart guides my quaking body over to a chair and lowers me into it. I notice he's left the gun on the worktop. He brings me a cup of water. I stare at it, as if I've never seen such a thing before. He lifts my hand up and encloses my fingers around it. Raising it to my lips, I watch the transparent liquid slosh from side to side and wonder if I'll manage without spilling any. Perching the rim of the cup on my lower lip to steady it, I tip some water into my mouth and gulp it down. The effect is immediate. Its coolness courses through me, reviving every cell. I take another mouthful and another. When the cup is empty, I hand it back to Stuart.

'Good,' he says, 'now I'm going to take you to the residential area.'

'Stuart, I don't think I can make it.'

'You have to, Sarah. I need to sleep and I can't leave you here.'

'You can trust me, Stuart.'

'No, I can't, Sarah. That's the point.'

'You can take the gun with you.'

'Do you think I'd be stupid enough to leave it with you?'

'No, of course not, I didn't mean…'

'What was the plan, Sarah? To unlock the Ascendor access, is that it?'

'Yes, but Stuart…I…'

'So, when Zack realises that you haven't succeeded, they'll be looking for other ways to get up here. I've locked the service elevator, so it can't go back down to the City. The only other way is the Maintenance elevator. It won't be long before they work that out.'

'We need to do something about that,' I say.

'*We*?' he says.

He throws a bag over his shoulders and picks up the gun.

'You don't need to point that at me Stuart, I'm not going anywhere.'

'You go first,' he says, ignoring me but lowering the gun to his side.

We exit the computer block and turn right. I glance over at the Jojo but it's, still stationary, so I force my legs to move in the direction of the administration building with Stuart following.

'The elevator is situated in the next corridor, on the side of the building,' he says, sounding more comfortable now that he's talking engineering, 'and it can be accessed from both sides.'

As we approach the corner, I hear a faint mechanical click.

'What was that?'

'The elevator,' he says, throwing the bag down and raising the gun into position in front of him, 'we're too late, they're already here.'

'What are we going to do?' I say.

He doesn't reply but I know the answer, he's already turned the corner into the corridor. I follow behind him. Then we hear the elevator doors open. Stuart's body tenses, as the first of them steps out into the corridor. There's a flash of yellow light and a sound, so deafening, I think it will puncture my eardrums. Stuart's body lurches backwards into me, jolted from side to side, as he fights to control the gun. Then, as quickly as it started, the flashing stops and Stuart's body flops forward released from the gun's momentum. The angry clatter is replaced by a high-pitched ringing in my ears and an acrid smell of smoke assaults my nostrils. Through the fog in front of me, I see a figure lying prostrate on the floor. Stuart steps forward, gun at the ready then stops dead.

'*Jonathan*!' he screams.

Chapter 36

I'm not dead. I may have broken my arm as I dived to the floor and my left leg is twisted at an awkward angle and hurts a lot…but I'm not dead. Wounded? I can't move, not yet. A mental audit of my body, checking each part for any sensation of seeping blood, finds nothing. I'm not dead, but I am, *too* late. Opening my eyes for the first time since I hit the floor, I stare along it, in the direction of the gunfire. A thin haze of white smoke hangs a metre or so above me but, at ground level, it's clearer. I can make out two sets of legs, from the knees down, one, wears an SRU uniform, the other, the blue of the Maintenance Department. I don't know which one has the gun and I'm not going to do anything to find out. If they're speaking, I can't hear them. My ears are battered into deafness. I stare out at the smoke-cushioned, sound-muffled world I now inhabit, and wait.

There's a voice, distant and indistinct, I can't make out the words. I notice, through the whitened gloom, a set of legs approaching me and cringe from them, spotting the end of a gun against the thigh. They kneel down next to me and I feel a hand grab my arm and roll me onto my back. A sharp pain shoots through my left shoulder and I can't stop myself from crying out.

'Sorry, sorry,' someone says above me, '*Jonathan*?'

The voice breaks and turns into a choking sob.

'Stuart?' I whisper.

'How...how, can it be you? What have I done?'

I see him wipe his dripping nose with his sleeve, his face contorted with emotion. Fear? Remorse? The gun lies on the floor next to me, next to him. It gives off a faint acrid smell and I realise that he was the one who fired it.

'Stuart, *why*...why did you...?'

'I thought you were the Fulcrum. I knew they'd work out this way of getting into the Council Chamber but Sarah *was* right, it was you.'

'Sarah's with you?'

'Yes, she is, but...'

'I don't understand, Stuart. Why have you got the gun?'

'I took it off her,' he says, looking back over his shoulder, 'she can't be trusted, Jonathan.'

'I know,' I say.

'How can you be alive?'

He looks at me with a puzzled smile.

'What you mean...after you shot at me?'

I laugh then stop, as it hurts too much.

'I'm so sorry...'

'It's alright, I'm alright...I *think*, despite your efforts to kill me. But, I tell you something, Stuart, you've changed. What happened to the shy, nervous person I used to know?'

'We've all changed, Jonathan,' he says, misinterpreting the words I meant only as a joke.

'I've got so much to tell you, Stuart but…' I glance over his shoulder, 'I'm not sure whether…'

'No, don't tell me now,' he says, 'let's get you up.'

He moves towards my left shoulder.

'Not that one,' I say, anticipating the pain.

Going around to my other side, he hooks his hands under my right shoulder. Then, using him for support, I raise myself onto my feet. He guides me over to the wall and props me up against it.

'I need to disable the access to this floor,' he says, 'before we do anything else.'

'Good idea,' I say.

I stare out in front of me and count the row of dents in the wall opposite. I can feel her presence only metres away from me and, despite all my good intentions, I glance sideways. She stands rigid, her eyes boring into me. Her hair hangs loose over her shoulders, a few strands across her face. I look down on the ground, searching for her hair band then, realising how ridiculous that is, I look back at the wall.

'Jonathan…' she whispers, the softness in her voice, chipping away at my resolve.

'I've got nothing to say to you, Sarah.'

But I *have*. I've got so much to say to her.

'You don't need to speak, Jonathan. I only want to…look at…you.'

On the last word, her voice wavers and, at the side of my vision, I see her hand slap into her mouth. Then I hear a staggered breath and I know that she's crying. Every part of my body wants to take her in my arms and comfort her, except my brain. That remains stubbornly, unmoved. I glance over at her. Her head is lowered, her whole body racked by a shaking beyond her control. But no tears, not yet. They're held, by a dam deep inside her, waiting to be released. Her stomach heaves in its effort to push them out, her breathing becomes shallow and fast. Then she keels over, falls to the floor, her face covered by a blanket of hair.

'Stuart,' I shout, 'quick!'

I rush over to her prone body and brush her hair from her face. Stuart runs up behind me.

'What happened?'

'She passed out…in front of me. Look at her face, it's so pale, drained.'

'That's shock,' he says, 'we need to get her warm.'

'Are there pods here?' I ask.

'No, but there's a residential area. It's a bit of a walk though. How will we…?'

'I'll carry her.'

'Can you manage that, Jonathan?'

'Yes.'

'Well…if you're sure. I'll take the rest of it…the bag, the gun. I've disabled the elevator.'

I crouch down beside Sarah.

'I'm going to need some help getting her up.'

Stuart puts down the bag again then we hook our hands under her arms and pull her limp body into a more upright position. I take the weight of her upper body onto my left arm, ignoring the shoot of pain as I do, and hook my right arm under her knees.

Hoisting her up, I shuffle her into my body. Her hair rests on my shoulder and the smell of it against my face is almost too much for me to bear.

'Are you sure you can manage?' Stuart says, noticing the give in my knees.

'Yes, yes,' I say but I know it's a lie.

'Follow me,' Stuart says, overtaking me.

I take a tentative step forward then, another. Her unconscious body repossesses mine and I tighten my grip on her, pull her in closer. Staggering forward, I glance down at her.

'Jonathan…' she says, her eyes staring up at me.

'It's alright, Sarah, it's alright, you passed out. We're taking you to the residential area.'

I feel a pressure on my right arm as she squeezes it with her hand.

'Thank you,' she says.

If I bent my head down, a little, I could reach her lips. But I don't. Then I feel her slipping from my arms, my muscles failing me.

'Stuart, help me, I can't hold onto her anymore.'

He turns, drops the bag and places the gun on the floor. She's on her feet now but she's putting no weight on them. With my arms still wrapped around her, I lift her up.

I don't know how we manage to get her to the residential area. She's dragged most of the way, with my right arm across her back under her armpit. Stuart does the same the other side of her, carrying the gun with its strap across his body. The bag was a problem because I couldn't bear the weight of it on my injured shoulder. In the end, I hooked it over my neck and let it hang down in front of me. After ten minutes of walking, we arrive.

I look up. In front of me, I see a block of small individual buildings arranged in rows.

'What are they?' I ask, as Stuart directs us to the first door on our right.

'They're quite something, Jonathan, wait and see.'

We have to negotiate the doorway sideways, as there's not enough width to get all three of us in at the same time. In front of me, I see a room many times bigger than my old pod. It's full of seats and tables. I stare open-mouthed at its splendour.

'That's only the start,' Sarah says, smiling up at me.

There's a click as the main door closes behind us then I watch fascinated as the room fills with light. Not the harsh, draining glare of the City pods but a soft glow, coming from various points in the room. Another click and we're engulfed by a wave of music, quite different from the brash, attention-seeking clamour of the COMSET. A shiver runs up my spine with every rise and fall of the notes. I've never experienced anything like it before.

'That's wonderful,' I say, as the white wall on my left transforms into a woodland scene.

'What was that?' I say, mesmerised, noticing a small grey animal scurrying out from under the trunk of a fallen tree.

'I have no idea,' Stuart says, 'but isn't it incredible?'

'It's Earth,' Sarah says, 'as it used to be before...'

'As it is *now*,' I say.

'What, did you say?' Stuart says, turning to me.

'I'm not dead…because when I stepped out from the tunnel, it was like…*this*.'

I point at the scene in front of us.

'And it's been that way for…centuries. The ozone layer repaired itself a long, long time ago.'

'But the Deathday candidates?'

'They're all there, Stuart, or *have* been. The Human Race survived.'

'So, *why*,' Sarah says, '*why* did you come back?'

'I came back to release the colonists from this prison, to save them from Zack and his craving for power.'

'You did it for the Colony?' Sarah says.

'No…I did it for you, Sarah…*for you*.'

Chapter 37

19/06/3042 06:42 hours
SARAH

Jonathan's alive. I have to keep repeating that simple fact to myself but still I can't believe that it's true. I turn onto my side, as I have done many times in the night, for confirmation. The solid evidence lies before me. I shuffle into his back and let my breathing take up his rhythm, our bodies, rising and falling together. But I can't trust my senses. How many times have I dreamt of doing this then woken to the brutal truth that it's not real? *Too* many. And yet I allow myself to sink into this comfort, this lie. It's so easy, so easy. I hear a moan, as he shifts position, onto his back. Moving a little to make room for him, I watch his face, soft with sleep, the tension of last night, gone. I rest my arm across his chest, holding onto him for a while longer. Then, I see that his eyes are open, staring up at the ceiling.

'Jonathan,' I whisper.

He doesn't respond and fear takes hold. It's not real. *It's not real.*

'Jonathan,' I repeat, 'are you awake?'

'Yes,' he says, indicating that he's heard me but that's all.

I start to breathe again.

'How long have you been in the Colony?' I ask.

'Two days.'

'Oh,' I say, hearing the flat tone in his voice.

227

We fall into an uncomfortable silence.

'Aren't you going to ask me why I didn't contact you sooner?' he says, his eyes still fixed on a point above him.

I don't reply. I don't need to.

'*Why*, Sarah?'

'I don't know.'

He sits up, pushing my arm from him and locks onto my eyes.

'That's not good enough.'

'I…was desperate…I was…alone.'

'You had Stuart.'

'It's complicated.'

'It didn't look complicated to me, Sarah.'

I avert my eyes from his accusing stare. He wants an explanation but I can't give him one. Not because I don't want to, but because I don't have one.

'Last night, you…'

I remember, his gentleness.

'Last night, I was…I don't know…tired, confused.'

'And now you're not,' I say.

He turns away from me.

'How can I trust you, after what I've seen?'

'Do you want to trust me, Jonathan?'

'Yes, but do you know what I keep thinking?'

'I…'

But he doesn't let me finish.

'I keep thinking Sarah, what you must have *done* to get Zack to look at you like that.'

'It's all in his mind,' I say, 'I've *done* nothing.'

'So, was it all in my mind too, what I believed

you felt about me?'

'No, Jonathan, *no*, how could you say that?'

'You're awake then,' Stuart says, walking into the room.

'Yes, I am,' Jonathan says, getting up off the bunk and shooting me a glance, 'wide awake.'

Stuart moves across and sits next to Jonathan on the bunk. Knowing that I will be ignored, I sit crossed legged, head down and listen.

'We need to formulate a plan,' Stuart says.

'I promised Naomi that I'd go back for them,' Jonathan says.

'Yes, we'll need everyone we can get hold of…that we can trust,' Stuart says.

I feel their eyes burn into the top of my head.

'There are three others still down in the City. Kyle, Oli, Marilyn, they came back in with me.'

'*Marilyn*,' I say, 'Marilyn's with you?'

'Yes,' Jonathan says, 'she saw it all, too…*everything*.'

In an instant, my happiness at the sound of her name is destroyed.

'When did you start to enjoy hurting me?' I say, close to tears.

He stares at me, bewildered.

'I'm sorry…that was unnecessary.'

'So, we've got thirteen people,' Stuart says, breaking the silence that follows, 'and one gun.'

'Plus…a screwdriver and a flashlight,' Jonathan says.

'*Fourteen*,' I say.

They don't respond.

'I'm with you too.'

'Look, Sarah,' Stuart says, 'I don't think…'

'I don't care what you think. I'm with you, whether you like it or not.'

'What do you think, Jonathan,' Stuart says.

'Maybe…maybe, we should give her another chance.'

His words fill me with hope.

'Thank you, Jonathan, I won't let you down, I promise. What about you, Stuart?'

'I agree, *in theory*, but you're on probation, Sarah. One false move and that will be it.'

'I understand. I wouldn't expect anything else,' I say, moving across to join them.

'I forgot about the Admin workers,' Jonathan says, 'four of the Ceremonial Chamber attendants have agreed to help us.'

'How did you do that?' I say, astounded.

'It's a long story.'

'So, the girl I saw…when I brought Andrea…was that one of them?'

'No, the one you spoke to was Oli. She's quite something. Only she could have passed herself off as an attendant and been that convincing.'

I see the admiration in his eyes.

'She's pretty,' I say, without thinking.

Jonathan smiles.

'She doesn't have a lot of good things to say about you.'

'Oh,' I say.

'Anyway,' Stuart says, 'that brings our total up to a respectable, eighteen.'

'We've already discussed an evacuation of the Colony with the Admin workers,' Jonathan says, 'they would co-ordinate it via the Ascendor.'

'That's going to take some planning,' Stuart says. 'It'll take a considerable time to get everyone up. We need to work out, how long.'

'Zack will stop it,' I say.

'Yes,' Jonathan says, 'so we need to get as many out before he realises what's happening.'

'What's the matter, Jonathan?' I say, noticing his worried expression.

'It's not going to be as simple as you might think to get people out safely.'

'What do you mean?'

'There's something up there...in the tunnel.'

'What?' I say.

'A huge machine that travels along its length, pushing anything in its way until...'

'The Sweeper,' Stuart says.

'You know about it?' Jonathan says, surprised.

'It's a Colony machine, like any other. It needs annual maintenance.'

'You've *worked* on it?'

'No, I haven't but I was due to go up there this year. I've studied the plans but we've not been told what it does, only that it's part of the Colony's original defence system. As far as I know, it's never been activated.'

'Oh, it's been activated,' Jonathan says.

'You activated it,' I say, horrified.

'Yes, but what I'm saying is that it's been activated, many times in the past.'

'How do you know that?' Stuart says.

'There's a pit…'

'Stuart,' I interrupt, not wanting to hear anymore, 'you could disable it…couldn't you?'

He stares at me.

'Maybe,' he says, '*maybe*.'

That's good enough for me…for now.

Chapter 38

19/06/3042   07:20 hours
JONATHAN

'Do you know how to use that?' I say, catching a glint of black metal in the beam of the flashlight from the gun, Sarah has resting against her right leg.

'Yes, but I'm hoping that I won't have to.'

'Believe me, it's terrifying,' Stuart says, positioning himself in front of the elevator doors, as we wait for them to open into the Maintenance Department.

I look around at the three of us, each wearing different coloured tunics, only Stuart staying true to the work area, he was allocated at birth.

'Do you think we should change tunics,' I say. 'It might give us a bit more time before we're spotted.'

'You could be right,' Stuart says, stepping out of the elevator followed by Sarah, the gun and me.

I shine the flashlight out into the corridor.

'We keep spare work tunics, in case they get oily, during the course of the day,' Stuart says, 'I'm sure we can find something to fit the pair of you.'

We walk down the corridor, dimmed still from the amber of the night lighting. I glance sideways as we pass the first office, half expecting to hear Daniel's thumps from the other side of the door. But all is quiet. Stuart stops outside one of the offices.

'You two go down to the workshop,' he says, 'there's some clean tunics on the shelves at the back.

I'll get the override code. But we need to be quick, the workers will be arriving soon.'

We leave Stuart and run down to the entrance of the workshop. Once inside, we make our way across the vast space, to the back. Sarah gets there first. She pulls tunics off the shelves, putting them up against her to find one the right size. Satisfied that she's found the best fit, she starts to take off her tunic top. I hold my breath, as her stomach then her breasts, come into view. She pulls her top up over her head then spots me watching and clutches it to her chest.

'Sorry,' she says, 'I forgot.'

'Forgot what?' I say, hurt by her actions.

'That you…me…'

'But I've seen you…'

'Yes,' she says, 'but…it doesn't feel right…I…'

Upset, I walk over to the shelves and search for a tunic that will fit me. There's one that's a little bit short but I decide it will have to do. I take off the Admin tunic, refusing to hide myself from her. As I pull my tunic top over my head, I see that she's facing away from me. Disappointed, I remove my tunic bottoms and scramble into the blue ones. Then, as Sarah did, I transfer the ID badge onto it.

'Looks good, Sarah,' Stuart says, as he enters the workshop, 'but…there's one thing that gives you away.'

'No, not that *again*, Stuart,' she says, yanking back her hair.

'All I'm saying, is that no Maintenance worker would be allowed to have hair that long, for safety reasons.'

He goes across to one of the drawers under the workbench and brings out a knife.

'*No*,' Sarah says, stepping back, 'you can't do that. There has to be another way.'

I grab the knife from Stuart and put it as far away from him as I can.

'I suppose, there are the caps,' he says, 'some of the girls wear them to keep their hair clean.'

'Why didn't you tell me about the caps before,' Sarah says, 'you'd have had my hair off, before mentioning them, if Jonathan hadn't stopped you.'

'I've only just thought of it,' Stuart says, a look of surprise in his eyes at the ferocity of the attack.

'They're over by the boots.'

Sarah rushes over and picks one from the shelves but, it's far too small, to take her mass of hair. She grabs another. I notice this one's a lot bigger and covers most of her forehead but still she struggles to wedge all her hair up into it.

'There's a bigger problem than your hair,' Stuart says, 'we need to find some way of transporting the gun without it being seen.'

I scour the workshop for something that might work.

'What's that,' I say, pointing to a long green case on the bench by the door.

'That's a good idea Jonathan.'

Inside it, lies a savage-looking instrument nestled in the shaped lining.

'What's that?' I say, impressed.

'It's a cutting tool for big pipes, metal beams that sort of thing.'

He lifts it out and places it down on the bench. I lay the gun inside the vacated space. It's not the same shape and it's smaller than the cutting tool, but it fits in.

'It needs some padding,' Stuart says, 'Sarah, bring me the SRU uniform.'

She comes up behind us and hands Stuart the uniform. She's unrecognisable. I stare at her, unable to believe the transformation.

'You could be a boy *or* a girl,' I say, without thinking, my eyes travelling down to her chest.

Straight away I wish I'd said nothing. Seeing the colour rising in her cheeks again, I look away. The awkwardness of the moment, is broken by the sound of voices approaching. Stuart snaps down the lid of the case and pulls it off the edge of the workbench by the handle.

'Right, let's go,' he says.

We march out of the workshop and back towards the elevator. A group of about six Maintenance workers are approaching us.

'*Stuart*?' one of them says.

'Can't stop, we've got an urgent job,' he says, pushing past him.

'Where have you been?' the Maintenance worker says.

Stuart doesn't stop. He and Sarah have reached the elevator now. I trail behind.

'And who are *you*?' he adds, eyeing me, as he passes.

'In a hurry, emergency,' I say, running to the doors that Sarah is holding open for me.

I jump inside.

'Wait,' I hear behind me, as the door closes.

At the City level, we push through the queue of dismayed Maintenance workers waiting to go down and make our way to the perimeter corridor. There, we turn left and approach the entrance to the Administration building. I make a mental note of the override code Stuart puts into the console, 7.1.9.1. We march into the foyer and Stuart heads for the desk.

'Emergency pipe work...' he says.

'Pipe work?' I hear the astonished novice repeat, as I disappear into the corridor on my way to the Ceremonial Chamber. At the door, I tap gently on it.

'It's me,' I say.

'Jonathan,' Marilyn says, letting us in, 'where have you *been*?'

'I said he'd turn up, didn't I,' I hear Oli say, from a seat in the corner.

She leans back with her hands behind her head and stares up at the ceiling.

'We've been so worried,' Kyle says, 'why did you go off like that?'

'It's a long story,' I say, 'but I've found...'

I'm interrupted by the sound of Stuart's voice outside the door. Realising my mistake, I rush over and let him in.

'This is Stuart,' I say, holding onto his arm. 'Stuart, this is Marilyn and Kyle and over there is...'

'So, this is the wonder man himself,' Oli says, getting up from her seat and marching over to him.

'This is Oli,' I say, 'don't worry she's not as scary

as she looks.'

'Well, well,' she says, scanning his body up and down, 'I'm looking forward to seeing what *you* can do.'

'You're making him nervous, Oli,' I say.

'And who's *he*,' she says, looking over Stuart's shoulder, at Sarah, behind him.

'Marilyn…' Sarah says, ignoring her and stepping forward.

I notice Marilyn's uncertain look.

'It's alright, she's on our side.'

'Sarah.'

Marilyn throws her arms around her. I watch as they cling onto each other, held by a bond I don't understand.

'So, just because she's changed tunics, we're supposed to trust her, are we?' Oli says.

'It's got nothing to do with the tunics,' I say, irritated.

'Are you sure, Jonathan,' Kyle whispers, looking across at Sarah and Marilyn, still holding onto each other.

'Yes, I'm *sure*.'

'I don't suppose anyone's interested in what I think,' Oli says.

'Yes, you're right, we're not.'

I turn my back on her. Then Tyler enters the Chamber, followed by the three other Admin workers, their faces fresh with sleep. I introduce them to Stuart and Sarah.

'What now?' Sherryl says, turning to me.

'Now, we take over the Administration Centre as

our headquarters,' I say, 'but first, we need to evacuate the workers.'

'They'll go up with today's Deathday candidate,' Kyle says.

'And how, exactly,' Oli says, 'are we going to keep out the SRU when they start noticing that the Colony is disappearing?'

'With *this*,' Sarah says, holding the gun out in front of her and pointing it straight at Oli's chest.

Chapter 39

'What are you *doing*?' I hear someone shout.

I don't respond. They're not important...none of them. I see only one other person in this room and that's, Oli. She stands facing me, a few metres from the point of the gun. Her eyes have lost their sharpness, dulled by a veil of fear. They're fixed on mine, as if connected, by an invisible wire, stretched out between us. Her mouth hangs open, caught mid-sentence but she's not saying anything, *not now*.

'Sarah,' Jonathan says, from somewhere to my left, 'put the gun down.'

The barrel of the gun dips, my attention diverted by his plea. Oli's eyes register it.

'Jonathan's right, Sarah, you should put that thing down.'

I lift the gun up again but I've lost my hold on her eyes.

'Do you even know how to use it?' she says, looking at Jonathan, not me.

I take off the safety catch. At the sound, her eyes dart back to mine, eyebrows raised in surprise. I've got her full attention, now.

'Put it *down*, Sarah!' Jonathan shouts.

He grabs hold of my left arm. I stumble sideways, the gun's weight pushing me off balance. Someone dives at me from the other side and wrestles the gun out of my grasp, as I fall into Jonathan. He puts his arms up as if to catch me but, instead, pushes me away from him with a violent shove. I stagger backwards then look up at him. His expression is one that I've never seen before and it frightens me. I watch, with a sick fascination, as Oli runs to his side, clutches his arm with both hands and rests her head against it. Her eyes are open, fixed on mine, bright with triumph. I look down at the ground to defend myself from them. Overcome by a feeling of nausea, I realise what I've done. I'm pinned to the spot by disapproval, disgust but it's only Jonathan that I care about. He looks down at Oli.

'Are you alright Oli,' he says.

He rests his hand on her arm. She doesn't reply. She doesn't have to. He stares back at me.

'What's going on, Sarah? I can't believe what you just did.'

My guilt-swollen tongue is incapable of forming an explanation, even if I had one.

'Why, Sarah? Tell me why you'd threaten Oli like that.'

'I...don't...' I manage to get out.

'You don't *know*,' he says, jumping in.

'No, I...don't...like her.'

It's out of my mouth before I can stop it. Of all the things I could have said to try and salvage the situation, this is the most pitiful. But it's the truth, or at least, part of the truth. I dislike her, yes. Her sarcasm, her barbed remarks, her pretty face masking a sharp mind. But, most of all, I dislike her because she wants what I want, what I had. I saw it the moment I walked into the room. And that scares me. I wait for Jonathan to say something but he doesn't. He shakes his head and turns away from me.

I call after him. But he's already guiding Oli to a seat across the room, his arm resting on her shoulder. One by one, the others move away from me to join them. I'm left alone, an island surrounded by a sea of disapproval. Only Marilyn remains. I glance at her, hoping to see something, anything in her expression that might give me some comfort. But there's only disappointment there.

'Marilyn...*please*,' I say, letting go of the sob that's been building in my chest, in my throat and allow it to take control of me.

Without a word, she steps forward and wraps her arms around my shaking body, holding me together.

'It's alright, Sarah, I understand,' she whispers, 'I understand.'

'Marilyn, why are you defending her actions?' Kyle says.

'I'm not defending them. But we've all done things that we regret, that we're ashamed of...*every* one of us.'

Kyle takes in a sharp breath, his eyes averted from hers.

'If she apologises...to Oli, can't we put this to one side, concentrate on what we're here to do?' she says.

'Apologise?' I say, my heart pounding again.

'Yes, Sarah, apologise,' she whispers, 'it's the only way.'

'Would you accept an apology, Oli,' Jonathan

asks.

She nods, that's all. She's become a mute victim and she plays the part well. I swallow hard. Can I do this? One look at Jonathan and I know that I have to. I feel Marilyn squeeze my hand then I walk the few metres to where Oli is sitting. It seems much further. I stand in front of her, avoiding her eyes, unsure whether to stay where I am, or sit down next to her. She takes the initiative and gets to her feet. Unable to put it off any longer, I take up her expectant, hurt look. It's convincing. I draw in a lungful of air and speak.

'I'm...sorry, Oli,' I say.

She doesn't respond, not a twitch, nothing. Does she want more or is she happy to savour her power over me for a little longer?

'What I did...was unacceptable...and I'm sorry,' I add.

She glances up at Jonathan then, without a word, she steps towards me, places her hands on my shoulders and kisses me on my right cheek. Then she removes her hands and smiles. The place where her lips touched my skin, burns. I can feel the shape of it as if she's left an indelible mark there. And still she says nothing, just turns to face Jonathan.

'Thank you, Oli,' he says, with that smile of admiration, he reserves only for her.

'Right, I think we need to move on, now,' he says.

There's nothing for me then? I'm forgotten. I move to the back of the group, with Marilyn, my only companion.

'We need to evacuate the Admin staff,' Jonathan says, scanning the group as he speaks.

I notice his eyes never quite meet mine.

'It will take several hours to get them up to the tunnel,' Jonathan continues, 'then they can go out with today's Deathday candidate.'

'We'll need to keep someone on reception,' Tyler says, 'to warn us if anyone approaches.'

'Yes, good, Jonathan says. 'Someone will have to guard the door of the Ceremonial Chamber. We must protect the Ascendor, at all costs. They'll have the gun.'

There's an uncomfortable silence.

'I had weapons training,' Oli says, 'when I was in the SRU. It was only theory, I never got to handle the real thing but I think I could do it...unless you have anyone else in mind.'

She looks around the group making sure, as she does, that she makes eye contact with me.

'You were in the SRU?' Stuart says, surprised.

She ignores him.

'Yes, Oli, you'd be ideal,' Jonathan says.

'Kyle and Marilyn, you stay here, help with the evacuation, keep everyone calm. Stuart you come with me.'

'Where are we going?'

'I'll explain later,' he says. 'Right, let's go.'

'What about *me*?' I say, from the back.

There's so much noise from the scrape of chairs, he doesn't hear me and carries on towards the door.

'Jonathan,' I call out, louder this time, 'what about me?'

They all stop what they're doing and look in my direction. He turns to face me.

'You…you stay here,' he says.

'Is that a good idea, Jonathan,' Stuart says, his eyes moving over to where Oli is standing by the door.

'Maybe, not. Alright, Sarah, you better come with us.'

And before I have a chance to comment, he's out the door, followed by Stuart. I weave my way through the displaced chairs, rushing to catch them up.

'Behave yourself, Sarah,' Oli hisses, as I push past her, out into the corridor.

'Wait, Jonathan,' I say, 'where are we going?'

But I get no reply. He doesn't even slow his pace. As they exit the building only Stuart bothers to check if I'm still following. We turn left into Corridor E and make our way down to the esplanade, past the Health & Wellbeing Centre. At Corridor C, we turn right then up the stairs to the top walkway of the Eugenics Centre pod block. Stuart's pod?

'Stuart get your toolbox, we're going to need it,' Jonathan says.

'I wish you'd tell me what we're doing,' he says, entering his pod.

I wait in silence with Jonathan. He doesn't look at me. I might as well be invisible. A couple of minutes later and Stuart joins us at the top of the stairs, carrying the box then we're off again. We cross Corridor C then Jonathan stops a short distance along the side of the SRU building. He looks down at Stuart.

'Take the air vent cover off,' he says.

'What?' Stuart says, staring at him, astonished.

'We're going to get the SRU prisoners out.'

'Now!' I say.

'Yes, Sarah…*now*.'

Chapter 40

19/06/3042   10:10 hours
JONATHAN

'I can't believe we're doing this,' Stuart says from the floor, his head inside the air vent opening, 'in full view of everyone. It's madness.'

'I think it's clever,' Sarah says, 'as far as the colonists passing by are concerned, we're three maintenance workers going about our work.'

I smile, forgetting that I'm still furious with her.

'And will they think the same,' Stuart says, 'when eight SRU officers crawl out into the corridor?'

'I'm sure Jonathan's thought that out,' Sarah says.

'Yes, of course I have,' I say, hoping that neither of them ask for details.

'Sarah, you stand guard,' I say.

'On my own?'

I crouch down by the toolbox and take out a heavy grey metal tool.

'Spread some tools around, make it look convincing.'

'With a thirty centimetre monkey wrench?' Stuart laughs, 'whatever do you think you'd use *that* for in an air vent?'

'Does it matter?' I say, ignoring him and laying it on the floor, 'I just like the look of it.'

'Well, if we're not going for accuracy,' he says.

He starts emptying the contents of the box placing each item, a little too hard, onto the floor around it.

'Calm down, Stuart,' I say as a Kindergarten worker walks past.

I push, a metal-toothed tool out of her path with my foot.

'Sorry,' I say, 'air vent maintenance.'

But she's not interested. She stares straight ahead and continues down the corridor.

'See,' I say, 'it's working.'

Stuart sighs and grabs a flashlight from the box.

'If anyone looks suspicious, Sarah, shine this down the air vent.'

'Like this?' she says, kneeling in front of the opening and ranging the beam from side to side like an off-kilter searchlight.

'No, more like this,' he says, 'less movement.'

'Stuart, we need to get going?'

I push him out of the way then take the flashlight out of my pocket.

'I'll go first. Oh, and bring the big screwdriver,' I add.

'As if I'd forget *that*,' he mutters.

Last time I did this, I crawled in backwards. It's going to be a lot easier dealing with the six-way junction this way round. We've gone about fifteen metres when my hand slips over the edge of the downward vent.

'Stuart, it's the junction. Don't look down.'

He says something I don't hear. I edge my chest over the rim, reach out with my right hand and throw the flashlight into the forward vent in front of me.

'Be careful with that,' I hear from behind me.

I peer right and left down the side vents but,

beyond the range of illumination from the flashlight, I'm met with a wall of blackness. Using my elbows, I shuffle forward then push my feet off the rim behind me and over the gap. I pick up the flashlight and shine it over my left shoulder.

'You alright, Stuart?' I say, but there's no reply. 'Stuart?'

'Yes, I think so, but I'm not sure…I…can…'

'You've done it before, Stuart. What's the problem?'

'I don't know, the gap looks bigger somehow.'

Despite his concern we negotiate the downward vent without any problem. We travel another ten metres or so to the next junction then take the right hand vent that leads to the cellblock. At the first grill, I stop and peer through it but can't see anything. I tap on the metal.

'Naomi,' I call out.

'Jonathan?' a voice says above me, as if she's been expecting me. I look up at her striped face through the grill.

'Stuart and I are here to get you out.'

'*Now*?' she says.

'It's, fine, Naomi, don't worry.'

'Give me the screwdriver, Stuart.'

I get to work on the clips and, in no time, I have the vent cover off. I poke my head up through the opening and my nostrils are assaulted by the acrid fug inside.

'What's that awful smell?' Stuart says.

I kick him with my left foot.

'Ow! What was that for?' he says.

I climb out into the cell and Stuart follows. He stands with his arms crossed over his chest as if to protect himself from the stench.

'Stay here,' I say, as I put the override code into the door console.

The door opens and I peer out into the corridor. There's no one around.

'Naomi, hold this door open.'

I move to the next cell and punch in the code. The door opens to reveal three SRU officers each sitting with their backs against a different wall, knees up to their chests, staring at a point in the centre of the cell. The smell in here is different but as pungent as that in the girls' cell.

'Quick,' I say, 'we're getting you out.'

'What *now*?' the one against the far wall says, astonished.

Not this again.

'Yes, *now*,' I say.

They get up, shuffle to the door and follow me out into the corridor.

'What was that?' I say, hearing a scream from further down the cellblock.

'He's in a terrible state,' one of them says, looking over his shoulder, 'I think the lights have gone out in his cell.'

'Quick,' I say, pushing them towards the open door of the girls' cell, 'get inside. I'll be with you in a minute.'

I run down to the far cell and press my ear up against the door. I can make out a muffled noise inside. Then a scream punctures the air. I punch in the code and wait for the door to open, spreading light onto the cell floor. At first, I can't see anybody in there. Then a figure, on all fours, shoots out from behind the bunk and scurries past me into the corridor. I turn round and see Finn, eyes wide with terror, curled up against the wall. *Finn's dead.* But as he stares, transfixed, at the light fitting above my head, he looks very much alive.

'Finn?' I say, stepping towards him.

He cowers away from me, his eyes fixed on the light and I know I can't do anything more for him. At least, he's not screaming any more. I charge back down to the girls' cell.

'Stuart, you go first, then me, then the rest of you,' I say.

'Down *there*?' one of the male SRU officers says, pointing at the air vent.

'Trust me, it's the only way.'

We watch Stuart's feet disappear down the vent opening.

Even over the six-way junction, we make good progress and everyone, including Stuart, gets over it without incident. Now, I can see the square of light from the corridor over Stuart's shoulder and notice his pace quicken towards it.

'Sarah,' I hear him call out.

The light from the vent opening is blocked by a set of bent legs. Stuart crawls out and I move forward.

'It's clear, Jonathan,' Sarah says, peering in.

I push myself out into the corridor.

'It's nearly lunch break,' Sarah says, 'we need to

get them out now.'

I look up and down the corridor. A lone pharmacy worker turns into the esplanade and I decide that it's time to go. I crouch down by the vent opening and look inside. An apprehensive face, belonging to one of the girls, stares out at me.

'You need to go, now,' I say, moving out of the way.

She crawls out of the vent and stands, disorientated, with her back against the wall, her eyes darting about her.

'Go to the Maintenance elevator and wait for Stuart. He'll take you up to the Council Chamber,' I say.

She looks at me, confused.

'Quick,' I say, 'I haven't got time to explain.'

She walks away from us, scanning the corridor as she goes. Three more emerge from the air vent and I watch the dishevelled group march away from us and disappear into the esplanade. Over the next ten minutes, we get the others out, only stopping to allow colonists to pass.

'Stuart get the grill back on,' I say, as the last of them walks away from us.

Sarah helps me put the tools back into the box.

'You take the toolbox,' I say to Stuart, 'we'll follow.'

But he's not looking at me. He's looking *behind* me. I turn and see Zack and Sean enter Corridor C from the perimeter.

'Stop!' Zack shouts.

Stuart drops the toolbox to the floor, with a

clattering thump and charges towards the esplanade.

'Run, Sarah!' I shout, grabbing her arm.

Chapter 41

'Split up,' Jonathan shouts as we enter the esplanade.

I feel his hand release mine and, before I have a chance to protest, he's gone. I watch him run in the direction of the Museum & Archive building. Stuart, in front of me, darts right into Corridor D. I start running again with no idea where I'm heading.

'Stop!' I hear behind me.

I swing round and see Zack charging towards me. Sean's with him, but he splits away and heads after Jonathan. Hoping that he hasn't recognised me, I turn back and continue my way along the corridor until I reach the entrance to Corridor D. I consider following Stuart down there but think better of it. Instead, I run along the back of the Health & Wellbeing Centre and fly into Corridor E and up the stairs to the first walkway of the Administration Block pods. Diving to the floor, I battle to control my breathing, to quell my pounding heart. I wait for the sound of feet on the metal steps behind me, but nothing happens. After a couple of minutes, I get onto my haunches and peer over the solid metal section of the walkway railing. Below me, two people stand, waiting. I can't tell if they're together or not, as they stare off in opposite directions. There's no sign of Zack. I get down on all fours and crawl back the way I came. Then I feel it, a vibration, through my hands and glance over my shoulder. Zack is on the walkway. I get up and stumble down the stairs into Corridor E, colliding with a Pharmacy worker at the bottom. I don't have time to apologise. I'm gone before he has a chance to react.

My lungs are straining and a sharp pain grips me under my ribcage. My body is screaming at me to stop but I can't. I career right and run along the Administration Block to the entrance. In front of the door console, I grapple to remember the override code. Numbers flash up inside my head but I can't recall the correct sequence. I thump the intercom button.

'How can I hel…?' a voice says.

'Let me in, it's Sarah!' I scream into it.

There's a faint sound as the door begins to slide open, too slow. I push myself through the gap and into the foyer. Sherryl sits at the desk.

'Zack's after me,' I gasp, trying to draw air into my aching lungs.

'Under the desk, quick,' she shouts.

'I'll be seen…'

But I'm already under it.

'He's outside,' Sherryl whispers down to me.

The bottom of the desk doesn't quite reach the floor, there's about a ten-centimetre gap. A metal bar runs round the base of the panels but it's narrow, four centimetres at most. Even so, I recognise it as my only option. I rest the palms of my hands on it then, with my legs at full stretch and my heels hooked over the bar opposite me, I perch across the width of the desk. Sherryl's legs brush against me. My arms are shaking so much, that I feel as if they will give way at any moment and send me crashing to the floor.

'Good morning...sorry, afternoon, Zack,' she says.

'Have you seen a Maintenance worker?' he says.

I can hear that he's out of breath despite his effort to keep control of his voice.

'Maintenance worker?'

I look down. Zack's feet are only centimetres away from my right leg. If I had a spare hand I could reach out and touch them. But the pain in my arm muscles is so intense now, that all I want to do is give up, let go and slump onto the floor. Instead, I force myself to concentrate on what's being said above me.

'Yes, that's what I said,' Zack snaps.

'No,' Sherryl replies, 'I haven't.'

There's a long pause. Please go. *Please*. I'm not sure how much longer I can hold this position.

'Contact the SRU if you see a Maintenance worker acting suspiciously.'

'I will,' Sherryl says, as my left arm gives out and I keel sideways onto the floor.

'He's gone,' she says.

I crawl out from under the desk and breathe again.

'We haven't seen anything of the SRU rebels,' Sherryl says.

'What about Stuart and Jonathan?'

'No, there's been no sign of either of them. What

happened out there?'

'Zack and Sean came after us. We split up. I don't know if they managed to get away or not.'

'They'll get here, don't worry,' Sherryl says, putting a hand on my shoulder.

'Beatrice and the Admin workers are ready to go up.'

'How did she seem?' I ask.

'Who?'

'Beatrice.'

'She was quiet but that's not unusual, they always look subdued.'

'The girls?' I say.

'Yes…I suppose it is mainly the girls. Why do you ask?'

'No reason,' I say, making my way towards the double doors.

At the Ceremonial Chamber, I tap on the door. There's an indistinct noise from the other side but nothing more.

'It's Sarah,' I say, assuming that the noise is coming from Oli.

There's silence.

'Let me in, Oli,' I say, irritated by the lack of response.

'Password,' she says.

'Password?'

'Nobody gets in without it.'

'What password? There isn't a password.'

The door opens and Oli stands, grinning, gun hanging down at her side.

'Just checking,' she says, as I push past her, 'can't

trust anyone.'

I avoid contact with her gloating eyes. The room is full of Admin workers, most are sitting, others, stand in huddled groups. There's an air of excitement about them, their voices animated by a new sense of purpose. I spot Beatrice perched on the edge of the podium, walk across and sit next to her, taking her cold hand in mine.

'Ready?'

'Yes,' she says, glancing in my direction, 'and thank you, Sarah…for everything.'

I squeeze her hand. It feels clammy.

'Right,' Oscar shouts, 'we're going to start the evacuation. We'll take four at a time. Marilyn and Kyle are at the top. They'll explain what to do. Beatrice, you go in first.'

'See you on the outside,' I say, as she steps into the Ascendor.

Another three join her, the doors close and she's gone.

It takes about an hour to get them all up to the tunnel. When the Ascendor returns from taking the last batch up, Fearne opens the doors to check that they're all gone. Then I hear a disjointed voice coming from the intercom, distorted by panic.

'Get out of there, *fast*.'

It's Sherryl. Oli dives across to me from the door.

'Behind the podium,' she screams and grabs me roughly by the arm.

'But…'

'*Do* it,' she hisses.

We fall to the floor, the gun between us. There's a

crash as someone hurls themself through the door of the Chamber and runs into the open Ascendor.

'What…?' I hear Fearne say.

But she doesn't get a chance to finish. We listen as more people enter the room.

'Close the Ascendor doors,' I hear Zack shout from the direction of the Chamber door.

'But…' someone says.

I think, it's Tyler.

'Do as you're told,' Zack shouts. 'Send him up.'

'Saves us a job,' Sean says, laughing, as the Ascendor door closes, 'he chose the wrong place to go, the idiot.'

'This is very irregular,' Fearne says, attempting to reinstate her authority, 'who was that?'

'I don't like your tone,' Zack says. 'I don't need to explain my actions to you. For your information…*Fearne*, the person you've sent to their death, helped the SRU rebels escape from detention this morning.'

'We'll still need his name for administration purposes,' she insists.

'Well I'm sorry, I didn't get the opportunity to find out his name,' Zack says, his voice thick with sarcasm. 'Oh, and by the way, he had two accomplices so expect them here shortly. I'll try and make sure that everything is in *order* for you, next time.'

'We'll deal with it,' Tyler says.

'*Yes*, you will.'

I hear the swish of the Chamber doors as they open then close again. The second they do, Oli pushes me away from her with the butt of the gun and crawls out from behind the podium.

'Who was it, Fearne,' she says.

'I didn't see. It all happened so fast.'

I walk up behind Oli.

'Did any of you see?'

There's no reply only a general shake of heads.

'Well, whoever it was,' I say, 'they're safe now.'

Chapter 42

19/06/3042   11:50 hours
JONATHAN

I charge along the front of the Eugenics Centre, managing a quick glance over my shoulder as I go. Two more officers have joined Sean but Zack's nowhere to be seen. Did he go after Sarah? I try not to think about what that means, if he did. One of the new officers is gaining on me. He looks athletic, fitter than Sean who is being left behind, red-faced and doubled over with exhaustion. I need to keep them away from the Maintenance elevator, give Stuart a chance to get the SRU rebels up to the Council Chamber. I keep going, past the Museum and Archive building, then decide to cut down Corridor A to the perimeter. *Big mistake.* Colonists are leaving their workplaces for lunch break, hundreds of them, making their way down to the Solarium. I look out of place as I run, too fast, against the flow of people.

When I reach the perimeter, I check behind me. My strategy has worked, there's no sign of them. I dive right and run along the front of the Museum & Archive building, doubling back on myself. They won't expect that. When I get to the entrance of Corridor B, I filter into the train of people walking down to the esplanade, slow my pace, trying to look like any one of them. The temptation to break out into a run is overpowering but I concentrate instead on the Health & Wellbeing worker in front of me. I mirror his pace, keeping my eyes on the back of his head.

Looking right as I enter the esplanade, I spot Sean about fifty metres away from me. He's given up the chase and stands panting, his eyes scanning the passing crowd. Maybe, it's my hesitation that alerts him. He stares in my direction and his eyes fix on mine then he's running towards me. I look across the esplanade to the Solarium. Door 2 is about to close. I fly across to it and push my way through the diminishing gap into the already tight-packed transition chamber. The door closes behind me, brushing my back. I hear a pounding behind my head and guess that it's Sean. But he's not getting in. A couple of colonists, squashed against me, glance over my shoulder at the scene, surprised at this unaccustomed commotion. Most are unconcerned by this display of impatience and remain, staring down at their feet.

After a few seconds, the inner door opens onto the Solarium. The colonists file out then disperse into the sun-drenched atmosphere, each making their way to a favourite spot. I take the path that dissects the Solarium in two and jog across to the other side, starting to relax. But it's too soon. An SRU officer is approaching me. There's another, coming from the other side. I know, before I check behind me, that there's one there, too. Abandoning the path, I take off and run across the grass to the Arboretum, weaving my way in and out of the trees looking for somewhere to hide. I stop under one that has copper-coloured leaves that remind me of Sarah's hair and stare up at its canopy of branches. What I'm about to do is strictly forbidden in the Colony, but I do it anyway. I hook my hands onto a low level branch and pull myself up onto it. Then, spotting SRU officers approaching, I scramble deeper into the heart of the tree. My height helps and, after several minutes of climbing, I'm at the top. I lie along one of the stronger branches with my arms hugging its girth and peer down. It looks a lot higher than I thought and I fight back a wave of vertigo, as I watch the tops of heads pass underneath me. Because I can see them so clearly, I feel sure that they must be able to see me too. It doesn't take me long to convince myself that I'm invisible to them.

After some time, I don't know how long, the number of colonists passing below me reduces. None of them have been SRU officers. I jolt, as I feel myself sliding again down the side of the branch and renew my grip on the textured perch. I decide it's time to make a move so I ease my body back towards the trunk then start my descent. When I get to the last branch, I realise that it's not the one I came up on. This one is a lot higher. Not wanting to go back, I slide my body over the edge and hang, letting my arms take the weight. A sharp pain shoots through my injured shoulder. I cry out in pain and let go. Landing hard, with my right leg bent at an awkward angle, I hobble towards the nearest exit. The paths and gardens are deserted now. Only a group of Kindergarten children are left, chasing each other around some pink-coloured shrubs.

I approach Door 3 and wait for it to open. Once inside, I peer out into the esplanade through the transparent walls of the transition chamber. All looks quiet. As soon as the outside door opens, I charge across to Corridor C opposite and I don't intend to stop until I reach the perimeter. To my amazement, Stuart's toolbox is still there where he dropped it, before he ran. It hasn't moved at all, not a single centimetre. I smile, visualising all the colonists that must have stepped around it, not considering for a second, the possibility of moving it out of the way. I pick it up and continue with it down the corridor. At the end, I look down the front of the Administration Block and notice a group of Pharmacy workers filing out into the perimeter corridor. I stare at them, puzzled, then it hits me. Beatrice is a Pharmacy worker. These are her colleagues who have attended her Deathday ceremony. So the first of the evacuees have gone. I walk, with an air of purpose, towards the entrance and push my way through into the foyer. Oscar is now at the reception desk and I wave at him as I pass.

I think that I hear him call out my name as I pass through the double doors, on my way to the Ceremonial Chamber, but I don't stop. Outside, I tap on the door.

'It's Jonathan,' I say.

The door opens at once and Oli stands behind it, gun resting at her side. One look at her dulled eyes and I know there's something wrong.

'Jonathan, am I glad to see you,' she says as I walk in and put the toolbox on the floor.

Sarah, Marilyn and Kyle are in a cluster over the other side of the room, looking down at someone sitting on one of the seats.

'Sarah, you're safe,' I shout.

She turns. Her eyes are puffy and bloodshot, her cheeks wet with tears.

'Jonathan,' she says, throwing her arms around me, 'it's awful, awful.'

Straight away I spot, that the person slumped in the seat with their head in their hands, is Stuart.

'What happened?'

He looks up at the sound of my voice. His face is almost unrecognisable, covered in red blotches from exertion or, perhaps, crying. His hair sticks up in damp tufts but it's his eyes that worry me the most. They're scoured with fear, or is it guilt?

'Jonathan,' he says, getting to his feet, 'it was my fault, my fault…'

His voice fails him. He stands, shoulders hunched in silent submission, in front of me.

'It wasn't your fault, Stuart, I keep telling you that,' Marilyn says, putting her arm across his shoulders.

'Can somebody tell me what's happened?' I say.

'It was going so well.' Kyle says. 'We waited for Beatrice to come up but Stuart arrived first, he'd been chased into the Ascendor by Zack, it didn't matter, he was safe. They all followed her down the tunnel and through Gate 1. We watched them go. Marilyn was standing in the doorway of the Ascendor, Stuart and I were talking, working out the next move. Then it started, the vibration, buzzing through my feet. I looked down but, before I could say anything, Stuart pushed me into the Ascendor. Marilyn stumbled backwards against the back wall and then the doors closed and we came back down to the Ceremonial Chamber. Stuart knew…'

'I knew…' Stuart says, '…I stood in front of the hangar doors…and watched the Sweeper emerge. I'd forgotten…forgotten to tell them…about the sensors at the Gates that detect any movement *towards* the Colony. The siren screamed around me, so loud, too loud. I couldn't think. I couldn't block it out. I walked backwards down the tunnel, never taking my eyes off it, not for a moment. It was as if…I could stop it…if I kept my eyes on it…I don't know…what I was thinking. Between Gate 3 and 4, I turned around. I could see three Admin workers, one was on the floor, the others helping her to her feet. Beatrice was holding the door open for them. Then she caught sight of it…the Sweeper…she panicked…went through, allowed the door to close. I didn't hesitate, I knew what was coming…I jumped up, threw myself at the scoop and clung onto it, screaming at them to do the same. But they were mesmerised…by the pit…opening up in front of them.'

His voice breaks.

'*And*…Stuart?' I say.

'I watched them…Jonathan…as they fell screaming into the darkness…all three of them. There was nothing I could do.'

Chapter 43

19/06/3042   15:11 hours
SARAH

'It's not going to work,' Oli says, 'the evacuation, not with that thing up there.'

'She's right,' I say. 'Imagine how difficult it'll be when we evacuate the children. It's far too dangerous.'

'Stuart, you said you could disable it?' Jonathan says.

He gets no reply. Stuart sits hunched, his arms across his chest, isolated by his grief...his guilt.

'For goodness sake, Stuart, it wasn't your fault,' Oli says, marching across the room towards him, 'you need to concentrate, stop feeling sorry for yourself.'

She leans into him, her mouth only centimetres from his left ear.

'Can it be disabled, yes or no?'

'Possibly,' he mumbles.

'Yes or no, Stuart.'

'Yes...I think so.'

'Stop bullying him, Oli,' I say, 'can't you see how upset he is?'

'How upset, *he* is. What about the three in the pit? How upset do you suppose *they* feel at the moment?'

'That's not fair,' I say, watching Stuart's shoulders slump, pushed down by her verbal attack.

'What you don't know, Sarah, is that in our

efforts to rescue *you*, I nearly ended up in that pit.'

'Did you?' I say, looking at Jonathan for confirmation.

He nods.

'So, I think I know a bit more about it, than you.'

'Alright, what do you suggest we do then?' I say.

'I don't know, that's why I'm asking Stuart.'

'We could try and rescue them,' I say, with little conviction.

'No, Sarah,' Jonathan says, 'to do that we'd have to activate it again. It would be…'

'We'd have to activate it anyway,' Stuart says, 'to disable it.'

'*At last*, the oracle speaks,' Oli says.

Ignoring her, Stuart gets up and walks across the room to where we're standing in a huddle by the door. Tyler and the other two Admin workers sit on the edge of the podium, watching us.

'I've been thinking…' he continues.

'That's what you're good at, Stuart,' I say, squeezing his upper arm.

'…it might not work…but I've got an idea. I'll need to go to Maintenance first and get something.'

'Is there anything we can do while you're gone,' Kyle says.

'Yes, you, Jonathan, Tyler and Oscar go up to the tunnel.'

'But…' Tyler says, his faced blanched with fear.

'I need the strongest up there,' Stuart says.

'I'll do it,' Oli says, 'if he's not keen.'

'No, I'll go,' Tyler says.

Oscar remains silent, staring out in front of him

with blank eyes.

'And Sarah, you go up too.'

I look at him, puzzled. 'Why…?'

But he doesn't answer.

'I'm stronger than Sarah,' Oli says, 'that's ridiculous.'

She lets Stuart out of the door then leans against the wall, her lips fixed in a surly pout. Fearne opens up the Ascendor and I step inside. Kyle is behind me but Jonathan pushes past him and gets in beside me.

'Take the next one,' he says, as the doors close.

The Ascendor jolts into action and we start our journey upwards, our bodies close but not touching.

'You're shaking, Sarah.'

'I'm frightened,' I say.

'I'm with you, there's no need to be scared.'

He wraps his arms around me, absorbing my fear into his body. I rest my head on his chest, eyes closed, and listen to the comforting beat of his heart through his tunic. All too soon, the Ascendor doors open and I feel a cold, damp draft of air on my arm. Jonathan guides me out, away from the warmth and into the tunnel. I gasp. I don't know what I'd imagined when I'd thought of this place, but not this. Not this hard, compassionless corridor of stone.

'Don't let go of me,' I say.

Next up are Kyle, Oscar and Tyler. Kyle jumps out of the Ascendor when it arrives, without hesitation. Oscar and Tyler take some coaxing to get them out into the tunnel. I understand how they feel. When they do emerge, they stand close together looking about them in silent awe, gripped by their own personal fears. We wait for Stuart to arrive. No one speaks. There's nothing to say.

A few minutes later and the doors open to reveal Stuart, the toolbox at his feet, a large coil of rope looped across his body. Jonathan grabs the toolbox.

'No, take these first,' Stuart says, 'we'll need the toolbox to keep the doors open.'

He bends down, takes two bulky metal tools out of the box then gets out and leaves it for the doors to close onto. They hum in an effort to complete their journey. Stuart has such a look of determined concentration on his face that nobody dares ask him about the two metal chair legs and the bag.

'Kyle, take the rope. Jonathan, you grab the chair legs and the bag of bolts. All of you go down to Gate 1.'

'What about you?' I say.

'Sarah,' he says, ignoring my question, 'when you get down to the Gate, wait a couple of minutes then I want you to walk back towards me, do you understand?'

'Yes, but…'

'Just do as I say.'

Knowing that I won't get any more out of him, I run after Jonathan and the others, my ankles turning with the uneven surface under my feet, so different from that of the City. I arrive at the Gate, its door barely visible in the metal expanse of wall, in which it nestles. I look back the way I came and see that Stuart has moved to the right wall of the tunnel. I start to count. Jonathan has his back to me talking to the other three. He doesn't notice when I start to move forward away from the Gate and towards Stuart. I walk slowly at first then quicken my pace feeling vulnerable, alone in the centre of the tunnel.

'Sarah,' I hear Jonathan shout behind me, 'what are you doing?'

Then I feel it, a strong vibration travelling up my body from the floor. A shrill wail cuts into my eardrums and I slap my hands over my ears to dampen the noise. Stuart is shouting at me. I can see his mouth moving but I can't hear what he's saying. Then the lights start to flash, on and off, with a regular beat. I stumble forward towards him. With each flash, I can detect that he's closer to me but I don't see him move. Then he's right in front of me. I jump with alarm. Then he has his hands on my shoulders, turning me round. But the pulse of the lights has disorientated me.

'Keep walking,' he shouts, 'to the Gate. Don't look back, Sarah, keep walking.'

'What's happening?' I shout but he doesn't answer.

Instead, he grips my arm tighter and guides me through the strobing space in front of me. The vibration has now become a rumble and I sense that there is something behind, following us. Through the on-off lighting, I see what I can't believe, the entire wall in front of us, moving upward into the rock ceiling.

'Get under it,' I hear Jonathan shout.

'Stuart, what's going on?' Kyle says.

His eyes flash up in front of me, wide with terror.

'Keep moving, Stuart shouts, 'keep moving.'

We stagger forward in a group through two more Gates.

'Stuart, do something,' Jonathan says, panic in his voice.

'Take the others to the pit edge, Jonathan,' Stuart shouts, 'and wait.'

'Get behind me,' Jonathan screams at us.

We follow him, too scared to argue. Then he slows his pace right down and edges forward bit by bit on his hands and knees, his fingers exploring the floor in front of him.

'Stop,' he shouts, after a few more metres, '*don't* go any further.'

He places the chair legs and the bag of metal down onto the ground.

'This marks the boundary. Stay this side of it.'

I turn for the first time and look behind me. I can make out Stuart standing by the right side wall, facing away from me. I catch a glint above him, as one of the light pulses flash off the metal tool that he has poised, above his head. I watch in fascination, as he throws it forward. It spins in the air then curves downward. There's a clank then a grinding noise. The rumble falters. Then the siren stops, creating a silence, so intense, it hurts. The echoing ring, still sounding in my ears. The tunnel disappears as the lights die and we're plunged into darkness.

'What's happened?' I shout.

But before anyone can answer, the light flashes back on again. I scream. The vibration starts again but I can only stare, at the towering silver monster in front of me. Another grind and a metallic clack, as it spits out the tool and edges towards us. Stuart stumbles back.

'Bring me the chair legs, Jonathan!' he screams.

Jonathan bends down, grabs them off the ground. Then he runs up behind Stuart who turns, long enough, to snatch them from him. And still the monster creeps its relentless way forward, like a beast stalking its prey. Stuart edges closer and pushes the two chair legs, in quick succession, through the gap between the wall and the edge of the machine. He staggers backwards away from it. This time the grinding is louder as I hear the metal of the chair legs being chewed, mutilated by the wheels. But still it moves forward.

'It's not going to stop!' I scream.

Stuart darts forward, pushing Jonathan aside, and drops the bag of metal across the channel, in front of the wheels. Stuart and Jonathan turn, then run back towards us, nowhere else left to go.

'There's nothing more I can do,' I hear Stuart shout.

I watch as it looms above us. Terrified, I step back away from its gaping mouth. My stomach lurches upwards, as my foot searches for a surface that's not there. I throw out my arms, clawing at the air with my fingers, in a desperate attempt to regain my balance. But it's too late. I'm falling, falling.

Chapter 44

I turn and run towards Gate 4. *It's not going to stop.* In front of me, Tyler and Oscar are on their knees beside the partially open pit, their heads lowered in submission, bodies rigid with fear. Kyle stands next to them, the rope still coiled about his body, staring over my shoulder, his eyes transfixed.

'Where's Sarah?' I scream but I already know the answer.

I hear a long, high-pitched screech followed by a clunk and the grind of metal against stone. Then silence. I look behind me. The machine, only ten metres away from the pit is still, tilted at an odd angle. The top left corner has gouged a deep channel in the stone wall and become wedged there, buckling one of the panels, in the process. The right-hand set of wheels have careered off the track and hang suspended above the tunnel floor. Turning my back on the twisted wreck, I fall to my knees and stare into the black void of the pit.

'I didn't think that was going to work,' Stuart says, coming up beside me. 'Jonathan, what's the matter?'

I look up at him. My eyes tell him all he needs to know.

'Not Sarah?' he says, staring into the pit that has taken her.

I can't speak, my tongue is held, by terror. I struggle to breathe.

'Sarah!' Stuart shouts.

'Quick,' he says, getting no response, 'Kyle give me the rope. *Kyle*!'

But Kyle is still transfixed on the machine, as if he thinks that it might be feigning. That, if he takes his eyes off it for one second, it will start up again and finish the job. Stuart walks over to him, lifts the coil of rope from his torso.

'It's not going anywhere Kyle, not now.'

He turns and walks back to us.

'Oscar, you're the smallest you'll have to…'

'No…I can't…I can't,' he says, close to tears.

'*I'm* doing it, Stuart,' I say, 'no one else.'

'But Jonathan, you're too…'

He stops mid-sentence, knowing logic won't stop me. He loops the rope around his waist then ties a knot, tugging at it to test its strength. Then he beckons to Tyler to stand in front of him, facing in the same direction.

'Jonathan,' he says, 'tie the rope like this around Tyler then do the same with Oscar and Kyle. We'll need to pull against your weight, using our heels to gain a purchase on the rough ground.'

I move as fast as I can but my hands are shaking so much that the knots keep slipping and refuse to tighten. After several attempts, I have them tied together, with Kyle's feet about a metre from the pit edge, the other three standing behind him.

'I can't see the bottom,' I say to Stuart, coiling the other end of the rope around my waist and staring down, 'how deep do you think it is?'

'Not more than the length of the rope…*I hope.*'

Once I've checked and re-checked the strength of the knot, Stuart pulls the rope slack towards him, along the line.

'Each of you grab hold of it so that it can be fed out in a controlled way,' he says, 'we don't want him falling down in one go.'

'How will you know when to pull me up,' I say.

'Give a couple of sharp tugs on the rope that should do it.'

'Stuart, I need the flashlight, I can't see a thing down there.'

'In my tunic pocket.'

I walk over, crouch down next to him then slide it out from under his tunic top.

'Are you alright, Jonathan…going down there, I mean?'

'I just want to get going.'

'Good luck,' he adds.

I approach the pit edge and kneel down, facing Kyle's knees.

'I hope this works,' he says, 'because if it doesn't, I'm going to be the next one down there.'

'It'll work,' I say, then put the handle end of the flashlight into my mouth.

I'll need both hands to lower myself over the edge. Easing myself backward, I push my legs down into the pit and hang, suspended by my elbows. I watch as Kyle takes up the slack then feeds the rope down the line to Stuart.

'Ready?' Stuart shouts.

I nod, then in staggered movements, using my arms, I ease myself over the edge and allow the rope to take my weight. The sharp jolt that follows leaves my stomach behind and I almost lose my grip on the flashlight. The rope, bites into my midriff but, holds.

'Lower me down,' I shout to my invisible anchors.

'Not until you're stabilised,' I hear Kyle shout back.

I push my feet onto the pit wall and wait for more rope to be fed to me, transferring the flashlight from my mouth to my left hand. Then I start to *walk* my way down the wall. I make steady progress for several metres and start to feel more comfortable, when the wall in front of me, disappears. I fight to control the panic that seizes me, as the rope lurches to one side, setting off a swinging motion.

'What's happening?' I hear from above.

'It's alright, it's alright!' I shout.

But it's far, from alright. I'm swinging, twisting out of control, the beam of the flashlight ranging around me in a blur of white light. I wait for the swinging to subside…for my heartbeat to slow, then stare down, feeling sick. That's when I see, what I couldn't see from above, that the pit curves away from me, creating a slight overhang. *So that's why I couldn't see the bottom.* Before I have time to take in the consequences of this, I'm fed more rope. There's a jolt as I drop about a metre. Another jolt, another metre. After a couple more drops, my heels hit the side of the pit wall behind me. I notice now, a mustiness in the air. I twist myself round to face the wall and realise that I'll be able to walk down this, as well, to the bottom. Clinging onto the rope and this comforting thought, I turn round again. I direct the beam down beyond my feet at a forty-five degree angle. The shaft of light punctures the dark and I catch a flash of white, below me, picked out in the circle of illumination it creates. I move the beam to the right and see, the empty-eyed grimace of a white face, staring up at me. I gasp. *What was that*?

Directing the beam back down, I force myself to look...to confirm my worst fears. The bottom of the pit is full of bodies...no, not bodies...bones. The skeletons of those who have fallen victim to the Sweeper, over centuries. They're old, picked white-clean by the soil-dwellers, creatures hungry for survival, tunnelling through the dampness beneath the Earth's sun-baked crust. Gaining control of my breathing, I shout out.

'Is anybody there? Sarah!'

I'm met with only silence. I wait, listening for any sound, any sound at all. Then I hear a crack and swing the beam of light towards the noise, picking out the wide-eyed stare of a girl buried up to her waist in bones. Her head rests over the ribcage of one of her long dead companions.

'It's alright, don't be afraid,' I shout, 'I'll get you out!'

She turns to look behind her and I follow her gaze with the light. Two others cower behind her, a dark-haired boy and another girl. All three stare up at me, traumatised, unable to speak.

'Where's Sarah?' I shout, as the rope lowers me

another metre and I struggle to keep the light trained on their faces. 'Where's Sarah, *please*?'

The dark-haired boy raises a trembling finger and points to a spot about three metres to his right. I move the flashlight, following his direction and see her…*Sarah*. She lies on her back, her arms above her head, legs splayed out. Her body rests, partially buried, in a bed of broken bones. Her eyes are closed. She's still, lifeless.

'Sarah!' I scream but she can't hear me. She hears nothing.

I look down at my feet dangling about three metres from the top of the mound of bones. Then, as if they've heard my silent request, there's a jolt and I drop two metres in one go and come to rest just above a twisted skeleton. I wait, hoping that they can find me another metre or so of rope, but nothing happens. Putting the flashlight in my mouth, I fiddle with the knot at my waist, pulled tight by my weight. But I can't loosen it. I direct the flashlight back at the dark-haired boy.

'What's your name?' I say.

He looks taken aback by my question, as if it's too ordinary, too commonplace, for the circumstances he finds himself in.

'Mitchell,' he says, with a lack of conviction, as if he thought he'd never utter it again.

'You have to lift my legs up, so that I can undo this knot, do you understand?'

Has he heard me, he looks puzzled, unsure of what I'm asking of him? Then he begins to wade through the sea of tangled bones towards me.

Sometimes, he's forced to scramble over the top, when the way through becomes too difficult. But, after a few minutes, he's by my hanging feet. With a renewed sense of purpose, he grabs my ankles and pushes up, giving me enough slack to work on the knot. He watches, as I ease the ends through and drop, with a crunch, onto the grim heap beneath me. I tie a double knot at the base of the rope then lift the boy, so that he can claw his way onto it. He curls his feet over the knot and I lift him up and tug twice, hard on the rope. There's a pause and I think that my signal hasn't worked then it rises, taking the white-knuckled boy with it. He looks upwards as he goes, as if sensing salvation. I glance over to Sarah, lying motionless, not wanting to accept her fate.

'You're next,' I say to one of the girls.

But her eyes are fixed on Mitchell's disappearing feet and she doesn't hear me. I leave her and wade across to Sarah, using my arms to propel myself. Pushing my arm under her back, I lift her up a little and shine the flashlight onto her face.

'Sarah, can you hear me?'

Getting no response, I repeat it, stroking her cheek with my finger. Her eyes flutter open. I direct the beam of light away from them.

'Sarah, it's Jonathan, you're going to be alright now,' I say, taking her cold hand in mine.

'Jonathan?'

'Yes, Jonathan,' I say, kissing her cheek. 'Are you hurt?'

'I don't know…I don't think so. How…?'

'Don't try and speak. One of the Admin workers

has gone up already. I'll get the two girls up first then come back for you.'

She grabs my hand.

'I promise, Sarah, I promise.'

I turn and direct the light above me, watching as Mitchell scrambles over the edge of the pit to safety.

It takes a while, perhaps half an hour, to get both girls up to the tunnel. I turn my attention back to Sarah. But she's injured her foot in the fall and isn't going to be able to hold herself on the rope. I manoeuvre her under it, lift her up onto my hips with her legs wrapped around my waist and tie the rope around her. Tugging at it twice, I hold my breath as I let go of her, hoping that the knot is strong enough to take her weight. It is and I watch her rise in a spiralling motion above me.

I don't know if the rescued Admin workers have joined forces with the pulling team but when it's my turn to be lifted out, it seems to take half the time it did to go down. It's as if I've somehow become lighter, no longer burdened by a weight of fear. As I rise to the surface, I switch off the flashlight, leaving the silent bones in darkness again, as they've been for centuries and will be for centuries to come. In death, their cushion of broken bones has saved the lives of four people. Saved the life of, my Sarah. And I thank them...these nameless saviours.

Chapter 45

'Sarah, you're safe,' I hear Kyle say above me, 'you're safe now.'

'Thank you,' I whimper, '*thank* you.'

It's alright, I'm alright. Then I remember Jonathan, still in the pit.

'Jonathan!' I shout, scrambling onto my feet.

Stuart catches me, as I veer sideways, overcome with dizziness. A pain spears my ankle, as it takes my weight.

'Sit down, Sarah, we'll deal with this,' he says, lowering me back to the ground.

All I can do is watch, helpless, as they haul Jonathan up from that terrible place. A place that still resonates with pain, suffering and fear, even now, after all the centuries. It takes the combined strength of them all to get him out, their tired, shaking limbs almost seizing up with the effort. I will them to find a little more of it. Then the top of his head appears and he's scrambling up into the tunnel, every part of me wanting, but unable, to help him.

'Sarah,' he says, pushing the rope from under his feet and stumbling over to me.

He kneels down beside me. I throw my arms around his neck and feel his body trembling under my fingertips. Then he pulls me closer, his grip so tight that I can hardly breathe. We stay locked together for some time, words redundant.

'Sarah, Jonathan, we have to go,' I hear Stuart shout across to us.

Jonathan helps me to my feet. I wince, as the pain in my ankle strikes again.

'You're injured,' he says.

'I don't think it's serious. I've twisted my ankle, that's all.'

'Here lean on me.'

I put my arm around his shoulder for support then hobble forward.

'There's a gap just big enough to get through, between the Sweeper and the wall,' Stuart shouts, pointing to the tilted, broken machine in front of us.

It stands reduced to a heap of useless metal, its days of terror over.

'Leave the rope here,' Stuart says, 'we might need it again.'

Oscar gathers it up and leaves it in a coil by the wall, next to the pit opening.

'What are we going to do about *them*?' Jonathan says, pointing to the hunched, trembling clutch of rescued Admin workers by the wall.

'We'll take them back down to the City. Let them recover,' Stuart says, making his way across to the wall and squeezing his body sideways through the gap.

Oscar, Kyle and Tyler go next, followed by the Admin workers. Then it's my turn. I'm fed through the gap, a set of hands on my arms, another on my legs. Waiting for Jonathan to join me, I look behind and see the full length of the corridor revealed before me through the three open Gates. When everyone is through the gap, we follow Stuart down to the Ascendor. We send the Admin workers down first, with Tyler. Then, with Stuart standing next to the toolbox, we manage, somehow, to wedge everyone else in, even though it would be easier to do it in two trips. It's as if no one wants to stay alone in the tunnel.

Back in the Ceremonial Chamber, Stuart and the others recount the full story to the waiting group. I'm glad to be left out of it. I sit on the edge of the podium, relishing the calm. But something's missing. *Someone's* missing. I scan the room to make sure I'm not mistaken.

'Here's the list of SRU pods, Jonathan.'

Fearne's voice distracts me.

'Oli, Sherryl and Oscar, stay here,' Jonathan says from the door. 'The rest of you come, with me and Stuart, up to the Council Chamber. We need to get ready for tonight's evacuation.'

My ankle is less painful now but, on the short journey to the elevator, I decide not to mention it to Jonathan and continue to lean into his body, wanting to keep him close for as long as possible. Stuart waits by the doors, as a group of workers come up from the Maintenance Department to make their way to the Gym, or their pods. They file out, looking surprised at us waiting to get in, but don't comment. As I step inside, I spot a group of SRU officers coming our way, their eyes darting about the corridor as if they're searching for someone. They don't notice us.

At the Council Chamber, we step out into the deserted corridor and Stuart leads the way to the surveillance room.

'This is incredible,' Tyler says, staring about him.

Fearne clutches onto his arm and turns to me, her eyes bright with excitement.

'Yes, I suppose it is,' I say, although it's held nothing but fear and misery for me.

As we enter the surveillance room, I hardly recognise the eight SRU rebels that greet us, so changed are they from the pathetic specimens we rescued. They've lost the filthy uniforms, the film of dirt on their faces and bodies but, most of all, they've lost the smell. Standing in a group like that, a wall of black crispness, they look imposing. Naomi steps forward.

'What's she doing here?' she says, pointing at me.

'Sarah's with us, relax,' Stuart says.

She turns to Jonathan, doubt all over her face.

'It's, fine, Naomi. She's with us,' he says.

She glances at our clasped hands.

'That remains to be seen,' she mutters.

'I need to get to work on the Ascendor access,' Stuart says, picking up the toolbox. 'It has to be situated in the administration building, somewhere. Fearne come with me, I might need some help.'

Fearne? When has Stuart ever needed help with anything mechanical? But there's a positive glow about him as he escorts her out of the room. A ridiculous pang of jealousy grips hold of me as I watch them leave, chatting away like old friends.

'I hope she doesn't distract him from the task,' I

say.

'What do you mean?' Jonathan says.

'Nothing. She's attractive, that's all.'

'Tonight,' Naomi says, 'we need to evacuate the pod blocks. We'll use the Council Chamber as a holding facility. Stuart will have to get hold of tomorrow's maintenance override code, before we start. How many people have we got that we can rely on?'

I notice she glances at me.

'Stuart, myself, Kyle, Marilyn and Sarah,' Jonathan says, 'the four from Admin and the seven other SRU rebels. That's it.'

'You forgot Oli,' I say, trying to disguise the delight in my voice.

'Oh yes, and Oli. That makes eighteen.'

'And one gun,' I add.

'Functioning?' Naomi asks.

'Oh yes, it's functioning.'

'That will have to be enough,' she says. 'We start at 21:30. I suggest we try and get some sleep before then.'

I wander over to the surveillance screens and watch the City below us, going about its business, unaware that the lives of its inhabitants are about to change forever. Then I spot someone, in the esplanade, a person picked up by the camera on the corner of the Pharmacy building. There's something about the expression, the manner. Something's very wrong. I make for the door.

Chapter 46

19/06/3042   18:42 hours
JONATHAN

Why would she disappear like that, without a word? The flashlight ranges from side to side in front of me, as I charge down the perimeter corridor of the Council Chamber, searching for Sarah. I charge into the refectory, weaving my way through the maze of tables and chairs. It's deserted. The last time I saw her, she was standing by the door talking to Stuart...yes, I'm sure it was Stuart. I went over to speak to Tyler and when I looked back, she was gone. I glance at the serving hatch, it's open. I scramble through it into the connecting room and march across to the elevator, opposite. The console indicates that it's still at this level. That's odd. I'm sure that Stuart told me that it's programmed to, automatically, go back down to the City. For some reason, it's remained on this level. It's not important. Sarah's not here.

Out in the corridor again, I direct the flashlight beam into the gloom of the no-man's land, between here and the residential area. This space unnerves me. I try to imagine what it was like when Councillors walked here on their way to a comfortable night's sleep, chatting about the day's activities. But it's no use. I feel the cold, forbidding atmosphere press me to keep moving, as I break into a trot and stare straight out in front of me. I watch the circle of light bob up and down to my rhythm.

Arriving at the first of the residential buildings, I discover that it's occupied by three of the SRU rebels.

'Find your own bed,' Naomi complains, as I walk into the sleeping area.

Andrea lies next to her on the large bunk, the cover pulled up over her face, her chest rising and falling in time with her muffled snores.

'Have you seen Sarah?' I say, as she turns onto her side, facing me and nestles back down.

'No, she's not with us. Get some sleep, Jonathan and leave us be,' she says, yawning, 'this is the most comfortable I've been for weeks…*ever*.'

She's right and I know it, but I'm not giving up yet. I check a few more of the buildings then find one that isn't occupied. Something makes me drift through into the sleeping area and I walk over to the bunk and press down on the surface. My hand sinks into the padded cover. It's met by a giving firmness beneath. I sit down on the edge and bounce up and down. Then, a feeling of tiredness engulfs me and I sink into its welcoming surface. Shuffling under the cover, I pull it up so that the soft fabric brushes my chin and the bottom of my ears. I'll close my eyes, just for a few minutes that's all, a few blissful minutes.

'Jonathan, wake up.'

I prise open my eyes and watch dismayed, as my cocoon is deconstructed in front of me. I claw at the retreating cover but it's too late, it's already down to my ankles.

'Get up, it's 21:00 hours. *It's time.*'

I peer out through sleep-encrusted eyes at Naomi looming over me.

'You didn't find Sarah, then?' she says, as if confirming something she suspected.

'What time did you say, it was?'

She doesn't answer, knowing that I heard the first time. With every part of my body craving more sleep, I sit up and push myself to my feet, suppressing a yawn. *I didn't find Sarah.*

Twenty minutes later and we're in the elevator going down to the City. Sarah's absence presses in on me, like a heavy weight on my chest, and I fight to draw in breath.

'Stuart's unlocked the Ascendor,' Fearne says, her voice full of admiration.

'Yes,' he says, 'not sure how long it will hold, though.'

'We need to get the other three from Admin,' Naomi says, 'then make our way to the first pod block for evacuation, Food Production. The corridors will be crawling with SRU officers. They know we're in the City somewhere, they'll be searching for us. Tonight is our chance to get as many colonists out as possible, but if we're discovered at the first pod block, it'll be over. There's too many of them to fight.'

'We've got a gun,' Tyler says.

'Yes, and they've got *two*,' I say.

A mechanical sigh signals to us that the elevator has arrived and I feel it jolt to a stop. We wait in silence for the doors to open. When they do, Naomi peers out into the corridor.

'That's odd, I can't see, or hear, *anything*,' she says.

She steps out and the rest of us follow. I look left into the perimeter then right along Corridor F to the esplanade but there's nothing to see. It's quiet, *too* quiet.

'Tyler, Fearne, get the others from Admin and meet us on the top walkway of Food Production,' Naomi says.

We split up. Naomi takes off down the corridor, the rest of us follow, hugging the side wall of the building.

'Sarah's missing,' I say to Stuart, as he comes up beside me.

He stares at me, a confused look on his face.

'No she's not. I helped her down to the City.'

I stop dead and he crashes into my back.

'*What* did you say?'

'I said, I helped Sarah…'

'How?' I say.

'Via the service elevator, I unlocked it. She said that she'd been given instructions to go down there.'

'And you believed her?'

'Yes, I did.'

'When was this?'

He pauses, perhaps sensing the urgency in my voice.

'Stuart, *when*?'

'I don't know…about 18:00 hours. What's wrong?'

'We didn't tell her anything. She's done this on her own.'

'Not *again*,' he says.

'What do you mean, *not again*?'

'She's warned Zack.'

'No, Stuart, I don't believe that,' I say.

But doubt lies at the edge of my words, ready to pounce.

'I don't believe it,' I repeat, trying to convince myself.

When we reach the stairs to the pod walkways, the others have already made their way up to the top.

'Right, we'll do it a walkway at a time,' Naomi says. 'Get them out of the pods and we'll take them to the elevator in batches of twenty. Fearne take the list of SRU pods and identify them as we go.'

I swing round at the sound of footsteps on the stairs behind me, Oli appears holding the gun at her side, followed by Oscar and Sherryl.

'Can someone else take this thing, I'm fed up with lugging it around,' Oli says, thrusting it into Stuart's arms.

'The place we need to guard, *at all costs*, is the Maintenance elevator,' Naomi says, turning to one of the SRU rebels, behind her.

'Lukas, take charge of the gun and go with Stuart. We'll need four people spread out in the corridor to encourage the evacuees on their way, keep them moving.'

'I'll go,' I say, 'Oli, Tyler, Kyle, come with me.'

Ten minutes later and we're in position down Corridor F, with me nearest to the elevator. I signal to Stuart standing between its open doors. In front of him, Lukas stands, with the gun poised ready, his eyes darting from side to side looking for movement. The lack of SRU officers is unusual, unnerving. I spot the first batch of pod evacuees running across the corridor towards Oli. One by one, they stumble forward, wrapped in their covers, water bottles clasped in their hands. As they pass me, I hurry them along to the elevator, directing them with my hands. The last of the batch, a young girl of novice age, stands on the corner of her cover that trails on the floor beside her, staggers to the side and almost falls. She puts a hand up to the wall to steady herself then hoists the cover up higher onto her shoulders and scurries after the others. She spots the SRU officer brandishing the gun and slows down.

'Keep going, it's fine, you'll be fine,' I say, giving her a gentle push, as she passes.

I soon lose count of how many batches have passed me. They file down the corridor, cloaked figures with guarded eyes but compliant, still. Despite the unfamiliarity of the situation, they trust us to look after them, as they've been looked after, for their entire lives. But the responsibility weighs heavily on me.

After about an hour, a signal travels down the corridor towards me to say that all the Food Production pods have been evacuated. I watch as the last of them enter the elevator and go up to the Council Chamber then I turn back to the corridor. Naomi and the other SRU rebels run down it towards me. Oli, Kyle and Tyler join them as they pass.

'Right,' Naomi says, reaching me, 'I can't believe it but that's the whole of that pod block evacuated and *still* no sign of the Fulcrum. So we carry on to the next, the Nursery & Kindergarten block.

She marches off in the direction of the perimeter, the others following.

'Something's not right,' I say to Stuart.

Kyle shouts something, behind me, that I don't catch. I turn and see a figure moving from the esplanade towards us, *Marilyn*. She has her hands clamped to either side of her head, as if it might explode. As she approaches, I can pick out her features. But they look, like I've never seen them before, twisted by fear, pain. No, not that, something else. She glances over her shoulder as if she's being chased but there's no one there. And then I know what it is, the look...in her eyes...contorting her features. I know what it is she's running from. It's *guilt*.

Chapter 47

19/06/3042   18:01 hours
SARAH

I feel bad about tricking Stuart when he was starting to trust me again. But I had to get down to the City, find Marilyn, find out what's, going on. Something must be wrong. It's out of character for her to act this way. I shift my position in the cramped space, shuffle round releasing the foot that's trapped under my left leg. It bangs, lifeless, into the door. Then it hits me, the flaw in my plan. How am I going to get out? It's gone 17:30, they'll be no one in Food Production, *no one*. As the chute slows then stops, I fight back the rising panic inside me. Stuart will realise the mistake. He'll bring me back up to the Council Chamber. But, as the seconds then the minutes pass, I know that he's gone, preoccupied by preparations for the evacuation and the pretty Fearne.

The chute feels smaller now, its metal walls pressing in on me in a terrifying embrace. I want to get out. I want to get out, now. I consider banging the door but what's the point, there's no one there. But then I hear something, a faint noise from the other side. I press my right ear against the metal focusing on the sound. A rustle, a movement. Someone's there. I raise my hand up ready to thump on the door then stop. It could be anyone out there. But does it matter who it is? My hand, clenches into a fist, as the doors start to open. I stare at them, fascinated, as air from the Food Production Unit, wafts in and brushes against the side of my face. Through the widening gap, I make out the torso of a person standing in front of the chute, packets of food in their hands. Their head is above the top edge of the chute door and I realise that they can't see me. The packets are thrust forward into the chute and a hand pushes into my arm. There's a gasp and the body lurches backwards away from me. The packets fall to the floor and I scramble out after them, my left foot losing its purchase, as it lands on something slippery beneath me. Then we're face to face in the blackness, our rapid breathing in unison.

'So, you're Zack's contact in Food Production,' I say.

I get no answer because, whoever it is, turns and runs.

'I know who you are,' I lie, shouting after them.

As my eyes adjust to the dark, I make out the solid shapes of the workbenches ranging out in front of me. I step out of the sticky mess under my feet and crouch down. Scooping the food off the floor, I put a handful in my mouth and chew, knowing that any floor in the Food Production Unit will be pristine, germ free. Then I remember that my feet, which have trampled over the food, are not. The skeletons of the death pit come into my mind and I spit the contents of my mouth out onto the floor, in disgust. I push the food sideways into a heap with my foot and step forward. Then I see them, packet after packet of food, lined up on the workbench in front of me. I reach my hand out to grab one but I'm distracted by the sound of someone approaching from the door. I dive under the workbench, pushing myself up against the side panel and clutch my knees up against my chest.

I listen as they walk along the gap in the workbenches behind me, then stop. I can feel their presence so close to me now. I want to turn, but daren't. Instead, I tense every muscle, every nerve in my body and focus on the spot where the person is standing. I hear the sound of food packets being opened then, after a few seconds, closed again. They're methodical, working their way down the bench. They move across to the food chute and I hear, what I think is, the sound of packets being loaded into it. After several trips, they finish. The doors to the food chute close then they walk past the workbench again and away from me. I stay where I am until I'm sure they've gone, wait a few seconds then crawl out from my hiding place. As I thought, all the food packets have been removed from the workbench and placed in the food chute, ready for collection. I decide to leave them where they are and think about my options. I can go out into the corridors and risk being spotted, or stay here until the Silence then go in search of Marilyn. Tiredness wins. I crawl back under the workbench and lie down. The minute my head hits the floor, I'm asleep.

My eyes flicker open and I stare about me, disorientated by my unfamiliar surroundings. It takes me a while to work out where I am. I don't know how long I've been asleep but the stiffness in my back and the crick in my neck, indicate that it must be hours, not minutes. I yawn, then shuffle out of my den on all fours. Walking over to the food chute, I press the button and the doors slide apart. It's empty. Hunger gripping me, I feel around the bottom of it, hoping that something's been left. But they've been thorough, taken everything. That means that it's late, gone 21:30 hours. I close the chute doors and, using my hands as buffers, weave my way through the workbenches to the door and out into the night corridor.

Outside, the perimeter is deserted. Marilyn could be anywhere. At the entrance to Corridor A that runs between the Pharmacy and the Museum & Archive buildings, I dart across and run down its length. The eerie, unnatural silence is worrying me. I haven't seen a single SRU officer. When I reach the end of the corridor, I slow down and peer out into the esplanade. The Solarium is shrouded in the black of night time. The only sound to be heard is the rush of water from the sprinkler system, inside. I hesitate before stepping out into the gloom then make my way along the back of the Museum & Archive building, keeping close to the pod block, looking about me as I go. Every nerve in my body is buzzing, alert and waiting. Part of me wishes that something would happen, *anything*, to release the tension, I feel, as I creep forward. Then I spot something a few metres ahead of me. Not something, *someone*, lying on the floor near Door 3 of the Solarium. I look up and down the esplanade then move towards them.

It's an SRU officer, prostrate on his back. I see

from his badge that his name is Niall. I jump in surprise, when I notice that his eyes are wide open, staring up at me. But there's no movement there. Beyond him, I see more of them about ten metres further down the esplanade, groups of two or three. I dart from one to another but everywhere I'm met with the same unblinking eyes, wide with fear, staring out from frozen bodies. There are twenty to thirty in this area, alone. Most are lying flat on their backs, some slumped against the outside wall of the Solarium's transition chamber. All are motionless, all caught in the grip of a death-like stillness. Ahead of me, I spot a movement. It surprises me, because it looks so alien, amongst all this stillness. There's a person standing with their back to me, over a group of three SRU officers lying on the floor. They're shouting, spitting out sharp, angry words from their mouth. But that's not all, the person's right foot jerks back and forwards, kicking into the bodies with a violent frenzy.

'This is what it feels like,' I hear them scream, their foot pounding into flesh, 'to be helpless, trapped inside a paralysed body, at the mercy of savages like you.'

Through the distortion of rage, I know that the voice belongs to, Marilyn. She moves across to one of the others, spits onto his face then starts the kicking again.

'Marilyn, what are you doing?' I scream, running up behind her.

She swings round, her face pinched with hatred, eyes wild. Only the voice is recognisable, as my friend. I look down at the bodies at our feet. Zack, Sean and Jevon stare up at me, their eyes pleading for help.

'What have you *done*?'

'Nothing they haven't done to others,' she says defiantly, 'I put it in their food, the rape drug.'

'It was *you* in the Food Production Unit,' I say, but she's not listening.

She's gone far beyond listening, beyond reasoned thought.

'I did it for the Colony...for the evacuation and...for all the poor girls who have suffered at their hands.'

I crouch down beside Zack, keeping my eyes away from his, unable to bear the stunned look there. I pull up his tunic top. A row of red-blue marks run up the side of his body. I brush a fingertip along his bottom rib and feel the jutting edges of a break there.

'You didn't have to do *this*,' I say 'did you?'

She stares at the battered body, a puzzled look on her face, as if it has nothing to do with her.

'*Did* you, Marilyn?'

'Yes, I did,' she screams, 'I *did*.'

Then she takes off down the corridor and disappears from sight.

Chapter 48

Overtaken by a crippling exhaustion, I look up and the corridor swims around me, in a fuzz haze of dirty orange light. Marilyn's taken over from Stuart at the Maintenance elevator, so that he can co-ordinate the final stage of the evacuation, up to the tunnel. I raise my head again, slowly this time, and glance towards her. She's not herself. Not since she ran towards me last night, with Sarah close behind, her face riddled with guilt and shame. I haven't been able to get a word from her. But, if it weren't for her actions, disabling the Fulcrum members with drugs, we wouldn't have got the colonists up to the Council Chamber. The plan was too ambitious. But she made it work, with one stroke of genius. So, why is Sarah so guarded about it? Why does she keep giving Marilyn those looks of *what*…concern…fear? Why did Marilyn remain silent throughout Sarah's explanation of what had happened?

The last stragglers from the Pharmacy pod block shuffle past me. I gave up cajoling them on their way, hours ago. Now, all I can manage is a grunt, a shove in the right direction. My brain is too fuzzy with lack of sleep, my body too heavy, to engage in niceties. Their blank eyes, dulled by sleep and the Supplement, give me only a cursory glance as they make their way to the elevator. Then I catch a movement to my right and swing round. The corridor rushes past me in a blur and I throw my arm out to the wall to steady myself. I lean against it, feeling vulnerable, waiting for my vision to clear. When it does, I see Naomi and the other SRU rebels trotting towards me. How can they look that fresh, that awake?

'That's the lot,' Naomi says, as she comes up beside me, still breathing steadily, 'thanks to Marilyn. We've checked the esplanade and they're all still there, although I did spot movement from a number of them. It won't be long before they're functioning again. So we need to concentrate on getting colonists up to the tunnel.'

Naomi makes her way towards the elevator. We take that as a cue to follow her. Lukas brings up the rear and, holding the gun ready in front of him, edges backwards, his eyes scanning the corridor from left and right as he goes.

'Hurry up Lukas,' Naomi snaps, pulling him into the elevator and pressing the button.

I notice the shadow of resentment in his look. She's taken charge of the SRU rebels, in fact, she's taken charge of the whole evacuation. She's a strategist, a quick thinker. That's what we need now but, it seems that not everyone is convinced of her leadership qualities. The elevator jolts to a stop and we file out. The corridor outside is full of colonists. Some sit huddled against the walls their covers wrapped around them, others are on the floor asleep. We step over the complaining bodies on our way to the administration building. A disorderly queue spreads from the entrance doors, along the façade of the building and down the corridor, in both directions. Oli and Kyle are at the head of the queues, trying to restore some order.

'How's it going?' I shout to Oli, as she pushes another two through the doors.

'I was before them,' a sallow-skinned boy with angular eyebrows, whines.

Oli steps towards him and pushes her face into his.

'*I* decide who's next,' she says, 'not *you*?'

His mouth clamps shut and he hoists his cover over his shoulders, avoiding her glare.

'I'm not sure how much more I can take of this,' she says, in a voice that's designed to be heard. 'It's going to take hours to get them up to the tunnel. Meanwhile, we have to listen to *that*,' she says.

'Can we get through,' Naomi shouts from behind me.

'Help yourself,' Oli says, a hint of sarcasm creeping into her voice.

She pushes one side of the queue back, Kyle does the same with the other and we hurry through the gap they've created.

'Are you alright, Marilyn?' I hear Kyle say, but she doesn't reply, doesn't even glance in his direction.

'Marilyn,' he calls after her, but she's not stopping.

Inside, it's not a lot better. There are people ranged along every corridor.

'Have you got any food rations,' one girl says,

grabbing my arm as I pass.

I shake her hand off.

'They'll be plenty of time to eat when you get out, up to the surface,' I say.

She looks away and, at once, I feel like a bully. They have no idea what's going on, they're hungry and scared. The damage done, I continue down the corridor. Ahead of us, Stuart is loading a group of colonists into the Ascendor. A young girl at the front is clutching onto the sides of the doors.

'No, I don't want to!' she screams.

Fearne tries to unhook her hands from the doors but she won't be moved. Stuart stares at her, dazed, unsure what to do. I can see that he's exhausted.

'Go and get some rest, Stuart,' I say, my hand on his shoulder, 'I'll take over for a bit.'

His eyes, full of gratitude, shoot up to mine then return to their previous state of tired resignation.

'It's alright, I'll stay for a while longer.'

I step towards the girl, still clinging with clawed hands onto the door. Her panic filters along the queue behind her and an exchange of nervous looks and whispered concerns, run along its length.

'There's nothing to be afraid of,' I say, 'I promise.'

She glances up at me, unconvinced.

'I've been up there myself and look, I'm fine,' I say, louder than necessary trying to calm those waiting.

Her left hand loosens its grip a little then, let's go.

'That's it,' I say, 'in you go.'

She peels her other hand off the door and steps in

joining the others already inside.

'See you soon,' I say, as the door closes on them.

'We could do with some sedatives to calm some of them,' Stuart says, 'keep them moving. Could you have a word with Marilyn, see if she can get hold of some for us?'

'What's the matter?' he says, seeing my expression change.

'Something happened to Marilyn last night.'

'What?'

'I don't know, I can't get any sense out of her but I think Sarah's got something to do with it.'

'I thought she'd be pleased with what she did. Look how many we've got up here in one night.'

'I know, but she's not.'

'To be honest, Jonathan, I've got more pressing things to think about than that.'

'What?' I ask, recognising that look.

This is serious. He guides me over to a quiet corner of the room, leaving Fearne to organise the colonists.

'I'm worried,' he says, '*very* worried.'

'About what?' I say.

'The system.'

'The system?' I say, knowing that I won't be able to speed up his methodical delivery, however many questions I ask.

'Yes, the computer system, I think we're overloading it.'

'Why do you think that?'

'I've been going down and checking on it. I'm no expert,' he says, 'but I think that the unusual activity that's been generated, particularly the intruder alerts, is taking its toll.'

'But it's been running the Colony for centuries without a problem.'

'Yes, but only maintaining routine tasks, familiar processes. Now, in a matter of days, it's forced to deal with an unprecedented level of activity, including attempts to hack into its systems. It should never have lasted this long, Jonathan. It should have failed centuries ago.'

'Is it going to *fail*?'

'Maybe.'

'I know what your "maybes" mean, Stuart. It's going to fail, isn't it?'

'Yes, I think it is,' he says, glancing behind him.

'And what would that mean?'

'It would mean disaster, Jonathan, *disaster*.'

Chapter 49

20/06/3042   08:24 hours
SARAH

I look across at Marilyn, wedged in the corner of the elevator, as far away from me as possible, her eyes fixed to a point on the back wall.

'Do we all know what we're doing?' Naomi says.

There's a murmur, perhaps of agreement, it's difficult to tell. It's clear from Marilyn's lack of response that she hasn't realised anyone's speaking.

'*Marilyn*,' Naomi says, a note of irritation in her voice.

'What?' she says, noticing that all eyes are on her.

'It's important that we all understand the plan. It's not going to be as straightforward as last night, so you need to concentrate.'

'If it wasn't for *me*…there would have been no *last night*.'

'I know, and we're grateful for what you did, but you need to focus now on today. Do you even know what's happening?'

'Not really,' Marilyn whispers.

'Right, for *Marilyn's* benefit, I'll explain again. We've evacuated the pod blocks. They'll gradually make their way up to the tunnel but it's going to take a long time.'

'What about the children inside the Nursery & Kindergarten building?' Marilyn asks.

There's a stunned silence. Several sets of eyes

look in Naomi's direction, with amused interest.

'*Remember*, Marilyn,' I say, trying to deflect Naomi's attention from her, 'we're starting *that* now.'

'You haven't listened to a word I've said, have you, Marilyn. Well, Sarah will have to give you the details, I'm not going over it *again*.'

She turns her back on Marilyn, dismissing her with a shake of her head.

'What about the skeleton crew we've left in the Power Station?' Anton asks.

'Yes, good question, they will need to keep power to the Colony right to the end. I suppose that they'll be the last to go,' Naomi says, as the elevator reaches the City and stops.

We step out into Corridor F and make off towards the Nursery & Kindergarten. Marilyn and I are co-ordinating things at the elevator. That's the plan, anyway.

'Are you alright, Marilyn,' I say, as we're left alone in the corridor.

I place the toolbox on the floor beside me.

'Don't keep asking, Sarah, I've told you, I'm fine, apart from this maintenance tunic, it's too tight.'

'At least I had the foresight to realise that you needed one,' I say, folding my arms tight across my chest. 'I had to guess your size. I'm sorry I didn't get it right but I was under a bit of pressure at the time and you aren't any help.'

'Why are you so angry with me, Sarah?'

'I'm *not*.'

'What I did last night, I did it for all the girls that

have suffered at their hands. You have no idea, what they would have gone through, how scared they would be.'

'I have though, Marilyn.'

'*You*?' she whispers.

'No, not *me*, Beatrice,' I say. 'Sean and Jevon were... I don't think I will ever forget the look of terror in her eyes.'

'They deserved everything I did to them, *everything*. Surely you understand?'

'But Zack didn't...'

'Zack didn't *what*?'

I look down at my feet. Now I know why I feel guilty.

'Don't think I didn't notice, Sarah, the way you flew to his side. The way you looked at me, as if I'd injured someone you cared about.'

'No, that's not ...'

But I can't continue, I can't explain my actions to her, to anybody. A wall of silence builds between us as she stares down the corridor.

'Marilyn, tell me what you're thinking?' I say.

She doesn't get a chance to reply, or not, because two SRU rebels, Anton and Callum turn into the corridor from the perimeter.

'Naomi says that they're ready to start evacuating the older children,' Anton says, 'they'll travel along the Jojo. We'll escort them from there down Corridor F to the elevator. It'll be up to you two to load them in and get them up to the Council Chamber. Is that clear?'

I nod. He glances at Marilyn. She doesn't bother

to reply. He turns and makes his way to the perimeter.

'I'll go and make sure their ready up there,' Marilyn says, putting Stuart's ID code into the console.

I keep watch, scanning the corridor for SRU officers. I'm alone, with only the toolbox for company and my guilt. I shuffle from foot to foot, not sure what to do. Then I hear a noise behind me, indistinct and low. I glance round and watch as two SRU officers stagger up from the esplanade towards me, leaning against each other for support. As they pass, I crouch down and open the toolbox, pulling out the only thing I recognise amongst all the unfamiliar objects. I hope they don't stop, don't ask me what I'm doing.

The elevator returns and the doors swish open, making me jump. When I look behind me up the corridor to the perimeter, the two SRU officers are too far away, for me to see who they were.

'What *are* you doing,' Marilyn says, staring at the screwdriver in my hand.

'Nothing,' I say, 'just trying to look convincing, in case...'

'Anything going on?'

'No, it's all quiet. I haven't seen any SRU officers,' I add, not wanting to open old wounds.

She looks up at me.

'Of course, you haven't, they'd all be in their pods by now, recovering.'

'Yes...of course...recovering,' I say.

Over the next hour or so, we get into a slick

routine. The children are excited, treating it as a game, a welcome distraction from their usual routine. They need no encouragement to get into the elevator. For them, this is forbidden territory. Marilyn accompanies them to the Council Chamber, as if she can't bear to be with me. She hasn't once offered to swap roles with me, so I remain in the corridor. There have been no more sightings of SRU officers. Perhaps she's right, they're in their pods but something about the ease with which the plan is going, makes me worried.

As Marilyn steps out into the corridor, I spot the next group of twenty children making their way towards us accompanied by a Kindergarten worker. It's not unusual for groups like this to be walking about the City during the day, so I relax, knowing that they must be one of the last batches left of this age group. One of the children has become separated from the others and trails behind the main group, a girl with mass of curly brown hair. She drifts down the corridor, inhabiting some unseen world of her own. Then her head swings round as if she's heard something behind her.

'*Sarah*,' I hear Marilyn whisper.

I turn round and see Sean, followed by a group of six or seven SRU officers, running towards us from the esplanade. I swing round, thinking about escape but a similar group is coming down from the perimeter, led by Zack and Jevon. *And Jevon has a gun*. They pass the Kindergarten group, without a second glance, their eyes on us.

'Quick!' I scream, grabbing Marilyn by the hand

and hauling her into the elevator. I stab at the button but not fast enough. Sean throws his body between the doors, as they start to close.

'Out!' he shouts.

He shoves me in the back and I stagger forward, stopping in front of Zack. Jevon has the gun pointing at my chest. Behind me, I hear Marilyn cry out with pain. She emerges, clutching her left cheek, a patch of red forming beneath her fingertips. I see the Kindergarten group turn and run back to the perimeter.

'What's going on, Sarah?' Zack says, glancing behind him, noticing my gaze.

I remain silent. His eyes have lost their sharpness, dulled by the after effects of the chemicals.

'*Well*?'

He turns to Marilyn.

'What about you…Marilyn?'

She eyes him warily.

'Yes…I know who you are, *now*. Last night, I was a little puzzled, as you kicked the life out of me, *Councillor*. Nothing to say?'

He looks back at me.

'I assume that because *she's* with you, that you made it to the Council Chamber. But, what I don't understand, Sarah, is why you were there last night. Perhaps, you could explain.'

Let him come to any conclusions he wants, I'm not saying anything.

'Where's the gun?' he barks.

'Up in the Council Chamber,' Marilyn says.

'Have you got others?'

'…Yes,' I say, but with too much hesitation.

He glances at Jevon. 'What do you think?'

Jevon nods. 'Let's do it.'

Zack grabs my arm and pushes me back into the elevator. Jevon puts the gun to Marilyn's head and directs her behind me. Zack orders six of the officers to stay behind, the rest pile in with us. The doors close.

'Up!' Zack shouts.

Chapter 50

20/06/3042   10:55 hours
JONATHAN

'Did you see that?' Oli says.

She's perched on the workbench, her legs swinging backwards and forwards, the gun resting across her thighs.

'What?' I say.

'The lights, they keep dimming.'

'I haven't noticed,' I say, keeping my eyes on the surveillance screens. 'Aren't you supposed to be guarding the elevator?' I add, hoping she'll get the hint.

'I got bored. The first three hours were the worst,' she says, laughing, 'wave after wave of whining colonists. You'd think they'd be a bit more grateful. Then, when the first of the children arrived, I thought I'd take a break.'

I grunt in response.

'You could take your eyes off *her* for a minute and talk to me,' she says.

'I need to keep watch, make sure everything's OK.'

'How many SRU officers have you seen, exactly?'

'None, as you well know, but that isn't the point.'

She shuts up. She's quiet for the best part of two minutes, before she starts again.

'It's all been a bit cool, hasn't it?'

'*What*?'

'The great reunion.'

I sigh. I know what's coming.

'I thought, as the love of your life, there would be a bit more passion involved. But she seems distant, almost ungrateful.'

'Ungrateful?' I say.

'Yes, considering the danger you put yourself through to get to her.'

'You don't know anything about it, Oli.'

'Maybe not, but if it was me, you'd know how grateful *I* was. There'd be no doubt…'

'No!' I shout, leaping to my feet, the chair crashing backwards onto the floor behind me. 'Zack!'

I point at the screen. Oli slides off the workbench and dives over to me.

'There's what…twelve…fourteen of them?' she gasps.

'Jevon's got a gun,' I say.

I watch, horrified, as he points it at Sarah.

'She might be able to convince Zack that she's still on his side,' Oli says.

'How would she do *that*?'

'She's done it before,' she says, shrugging.

'They're getting into the elevator.'

'Jevon's got the gun at Marilyn's head,' Oli says, 'what a thug.'

'They're coming up, *quick*'

I make for the door.

'We have to warn the others,' she says, as we jump over the waiting bodies of colonists in the corridors and sprint to the administration block.

'We haven't got time,' I shout.

We swing into the connecting corridor between the administration building and the health centre and charge along the back of the computer building, screaming at colonists to move out of the area, as we go. They seem reluctant to give up their hard fought for territories and stare at us, with a puzzled lack of concern. As we approach the elevator, I see straight away that we're too late. The SRU officers are standing outside it. Jevon still has the gun at Marilyn's head, enjoying her terror. Sean has Sarah's arm twisted up her back. They look about, confused, unable to make sense of what they see. The colonists in the corridor haven't moved. They must think that this is all part of the evacuation. Why wouldn't they, one SRU officer is the same as any other to them. Jevon pulls Sarah's arm further up her back. She jerks backwards, face creased with pain. Then she spots me. Her attention caught for a little too long. Zack notices and follows the direction of her gaze. He peers through the dim lighting of the corridor then moves towards me, growing recognition in his eyes.

'*Jonathan*?' he says, when he's about five metres away from me. '*What*…I don't understand.'

'Don't come any closer, Zack, or we'll shoot,' I say.

'*We*?' he says.

I look behind me. Oli, and the gun, are gone.

'Ever delusional,' he says. 'How can you possibly be alive? Where's the Council? What are this lot

315

doing here?'

He waves a hand at a group of huddled colonists, staring up at him. He hasn't worked out what's going on. He's trying hard to hide it but there's a shadow of real fear in his eyes. He doesn't understand and that's scaring him.

'Too many questions, Zack, which one do you want answered first?'

'Just take us to the Council. But I'm warning you, Jonathan, if you try anything clever, *anything* at all, we'll shoot Marilyn's head off and that's going to make such a mess of this corridor.'

He manoeuvres behind me then shoves me in the back towards the elevator.

'Grab him,' Zack says to two of the officers.

They take an arm each, their grip so tight that I begin to feel a tingle in my fingers, as it cuts off my blood circulation.

'Jevon, bring her over here,' Zack says, indicating Marilyn, 'she's our bargaining tool.'

Jevon pokes the butt of the gun into the back of her head. She gasps and I can see, even from this distance that she's shaking. Sarah, still being held fast by Sean, looks angry, defiant. I hope she doesn't do anything stupid.

'Which way?' Zack says.

I point in the direction of the Solarium dome. I haven't got a clue where I'm taking them, but that way seems as good as any other. We start off down the corridor. The few lights that are still working flicker on and off, for a second. It happens so fast, that I think I might have imagined it.

'What's going on?' Zack says, staring up at one as he goes.

'Your computer hacking activities have started to take their toll, Zack,' I say, 'even up here.'

'Shut up and keep moving,' he barks but I can sense his increasing anxiety.

We take a few more steps and it happens again. This time, the lights stay off for longer.

'How much further is it?' Zack says, as they flicker on again.

'Not far,' I lie, as the corridor is plunged into darkness.

I wait for the lights to come back on, but they don't. Taking advantage of their disorientation, I twist my body out of their grasp, turn and stagger back the way we came, my arms out in front of me, groping out into the blackness. I only manage a few metres before my feet come up against a soft bundle. My balance deserts me and I fall forward, landing on top of it. There's a surprised cry beneath me. I crawl over the complaining mound and my hands touch the cold of the floor. Scurrying forward, on all fours, I reach out my hand and feel a solid surface in front of me that could be the side wall. I make my way along it with my hands, pressing my body against the hard surface to guide me. After negotiating two more bodies, my fingers slide around a corner and I guess that I've reached the perimeter corridor. I ease my body around it and follow the front of the building, on my feet now. I edge my way along. Then the lights flash back on. I'm only metres from the entrance of the health centre. I glance both ways then make a dash for it. Half way across, I hear a ricochet of gunfire to my right. I push through the doors and dive onto the floor of the foyer, out of view.

Lying flat on the ground, I wait. All I can hear is the pounding of my heart and my staggered breathing. Nothing else. After a while, curiosity gets the better of me. Getting to my feet, I creep towards the entrance. Through the half-glazed door, I peer out into the corridor. A number of colonists wander about, aimless, unsupervised. Their eyes dart back and forth, they clutch at their covers, wrapping them tighter around their hunched shoulders, lost, unsure of what to do. I push open one side of the entrance doors and look out. I can't see any SRU officers, so I slide my body through the opening and out into the corridor. A boy stands hunched, opposite me. He looks up but loses interest in me, when he realises that I have nothing to offer him. Then his eyes move behind me. Something has caught his attention. I feel something hard being pushed into the centre of my back.

Then there's a click.

Chapter 51

20/06/3042   12:03 hours
SARAH

I stare at Jevon's back, broad and muscled and consider my options. With every step, Sean's grip on my right arm gets tighter, as if he's trying to cut it in two with his fingers. It's pointless, struggling, I've tried. It only made things worse. I can't see Marilyn, Jevon's body is obscuring my view but I know she's at breaking point, I saw it in her eyes. This could push her over the edge. The lights flicker on and off again. A wall of black uniform looms up, only centimetres from my face, as Jevon slows his pace. My hands go up to stop myself colliding with his back but he speeds up again. His shoulders are tense, his head swings from side to side as if he's expecting trouble. Sean tugs at my arm to get me moving and I feel a shoot of pain as he twists it out of alignment.

'You're hurting me,' I say.

'Good, now *move*,' he grunts, wrenching my arm up even further.

I do what I'm told and stumble forward fighting back tears. I wonder where Jonathan is taking us. He can't keep up this deception for much longer. Zack's not stupid, he'll work out that there's no Council.

Then the lights flash off. We're plunged into darkness. It takes me a few seconds to realise that they're not coming back on again. Sean's grip on my arm loosens and I take my chance. Pulling my arm from his hand, I turn into him. My knee thrusts upward and makes contact. He cries out in pain and I sense him backing away from me…hear his groan. Whichever part of his body I hit, it's got him off me. There's a crash as something heavy, metallic, falls to the ground in front of me.

'Marilyn,' I call out into the black void.

'Over here,' she says.

I stretch my arms out in front of me as a buffer and creep forward feeling the air with my fingers.

'Marilyn,' I say, trying to locate her.

A hand clasps mine, squeezes it then pulls me in. I come up against a body and throw my arms around it, holding on with all my strength, everything forgotten, except our friendship.

'I'm sorry,' I whisper, resting my head against her hair.

'Come on,' she says pulling me forward.

I have no idea what direction we're facing but it doesn't matter. We have to get as far away from them as we can before the lights come back on. I try not to think about the possibility that they might never come back on.

We stumble forward, Marilyn taking the lead. I sense that we're in the middle of the corridor but I can't be sure. All I know is that I can hear frightened voices on either side of us, where people have remained huddled against the walls. Marilyn's body jolts back into mine and I hear her cry out in surprise, as someone brushes past me with a frightened whimper. Still the lights stay off. We're making faster progress now and I can make out

Marilyn's shape in front of me as my eyes accustom to the dark. Then she stops and lurches forward. It feels like her feet are glued to the floor. I fall onto her curved back and put my arms around her to stop myself from toppling sideways.

'What is it?' I say.

Moving to Marilyn's side, I put my hands out in front of me. We seem to be up against a barrier about a metre high. I follow the top edge with my fingers then it comes to an end but, moving a little to my right, I pick it up again.

'The Jojo,' I say.

The lights flash back on. We freeze, feeling exposed. A clatter of gunfire reverberates behind us.

'Quick,' I shout.

I dive through the gap and flatten myself on the floor. Marilyn tumbles in on top of me. Despite her weight, I shift forward using my elbows to make room for her. She rolls off me, onto the floor. Shuffling round so that we can look out of the gap, we lie side by side, our breathing shallow and fast.

'What's going on,' I whisper.

I peer over Marilyn's shoulder into the dimness of the perimeter corridor. I can make out the entrance to the connecting corridor a little to our right and beyond that, the elevator. There are a lot of people around it. Some stand, others sit, one or two move away from us, uncertainty slowing their pace.

'Can you make out who's there?' I ask.

'No, there's not enough light.'

'We need to get to the Ascendor, warn Stuart.'

'I know,' Marilyn says.

We turn ourselves around again and crawl along the Jojo. Every time we get to a gap, I turn my head left to check it's safe to cross. After a few minutes, we reach the gap in the barrier that's opposite the entrance to the administration building. I scurry across it on all fours and crouch. Marilyn stays put, kneeling opposite me. We peer out. There are evacuated colonists everywhere now but no sign of Zack, or any of the other SRU officers.

'Ready?' I say.

I give the signal and we fly out from the Jojo and across the perimeter corridor, dodging drifting colonists as we go. We push through the entrance doors and fall headlong into the foyer. I charge down the corridor with Marilyn close behind me. The first thing I notice is that there are no colonists, anywhere. We reach the door to the Ascendor room. Something, the quiet, makes us pause. I put my ear up against the door and listen. I hear low voices but can't make out any words.

'What's happening?' Marilyn says.

'I don't know. Are we going in, or not?'

'We have to,' she says, her finger poised over the button, 'we have no choice.'

I nod. She stabs at it, the door glides open and we step inside. The only thing I see is the gun directed right at us, nothing else. Marilyn's hand, damp with fear, finds mine.

'I thought that door was locked.'

I glance up. Oli stands in front of us, the gun in her hands. Someone runs across to the door and we hear a faint click as it's locked behind us.

'Well, well,' she says, 'this is what it feels like, Sarah, to have a gun pointing at your chest.'

She steps forward and my heart almost stops dead. I gasp air into my lungs, my eyes fixed on the barrel of the gun, nothing else in the room visible to me.

'Unpleasant, isn't it?'

She lowers the gun and turns away from us. She's made her point. I let out the breath I've been holding then my knees melt and I keel over sideways onto Marilyn, her body preventing me from crashing onto the floor.

'*Jevon*,' Marilyn says.

I look up and see a group waiting by the Ascendor. Oli has the gun trailed on them now and, one of them, is Jevon. Confusion and fear dull his features. Two more of the SRU officers are in front of him. I spot Stuart standing by the Ascendor door.

'It's moving again,' he says, looking at the console lights, 'it must have got stuck on the way back down because of the power cut.'

The silence in the room is intense now, so much so, that the hum as the Ascendor arrives seems loud. Stuart presses a button and the doors open.

'Stuart, what's going on?' I say.

'We're sending them up,' he says, 'like the others.'

'Best place for them,' Oli says, 'let them burn.'

'*Please*,' Jevon says, 'don't...'

'*In*,' Oli shouts, shoving the gun into Jevon's back.

'No, *please*,' he screams, being forced to push the

other two into the Ascendor.

His hands grip the sides of the doorway, knuckles white with terror. He's crying now, strangled sobs catching in his throat. The faces of the other two are held by a silent scream, as they press their bodies up against the back of the Ascendor.

'*Tell* them' I shout, 'for pity's sake, tell them!'

But she's not listening.

'Let go of the doors, Jevon, or you die here.'

She thrusts the gun at him as his grip on the doorway loosens and he staggers inside. He turns to face her. Then, pinning him inside with the gun, she shouts at Stuart to close the doors. Three sets, of traumatised eyes disappear behind it.

'It's alright,' I shout, 'you'll be alright!'

But it's too late. The doors are already shut. There's not a sound, not a single sound, in the room.

'That was cruel,' I say, breaking the silence.

Oli swings round, her eyes dark with revenge.

'It's what they deserve,' she says, defiant.

Marilyn gasps at the words…*her* words.

'What have we become?' she whispers.

Chapter 52

20/06/3042　12:15 hours
JONATHAN

'So, you weren't delusional after all,' I hear Zack say behind me. 'Now, turn round…slowly.'

'I don't know what you're talking about,' I say, facing him.

'Your friend, the crazy girl with the gun, she turned up to rescue you but she didn't get the timing right. You'd disappeared. I assume Sarah, and that vicious girl, the Councillor, are with you?'

Sarah and Marilyn escaped. I stay silent, hiding my relief.

'Sean, give me the gun and check the building,' he says. 'Where's Jevon?'

'I don't know. I grabbed the gun off the floor and ran after you. I assumed he was following.'

'If you had the gun, why didn't you stop her?'

'I didn't like the look in her eyes. She meant it, Zack, I could tell.'

'So you ran off?'

Sean gives Zack a look. A look, I can't read.

'Why did *you* run off, Zack?' he says.

'I didn't have the gun, Sean.'

Sean holds his glare, but doesn't comment.

'I wouldn't waste your time,' I say.

'What?'

Zack takes his eyes away from Sean's and transfers them to me.

'I wouldn't waste your time searching the building, they're not here.'

'And why should I believe that?'

'Believe what you like, but they're both safe, somewhere you can't get at them.'

I notice a furrow between his brows that I haven't seen before.

'Where is she?' he says.

'Who?'

'Stop playing games, Jonathan…Sarah.'

'Zack, we need to get out of here. They might have more weapons and without the others…'

'*Shut* up, Sean,' Zack says then turns his attention back on me.

'Tell me where she is or I'll…'

'Or you'll *what*…kill me? Then you'll never know, will you?'

'Zack, we should go *now*,' Sean says, scanning the area around us.

'Right, move,' Zack says, indicating the corridor, with a flick of his head.

'Where are we going?' I say.

He hesitates.

'Back to the City…to get reinforcements. You lead the way, in case your friend turns up again.'

We walk back along the front of the health centre towards the administration building. I'm in front, with Zack and the gun behind me. Sean hovers at the side, his nervous eyes darting back and forth.

'What's happened to the others?' he says.

'How should I know,' Zack snaps.

'She fired the gun, Zack, I heard it.'

'They're probably dead then,' he says, 'forget them.'

'Is that all you think of your loyal followers, Zack?' I say, edging my way into the crack that's forming between them.

'Shut up and keep moving,' he says, but I know I've hit a nerve.

We continue forward until we reach the entrance to the corridor, then I stop, searching for anyone who might help me.

'Keep going,' Zack says.

As I walk over to the elevator, I notice that it's at this level. I press the button and the doors open. I'm relieved to see that it's empty and wonder what's happened to Naomi and the rest of her team. We get in. It starts to move down.

'How long has this been able to go up to the Council Chamber?' Zack says.

I don't answer.

'I'm talking to you, Jonathan,' he says, raising the gun.

'Look at the console, Zack, it's always been like that, you're just not clever enough to have worked it out, that's all.'

He glares at Sean.

'I checked it,' Sean says, 'the access was locked…I know it was.'

'Well, it's not locked *now*,' I say, grinning at him, 'so maybe you missed something, Sean.'

'You…'

He raises a fist and I brace myself, for the blow that I know is coming my way. But, as he draws his arm back ready to strike, the lights flicker off and on and then, off again. At the same time, I hear a mechanical sigh as the elevator operating system dies and we come to a graceful halt. I tense, aware of the two other bodies in here with me but, most of all, aware of the gun. I can't see it, but I feel its presence in front of me and respect its unseen dominance over me.

'A power failure,' Sean whispers stating the obvious, his voice apprehensive.

'Keep perfectly still, Jonathan,' Zack says, 'don't try anything or I'll use this.'

'Then you're more stupid than I thought. Are you seriously considering firing that weapon in this confined space?'

'Supposing it doesn't start again, we'll be trapped,' Sean says.

I can hear the growing panic in his voice.

'Shut up, Sean,' Zack says.

'Where's the console, where is it?'

I track Sean's movements by his staggered breathing then hear him thumping on the doors, or is it the wall? Neither. I know what he's doing, he's pounding the buttons on the door console.

'Stop that, Sean,' Zack shouts, 'and calm down.'

'We're trapped, you idiot, don't you understand?'

The tension around me is electric, unbearable. Then, the light flickers on and the elevator comes back to life, resuming its way down to the City. Zack, without a word, steps over to Sean and slaps him across the face. His head jerks to the side with the force of it, crashes into the wall, his eyes wide with surprise. Zack returns to his position in front of me and raises the gun to my chest, as if nothing has happened. I glance over at Sean. He stands with his head lowered, eyes on the floor, mute. His mouth is clamped shut, his teeth clenched within it. His jaw muscles shake with the effort that he's applying, to them.

The elevator jolts to a stop and the doors open. Sean steps out first, his eyes still fixed on the ground. Zack pushes me out with the point of the gun and the three of us stand in the deserted corridor. I notice the abandoned toolbox by the doors. The quiet has become an entity in itself. It's as if I could reach out, push my fingers through it and tear it apart.

'Where is everyone,' Zack says, looking around him, 'isn't it lunch break?'

Sean doesn't answer, his rage transformed into a sullen silence. I watch Zack's face as he battles to understand what's happening to his kingdom, his mouth half open, his brow furrowed with concentration. But still he maintains the pretence of a control, he doesn't have.

'Move,' he says.

'I assume we're going to the SRU,' I say.

He stares at me then, as if I've prompted him with my suggestion, he pushes the gun in my back, 'Yes, the SRU.'

We make our way towards the perimeter corridor and turn left. We've gone about fifty metres when I see a figure, a boy, moving towards us, hunched over as if the ceiling is pressing down on his back. He careers wildly about the corridor, dodging imaginary obstacles, as he goes. He's holding something in his hands but not with any conviction. It looks like, whatever it is, has dropped there without his knowledge and he has no idea what to do about it. He's shouting, no not shouting, screaming. I catch a word, "lights". That's when I know that it's Finn. And that he's carrying a gun.

'*Finn*?' Zack says. 'How did he get out?'

'He's got a gun,' I say, in case they haven't noticed.

'*What*?' Zack says, raising his weapon in response to my statement.

'Drop the gun,' he shouts, as Finn approaches.

The lights in the corridor flicker for only a second, no more, but it's enough.

'Don't turn the lights out,' he screams.

Then he's pointing the gun out in front of him, towards Zack.

'Drop the gun, Finn, I'm warning you,' Zack shouts.

But it's too late. I dive to the floor as a clattering barrage of bullets fly over my head.

Chapter 53

20/06/3042   13:01 hours
SARAH

'What's happening down there,' Stuart says, loading another batch into the Ascendor, 'where's Jonathan, Naomi and the rest of them?'

'I don't know,' I say, 'Zack and six other SRU officers forced us up here. Marilyn and I managed to escape them, but Jonathan...he disappeared.'

'Jonathan's *missing*,' Oli says from the door.

I ignore her and keep my eyes fixed on Stuart.

'I don't know how much time we've got left,' he says, guiding me out of earshot of the queue of waiting children.

'What do you mean?'

'The whole system's failing. I need to get down to the lower level of the City, get them out before...'

His voice trails off.

'Before *what*?' Oli says.

I look up surprised, I hadn't noticed her standing there.

'Before...it's too late.'

'I'm coming with you,' I say.

'No, Sarah, it's too dangerous. Besides, you're needed here.'

'I'm coming and that's the end of it.'

'And me,' Marilyn says.

'No, you're not,' Kyle says, 'you're staying here with me.'

Marilyn shoots a look across to him, a look that can't be argued with. He holds it for a couple of seconds then glances down, defeated.

'Kyle,' Stuart says, 'you'll need to take over from me. We have to keep going with the evacuation while we still can, get as many of them up to the tunnel before 14:00 hours.'

'You'll need cover,' Oli says, 'they've got two guns down there. No one will be going *anywhere*, if that elevator isn't guarded.'

'She's right,' Stuart says, 'we've got to keep that access secure.'

'I don't think Zack knows,' I say.

'Knows what?' Oli says.

'I don't think he knows…that there is no Council.'

'That's ridiculous,' she sneers, 'he *must* know.'

'It's not ridiculous, Oli,' I say, 'you weren't there. You didn't see the confusion on his face. He doesn't understand what's going on, I'm convinced.'

'She's right,' Marilyn says, 'I saw it too. We need to take advantage of that fact, stop bickering and *do* something.'

'Fearne help Kyle,' Stuart says, 'Sarah, Marilyn and Oli come with me.'

'No, we can't go via the elevator, they'll be guarding that,' I say, 'we'll have to use the Ascendor. Come on, *move*.'

There's a faint whirring behind us as the Ascendor returns from the tunnel. The minute the doors open, Stuart's inside, despite the expectant surge forward from the children. Marilyn and I follow then Oli, holding the gun down by her side. But when it starts to move, we get a surprise because it's going, *up*.

'No,' Oli screams, banging on the door, '*down!*'

But it makes no difference, we continue on our way to the tunnel. The scene, when the doors open, is complete mayhem. Colonists crowd around the immediate area of the Ascendor, some crying. In front, closest to the doors, is Jevon, his panic infectious. Tyler and Sherryl have hold of his arms in an attempt to restrain him.

'You're safe, calm down,' Sherry shouts.

But he's not listening to her, he's not listening to *anybody*. Instead, at the sight of the open Ascendor, he lunges forward and grabs Stuart by his tunic.

'Get out,' he screams, 'I want to go back down.'

'*You* really don't,' Oli says, from the back.

'You caused this,' I say, swinging round to face her, 'this chaos.'

She shrugs. I grab Stuart's right arm, Marilyn takes his left and we haul him back inside, clearing the doors. Tyler has a hold on Jevon now, but he's struggling to restrain his bulk. The doors click and start to close. The last thing we see, as they do, are Jevon's flashing, desperate eyes.

'Idiot,' Oli mutters behind us.

The Ascendor travels down to the City without stopping at the Council Chamber. I relax a little. Oli looks worried, despite her bravado, the muscles in her back, pressing against mine, tighten. All four of us are doing the impossible and avoiding eye contact. I watch as a bead of perspiration forms on

Stuart's forehead, as we come to a stop. There's an air of expectation, *hope*, as we wait to see if the doors will open. There's no surprise when they don't. It's so quiet, that I hear Marilyn gulp down a mouthful of saliva.

'Open the door,' Oli shouts.

She bangs against it with her left fist, her right, clasps the barrel of the gun that she has resting upright on the floor against her leg.

'It's useless,' Marilyn says, 'no one's there.'

Oli thumps the door again, harder this time.

'Let us out,' she screams.

'Don't,' I say, 'there's no one there.'

'Shut up, will you?' she says, pressing her ear against it.

'Who's there?' a voice says from the other side.

She jumps back, her head banging into mine. Her hand shoots up to her mouth, stifling a gasp, but she doesn't answer.

'Tell them to open the door,' I whisper, sensing her caution, my head throbbing.

'We don't know who it is,' Marilyn says.

'It doesn't *matter*, does it?' Oli says.

She pauses, takes in a breath, then speaks.

'Open up, we've come down from the Council Chamber on official business,' Oli says, addressing the metal door in front of her.

Surprised, we watch as the doors open onto an empty Ceremonial Chamber. Oli pulls the gun up from her side, holds it out in front of her and steps out. A hand grabs her arm. Someone else, wearing the black of an SRU uniform, wrestles the gun out of her hands. Then she's being held, arms behind her back, facing the door.

'Naomi!' I shout.

'Let go of me, you stupid…' Oli says, shaking her off.

I step out and notice, at the periphery of my vision, the rest of the SRU rebels lined up either side of the doors, ready to pounce.

'It's alright, it's us, relax,' I say, holding my hands up in a gesture of submission.

'Sorry,' Naomi says, 'we weren't sure who it was. We saw Zack and the others take you and Marilyn. Are they still up there?'

'We sent Jevon and two others up to the tunnel. We don't know where Zack and Sean are…or Jonathan.'

'We came here because there were too many SRU officers around, we took advantage of the power failure,' Andrea says.

'Stuart, we found this outside the elevator.'

Naomi says, pointing to the toolbox by the wall.

'Thank goodness,' he says, rushing over to it and checking the contents.

'We had to put a hold on the evacuation of the Nursery & Kindergarten. There's still a thousand young children to go and about sixty staff. Apart from them, there's the Fulcrum and the skeleton crew down in the power station.'

'We have to get them out of there,' Stuart says, 'I'll need help.'

'Anton take the toolbox up to the Council Chamber, we can't afford to lose it again,' Naomi says.

She indicates to the others to follow her.

'Right, let's go.'

Outside in the perimeter, all is quiet. The City has lost its daytime lighting, replaced by the amber of the night corridors. Naomi leads the way along the front of the Admin building. She walks, knees bent, the gun ready out in front of her. When she reaches the entrance to Corridor F, she waves her left arm and four of her team charge across to the other side and peer around the corner. Naomi does the same.

'It's clear,' she says, 'let's go.'

She launches off again. We follow, running the short distance to the elevator. Stuart punches in the code.

'Who's coming with me?' Stuart says.

'I will,' I say.

He doesn't argue knowing that there's no point, no time.

'We'll guard the elevator,' Naomi says, 'we'll send two teams out to scour the City for anyone we've missed, get them up to the Council Chamber. Oli, you join Andrea's team. Marilyn you go to the Nursery & Kindergarten, tell them to get ready for their final evacuation. We should have this City clear in two hours.'

'Since when have you been in charge?' Oli says, arms folded.

'We haven't got time for your tantrums, Oli…*do*, it.'

'What about the Fulcrum,' Marilyn says, 'are we going to get them out?'

'Any that will listen to us, we'll evacuate, but if they don't …well, that's their decision.'

'Good luck,' Stuart says, as he steps inside, 'and, Naomi, don't leave it too long to get yourself and your team up to the Council Chamber.'

'I won't,' she says.

I get in and stand next to Stuart facing out into the corridor. Naomi's head swings round as her attention is caught by something happening to her right.

'Oli,' she shouts, 'where are you going?'

The last thing I hear, as the doors close is Oli's voice.

'To find Jonathan…nobody else is worried about him.'

'Open the door,' I scream at Stuart.

But we're already moving downwards. It should be *me*, not Oli.

Chapter 54

20/06/3042   13:01 hours
JONATHAN

I open my eyes and stare out across the floor of the corridor, trying to make sense of what I see. A figure...*Finn*, is running away from me, with zig-zag movements. He careers from side to side, as if he can't make up his mind where he's going. To the right of my vision, I see the feet of someone else lying on the floor. Other than that, the corridor is deserted. I squint into the distance again but Finn has disappeared from view. Then a blanket of amber descends on me, as the light in my eyes, fades. I'm dying, I think, as it closes around me in a comfort of softness. Then I feel a sharp pain in my ribs as a foot makes contact with them.

'Get up!'

I raise my head and see Sean above me, brandishing a gun at my temples, a halo of smoke drifting around his head. Propping myself up on my elbow, I look around. Zack is behind me. He lies, quite still, on his back, eyes closed. Sean kicks me again, selecting exactly the same place as before, as if for emphasis. I push myself to my feet and stand on unsteady legs. My hand goes to my throbbing side.

'Is he alright?' I say, indicating Zack with my eyes.

He shrugs, but doesn't move. I walk over to

where Zack is lying then crouch down beside him. His eyes flicker open as if he senses someone's there.

'What…?' he says, trying to get to his feet.

A note of panic creeps into his voice, as he slumps back to the floor, his hand clutching his shoulder.

'Help me Sean.'

Sean hesitates, moves across to him then grabs hold of his arm and tugs at it. Zack screams out in pain.

'Not that arm,' he says, 'the other one.'

Sean hauls him to his feet. I notice a blood red hand print on the floor.

'You're wounded,' I say.

Zack stares down at his hand, puzzled, as if it doesn't belong to him then places it again to his shoulder.

'How did Finn escape,' he shouts, turning on Sean, 'and *how* did he get hold of a gun?'

'I don't know, Zack, do *you*?'

'Does it matter how it happened?' I say. 'Finn is loose in the City with a gun and he's very dangerous. You need to stop him.'

'Don't tell us what to do,' Sean says, moving towards me, the gun poised, 'you're in no position to do that.'

'And neither are you,' I say. 'Look around you. Where's the Fulcrum, Sean, where? I can't see them, can you?'

'I've still got this,' he says, waving the gun in front of me, 'that's all I need.'

'But…'

I don't get a chance to say more. There's a distant clatter of gunfire. Sean's head shoots round in the direction of the noise. I seize my opportunity and dive at him. He's taken by surprise and topples over backward onto the floor, still holding the gun that clunks down next to him. I take off down the perimeter corridor, trying to put as much distance between us as I can. At Corridor G, I turn and charge down towards the esplanade then double back on myself, moving across the back of the Food Production Unit. When I swerve right into Corridor F, I've gone full circle. I peer down the corridor and make out, through the orange dimness, a group standing outside the elevator. At this distance, it's hard to be sure but I think they're all wearing SRU uniforms. As I approach, I recognise one as Naomi. She trains the gun from side to side. Behind her, Lukas and Andrea scan the corridor, shoulders hunched with concentration.

'Naomi,' I shout, 'I need to go up *now*.'

She nods, not once taking her eyes from the corridor.

'Sean and Zack are following me and Sean's got a gun.'

She nods, staring over my shoulder.

'And, Naomi…Finn's escaped.'

She nods again, snatching a quick glance at me.

'And he's got a gun.'

'*Finn*? How..?'

'I don't know, but…'

A scream of bullets sweeps across the corridor

340

from the perimeter. I look up and make out a crouched figure holding a gun, using the corner of the Food Production building as a shield. Naomi gets down on one knee, resting the butt of the gun on her leg and fires.

'Quick,' she screams.

I jump inside the elevator and stab at the button as a flash of yellow pierces the gloom. The door closes muffling the deafening crash of bullets and then jerks into movement. It takes only a quick glance to see that it's occupied by six SRU officers, Fulcrum members.

'What are you doing in here?' I say.

'We're evacuating the Colony,' one of the girls says, lowering her eyes at my surprised stare.

I recognise her but can't see her ID badge.

'Come to your senses, have you?'

She doesn't respond. Despite their cowed expressions, I don't trust a single one of them.

At the Council Chamber, I jump out into a deserted corridor. I smile. The backlog of evacuees has disappeared. Turning around, I expect the others to file out behind me but they stay put. The doors begin to close and I step forward, blocking their path with my foot.

'Get out, quick.'

They stare at me, frozen. I grab the arm of the younger officer, pressed up against the side wall and tug at it.

'Get out!' I shout.

He has no choice but to move. I haul the others out.

'Follow me,' I say, as I hear the elevator doors close behind me.

I don't know if they're behind me or not and I don't care. Storming into the administration building, I make my way to the Ascendor.

'Jonathan,' Kyle says as I enter, his eyes bright with relief.

He stares beyond me, at the Fulcrum members standing in a huddle by the door. I watch that brightness dull into suspicion.

'They're going up,' I say.

'Have you seen Marilyn?' he asks.

'No. Where's Sarah?'

'She went down to the City with Stuart, Marilyn and Oli.'

I take in a quick breath, fear gripping me.

'It's getting bad down there,' I say. 'Is the Deathday candidate up in the tunnel?'

'Yes, he's there, waiting,' Kyle says.

'Right, you three get in,' I say to the SRU officers nearest to me, 'I haven't got time to waste, so don't mess me about.'

They file in, without a word and I follow.

'Fearne, I'll need your help,' I say.

She gets in beside me.

'Jonathan, will I see you again?' I hear Kyle say, as the doors close.

'Yes, of course.'

But I'm not sure he hears me.

At the tunnel, I push the SRU officers out into the throng of people congregated around the Ascendor. I'm hit by the pungent smell of urine.

'Jonathan,' Sherryl says, 'am I glad to see you, it's chaos up here. What time is it?'

'It's gone 14:00 hours,' I say, using my body to prevent the doors from closing.

'Fearne hold these doors for me. Where's the Deathday candidate?'

She points towards an ashen-faced boy that Tyler has by the arm. Fighting my way through a mass of blanketed bodies, I move across to them.

'What's your name,' I ask, pretending I haven't read his ID badge.

'Brendan,' he mutters.

'Well, Brendan, you are the man of the hour. You see all these people, thousands of them. You're going to lead them out to safety. No one else can do it, only you. Do you understand?'

'Yes,' he says.

'I'm going to be with you, Brendan, to help, but you will be the one who saves their lives.'

I take his arm. 'Come with me,' I say, pushing my way back to the Admin workers.

'Right,' I say, 'I need one person to volunteer to keep the Ascendor open for me so that I can get back down. The rest of you have done your bit and need to get out now.'

'I'll do it,' Fearne says.

'Are you sure?'

'Yes, I want to.'

'Good,' I say, clutching her shoulder.

'I'll get in front of them all with Brendan. Sherryl, you join us. Tyler and Oscar, you bring up the rear. I'll see you later Fearne and, thank you,

you're very brave.'

Tyler and Oscar fight their way through to the back towards the gaping entrance of the empty Sweeper hangar. They herd stragglers, who have fled inside it, out into the tunnel. The colonists, realising that something is happening at last, have quietened down, their eyes expectant. We make our way to the front of the waiting colonists, their numbers making the tunnel appear, narrow and claustrophobic. They draw aside to let us pass. I give Brendan's arm an encouraging squeeze as we get to the head of the phalanx of colonists. Sherryl takes up her position on the other side of Brendan.

'Get into single file and follow us!' I shout to the front rows then march off in the direction of the Renaissance Gate.

We make steady progress through Gates 2 and 3. Every now and then I glance behind me to check they're still following us. Ahead, I see the bulk of the derailed Sweeper and slow down.

'We'll have to get them all over this,' I say to Sherryl.

She nods and I'm grateful that she doesn't voice the questions I see are in her eyes.

'I'll go first,' I say, squeezing through the gap between the wheel mechanism and the tunnel wall.

Brendan follows me, then Sherryl. I walk up to the edge of the partially closed pit. There's a gap of about a metre. His curious eyes move downwards.

'Don't look down, Brendan…jump.'

He leaps across, clearing it by a good thirty centimetres. I take hold of his arm again and lead him to the door console.

'Take a deep breath,' I say, 'then put in your ID code.'

He looks at me, his expression blank.

'You do remember it, Brendan,' I say, trying to keep my voice calm, 'don't you?'

He nods, then raises a trembling finger to the console and punches in his number, as he has done for the eighteen years of his life. We wait. A terrible thought comes into my head that it won't work, that the system has already failed. Then we hear a noise, barely audible and the door creeps open. I pull a staggered breath into my lungs then guide Brendan through to the other side. Sherryl brings through a group of ten who are standing on the pit edge.

'Come on,' I say to the one in front.

He jumps across the gap, the other nine follow without hesitation.

'Sherryl,' I shout, 'we need to keep a steady flow through the Gate, to keep it open.'

She waves her hand indicating that she's understood. I join Brendan on the other side and we walk forward.

'Nearly there,' I say.

When we get to the Renaissance Gate, we stand in front of it, Brendan staring up.

'This is your destiny,' he says, reading the inscription above the door.

'Yes, it is,' I say, putting an arm over his shoulder. 'Now, put your hand over your eyes. When that Gate opens there'll be more brightness than you've ever seen before. Sunlight, Brendan, *real* sunlight. But you have to give your eyes time to adjust. Whatever you do, don't look at it, do you understand?'

He nods. After a few seconds, the Renaissance Gate glides open and a shaft of light slices through the gloom of the tunnel. Putting a hand up to shield my eyes, I squint out at the outside world, as I did only a week ago. There are crowds of people in front of us, no way will they be prepared for the numbers of colonists that are behind me. I give Brendan a little push, and a pair of hands grab him and guide him out into the afternoon glare. I could go out, right now, save myself. But I know that isn't an option anymore. I turn away from it. There's a shout from behind, but I don't stop.

'Keep going, Sherryl and tell them to shield their eyes,' I say, running up to her.

I crawl back through the gap and push my way down through the crowd to the Ascendor, never looking back once. When I reach Tyler and Oscar at the end, I call across to them.

'Thank you both…thank you.'

Then I fly over to Fearne and the waiting Ascendor and jump in.

'You can go now, Fearne,' I say.

She doesn't reply just steps in, releasing the doors.

'We did it,' she says, her eyes brimming with tears, 'we *did* it.'

Chapter 55

'Stop sulking, Sarah,' Stuart says, standing by the elevator door.

'I'm not…sulking.'

'I need your full attention, your full co-operation, you know that. Why did you volunteer to come with me, if you really wanted to go and find Jonathan?'

'I don't know.'

'Exactly. You're annoyed with yourself because Oli thought about it…about him and not you.'

There's no point saying anything. Of course, he's right.

'She's no threat to you, Sarah.'

'Isn't she?'

'Not unless you let her be.'

'What do you mean?'

'Jonathan's confused, she'll take advantage of that…she's an opportunist. You need to work out what you want, who you want.'

Who I want? The elevator arrives before I have a chance to ask him what he means. I'm relieved. His words have made me uneasy.

'Right, Sarah, full attention, okay?' he says, as he steps out into the corridor.

'Full attention,' I repeat, following him down to the workshop area.

'There's no one here,' I say.

'That's good. There should only be the skeleton crew in the power station.'

'Where is the power station?'

'No time for questions, follow me and you'll find out.'

I do as I'm told. We reach the end of the corridor and enter the workshop. This time, I look around it with fresh eyes and see that, what I thought was a solid metal wall over to the left of us, has a large double door incorporated within it, almost as big as the wall itself.

'This way,' Stuart says, walking over to it.

He stops in front of it and presses the button on the console. I'm dwarfed by the height of the doors as they slide apart. A metallic smell wafts through on a blast of cool air. I gasp in astonishment, my mouth open, at the sight before me. I've never given the power station a second thought but this…this is…

'Beautiful, isn't it?' Stuart says, smiling, his eyes bright with pride.

I stare up at the cylindrical metal structures towering over me, at the pipes interwoven in a complex pattern around them, over them and underneath. There are pipes everywhere. My eyes catch a glint of silver, as I look up at the larger of them suspended from the ceiling, high above my head. Everything is connected in a working, humming whole.

'It's the heart of the Colony, Sarah,' he says, his voice lost in the hollow space, 'and has been for centuries.' He looks down, 'but …now.'

'It might be alright,' I say.

'Yes…it might. Come on.'

He walks across to a metal staircase. I glance up it to a walkway that goes all the way around the edge of the huge space, about ten metres above the ground. Putting my hand on the red handrail, I feel a vibration run up my arm and allow the power of the place to course through my body. Then prompted by a shove from Stuart, I pull myself up the stairs. On the walkway, it's easier to see how the different parts connect together and I can make more sense of the structure. I want to stop, wonder at its complexity.

'Keep going, Sarah,' I hear behind me, 'right to the end. They'll be in the operating room.'

I look down through the metal mesh beneath my feet, at the drop below. The slight movement the walkway makes with every step, worries me and I cling onto the rail, even harder. We walk the eighty metres or so to the back of the room to a red door. I sense Stuart gaining on me and look behind. He walks as if he's on solid ground, his hands by his side not once touching the rail.

'Go on, he says, pushing me forward, 'keep moving.'

When I reach the door, I wait for Stuart, unsure of what to do.

'Push it,' he says.

I put my arm to it and push. It's heavy and Stuart has to help me. Inside, is a long rectangular room, every centimetre of wall space covered in a panelled, grey-blue metal. On it, is a mass of dials, meters, flashing lights and switches. In the centre stands a white double-sided block of computer consoles with workers on either side. They stare at the screens in front of them with a quiet intent. The silent frenzy of activity of the dials and the flashing lights mesmerises me and I don't realise that one of the workers facing us on the other side of the console block, is speaking.

'Sarah?'

I look up and recognise Malik, whose pod is, was in the same block as mine on the back of the Nursery & Kindergarten building.

'Do you know, Sarah?' Stuart says, surprised.

One or two of the other workers are staring at us now but most have their eyes fixed to the screens in front of them, uninterested in our presence.

'Yes, the last time we spoke, was when we were both taken in for questioning by the SRU, remember? I thought you…'

'It's a long story, Malik,' I say, not wanting, or able, to explain what has happened to me since that day.

Stuart wanders over to a set of dials on the wall facing us, and peers at them.

'Everything functioning alright?' he says.

'Yes, surprisingly, considering the power fluctuations we've had,' Malik replies, 'it's a magnificent piece of engineering.'

'We need to evacuate you,' Stuart says, 'that's why we're here.'

'Yes, I know,' Malik says, 'we're doing final readings to check that the system is stable before we leave. I can't believe that we're…'

He looks away, a sadness about his eyes.

'There's sure to be magnificent machines on the outside, Stuart says, 'machines that will need engineers to maintain them, engineers like you.'

'Yes, I'm sure you're right.'

He sighs then turns to the others hunched over the consoles.

'Right, everyone, it's time to go.'

One by one, they tear themselves away from the screens as if they're physically held by them and gather by the door. Only, a slight girl with shoulder length brown hair remains, staring at the screen in front of her.

'Keira,' Malik calls across to her, 'we need to go.'

'Something's not right. I'm getting some odd readings.'

'What do you mean?' Malik says.

He walks across to her and peers over her shoulder at the screen.

'I can't see anything.'

'Look, *there*,' she says, pointing, 'that figure has changed significantly in the last hour and it's continuing to change…to increase in number.'

'Stuart come over here, have a look at this,' Malik says.

Stuart walks over to them and I follow, interested by what's going on. The screen in front of us, shows a mass of figures displayed in columns. I notice that some fluctuate a little every now and then. But the one that Keira points to, is increasing in size, with relentless consistency.

'What is it?' I ask, realising that I'm the only one who doesn't know.

'It's the pressure gauge,' Stuart says, 'relating to the cooling tower.'

His answer means little to me. The others have congregated around us now, all trying to get a view of the screen. I edge sideways, out of their way and let them move in closer.

'If it keeps going up at this rate, it's going to reach critical status,' Keira says.

'It could be just a glitch in the software,' Malik says.

'No, that was the first thing I checked. What we're witnessing here, is happening.'

'It's speeding up,' Stuart says, alarmed, '*look.*'

'What will happen if…?'

But I don't get any further with my question. A piercing noise cuts through the room, with a rhythmic high-pitched scream. A large red light flashes on the wall opposite us, illuminating the white of the console block with splashes of orange.

'Get out,' Stuart screams, 'it's too late. There's nothing we can do.'

Malik flies to the door and the others follow. I stand and stare, held by the mesmerising pulse of light pumping at my eyes.

'Sarah, *move!*'

Stuart's voice pierces my consciousness, I turn and run out of the wailing room. We clatter along the shaking walkway and down the steps. I don't know what I'm running from but, their combined fear, carries me forward. We dive through the double doors into the workshop. They close behind us, muffling the noise of the siren, but not enough to ease the panic. Then we're out in the corridor, charging towards the elevator. Malik stabs at the button but it's at another level. It can only be seconds before it arrives but, every one of them, seems like an age. No one speaks.

At last, we're inside and going up to the City. There are seventeen of us packed in here and I can smell the fear.

'How long have we got,' Stuart says, 'before it...?'

'Blows?' Malik says, 'I don't know. It could be minutes, or hours. I really don't know.'

I grasp Stuart's arm, my pulse racing.

'The children,' I whisper, 'what about the children?'

Chapter 56

'They've gone,' I say to Kyle, trying to shake off a small, red-faced girl clinging to my knee.

'All of them?'

'Yes, I think so, I didn't wait around.'

'Where are the rest of the Admin workers?' he says, puzzled looking at Fearne.

'I told them to go out, with the others. They've done their bit.'

'Where's Stuart?' Fearne says, patting the head of one of the milling crowd of toddlers who clutch at her tunic bottoms for attention.

'I don't know, in the City somewhere,' Kyle says.

I glance around the room.

'What's going on here?'

'We decided to halt the trips up to the tunnel for colonists from the pod evacuation and concentrate on getting the children up. They're a handful,' he says, manoeuvring a boy to face the right way round, to enter the Ascendor.

'Where we going?' the boy says, wiping his dribbling nose on the back of his hand.

'For a ride,' Kyle says, his voice dulled by repetition.

He turns to me. 'They never stop asking questions. I'm exhausted.'

'How long will it take to get this lot up?'

'We can squeeze eight children, at a pinch, into the Ascendor. So, if it keeps going, we should get them up by about 16:30.'

'*If* it keeps going?' I say.

'We've had a few scares, with it stopping half way. It's struggling to cope with the traffic and we've still got the rest of the Nursery & Kindergarten to evacuate.'

'How many of them?'

'Over a thousand, plus about sixty staff. The strange thing is that we haven't had any up from the City for a while.'

'I'll go down, see if I can speed things up a bit. I'd feel happier if we could get them up here.'

I wade my way through a clinging sea of excited children, back to the door. Out in the corridor, two Nursery & Kindergarten staff are attempting to keep about forty children in a straight line. As I pass, I trigger a wave of sticky hands. I smile at them, infected by their enthusiasm. Raising my hand to them, I make for the elevator.

Down in the City, there's an eerie silence. I run down the corridor to the perimeter and over to the Jojo, straining my eyes against the dimness around me. But, instead of the train of toddlers I was expecting, it's deserted except for a single tiny shoe, resting up against the barrier. My pulse quickens and I'm gripped by the certainty that something is wrong. I make my way along the front of the Food Production building hugging the walls, past the entrance to Corridor G and onto the Nursery & Kindergarten. I haven't been inside this place since I was a child.

The first thing I notice is that the door is half open. I step inside the cheerful foyer, loud with walls and furniture in primary colours, designed to appeal to its younger audience. Now, in the quiet and the emptiness, its gaudiness looks out of place. I walk over to the far doors and they glide open, revealing an equally colourful corridor. What grabs my attention is not the bright images of animals, real or imagined, lined up along the walls, but the continuing silence. I creep down its length, my eyes darting left and right, taking in the deserted classrooms, on either side of me. Still there's not a sound. In front of me is a set of double doors. I glance behind me then approach them.

'Jonathan,' I hear someone whisper, to my right.

I swing round, heart pounding, but can't see anyone.

'Over here.'

There's a dark alcove about two metres from the doors and the voice is coming from there. I walk towards it.

'Who's there?' I say.

Then I spot Marilyn crouched down, pressed against the wall.

'What's going on?'

'*Quiet*,' she says, beckoning me over.

I squat down beside her.

'Thank goodness you're here. I don't know what to do.'

She clutches at her bottom lip, her fingers trembling.

'It's alright,' I say, grasping her hand in mine, 'I'm here now.'

'He's in there…with a gun,' she says.

'Who's in there?'

'Finn…with the children…I managed to get out…without being seen but I…I couldn't think what to do…he…he looks so wild.'

'Stay here.'

Creeping across to the door, I peer through one of the small glass panels. The space is full of toys, scattered around the floor space, abandoned. In the far corner, I see a play area with a slide, a climbing frame and other things that are partly obscured by the edge of the window. I push the door a little and look to the left through the crack. A mass of children huddle together on the floor, arms touching. Dotted amongst the hundreds of children are about thirty members of staff. They all stare straight out towards a raised platform in front of them. The children are quiet, held by the tension that pervades the whole space. On the platform, sitting cross-legged, is Finn. He has the gun resting on one of his knees, directed at the frozen mass of bodies in front of him. His traumatised eyes dart from side to side, the only discernable movement in the stillness. I close the door and walk back to Marilyn.

'Is there another entrance,' I say, 'behind him?'

'I don't know…I didn't notice…sorry.'

'Come on,' I say, grabbing her wrist and pulling her to her feet.

We run round the corridor that surrounds the play area searching for a door, a window, anything to gain access. Turning a corner, we make our way along the back of the space then I spot a door, smaller than the other one. I press my shoulder up against the opening side and peer in. All I can see is the edge of the platform, I haven't got a view of Finn. A girl, sitting by the far right corner of the podium, spots me, her eyes light up with surprise. I put my finger to my lips to stop her speaking but it's too late. The boy, pressed up against her, notices that her attention has been distracted and looks in my direction too. This sets off a chain reaction along the front row. A buzz of conversation starts up. Then the eyes of one of the staff members, sitting a few rows behind, widen and I know that Finn has noticed. I dive through the door. Finn's head jerks to the right as he looks over his shoulder at me. I charge the five metres to the platform and jump up onto it in one movement, just as the lights flicker, then fail. A child screams. I hear the muffled sound of frightened crying.

'The lights, put on the lights, the lights…!'

In the dark, I sense his panic.

'Finn, it's alright, it's alright. They'll come back on, they will, they will.'

Edging forward, I reach out my hands into the blackness. But he's gone beyond reason, beyond comfort.

'Put them on,' he screams, 'put them on!'

Then, a deafening clatter starts up and, a flash of yellow light arcs from side to side, as if with no human intervention. I dive to the floor, my hands clamped over my ears and wait for it to stop. When it does, I lie on my front and listen, through the whine in my ears, to the whimpers of terrified children. It starts with one or two then more join in, as the need for emotional release spreads, like a disease, through their ranks. The light flickers back on, as I'd promised Finn it would, and I stagger onto my shaking legs. He's only an arm's length away from me, curled up now, in a foetal position, a line of saliva running down his chin onto the surface of the platform. The abandoned gun lies next to him. I force myself to look out through the hanging cloud of smoke at the rows of children, searching for injuries...fatalities.

'They're fine...fine,' one of the staff members shouts, her voice breaking with emotion, 'shaken up, but otherwise, fine.'

Another confirms this from the back.

'I can't believe it,' Marilyn says, 'the gunfire must have gone over their heads.'

'We need to get them out of here...*now*,' I say.

I'm about to jump off the platform, when there's a muffled boom from under my feet, knocking me off balance with its immense force. I topple over the edge onto the floor. Marilyn screams behind me. I claw my way back to my feet and see her in front of me, on her knees, her hands splayed flat on the floor of the platform.

'What was *that*?' she says.

Chapter 57

20/06/3042   15:42 hours
SARAH

'I have to get out at the City,' I say, pressing the override button.

'No, Sarah, you're needed up in Council Chamber to help with the evacuation of the children up to the tunnel.'

'But what about the ones still left?'

'It might be…too late for them, Sarah,' he says, avoiding my eyes, 'we need to concentrate on the ones we *can* save.'

But I've already made up my mind. As soon as the elevator comes to a halt and the doors open onto the amber of the corridor, I charge out.

'Sarah!' I hear behind me but the doors are already closing on him.

I refuse to accept that it's too late. It *can't* be.

I swing round into the perimeter and run down the front of the Food Production building then spot Sean, with five other SRU officers, coming out of the entrance only metres away from me. Even from this distance and in the dimness, I feel, more than see, the hatred being directed at me. He raises the gun and points it at my chest. Without Zack's protection, I'm finished. I turn and run back the way I came, crouching down, in a ridiculous attempt to make myself smaller, less of a target. Then I feel the force of a barrage of bullets fly over my head, as I dive into Corridor F and run, faster than I've ever run before, down its length. Another burst of gunfire falls just short of me and the clatter at my heels pushes me forward. My lungs ache with the effort and I know that I won't be able to outrun it, for much longer.

At the esplanade, I hesitate, unable to decide whether to go left or right. I choose right. Careering round the corner, I collide with Zack. He cries out in pain as my hand makes contact with his shoulder. I stare at his drained face, the dark wet patch on his tunic, and the blood staining my fingers then snatch it back, shocked.

'Sarah, what's wrong,' he says, lightening his grip on my arm.

'Sean…he's…'

He looks over my shoulder then pushes me behind him. Four SRU officers stand in the corridor, facing us. I take hold of Zack's upper arms, using him as a shield and watch as Sean turns into the esplanade from Corridor F, ranging the gun from side to side. He slows down, seeing us and then moves forward, signalling to the others to follow. Two metres away, he stops, his eyes fixed on Zack.

'You can't protect her anymore Zack, she's mine, to deal with at my pleasure. You're finished, a spent force. I'm in charge of the Colony now.'

'There *is* no Colony,' I shout, 'nothing to be in charge of.'

Sean's eyes move from Zack's to mine, as if I'm confirming something he already knows. But he says nothing.

'Look around you, where are the colonists, Sean, *where*?'

'There's been no one in any of the work areas we've searched,' one of the SRU officers says, behind him.

'Shut *up*,' Sean says.

His eyes dart about, as he tries to make sense of what's being said.

'Where are they?'

I don't reply.

'*Answer* me,' he says, raising the gun level with my head.

'Tell him,' Zack pleads.

'Do *you* know?' Sean says, directing the point of the gun at him.

'No, but I'm not stupid enough to pretend that everything's normal. Any fool can see that the place is deserted, *look* at it.'

'Get away from her Zack.'

'No, you'll have to kill me first.'

'Don't underestimate me. I'm prepared to do that.'

I step out from behind Zack.

'Move away from him,' Sean says, directing me with the gun.

He watches as I step forward.

'The rest of you,' he says, addressing the five officers spread out around him, 'look at him, *look*. Do you want to continue with your allegiance to this…loser, or do you want to join forces with me?'

They stand in confused silence, unsure, still held by Zack's authority.

'I've got the gun,' he says, 'in case that makes a difference to your decision.'

One by one the officers slink towards Sean and take up their half-hearted positions behind him.

'Pathetic,' I mutter under my breath.

'Good,' Sean says, smiling at Zack, 'not looking quite so confident now, are you?'

'I'll ask you again,' he says, directing his attention back to me, 'where are they?'

'Who?'

I hold his eyes. He stabs the gun into my chest with such force that it knocks the breath from me.

'That's what you get for being clever,' he says, '*speak.*'

'Some are up in the Council Chamber,' I say.

'And the rest?'

'They're outside.'

'Outside *what*?'

'Outside the Colony,' I say, 'on the surface.'

'Dead?' Zack says, glancing at me.

'No, *alive.*'

'What are you talking about,' Sean says, a note of panic in his voice, 'alive.'

'The ozone layer has repaired itself. How do you think Jonathan survived? Think about it, Sean.'

'You're lying.'

'Alright, I'm lying, if that's what you choose to believe. But I tell you something, Sean...*all* of you,' I take each one of them in with my look, 'the computer system's failing. I've been down in the power station...the Colony's finished. If you've got any sense, *any* sense at all, you'll get out of here,

363

join the others waiting to get up to the surface, to safety.'

'Is this true, Sarah?' Zack says.

'Yes, I promise you, it is.'

'She's lying. You might be taken in by her, but I'm not.'

Sean grabs my arm and pulls me towards him.

'Let go of me!' I scream.

'Take me, Sean,' Zack says, 'let Sarah go.'

'And miss out on the fun?'

His sneer lasts only a second, wiped from his lips by an echoing, booming sound, deep and resonant. I feel the ground shake beneath us, with the intensity of it. I stagger sideways. My hand shoots out as I steady myself against the wall. The vibration runs the length of my arm, to my chest, as the blast reverberates through it.

'What was that?' I hear someone shout.

Then Zack takes my other hand and hauls me along the esplanade.

'Quick!' he shouts.

'It's the cooling tower,' I say, as we run but he's not listening.

I take a quick look behind me but no one's following.

'Where are we going?' I say.

'I don't know,' he says, a desperation in his words that I've never heard before.

He clutches his shoulder and I realise that every jolt of his body, as his feet hit the floor, must be like a knife stabbing into him.

'We need to get up to the Council Chamber,

Zack' I scream, 'we're going in the wrong direction, *Zack*!'

I point down Corridor E.

'This way.'

We reach the stairs leading up to the pod walkways on the back of the Health & Wellbeing Centre.

'Up the steps,' I scream.

He slows down and I think that he's heard me, that he's listening to me, at last. I push him up towards the first walkway. Then he comes to a complete halt.

'Zack, keep going,' I say, overtaking him.

But he's not moving. I turn around and look down at him. His eyes swim up to meet mine, clouded with pain. Then he sways, his head flops forward and he crashes down onto the metal steps, at my feet.

Chapter 58

20/06/3042   16:33 hours
JONATHAN

'Sounded like an explosion,' I say, helping Marilyn to her feet, trying to make myself heard over the terrified wailing of the children.

They mill around us, disoriented, their faces screwed up with panic, seeking comfort.

'Zack?' Marilyn says.

'Has to be.'

'Whatever it was, we need to get the rest of them out and fast,' she says.

Her eyes dart to the door behind us, distracted by a movement. I follow her gaze and see Oli run in and jump onto the platform.

'Jonathan,' she says then notices Finn curled up on the floor, the gun still next to him. She bends down and picks it up, 'what's going on?'

'Finn went berserk, started firing at the children.'

Oli points the gun down at Finn and I watch her finger hover over the safety catch.

'No, Oli,' Marilyn shouts, '*don't*. Can't you see what a terrible state he's in?'

'And *they're* not,' she says, indicating the traumatised children with a flick of her head.

'We haven't got time for this, Oli,' I say, 'leave him. He's no danger now. Have you seen Naomi and the others?'

'No, but I heard shooting then the explosion.'

'It's not safe to take the children out there,' Marilyn says, 'wouldn't it be better, to leave them here.'

'No, we have no choice, we've got to move them,' I say.

I walk across to a group of Nursery & Kindergarten workers. The one called Laurence turns as I approach, his eyes full of questions.

'Why did he fire at us, like that…an SRU officer? It's a miracle nobody was killed.'

'Look, I could stand here and explain but it would take too much time. All you need to know is that things are getting very dangerous out there. We need to do something about these children.'

'And the babies,' the one called Amelie says.

'Babies?' I say.

'Yes, in the Nursery, hundreds of them. What are we going to do about them?'

I'd forgotten the babies.

'They'll need to be carried,' Laurence says, 'and we've only got sixty staff left. How are we going to manage that?'

'We'll manage,' I say.

But it's only said to calm him down, calm them all down. If I'm truthful, I have no idea how we're going to do it.

'Get the ones that can crawl, ready and by the door in fifteen minutes,' I say.

His bewildered look indicates that what I'm asking may be impossible but he says nothing.

'One of you go and tell the Nursery staff to get ready. We'll be back for the babies.'

Twenty minutes later, we've somehow got the children into groups of fifty, with a staff member with each group. I stand on the platform and wait for their attention.

'The five spare staff will help get the ones who can't walk across to the Jojo. Marilyn you join them, I'll help. Oli you'll need to cover us. We have to make this a game…a game where the children must be quiet and keep hidden.'

I glance down at Finn, his face is turned away from me, not a sound or a movement, comes from him. I decide to leave him where he is for now. I leap off the platform and across to the door, weaving my way through the huddles of children. Oli pushes in front with the gun.

'Ready!' I shout behind me.

I assume from the lack of a response that they are or, at least, as ready as they'll ever be. We shepherd the first fifty children out through the door and they totter down the corridor. It's easy to spot the ones that, despite their determination, are not going to make it. They fall forward, after a few teetering steps, onto all fours and crawl, reverting to their favoured way of travelling. I grab two, one under each arm and carry them down the corridor. Glancing behind, I see that most are managing to wobble their way along, swaying from side to side, faces fixed in silent concentration.

At the main entrance, Oli runs out into the perimeter corridor then signals to me to move. We shepherd the toddlers, in single file, across the corridor. Most of them, we have to carry. The City is still shrouded in amber light. But now, even this inadequate light is diminished by a rhythmic fluctuation, pulling the City in and out of darkness. I hope that it holds long enough to finish the evacuation. On the Jojo, the children make better progress down on all fours where they feel more comfortable. They scramble forward with surprising speed. If one gets faster, the others follow, as if in competition. The confines of the Jojo and the enveloping gloom hold them together as one entity. When Oli reaches the entrance to Corridor F, I see her jump off the Jojo and take up position in the centre of the corridor. We half guide, half carry the children across the perimeter in batches of twenty-five, the number we can get into the elevator at one time.

It takes over an hour to get all the children from the Kindergarten, load them up and send them up to the Council Chamber. During that time, there's been no sign of anyone in the corridors and no further sound of gunfire. It's eerie, quiet. I watch the last of them get in, then the doors close. As they do, I feel a tickle play at the back of my nose and sneeze, surprised at the force of it.

'Look!' Oli says, pointing down the corridor.

Following the direction of her finger, I see a curled shadow of grey, drift out of the air vent about ten metres from where we're standing.

'Smoke,' Oli says.

'The *babies*.'

Marilyn doesn't hesitate. She's already running in the direction of the Nursery & Kindergarten

369

building. We charge after her. All the way, I'm calculating in my head how fast we can do this, how many of them we can get into the elevator. I overtake Marilyn and dive through the entrance. Oli stays outside.

'Be careful!' someone shouts.

A mass of wriggling bodies are lined up on the floor of the foyer in front of us. I veer sideways, in time to stop myself crushing one underfoot.

'We thought we could speed things up,' she says, staggering backwards in an effort to break my fall.

'Grab two each,' I scream regaining my balance, 'three if you can manage it and follow me.'

Bending down, I scoop up three of the tiny bodies into my arms. Three sets of eyes stare up at me, trusting and fearless, and my stomach wrenches. Then I run out into the corridor behind Oli. I glance behind me and see Marilyn and the Nursery staff running with their precious loads, urgency in their smarting eyes. When we arrive, I stab in the code and wait for the doors to open.

'Pile them in,' I scream, 'pile them in.'

'No we can't…' Marilyn says.

'They'll be alright, they *will*. Get as many as you can in. They'll sort them out at the top.'

Marilyn places the two she's holding on top of the pile. The babies seem unconcerned, comforted by the mass of bodies around them. Then we're charging back to the Nursery & Kindergarten to do it all over again. The next batch are not so compliant. Whether they pick up the tension emanating from our bodies, or can smell the smoke, I don't know. But I watch as the face of the middle baby I'm carrying screws up into a wrinkled mass and then it's howling, distraught at the interruption to its afternoon routine. And it's infectious. Soon all the babies take up the cry, thrashing their arms and legs about, in protest. It takes six tortuous trips to get them all to the elevator. Before I leave for the last time, I run down to the play area and over to Finn, still in exactly the same position as I left him.

'It's time to go, Finn.'

He looks up at me, his eyes vacant but he does not move. I put the screaming babies down onto the floor and get hold of his arm to pull him to his feet.

'No,' he whimpers, lashing out with his hand.

It's the babies or Finn. I choose the babies. I pick the squirming mass off the floor and run.

The corridor is heavy with smoke and it's hard to make out where I am. Before I realise it, I find myself at the Admin Block entrance. I've missed Corridor F and the elevator. Hugging the wall, I retrace my steps and, after five minutes, spot them, hazy figures in front of me. I run up behind them. The last batch of babies and Nursery workers are inside ready to go up. I thrust the three babies at Marilyn.

'Aren't you coming with us?' she says.

'I'll be up in a minute. There's something I have to do.'

'Jonathan, where are you going?' I hear Oli shout behind me.

I feel my way along the wall and turn into the perimeter. Then, pulling the bottom of my tunic top over my face to provide some protection against the smoke, I stumble forward blind and choking. I check off the City buildings as I go. When I reach the one I want, I see that the door is wide open.

'Jonathan, what are you doing,' Oli comes up behind me, coughing and grabs my shoulder. 'We've got to go.'

I shake off her hand and march across the reception area to the door, the lights buzzing with intermittent life.

'You go, Oli. I'll be alright.'

'No, Jonathan, I'm not leaving you…even if you are an idiot.'

I stop outside the half-glazed door of the Assisted Hatching facility and peer through the glass into the darkness, so different from the medical brightness, the last time I was here. I open the door.

'Why are we here?' Oli whispers, infected by the ominous atmosphere inside.

'We have to save them,' I say, '…the babies.'

I run up to one of the incubators and look inside at the curled creature inside.

'They're not babies, Jonathan.'

'Yes, they *are*!' I shout, searching for a way to open it, 'one of them is my baby. Don't you understand, one of them is *mine*?'

'They're dead.'

'*What*?'

I swing round to face her, fear clawing at my heart.

'Look at the monitors. They've failed. They're all dead, Jonathan.'

'Dead,' I whisper.

'Come on,' she says, 'we've got to go.'

She takes hold of my hand and I allow her to lead me to the door. I follow her to the entrance in a trance, numb. Out in the corridor it's impossible to see. It feels hotter. Oli is only a metre in front of me but I'm finding it difficult to keep sight of her, through the tears that course down my face, from the smoke…the pain. A misery, I don't comprehend, has taken hold of me and won't let go.

As the elevator doors slide open, I hear a choking cough behind me. Oli hears it too and twists round, the gun raised and pointed in readiness, into the gloom.

'Who's there,' she shouts.

'Help us, *please*.'

A person pushes past her into the elevator and falls to their knees in front of me. Another four, all wearing SRU uniforms, push in after them.

'Come back,' I hear someone shout out into the smoke-muffled corridor.

Then Sean looms into view in front of Oli.

'Oh no you don't,' Oli says, a cold edge to her voice.

I hear the click of the safety catch, as she releases it.

'Let me in,' he screams, 'let me in!'

'*Beg*,' she says.

'What do you mean?'

'Beg…like I did, when you…forced yourself into me.'

'*Please*,' he whispers.

She thrusts the gun into his chest with such violence that he topples back away from the doors, then she stabs the button. I watch as they close on his screaming eyes.

Chapter 59

20/06/3042   18:50 hours
SARAH

'Zack, *Zack*!' I shout, tapping him on the side of his face to keep him conscious.

He moans and his eyes flutter open again. Then his head jerks upwards caught by a choking, smoke-fuelled cough. His face contorts with pain as he struggles to sit up. Then he collapses, exhausted, back down onto the walkway floor.

'Keep still, Zack, you need to conserve your strength.'

'Go, Sarah, I'm not going to make it, save yourself.'

'I'm not leaving you.'

He sighs, that's all. He doesn't have the energy to argue, not now. I don't know how long we've been here. But I know we can't stay here for much longer.

'I need to take a look at your shoulder, Zack,' I say, staring at the ever-growing sticky patch on his tunic top.

The acrid smoke catches at the back of my throat. It starts as a tickle, then degenerates into a hacking cough. Then I'm vomiting, with a violent wrench of my stomach muscles, onto the floor next to Zack's right leg. I look down at the creeping liquid pool beside me.

'Sorry,' I say wiping saliva from my mouth.

But Zack's eyes are closed again, he hasn't

witnessed anything. I breathe in deeply and take hold of the hem of his tunic top, pushing it up as far as I can. But it's not far enough, I can't see his wound. I raise his right arm above his head then move to the other side. Taking his wrist in my left hand and supporting his elbow from beneath with my other, I start to move his left arm away from his body. He screams out, his eyes wide open now, lit by agony.

'I'm sorry, Zack, I'm sorry. I need to get this off so that I can look at your wound.'

'Leave it, Sarah, leave *me*.'

'Listen Zack,' I say, ignoring his plea, 'can you move it at all, if I help you?'

He nods. Bit by bit we manage, between us, to raise his left arm above his head like the other, stopping every few seconds for him to recover from the effort. Now, his arms are stretched out above his head, as if he's about to dive into the air above him, defying gravity. He looks vulnerable like that. I feel a tightness grip my stomach, as I continue to work his tunic top up over his torso. Easing the sleeves over his hands, I pull them through and then over his head. He lets me do this without complaint apart from an occasional low moan. I manoeuvre his arms back to his sides and examine the wound. It's smaller than I thought it would be.

'I don't think the bullet went in,' Zack says, staring up, 'it glanced off me.'

I daren't do too much probing but I see, straight away, that he's wrong. There *is* an entry hole and, although the edges are drying a little, there's still a relentless seep of blood coming from its glistening centre. I have to do something, or he'll bleed to death.

'I won't be long,' I say, crossing to the nearest pod, its door half open.

Once inside, I grab a cup and fill it with water. Then I walk into the hygiene cubicle and press the button for a clean tunic. To my surprise, a white tunic of the Museum & Archive Department drops into the chute in front of me. I wonder whose pod this is, *was*, and whether I know them. It doesn't matter now. None of it matters anymore. Back in the pod, I push a hole through the thin material of the tunic top using the edge of the dispenser unit and tear it into strips. The bottoms, I tear into pieces and place two of them under the water dispenser, pressing the button. A spout of water, a measured cupful soaks into the material. I run back out into the walkway.

'Zack, drink this,' I say, raising his head up from the floor and putting the cup to his lips, he gulps it down.

I fold up one of the dry pieces of fabric and press it against the wound then set about bandaging his shoulder as best I can. It looks a mess but, at least, it's covered.

'We need to go,' I say, 'can you walk, with my help?'

'I don't know,' he says, 'I'll try.'

I lift him into a sitting position then, with one hand on the railing and the other under his right armpit, I help him to his feet. He sways against me. I place his hand on the rail while I tie the damp material around his nose and mouth with a tight knot at the back of his head.

'That'll help with the smoke,' I say, to his surprised eyes.

Then, I tie the other piece around my own face and place his right arm across my shoulders.

'Lean on me,' I say, as we step forward towards the pod stairs.

We stumble down them into the corridor and turn left. The smoke is thinner down here. A dense cloud hovers above our heads. Step by step, we make our way down to the Administration block until we reach the Maintenance elevator, hugging the side wall, as we go. I prop Zack against the wall and punch in the code. Out of the corner of my eye, I see him slip sideways towards me and step back away from the doors to stop him falling. The doors slide open next to me, releasing an explosion of fire that shoots out into the corridor, a raging ball of flame, engulfing everything in its path.

'*Run*!' I scream.

We stumble back down the corridor the way we came in the direction of the esplanade. I don't know where we're going, panic has seized hold of me. I can't think, daren't think. If I do, I'll be forced to accept the awful truth that there is nowhere to go. *Nowhere*.

'The Solarium,' Zack says, through the fabric around his nose and mouth.

'But we'll get trapped...we'll die.'

'I'd rather die in there, than out here,' he says.

I stare at him, taking in his stark words. *It's over*.

Now that I've accepted the inevitability of my death, I see that it's no different than before when I knew...embraced, it. I've been preparing, all my life, for a death by burning. Nothing's changed, after all. The fact that I wanted to believe in a different destiny, a future...a life beyond the Colony, is irrelevant. I will face my Deathday with dignity, as I've been trained to do. And that day...is today.

We run up to Door 6 of the transition chamber. The Solarium is in darkness, the shadowy shapes of the plants inside, its only inhabitants. I press the door button and wait.

'Is it locked, in night mode?' I say to Zack, alarm in my voice.

But before he has a chance to reply, the door opens and we stumble inside. I watch wafts of smoke drift in through the opening, contaminating the space around us. The door closes and we wait. I cling onto Zack and stare, in silence, at the inner door, willing it to open. And it does.

Inside, I fumble with the knot at the back of my head and pull off the fabric. There's a stuffy, warm quality about the air, as I pull it into my lungs.

'There's no smoke in here,' I say, removing Zack's mask, 'it's closed down the ventilation system against the pollution from outside, but there's still plenty of clean air.'

Zack takes in several deep breaths and sighs.

'That's good,' he says, throwing his head back.

My eyes adjust to the dark helped by the faint amber light, filtering into the Solarium from the esplanade.

'Where shall we go?' I say.

'I don't know. Have you got a favourite place, Sarah, somewhere special?'

I think about the Arboretum and my meetings with Jonathan. They seem such a long time ago, an age. *Jonathan*.

'Jonathan,' Zack whispers.

'How did you know I was thinking about him?' I say.

'You said his name.'

I hear the disappointment in his voice. We fall into an awkward silence.

'The Arboretum,' I say, at last, 'let's go there.'

Then I realise the selfishness of my suggestion. He hasn't got the strength to get there, of course he hasn't.

'We could stay here, if you like,' I say.

'No, I want to go to your favourite place, Sarah.'

I take hold of his good arm and place it over my shoulders. His half-naked body presses against me, closer than before, his hand clings onto my arm.

'Are you ready?' I say, as we step forward.

We both hear it, a dull thump…a muffled scream. We turn to face the Solarium door behind us, peering through the glass panels across the transition chamber. Silhouetted against the flickering glass, is a figure, arms raised, fists pounding against the strengthened panels.

'Zack, let me in! I can't open the door…it's locked!'

The words disintegrate into a hacking cough.

'*Sean*,' Zack says.

'Zack,' I hear, but it's fainter now, as if the hope it contained at the sight of us, has been sucked into the searing heat of the corridor.

'There's nothing we can do for him,' Zack says, 'it's too late.'

There's an agonising scream, then another. Zack's grip on my arm tightens. Then silence. And, in that moment, we both know. Sean's fate will be, our fate. There is no escape.

Chapter 60

'It would have been kinder to shoot him.'

Oli stands opposite me, her head tilted back resting against the elevator wall, the gun at her side.

'And *that*, Jonathan, is why I didn't.'

She stares up at the ceiling, refusing to meet my eyes. The Security Response Unit officers have taken up position as far away from her as possible, knowing *now* what she's capable of. They huddle together, coughing intermittently, eyes streaming from the smoke, from the corridor…from in *here*.

'It's hot,' one says, jerking his back away from the metal wall of the elevator.

When we arrive at the Council Chamber, Oli dives out, as if she's been released from captivity, and storms off down the corridor without a word. The first thing I notice, is the smell of smoke, not as strong as in the City but there, nevertheless, an ominous presence. I haul in a lungful of air then cough it back up again.

'Follow me,' I say with a little more urgency.

They're reluctant to move. *I haven't got time for this*. They force me to go in and push them out. We walk towards the perimeter and, as I turn into it, a body catapults into me, head making contact with my groin. A sharp pain rips up my spine. I gasp. Looking down, I see a pair of guilt-filled eyes staring up at me, belonging to a boy that I guess is about five years old. Behind him, a girl of a similar age stands, frozen, held by an invisible force.

'What are you up to…Lee?' I say, pushing him away from me and looking at his name badge.

There's no response from him, from either of them, but Lee fiddles with something in his tunic pocket.

'What have you got there?'

He thrusts his hands further into his pocket and I hear a clink.

'Nothing,' he says.

I crouch down, take hold of his right hand and pull it out. He grasps an object that I don't recognise.

'Give it to me,' I say.

He hesitates but, realising that I won't be deterred, places it into my hand. I've never seen anything like it before. A thin glass tube, tapering towards its tip with an oval of rubber fixed on the top.

'Where did you get this?'

The boy points behind him down the perimeter corridor.

'Look,' he says.

Taking an identical object from his pocket, he places it a few centimetres from my cheek. Then pressing the rubber part between his thumb and finger several times, he expels a faint puff of air onto my skin. I smile, rubbing my fingers against the spot.

'It tickles,' he says.

'Yes, it does,' I say, 'but you shouldn't have these, if they broke they'd be dangerous.'

Lee flashes the briefest of glances towards the girl who I see is called Sophie.

'Have you got some of these too, Sophie?' I say, spotting the look that passes between them.

Her mouth falls open in concentration as she considers her reply.

'No,' she says at last, shaking her head from side to side, lips pursed together for emphasis, 'look.'

She holds out her empty hands to me and I take hold of them, shocked by the difference in temperature, between them. The left is warm and has a stickiness about it, the other is ice cold. I stare at her puzzled.

'*There* you are,' a Nursery & Kindergarten worker shouts, running up to us, 'where have you two been? You should have gone up to the tunnel hours ago.'

'They had these,' I say, handing the two objects to her.

'What are they?' she says.

I shrug.

'You've been very naughty,' she says, shepherding them by the shoulders down the corridor towards the administration building.

Sophie glances back at me before she disappears. Then a gagging cough behind me, reminds me what I was doing.

'Come on,' I say to the bedraggled group, 'let's move.'

As we walk down the corridor between the administration foyer and the Ascendor room, I notice that the grills have been removed, propped up against the walls, and bunk covers stuffed into the openings. At first, I'm confused then realise it's an attempt to keep out the worst of the smoke. The offices we pass on the way are packed with babies, toddlers and staff. A kaleidoscope of sounds, crying, laughter and singing, fill the air. I charge through the Ascendor room door. Fearne is loading Sophie and Lee into the Ascendor, along with four of the pod evacuees.

'Jonathan,' Stuart shouts across at me, 'where have you been? I can't get any sense from *her.*'

He indicates Oli with his eyes.

'You've got lights,' I say, ignoring his question and looking up.

'Yes, we've been busy,' he smiles at Fearne as he speaks. 'We're getting our power from the back-up generator now. I'm hoping it will last the course. I estimate we won't get them all up much before, 04:00 hours.'

'Naomi!' I shout, spotting her and Lukas by the far wall, through the mass of bodies.

'Jonathan, thank goodness you're safe. We came up here after the explosion.'

'What was it…the explosion?' I ask.

'The cooling tower in the power station,' Stuart says, glancing beyond me to the door.

'Where's Sarah?'

'*Sarah*,' I say.

'Isn't she with you?' he says.

My heart falters.

'No…I thought…she was…here, with you, Stuart.'

'Oh no,' Marilyn gasps, slamming her hand across her mouth, 'oh no, *please*, no.'

I stare at her stricken eyes fighting back the panic rising inside me.

'She's not still down…?' I start.

But I need no answer. Stuart's expression is confirmation of my worst fear. I spin round and charge through the crowd to the door.

'Oh no, you don't,' Oli shouts, blocking my way with the gun.

'Let me *out*, Oli, I'm warning you!'

'You're not going anywhere,' she screams back, 'tell him Stuart, Naomi, tell him!'

'It's too late,' Stuart says, his voice shaking, 'I'm *so* sorry, Jonathan, but it is too late…now.'

I run back to him, my only hope, and grab him by the shoulders.

'*No*, Stuart, please listen to me, *listen*.'

'It's too late,' he says, 'she couldn't survive…'

'No, *listen*, Stuart. If *you* were down there, where would you go?'

'There would be nowhere…'

'Where!' I scream, trying to shake an answer from him.

'I don't know!' he says.

'*Where*, Stuart, I'm begging you. *Think*!'

'The Solarium,' he whispers.

'Of course,' I say releasing my grip on him, '*the Solarium*.'

'But it would be in lock down,' he says.

'But if she managed to get in…*somehow*.'

'Even if she *did* manage to get inside…which I

386

doubt...she'd be trapped there. She'd buy herself more time, but that's all, Jonathan, that's all.'

'That's enough...maybe, that's enough.'

'Come with me to the surveillance room.'

'I'm needed here.'

'But *I* need you, Stuart. *Sarah* needs you.'

'Alright, Jonathan,' he says, 'alright.'

'Don't let him out of your sight, Stuart,' Oli says as I push past her and run down the corridor to the exit, Stuart following behind me, coughing against the smoke.

'Wait for me, Jonathan.'

Inside, I stare at the banks of screens on the wall in front of me. Some, are blank, others display indistinct images that scroll up and down. One, or two have been reduced to a fuzz of dots and buzzing static but, a third of them, are still functioning. But it's difficult to make which ones they are, as the images are hazy with smoke tinged with the flashing amber lights of the City. Some flicker with the yellow of flames. I drag my eyes from these, refusing to accept the evidence they display, that the City is being consumed by fire.

'Stuart, which ones show the Solarium?'

'That block there,' he says, pointing to the far right edge of the top row of screens.

'None of them are working,' I say, walking across to them, racked with disappointment.

'They *are*, Jonathan, it's just that the Solarium is in darkness. You won't see anything.'

'Which ones show the Arboretum?'

I swing round to face him.

'Which ones, Stuart, tell me?'

He points to four. I put my face up to the first, searching for any sign of movement, anything at all.

'Stuart, help me.'

He sighs. I take two, he takes the other two. I stare at them, until my eyes lose focus then blink and stare again. But I can't make out a thing.

'What's that?' Stuart says.

'Where?' I say abandoning the screen I'm studying.

'There, can't you see it. Isn't that a leg?'

I squint at the point he's indicating.

'Is it?' I say, unsure.

'It moved,' he says, 'I'm sure it did.'

'Is it Sarah?' I say.

'I don't know but, whoever it is, they're still alive…*still alive*.'

There's something about the tone of his voice.

'Stuart?' I say.

Chapter 61

21/06/3042   00:24 hours
SARAH

I sit, aware of the rough bark on my back pressing through my tunic top and stare out into the gloom. The trunks of the trees around me are picked out solid and black, against the flickering orange background of the inferno that is now, the esplanade. I wonder, with a morbid fascination, how long the Solarium can hold out against such an assault. I pull at my damp tunic top, lifting it off my sweat-covered skin. The heat has increased over the hours we've been here. It crept up on us. Now it has gone past the point of comfort, soon it will become intolerable.

'Sarah,' Zack moans, his head resting on my shoulder.

I place the strip of fabric over his burning forehead and hold it there, soaking up the beads of moisture.

'It's alright, Zack, I'm here.'

'I'm so thirsty,' he whispers.

'I know, I know, but there's no water. I'm sorry.'

'How long have we been here?'

'I don't know,' I say, looking around at the onslaught beyond the glass frame of the Solarium, 'I can't believe it's still holding.'

He falls silent and I think that he's drifted off again into a fevered oblivion.

'It won't be long, now,' he says. 'Sarah…'

'Don't speak, Zack, save your strength.'

'No, Sarah, I need to tell you something before…'

'There's no need, Zack, I know.'

He sighs. It comes from somewhere so deep inside him, that his chest heaves with the effort of drawing it up.

'I've never felt happier…than I do, with you…like this.'

'Zack…I…'

He lifts his head from my shoulder.

'Don't say anything, Sarah, please.'

He leans forward away from the tree trunk and turns his head to me, twisting his body, his eyes shut against the pain. He recovers, places his hand on my clammy cheek and moves into me. Then his parched lips are on mine, with such a lightness, I can barely feel them. I don't know what to do. He doesn't move. It's as if this delicate point of contact, is all he needs. Then his mouth opens and he gathers my lips into his, with a sudden urgency. I keep quite still, unsure of how to respond. I feel the pressure release and he peels his dry lips from mine.

'Thank you,' he whispers, his head resting back against the tree.

'For what?'

'For giving me that…despite what you think of me.'

I can't think what to say, so I remain silent. After a while, I voice the question that's been hovering between us for hours, unspoken.

'Zack,' I say, 'why did you do it?'

He doesn't answer and I think that he's returned

to the comfort of unconsciousness.

'Zack?'

'Because I *could*,' he says, at last.

'That's not a good enough reason,' I say, needing more.

'It's the only reason, I've got.'

I decide to leave it at that. What's the point now, of pushing it further?

'I've been thinking,' I say, 'while you were resting, about the outside. About what sort of life I would have had with…'

I stop and glance sideways at him. His features stand out in sharp relief, against the orange glow beyond.

'…with Jonathan,' he says, his voice flat with resignation.

I try to weigh up his ability to cope with the truth.

'Yes,' I say, 'but, what about *you*, Zack? What would you have…?'

'There was never going to be an *outside* for me, Sarah.'

'Why not? You could have made a fresh start. You could have…'

'No, I couldn't, Sarah, you know that.'

'I don't…*know*,' I say, exasperated by his refusal to accept my vision, my dream of a future for him.

'You don't understand.'

'No, I don't, Zack, explain it to me.'

'I can't.'

'You *must*,' I say kneeling beside him, forcing him to look at me, tell me to my face. 'Why?'

'I'm scared,' he whispers, averting his eyes from

mine.

'Scared…of what?' I need answers. 'Zack, of *what*?'

'The outside…a life outside.'

'That's ridiculous.'

'I knew you wouldn't understand.'

'There has to be more to it than that. What are you really scared of, that people will judge you, that you'll be punished, ostracized?'

'The unknown,' he says, 'I'm scared of the unknown.'

We *hear* it first, a sudden rush of air. Then there's a patter above our heads, as leaves are assaulted by a million droplets of water, raining down from above.

'The sprinklers,' I shout, 'quick!'

I grab his good arm and pull him from the shelter of the canopy. He crawls out onto the grass.

'Lie down, Zack, lie down!'

I take up position flat on my back, facing the deluge. Zack lies next to me, our bodies touching.

'That's so good,' I splutter, water pouring down the sides of my mouth and onto the ground, as I speak.

Zack gulps down several mouthfuls. Then I feel his body shaking next to mine and I turn my head.

'What's so funny,' I say.

But I see now that his face is twisted by a different pain, sobs racking his body, his tears invisible against the water from the sprinklers. I put my hand up to his face and feel them there, warm against his skin, cooling as they run down his cheek. There's nothing I can say, nothing I can do, to help him. He's drowning in misery. I can't watch it. I face upwards again and allow the water to drench me and wait for it to be over, all of it, the dreams, the hopes, the longing…my life. *I want it gone.*

Then I see it, through the blur of water. I think, at first, that my eyes are playing tricks on me or that, the Solarium lights are coming back on. But no, there it is again, a white flash above me. This time I know, with a certainty so strong that it clutches at my heart, that I'm not imagining it. I wait, my chest tight with hope. There it is again, three flashes in quick succession. I sit up, wipe the water and the wet strands of hair from out of my eyes, and peer up again. But it's not there…not there. I wait and wait, but it's gone. *It's gone.*

Chapter 62

'Jonathan, they're ready to go,' I hear Kyle say, pointing to the closed doors of the Ascendor.

I stab at the button then go back to staring at the door, willing Stuart to come through it. He's been missing for over an hour, left me here to deal with the last of them before the back-up generator fails. All I can think about is the possibility that Sarah is still alive. It's been hours since we saw the indistinct image on the surveillance screen. And, even if what we saw was someone in the Solarium, the likelihood that they'd still be alive now, is slim. The likelihood that it was Sarah, even slimmer. But I hold onto the hope, I have to. It's all that's keeping me going.

The heat in the room is becoming unbearable. My parched tongue sticks to the top of my mouth. I work it, trying to generate saliva, but it's useless. I search the sea of orange tunics below me, trying to find water, and spot a fair-haired toddler clutching a bottle to his chest. It's a quarter full of liquid.

'You,' I say, pointing at the child, 'come here.'

His sleepy eyes swim to meet mine then he walks forward, weaving his way between his companions, towards me. I push him into the waiting Ascendor.

'You're next,' I say, 'you won't need this.'

I prise the bottle from the tight grip of his fingers then push more children in beside him, blocking any protest. The door closes, I stab the button and gulp down the tepid, cloudy liquid in one go. It doesn't do much to quench my thirst, but it's enough.

'That was unkind,' Marilyn says, breaking her silence of several hours.

'He'll get water when he's out,' I say, 'whereas we'll probably die of thirst by the time we've got them all up…assuming that it keeps going.'

'Isn't that where Stuart's gone,' Oli says, still clutching the gun, 'to check on the generator?'

'Is that what he said?' I ask.

She doesn't respond.

'Oli, is that what he *said*?'

She glances at me and shrugs her shoulders, heavy with fatigue.

'No, he didn't say anything, I assumed that's where he was.'

The door to the Ascendor room opens. My heart jumps into my throat, but it's only Naomi.

'We've got about one hundred and fifty still to evacuate. Is it going to hold out?'

'How should I know?' I snap. 'I just load them in and send them up. I didn't know I had to do any more than that.'

'Are you alright, Jonathan?' she says.

'Yes, I'm fine. I wish everyone would stop asking me that. Instead of asking me, what they really want to know…whether I'm upset because Sarah's dead.'

'We're all upset about that, Jonathan, you don't have a monopoly on it,' Marilyn says, turning away from me.

'Put that gun down, Oli, do something useful,' I

say, 'take over from me.'

'Don't take it out on me,' she mutters, putting the gun on the floor next to the Ascendor and herding a group through the gap between the partially open doors.

I walk across to the side of the room, lean up against the wall and let myself slide down it, onto the floor. *I can't do this anymore.* Sitting with my head resting on my bent up knees, I block out the heat, the noise, the mayhem and allow myself to retreat into a world where I can be with Sarah. Will this be enough, when I'm on the outside? To conjure her up in my mind, relive our time together, in my mind. *In my mind.* Or what? Wouldn't I rather be consumed by the flames, have a few moments of agonising pain, than a lifetime of suffering? *A lifetime.* I don't know how long that is anymore. Too long, without Sarah.

I feel a tug at my tunic sleeve. I raise my head and my gaze meets that of a girl, her hair stuck to her forehead in damp strands, her cheeks flushed red with the heat. She thrusts a half-full water bottle at me that she's holding in her right hand. The thumb of her other hand creeps, without conscious thought, into her mouth. She sucks on it, keeping her impassive eyes on mine.

'No,' I say, 'you keep it. You might need it.'

Undeterred, she places the bottle on my sloping legs and watches it slide down my thighs. Then she turns and takes up her position again in the queue, unaware that, her small act of kindness has saved my life. I get to my feet and walk back to the Ascendor, brushing my hand over the girl's head as I pass. I've got a job to do and it's not finished yet.

'I'm going to have a scout round the building,' Naomi says, 'check that we've got them all. Callum you come with me.'

Half an hour later, I have the last batch of children loaded in the Ascendor and send them on their way. My head goes back, I look up at the ceiling and let out a sigh of relief. *It's done.*

The room is full now of nothing, but silence. The stale smell of hot bodies lingers as a reminder of its previous occupants. But after a while even this fades.

'That's everyone,' Naomi says, as she charges through the door, followed by Callum.

Then, seeing my expression, she looks away. *Not everyone.*

'It's time,' she says. 'Marilyn, Kyle, Oli, Jade, Anton and Andrea, you go first.'

'See you up top,' Oli says, as she steps into the Ascendor, '*Jonathan*, did you hear me?'

'Yes, I'll see you,' I say without turning round.

'We did it,' Naomi says, as the door closes on them, 'can you believe it?'

'I thought we'd get some up,' Richard says, 'but this…this is incredible…with so few casualties.'

My throat tightens.

'It wouldn't have worked without Stuart,' Fearne says, looking towards the door, her eyes giving away her concern.

When the Ascendor returns, they gather in front of the doors.

'You all go. I'll wait for Stuart,' I say.

'No, I'm not going without him,' Fearne says.

'We should *all* go, Jonathan,' Naomi says, pushing Fearne inside, 'Stuart can make his own way up.'

They pile in. Fearne has given up her protest. Naomi gets in last and, as soon as she's clear of the doors, I push the button.

'Jonathan,' I hear her shout, as they close behind her.

As I step out of the room, I notice a strong smell of smoke that wasn't there before. It claws at the back of my throat, making me gag. I pull up my tunic top to cover my nose and mouth but it's too late. I convulse into a fit of coughing, my chest heaving to find air fit to breathe. I run to the administration block entrance, knowing that to venture outside would be suicide. That's when I see a figure running towards me through the haze. Stuart. He dives into the foyer, through the door I'm holding open for him and sucks air down into his chest, in staggered breaths. We feel the rumble of another explosion from deep below us and fall to our knees.

'*Move*,' Stuart shouts, hauling himself up to his feet and running faster than I've ever seen him run before to the double doors. We charge down the corridor and fall into the Ascendor room.

'Quick,' he screams, 'we don't have much time.'

'Sarah?' I say.

'Get in Jonathan, *get in*.'

I see him glance down at the gun lying on the floor where Oli left it.

'Don't make me…' he says.

I step inside and he follows, leans out and presses the button on the console. He pulls his arm inside as the doors glide shut. Then his hand clamps down onto his mouth. His eyes close. The Ascendor moves upward to the tunnel.

Chapter 63

21/06/3042   02:01 hours
SARAH

I haven't mentioned the flashing light to Zack. There's no need. It was in my imagination. Something I wanted to believe was there, but wasn't. Still my eyes keep wandering up, hoping to see it again. The sprinklers stopped about an hour ago, as suddenly as they started. My drenched tunic feels warm on my skin. Zack sits next to me, resting up against the trunk of the tree, his face flushed, not from the external fire but from a burning inside of him. I put my hand up to his forehead and feel the heat there.

'I'm cold,' he says, his eyes closed.

I glance at his shaking body, each hair on his arm picked out by a raised bump. He looks weak, ill.

'Zack, move away from the tree a little.'

He shuffles forward on his bottom and I slide in behind him, with my legs either side of his body. I pull his back towards my chest, with my arms wrapped around him, trying to quell the spasms of shaking that have taken hold of him. His head flops back onto my right shoulder and I feel his wet hair against my cheek.

'Is that better?' I say, as I feel his body relax.

'Yes,' he whispers.

After a while, I don't know how long, his staggered breathing becomes more regular and I know that he's fallen into the arms of sleep. Every now and then, he lets out a moan, a plaintive sound that emanates somewhere deep in the back of his throat. It's easy to say that you will go somewhere to die, but the reality isn't that straightforward. By now, I thought that we would both be dead, consumed by fire, reduced to ash amongst that of the trees and plants, that surround us. But the Solarium has held out against the furnace, in a way that I never believed was possible. I feel alone, despite Zack's physical presence. How long must I wait?

Then, as if I'd willed it with my thoughts, I hear a tremendous crash, a roar that thunders around the Solarium as the transition chamber is breached by the flames. I scream.

'What happened?'

Zack's head jolts upright, his muscles tense.

'The transition chamber's gone,' I say, 'it won't be long now, Zack.'

A few moments of silence elapses, as we accept this terrifying fact.

'Are you frightened?' he says.

'Yes.'

My chest tightens and I struggle to breathe, knowing that each intake of air might be my last.

'I don't think I can be brave,' I say.

'You don't have to be, Sarah,' Zack says, taking hold of my hand and putting it to his lips, 'we'll face it together.'

Now that the fire is only one partition away, the heat in the Solarium has become more intense.

'If the sprinklers come on again that might put it

out,' I say.

But my words sound hollow, impossible to accept. A gentle rain will not extinguish the inferno that rages around us.

'I thought I saw something…earlier…up there,' I say, pointing in the direction of the imagined flashes.

I peer up into the gloom. Something catches my attention.

'What's that?'

But he's not listening. His head has flopped to the side at an awkward angle. I ease myself out from behind him and rest his torso back against the tree. What I thought was only a trick of the light, is not. There's a rectangular patch at the base of the dome. I can't tell if it's lighter, or darker than its surroundings, but it's *different*. And it wasn't there earlier.

'Zack, I'm going to have a closer look.'

But he doesn't hear me. I walk towards the transition chamber, until an invisible wall of heat forces me to stop. I glance up and I see that it's a hole, an opening, I'm sure of it. A surge of hope takes hold of me, only to be dashed down again as I realise that it might as well be a kilometre, a hundred kilometres away, I can never reach it. An image comes into my head, indistinct at first, then clearer. Something I've seen in the Solarium many times but not taken much notice of. It's an image of Solarium workers, or perhaps they were Maintenance workers, I can't remember, it doesn't matter. They were up there, on a walkway. A walkway. I swing my head round searching for some way of getting up there.

Then I spot it. An enclosed green metal ladder, mounted several metres away from the transition chamber, running in a curve up the wall of the Solarium. I can't make out where it goes but it must lead to the walkway, it *must*. I run back to Zack.

'There's a ladder, a way up, Zack,' I say, pulling him up by his good arm.

'I don't think I can…,' he says, swaying, as if his legs have melted with the heat.

'You *can*, Zack, I'll help you.'

I place his arm across my shoulder, as he picks up the wet fabric from the ground and we stagger forward towards the ladder. I step onto the first rung, grab hold of the handrail and scream. A searing pain shoots through my hand and up my arm. I jerk it away from the intense heat of the metal, knowing that I've left the skin of my palm there, too. I look down at my red raw hand, faint with a sick agony and whimper. Zack wraps a wet cloth around it then takes the other one and wraps it around his right hand. The sound of a crack behind us, makes me turn. I watch, fascinated, as a line creeps along one of the panels of the inner wall of the transition chamber. Ignoring the soreness, I grab the handrail with my bandaged hand and begin the climb. Zack follows.

It's easier than I thought it would be. The ladder curves away from us and we're effectively inside a cage. Every now and then, I rest back on the rail behind me, feeling the heat through my tunic and look down at the top of Zack's head, someway below me. I can tell he's struggling to keep up with me. I glance down at the trees. They appear strange, mysterious, viewed from this angle. The foliage is inviting, as if I could dive off into their outstretched branches and lie there, cradled against the world of fire below. An orange flash catches my attention. I spot, a lick of flame, break through the partition wall, only a few metres below Zack's feet.

'Hurry up, Zack!' I shout, speeding up.

After a five minutes of climbing, my head emerges through the gap into the walkway. I turn and reach down my hand to help Zack up. The metal up here is warm but not yet, hot. He joins me on the walkway. I notice that his body is slick with perspiration, as he collapses on his knees beside me. I use my bandaged hand to wipe his glistening brow and wait for him to recover from the exertion of the climb.

'Look,' I say, 'it's there, the hole. Can you see it, Zack?'

He nods but he isn't looking at it. I help him to his feet. The walkway is too narrow to take both of us side by side, so we go in single file, with me leading. As we approach the gap, it becomes clear what it is. A whole panel in the roof of the dome has been removed, revealing the inner corridor of the Council Chamber. I stare, transfixed, at the wisps of smoke coming from the hole. They swirl upward, across the top of the dome, forming a cloud about three metres from its highest point. We clamber over the metre high barrier and out into the corridor. On the floor, next to my feet, is a toolbox. A screwdriver rests on top of it...a sign and, I know without any doubt, who has given me this lifeline.

An acrid, suffocating smoke thickens the atmosphere around me and I fight to find air to breathe. Holding my bandaged hand over my nose and mouth, I stare about me trying to work out where we are.

'It's hot,' Zack says, lifting his left foot up, 'the *floor*, it's hot.'

'Keep moving,' I say.

I turn right and stagger down the corridor towards the administration building. Then a noise makes me stop dead in my tracks.

'What's the matter?' Zack says, colliding with my back.

'I heard…'

But before I can say more, there's a creak and a large section of floor opens up in front of us. A second later, a column of flame pushes through it, clawing at the air above it. I spin round and run back in the direction we've just come, until I reach the connecting corridor between the science and computer blocks then make my way down to the perimeter. At the side of my vision, I see flames shooting out from the air vents, as I go. I glance over my shoulder. Zack staggers behind me, his features obscured by smoke. At the perimeter, I turn right and run, choking, along the face of the computer building towards the administration block, smoke tearing at the back of my throat. My eyes scan the floor, searching for cracks. Arriving at the entrance, we fall through it into the foyer. The air is a little clearer but it's stifling hot.

'Come on, Zack, not far now.'

We walk along the corridors strewn with the debris of the evacuation. Abandoned covers and water bottles lie on the floor, all that remains of the human mass that inhabited this place, only hours ago. As we enter the Ascendor room, we spot our means of escape standing open before us, redundant now that the evacuation is complete.

'I can't believe it, Zack,' I say, 'it's here, waiting for us.'

His silence makes me turn.

'We have to go, quick, Zack.'

He hesitates, as if he hasn't heard, or understood my words, then moves forward, streaks of black running down his face, his bandaged shoulder covered in dried blood. He looks half dead with exhaustion. I rush across and help him to the Ascendor. His right hand grasps the edge of the door and I feel the resistance in his body as I manoeuvre him inside then lean out to press the button. We're so close. *Please*, don't fail now. The doors swish shut as they have done hundreds of times then it jolts into movement. I start to cry, tearless, racking sobs of relief.

The Ascendor slows, then stops and the doors open. The tunnel is deserted, cold and smoke-free. I step out and gulp the clean air down into my lungs. Then I run, crying…laughing, with a relief so strong, it hurts. I don't know what makes me turn round but, when I do, I see Zack standing by the Ascendor, holding onto the side of one of the doors. His head is down. He needs help. I run back towards him. As I approach, he lifts his head and stares at me, with a look of such sadness, it makes my heart lurch inside my chest. Then he steps into the Ascendor.

'Zack!' I scream, '*Zack*!'

But it's too late. The doors close, as he allows the Colony to claw him back down into its burning depths.

Chapter 64

'We're clearing the area, Ryan, you can't stay here, it's, dangerous. All able-bodied colonists need to go on the transport down to the city. *Ryan...*'

I tear my eyes away from the Renaissance Gate, prompted by the vague familiarity of the name. In front of me, stands a uniformed woman with cropped brown hair and lines around her eyes and mouth.

'His name's not Ryan,' Stuart says.

'But his ID badge says...'

'His name is Jonathan and you won't get him to go anywhere, I've tried.'

'I can make him move,' she says, fingering a weapon in a holster around her hips.

'I'd like to see you try,' Oli says.

I turn to face her, wondering how long she's been there.

'You need to go, too,' the woman says, 'you three are the last.'

'We're *not* the last,' I say, 'there's someone else.'

'What does he mean,' she says, dragging her eyes away from Oli, 'how could there be anyone else alive down there?'

I don't get a chance to explain because there's a muffled boom from the tunnel that vibrates through my body and up my arms.

'Right, that's it,' she says, 'we're getting out of

here, now.'

She shouts across to two officers by the Renaissance Gate. They stare down the tunnel, hands out supporting themselves on the rock face, lit now by a dappled light from the sky behind us.

'Grab them,' she says, 'they'll be no more arguments.'

I'm hauled to my feet by one of the male officers, my arm twisted almost to breaking point, behind my back. I feel a sharp pain as the bones of my shoulder socket grind together.

'Let go of me,' I scream, legs flailing in all directions.

My foot makes contact with his shin and he leaps back losing his grip on me, enough that I'm able to wriggle free. Stuart and Oli are being pushed up the steps of the transport vehicle, Oli fighting all the way. The officer has recovered from my kick and approaches, his gun cradled in his hand, pointing in my direction. He advances towards me his finger poised, his patience spent.

'Wait!' I hear Stuart's voice, carried to me through the clear, silent air of dawn, 'look!'

He points in the direction of the Renaissance Gate. I hesitate before I turn, my body shaking, legs barely holding me up. My eyes are closed, protecting me from the disappointment. But I know I have to face it. I have to look. I have to. I gulp down a breath of air and open my eyes. In front of us, I make out a kneeling figure, picked out by the golden light of the sun, as it clears the top of the ridge behind me. The head is down, shoulders sloped forward, a blanket of hair, in damp coils, falls across the face. The body heaves up and down and I see a trickle of liquid slide from the bottom of the hair, onto the ground, next to the hands splayed out on it. Then, as if aware of the warm embrace of the sun, the person looks up. The face is blackened, white tear streaks run down it to the chin, on both sides. But still I can see that, it's Sarah.

I run, stumbling, towards her, fall to my knees in front of her, draw her body into mine. A smell of smoke and vomit fills my nostrils, as I press the side of her face against my chest, my hand in her hair. I know that this strange combination of smells will always remind me of the joy I feel here, at this moment. Her body shakes against mine as she lets go of it all, and sobs. I tighten my grasp on her, holding her together, wanting to absorb some of the emotion that overwhelms her, overwhelms me. Over and over again, she whispers my name, as if by doing so, she will confirm that I'm here with her.

'Let it all out, Sarah, let it all out.'

After a while, her body relaxes, the crying stops. She pushes away from me a little so that she can look at me. Her hands go up to my face.

'Jonathan,' she says, out loud this time, 'I didn't think we'd…'

'Sarah,' Stuart says, 'I can't tell you how good it is to see you.'

She looks up at him standing, a little apart from us, awkward, unsure what to do.

'You saved my life. Thank you, Stuart…thank you, so much,' she says.

410

I jump to my feet and charge towards him. The last thing I see, as I grab hold of him are his eyes, wide with alarm.

'Stuart, I'll never forget what you've done, *never*, do you hear me? No one will ever upset you or harm you, not while I've still got a breath left in my body. You will always have me as your friend, Stuart, *always*. You've saved Sarah's life, you've saved mine. Thank you, thank you so much.'

I feel a gentle pat on my left buttock.

'Jonathan, I'm finding it hard to breathe,' he gasps into my left ear.

I release my hold on him. He stands in front of me, red-faced, pulling air into his lungs. Then Sarah is there, beside us. She places her arm on his shoulder and draws me in. We stand, arms interlocked, clinging to each other.

'Sorry about the vomit,' Sarah says.

'That's fine,' Stuart says, wiping a streak from his cheek, 'can't be helped.'

After a while, I become aware of a group of people standing around us and let go of Stuart but keep my arm around Sarah, giving her support. Several, Rehabilitation Centre staff, have joined the uniformed officers. One of them approaches Sarah.

'I understand that your name is Sarah,' she says, 'despite your badge. The girl, Oli, has told me.'

I look over at the vehicle. Oli stands on the top step. From this distance, she looks small, almost fragile. She stares at me, watching. I can't read the look in her eyes. Then she turns and walks inside.

'Well, Sarah, we're taking you to the Centre to be

checked over. You two boys need to get onto that bus.'

'No,' Sarah says, 'I'm not going anywhere, not without Jonathan.'

'Fine, he can come too,' she says, perhaps sensing a fight she hasn't the time, or energy, to take on.

'I'll see you later,' Stuart says, as he walks towards the vehicle.

'I meant what I said!' I shout after him.

'I hope so,' he says, over his shoulder, 'because you nearly killed me in the process of telling me.'

He walks up the steps of the vehicle, turns and waves, then he's gone. Sarah and I watch as the vehicle coughs into life and trundles down to the city.

'Fearne's, a lucky girl,' Sarah says.

'Fearne?'

I stare at her, puzzled.

'Yes, Fearne,' she smiles, 'you'll see.'

Sarah is offered a stretcher but refuses it, insisting that she can walk the short distance to the Centre, with my help. Inside, they take her away. I'm told to sit and wait. I'm struck by the number of people milling about in the corridors, so many more, than last time I was here. Somebody pushes a cup of water into my hand and asks me if I'm hungry. I say that I'm not. A stale smell is coming off my tunic and I rub a splash of vomit off my sleeve. I need to get clean. I ask the next person that passes where the hygiene unit is. It's a man. I can't be sure what age, but older than me. He stares at me with blank, overworked eyes.

'Do you mean the toilet?'

I remember this word from before and the terrifying rush of water that comes with it.

'I'm dirty,' I say.

'Marcus,' he calls to another worker, 'can you organise a shower for this one and clean clothes?'

'But I'm…' he complains.

'Just do it, will you. I can't, I'm tied up for the next hour at least.'

Marcus sighs then, without a word, turns and marches off down the corridor, the way he came. After a few metres, he stops and looks round.

'Come on then,' he says.

I get off the bench and trot after him. He leads me into a room full of people standing naked in stone trays with water pouring down on them. I stare, astounded.

'Stop gawking and get those filthy clothes off,' he says.

I scramble out of my tunic and wait for instructions.

'In you go,' he says, 'indicating an empty tray.

I step into it and watch as he turns a lever on the wall. Water pounds down onto my head from above. I gasp.

'Too cold, or too hot?' he says.

I don't understand what he means but raise up my face to it and gulp down the warm water.

'Don't *drink* it,' he shouts, 'what is it with you CB's?'

He pushes a cloth into my hand.

'Rub yourself down, get all that dirt off.'

I forget about the wastage of water pouring down the hole by my feet and start to enjoy the sensation of it against my skin. All too soon, the water slows then reduces to a trickle. I'm handed a larger cloth.

'Dry yourself.'

He rubs the cloth against my arm in demonstration.

'That's right,' he says, 'I've got some clothes for you, over there on the bench. I have to go now. You'll be alright, won't you?'

Before I have a chance to reply, he's gone. I finish soaking up the water from my skin with the cloth then walk over to the bench where my new clothes are folded in a neat pile. I look up and spot a boy, tall and thin, with wet hair hanging into his wide blue eyes and realise, that it's me caught as a reflection. It's clearer than those I used to catch sight of, sometimes, in the windows of the City buildings. This is what Sarah sees, when she looks at me. *Sarah.* I have to get back to the waiting area. I pull the clothes over my half-dry body and charge down the corridor, slumping down on the still empty bench. Minutes later, Sarah is led out of one of the rooms by a woman wearing a light blue tunic. She looks beautiful with her hair clean and fluffy, cascading over her shoulders but her face is tight with thought.

'Is that him,' the woman says, pointing to me, 'Jonathan?'

Sarah nods.

'Well, young man,' she says, smiling, 'we need to have a word with you.'

'I'm...preg...nant,' Sarah says, the unfamiliar word sounding strange on her lips.

'Preg...nant?' I say, 'what...?'

'Don't worry, Jonathan, we'll explain it all to you. You're going to be a father.'

Chapter 65

'I'm scared, Jonathan.'

His grip on my arm tightens. We sit, side by side, united by the human being growing inside me.

'*Nine months*.'

'That's the age they're transferred to the Nursery,' he says, looking down.

'I don't understand how they…'

I think about the size of the babies at that age.

'They'll explain it to us, Sarah. They told you not to worry, that it's all perfectly natural.'

Those words sound as unconvincing to me, as the doctor's did, earlier this morning. He grinds the fingers together, his brow creased with worry. He's making me nervous.

'If it's *perfectly natural*, why didn't they explain it then? Why send us away to get some sleep first?' I say.

'I don't know.'

'Maybe, it's because they didn't think we could cope with it.'

'Maybe.'

His shoulders drop even further.

'They'll have to cut it out, there's no other way.'

My hearts starts hammering, again.

'We'll face it together, Sarah, I'll be with you.'

'It's growing in me, Jonathan, not *you*,' I snap,

then regret it.

He looks so helpless, so vulnerable. I put my hand to his cheek and guide his face towards mine.

'Jonathan, it will be alright. They'll help us.'

My lips touch his in a light kiss.

'They said they'd be with us every step of the way.'

'It's not my fault, is it, Sarah?'

'*No*, we created it together, weren't you listening?'

He smiles, the first since I told him.

'To be honest, I don't remember much after they said that it was, inside you.'

I look up and spot a group of children huddled in a group, a little way down the corridor. One of the girls is staring at us. No, not at us, at Jonathan.

'I wonder if it will be a girl, or a boy?' I say.

The young girl drifts away from the group and makes her way towards us, never once taking her eyes off Jonathan.

'I think you've got an admirer.'

She stops in front of him, her arms folded defensively around her chest.

'I'm sorry,' she says, her eyes staring at a point on the wall above his left shoulder.

'Sorry,' he says, 'what for?'

'I shouldn't have taken it. It wasn't mine. It was *his*.'

'I recognise you,' Jonathan says, 'your name's Sophie, isn't it?'

She says nothing to confirm or deny the fact.

'She wandered off up in the Council Chamber,'

Jonathan says, turning to me, 'with a boy. He'd found some glass objects. They looked like they'd come from the science block. I took them off him, they could have been dangerous.'

He turns back to her.

'You had something too, didn't you?'

She nods.

'And you took it from the boy?'

'No, I didn't.'

'I thought you said, it was his.'

'Not Lee's, *his*,' she insists.

She glances up at a Rehabilitation Centre worker passing behind her.

'*They* took it away from me.'

'What was it?' I say.

She glares at me, as if I'm an impostor then fixes her gaze back onto Jonathan.

'It was better than Lee's.'

'Better?' Jonathan says.

'Mine had pink water in it. You could do *this* and it didn't fall out,' she rocks her hand backward and forward in a 180-degree arc. 'Lee wanted to swap, but I wouldn't.'

'So, who did it belong to?' I say.

'I told you, it was *his*, it said so…on the label.'

My heart hammers inside my chest, as a terrifying thought prises its way into my consciousness.

'Sophie, *tell me*, where it is,' I shout, grabbing her by the upper arms and shaking her.

'You're hurting me,' she cries, her eyes screwed up tight.

'Sarah, what are you doing? You're frightening

her.'

'Sophie *listen*,' I say, softening my voice, 'you're not in trouble. I just need you to tell me, where it is.'

She points to a door, where a group of children, shepherded together by six or seven Nursery & Kindergarten workers, are standing. I place my hands on her shoulders and guide her back to the group.

'Where are you going?' I hear Jonathan say behind me.

'In here, Sophie? Was it, in here?'

She nods. I hand her over to one of the staff then push my way past them and through the door.

'You can't...,' I hear, as the door closes behind me.

Inside, a young boy has his top rolled up under his armpits and a doctor, sits in front of him, tapping at his chest.

'You can't come in here,' he says, looking up at me.

Ignoring him, I scan the work surfaces that run along two sides of the room.

'Did you hear what I said?' the doctor repeats.

'I'm looking for something,' I say.

Then I spot it, lying on its side on the shiny white surface, only centimetres from the edge. The light from above makes the pink of its contents iridescent. The doctor gets up from his seat but I push past him and grab the glass tube, noticing two things, the cork wedged into it and the label. I turn the glass tube around in my fingers, they're trembling so much that I think I might drop it. The label has been half worn away by the sticky damp fingers that have held it since its removal from the Colony, its right edge rolled into a greyed ridge of paper. H15, it says, with a downward stroke of another letter that I know, with a terrifying certainty, is an N. The 13, has been rubbed away. I can see now, why Sophie saw it as *HIS*. But it should read, H15N13. The flu virus that annihilated the Council, all those centuries ago, is here in my hands, *in this tube*. My legs weaken under me and I grasp hold of the work surface for support. My stomach heaves then I'm vomiting into the sink. With saliva and mucus, running down my chin, I make for the door, clutching the tube with its deadly contents, in my sweating hand.

In the corridor, I swing my head from left to right. I don't know what to do, where to go.

'What's the matter?' a woman passing, asks.

'How do I get rid of something dangerous?' I say, trying to control the shake in my voice.

'Medical waste?' she says, eyeing the tube in my hand.

'Yes.'

'The incinerator, in there,' she says, pointing to a door with a skull on it, 'but…'

I don't wait to hear what she has to say. I push my way through the door and make my way to the chute opposite. I look around for something to wrap it in and spot a large cloth on the worktop next to me. I place the tube with extreme care into it and pull the cloth around it, tying a knot at the top. Then, pulling up the handle of the chute and pushing my hand in as far as possible, I release it into the fire below.

Outside in the corridor, I charge down to the exit. I have only one thing on my mind, to get into the fresh air, calm myself.

'Sarah,' I hear Jonathan shout behind me, but I'm not stopping.

I push through the doors and walk out into the glorious sunshine and gulp down the clean air. Leaning up against the wall of the building, I hear the sound of excited voices to my left. I turn and watch as a line of children walk down the path to a waiting vehicle. A little apart from the rest, I see Sophie. She notices me and I see recognition in her eyes but then she turns away. I run over to her, gripped by a feeling of guilt.

'Sophie, wait. I'm sorry I shouted at you.'

She stares up at me, sensing her new power.

'That's alright,' she says.

I bend down and kiss her on the forehead.

'It's just that a glass tube like that, could be dangerous. You could cut yourself, if it got broken.'

She nods.

'Like the other one,' she says.

'Sophie, hurry up!'

She swings round, looking in the direction of the shout and the vehicle, full now of children, their faces pressed against the steamy windows.

'*What* did you say?' I shout after her, 'Sophie, wait. *What* did you say?'

She reaches the steps and a Nursery & Kindergarten worker lifts her up and carries her into the vehicle, her face resting against his cheek. The door hisses closed and I watch the vehicle move off towards the city.

Chapter 66

22/06/3042   12:30 hours
JONATHAN

We look out towards the Renaissance Gate. Sarah sits next to me, knees bent up, her right arm touching mine. She's been so quiet, withdrawn, since yesterday. It doesn't matter how hard I try, there's a part of her that I can't reach. A part she keeps hidden from me, from the world. There's so much I want to ask her. I need to know about her last days in the Colony. What she feels about giving birth and what happened with Sophie. But it's as if she's filed it away, like all the books she's worked on over the years. The books we worked so hard to preserve. Gone, every single one of them, reduced to ashes.

'What are you thinking?' I say.

She hesitates a little too long before answering and I know, what she will say, is not the truth, only something she thinks will stop me probing.

'I was wondering what they're doing,' she says.

I sigh, but answer her anyway.

'They're filling in the tunnel, blocking it off, returning it to the Earth.'

'Are you scared, Jonathan?' she says, breaking another long silence.

'Scared?'

'Of the outside...of life on the outside.'

'No, are you?'

'I don't know. It's so uncertain, so fragile.'

'But we've been given back our lives. We've been given time, a lot more time.' I take hold of her hand. 'There are so many things I want to do, Sarah, to experience…with you.'

'We have to live each day, as if it's our last.'

Her grip tightens on my hand.

'Yes, of course,' I say, noticing the sadness in her eyes.

'I mean it, Jonathan, we *must*.'

'Yes, we will,' I say.

'We don't know…when our Deathday, will be,' she says.

'Deathday? We don't have to worry about that, now.'

'We *do*, Jonathan. We're going to die *someday*. The only difference is, that we don't know *when*. It could be today, tomorrow, we don't know. Every year that we live, we will pass the anniversary of the day that we will die, just like in the Colony, except we won't know what date that is.'

'There you are.'

I look around, puzzling at Sarah's words.

'Alice,' I say, recognising the first person I saw when I came out of the Colony, on my Deathday.

'I've been sent to fetch you. You're to go down to the city, the pair of you.'

She glances at Sarah then back at me.

'This is Sarah,' I say.

'Pleased to meet you,' she says. 'Do you know what, Sarah, in the first few seconds of meeting *your* Jonathan, I knew he was going to be a handful.'

She smiles at me.

424

'What's all this I hear about you making a baby? Love will always find a way, always. Still, you're the first and...now...the last.'

She looks towards the men, working below us.

'That's what you get for playing God,' she mutters.

'*Playing God*,' Sarah says, 'I've heard that before. What does it mean?'

'I see you've picked up the inquisitive ways of your young man,' she says, grinning, the lines around her mouth deepening, 'full of questions he was from the start.'

She pauses.

'It means...how can I explain it...? It means that you can never beat Nature. It will always have its way, the Colony being a good example.'

'But the Colony *saved* the Human Race against extinction,' I say.

'Yes, it did. But perhaps...perhaps, it was our time.'

'Our time?' Sarah says.

'Yes, our time to go...to die,' she says, 'and, if it *was*, then playing God will not stop it. Nature will have its way...in the end. It always does.'

She stares out in front of her, then looks down at our upturned faces.

'Oh dear, look at the pair of you, so much to look forward to and yet such miserable faces. Don't listen to the ramblings of an old woman. What do I know? *Nothing*, that's what.'

And with that, she turns and walks away from us.

'Come on,' she says, over her shoulder, 'we'll

walk down to the city. It's such a beautiful day.'

I would like to thank my family and friends for their encouragement and support during the writing of this novel. Especially, my husband Rob, for his technical know-how and infinite patience; Justin, for the cover design and photography and Jackie, for her remarkable eye for detail and the hours of copy editing she did for me.

About the author

British author, Sue Yockney, was born in London. After studying art at Central St Martins, she went on to qualify as a chartered librarian. Now settled in Somerset, Sue and her husband enjoy travelling and discovering new places. Her family and friends often ask them why they don't have 'relaxing' holidays. The answer is simple - they prefer adventures. They have been to Alaska twice, using the local ferries to travel the Alaskan Marine Highway and did a five week road trip of New Zealand. Their most exciting and challenging trip to date, was driving the Dempster Highway (the Ice Road Truckers road) up to and beyond the Arctic Circle, in the summer. As Sue points out, doing it in the winter, would just be suicidal.

Find Sue on Facebook and Twitter.

Made in the USA
Charleston, SC
13 January 2014